Tynged
a tasting of wine history

Donald Furrow-Scott

ISBN 978-1-7338919-3-6

For Carl Weber

Table of Contents

andante

agité mystérieux

allegro bond

Acknowledgements, Author Bio, and series

PART ONE

ANDANTE

Script

Mur Castle, Kingdom of Neustria (North-West France), early Middle Ages

"Stay behind me, your Majesty! I shall protect you!" Gisela urged, her arm sweeping her Queen behind her. The gnarled witch grabbed at Gisela repeatedly, her long boney fingers snatching up snood, veil and dark locks. Gisela swirled and snapped her quirt up against the old woman's face, sending the witches hair and arms flying with a shriek. Another three witches rose up from the gray snow, blocking her and towering above them, forcing her to sidestep with a Queen who seemed to be lost in an otherworldly waltz of a dance.

"Back you, demons of Conomor and Dahut!" Gisela cried out at the witches. The sky grew blurrier. "I have been trained against your faery-craft by Saints Illtud and Saint Samson! I am as fearless as Saint Gildas!" she yelled, striking the left witch with her quirt, sending it exploding into a white cloud of smoke. "Trained in war by King Gradlon..," she kicked her great boots at the right witch, knocking it backward as it grabbed at her leg. "...And schooled by the scrolls of Moses in defense against your evil sorcery!" her voice as chilly as her breath in the air, the words forming a wispy shield facing the third witch. The witch's long fingers grabbed her arms and neck, tangling the magical quirt for only a moment before Gisela banished the witch into a white cloud with a strike of her gloved hand.

"For our wrestling is not against flesh and blood; but against vile kingdoms and power, against the rulers of the dark world, against the spirits of wickedness!" she called out in defiance.

The sky suddenly sank upon hearing her powerful warcry. More and more witches rose up from the snowy field, creating an army, closing in like a maze to trap them. "You will not claim the Queen, or her unborn child!" she growled determinedly as the thick clouds of the gray sky above, pregnant as the Queen herself, burst forth wafting walls of snowflakes and stinging crystals of ice down upon them all.

The Queen continued her waltz, brave young Gisela spinning about her, striking first this way then that at the witches, keeping them at bay as the Queen one-two-threed her way through the witch maze. Her Majesty seemed lost in some song in her own mind; guided by some magical tune whispering in her inner ear that Gisela could not hear.

Laughing, Gisela ran around her mother and danced through the snow, her oversized boots clomping and crunching amongst the wintery grapevines. Drab gray canes of the vines stuck out, gnarled and hardened off like old fingers, mostly empty of leaves for winter. The vines themselves were tied up goblet style, like so many bound hands above a captive's head, or perhaps a cruel hair bun on an old hag, all covered in a layer of icing-like fresh snow. Gisela tugged and pulled on her mother's extended arm as the older woman struggled to keep both protruding belly and youngster equally balanced while they walked through the snowy, sleeping vines.

It was an early snow along the Loire Valley, and from its banks up through the village hillside to the Mur castle where the royal family was staying, it was a quiet, solid white blanket, stained here and there with ashy gray patches. Above the castle and the chaotic vineyards surrounding the village, the sky let loose more snowflakes in sweeping, blowing clouds that would briefly obscure the Queen and her daughter's mid-day walk from the two watchful guards on horseback pacing them along the field edge.

Suddenly Gisela found herself looking at a field of stumps instead of full grapevines, as if her imaginary witches had all vanished and left one boot behind each. She twirled a lock of her hair sticking out from a braid and made a face, taking up her mother's hand when she had caught the few steps up to the girl. Gisela looked up at her.

"Mother? Why did His Majesty kill the grapevines here?"

Bertrada sighed as she squeezed her daughter's gloved hand, and looked around at the decimated vineyards stretching off towards the snow drifted fence lines.

"He did it to punish the people here who revolted against us. Those are Pineau d'Anuis, the grapes of Saint Martin for communion, but their wine also made the local rebels rich enough to think they could challenge the Crown."

"Saint Martin's grapes?"

Bertrada nodded.

Gisela twirled her hair more. "But these vines are chopped down. All the ones over by the castle moat were dug up instead."

"His Majesty is temperate about drinking, and wished to pull up every plant as punishment, but when his men told him even with the oxen and digging it would take all winter, he changed his mind and settled for chopping them down until he returns. He had to follow rebellious King Waiofar quickly, and chase him and his counts from Poitiers south to Wasconia!" the Queen laughed, shaking Gisela's hand excitedly.

"His Majesty killed the vines of the rebellion," Gisela repeated, trying to understand.

"Much like the revolt, the biggest and most important leaders he made an example of and slew, the rest he punished so they would remember. These strong roots will grow vines up again next summer if His Majesty doesn't pull them up, and these cut grapevines will return."

Gisela stopped twirling her loose lock. "Does that mean the rebels will come back too?"

"Only if they didn't learn their lesson!" the Queen tapped a finger on Gisela's pink nose. "As a dog that returneth to his vomit, so is the fool that repeateth his folly."

Gisela thought again. "Twenty-six!" she suddenly bubbled out.

"Very good!"

Gisela nodded. "As snow in summer, and rain in harvest, so glory is to a fool," she rattled off, for repetition brought wisdom. "Do we go down into the village to worship the Lord with the prisoners now?"

Bertrada caught her breath again, her hand uncovering her white fur cape and rubbing over her blue damask covered pregnant belly. "No evangelizing today, ma douce. This sudden snow is too deep."

Gisela led Bertrada through the snow back towards Mur castle, stomping a breaking path in the drifts for her odd waltzing gate as if now Gisela could hear the same mind's music as clearly as her mother.

The castle was a rectangular keep with an imposing height of straight walls, a true donjon, but cut off at the top, as if by a giant's ax. It had even been appropriately nicknamed "the Trunk" by His Majesty.

Through the lower curtain walls and up to the moat they walked together, under the watchful eyes of guards and archers. One archer, in particular, waited at the edge of the drawbridge. He was dressed richly, in a black pill hat with three feathers, one of them gold, and a twill cloak big enough to hide a couple of Gisela's under along with his legs. His cloak's collar was gathered up higher than his neck to keep the snow off, and his bay Jenet horse was liveried in the red caparison of the Royal Court. Off to their side stood a shivering woman, wrapped tightly in a worn woolen cloak and hood.

Bertrada struggled to pick up Gisela onto her hip as they approached the icy drawbridge and the waiting archer and woman.

"You are getting too big for me to do this," Bertrada teased Gisela before turning her attention to the stoic soldier, who half bowed before her. "Captain. How fares Archbishop Gravien this moon?"

The Archer's horse nuzzled Gisela, and her hand rubbed his snout and forehead before the horse turned away.

"The Archbishop is his usual avaricious, curmudgeonly self, your Highness, " the Archer advised, removing from his horse's saddle a leather scroll case ornamented with silver lions carrying crosses.

Gisela pulled a wafer of almond candy out of a hidden pocket in her fine blue kirtle and recovered the horse's attention.

Bertrada huffed, from a heavy child, being heavy with child and a heavy exasperation at the sight of another petition of the bothersome Tour's priest. She motioned for the Archer to keep the scroll case for now.

"This question of a Romefeoh tithe for his pilgrimage to the Pope is becoming my twin labor this winter. Sacré dieu! Why can't archbishops be more like Boniface than Justinian! Already we eat this land barren with the Royal house in residence and our troops at war, and now with my husband's Wascon prisoners and refugees from Poitiers arriving, there shall be naught left remaining here come spring but the Loire and the Archbishop's fat arse."

"Don't say curses mother," Gisela tisked. The Archer's face broke into a smirk.

"Lord, forgive me," Bertrada asked of the sky and falling snow before nodding to Gisela.

Gisela herself did not see her nod or hear the apology, for she was chuckling as the Archer's horse nosed her pockets after more of the marzipan treats he now obviously knew she kept hidden. She produced another one of the wafers for the horse, but it bumped her gloved hand in eagerness, and she dropped it. It fell down into one of her big boots, and the horse decided his mouth might fit in the big boot as well. The Archer pulled the horse's nose up and dug out the wafer out from her boot, amidst tickled laughter from Gisela.

"Now we know how you did so well on your riding lessons last summer. You bribe the palfreys with sweets!" the Archer accused the giggling girl before turning back to the Queen. "Precentor Gervold did not wish to travel back with me through this blizzard. He has remained with the Archbishop, where he is hopeful of arranging for some rye to be sent here, to help feed the prisoners."

"Now Gravien even takes my Chaplain!?" Bertrada shook her head as if deciding enough was enough. "We have funded Marmoutier Abbey well. We have funded Archbishop Gravien's repair of the roof of the Church of Tours. His Majesty generously donated a new pulpit, golden lectern and silken bookmark for the *Turonensis* for last summer's synod. Here in Mur, we build a new church to good Saint John, copying a gathering for a new book of hours for the psalter and feeding the many starving at our doorstep. Now Gravien wishes to ask even more of the people here, people who are only months subdued. No! No, I will not be drug into this haranguing of his again today," Bertrada commanded and stepped bruskly past the Captain of her Archers to enter the castle. "Come along Bérénice." The wrapped woman obediently followed.

"Your Highness, if you please, there is other news from the Archbishop," the Archer pointedly urged the Queen.

"Can't we discuss this inside?" the Queen demanded as she spun around, before noticing the Archer's hesitation. "Or perhaps this why you waited out here in the snow for me?"

"Forgive my impudence, your highness. Your welfare is far more important to me than either snow or gossip. I'm ...uncertain...whose ears you would prefer hearing this rumor of Tassilo," the Archer warned, his voice growing quieter as he stepped towards her, his eyes making a quick glance at Gisela, Bérénice and the open gates of the castle.

The Queen let Gisela slide down her hip and leg to the snowy landing of the drawbridge and to the waiting nanny. "Go inside with Bérénice, ma douce, and back to the chambers. Go take up your scriptorium studies again."

"Yes mother," Gisela quickly feed another marzipan wafer to the Archer's horse before she ran over the icy drawbridge and into the castle, her wrapped nanny in close pursuit and her mother semantically cringing in fear until Gisela made it safely across the ice and under the barbican.

Mur castle was warm enough to melt the snowflakes from her surcoat before Bérénice even got her out of her boots. Up in their chambers, her governor unwrapped himself from his blankets to retake his position behind Gisela at her low desk.

"If you are done playing, take up where we left off, Gisela. Copying Proverb thirty."

The young girl seemed oblivious to the instructions yet grabbed up a goose shaft as clean as any of the Archer's arrows, looked at the Proverb written on her left and began writing a copy on her right with the ink in a practiced hand.

Four things on earth are small, but they are exceedingly wise: the ants are a people not strong, yet they provide their food in the summer; the rabbits are a people not mighty, yet they make their homes in the cliffs; the locusts have no king, yet they all go out by their bands; the spiders you can catch in your hands,

<u>yet it is in kings' palaces.</u>

Every character, even every line of every character, seemed as precise as if his Holiness himself were destined to receive the illuminated vellum.

<u>Three things are stately in their tread; four are stately in their stride: the lion, which is mightiest among beasts and does not turn back before any; the strutting rooster amongst the hens, the ram leading his flock, and a king whose army is with him.</u>

The nun raised her quill off the vellum with a smooth stroke, making the Abbess smile.

"Wonderful Rene! Your determination has brought you through, and your practice made you skilled in the word of our Lord!"

"Do you think so, Abbess? The edges of the first three lines seem to waver, and the clubbing on the f's is rarely the same," Sister Rene pleaded, pleased but still uncertain.

"Sister, you do the Lord and the convent proud. You are one hand of God in this simple yet noble endeavor. Where the warrior's sword and ship take the baptism to the heart of the heathen, these pages will help the new priests and missionaries amongst them to reach the minds of God's newest flocks. We cannot take up spear and shield, but we can take up quill and ink to join the fight." The Abbess rubbed the back of the nun's shoulders in encouragement before stepping away.

The candle flames flickered as the tall abbess left one escritoire for the next, like a captain of the guard inspecting posts.

At the next desk, a nun was busy practicing letters on wax tablets. No expensive ink to be wasted yet on untrained hands.

The Abbess's calm demeanor and strong hands helped the nun with a few strokes and precise motions. Smiles seemed contagious around the Abbess as she left one candled shrine to knowledge for yet another. The desks occupied alcoves in the stone walls, and the hallway formed a great semi-circle around the alcoves.

"Mother," asked a nun approaching her down the hall. "The snow is growing much worse."

"If it keeps up till nightfall we'll be snowed in indeed. Have Sister Sandrine move all the cows into the undercroft of the refectory, and ask the Abbot to have lay brother Rupert to go over to Calae to fetch more hay before it gets too deep. Tell Sister Nadette to keep the chickens out of the officina!"

"Yes, Mother."

"Oh, Vespers is too close. Don't bother with the Abbot, I'll talk to him about Rupert myself."

The Abbess paused a moment in the darker space between the alcoves and kissed the honeysuckled cross hanging from her neck. "When I am afraid, I put my trust in you," she whispered and continued her pace to come to a nun with her head down on her desk.

"Sister Sophie!" she scolded the nun, who awoke to the horror of her Mother Superior shaking her.

"Abbess! I'm so sorry!"

"You should be ashamed! I don't know what they allowed at Fécamp, but this is unacceptable here!"

"Yes, Mother," the nun began weeping at her failure.

The Abbess relented, her softer face reappeared,

and she hugged the nun against her hip. "Too much Advent fasting preparing for Octave, I should think. And you have been practicing very hard since your arrival. I'll talk to Sister Gabrielle about reducing your chores for a day, but you should rest and reflect on what it means to this abbey for you to be here. Ask the Lord for guidance...and a good night's sleep." She hugged her once more and left the nun drying her tears.

The Abbess slowed her pace, the smell from the ovens of the kitchen now joining the warmth of the kitchen's shared walls with the scriptorium.

"Sister Claire," she came to the next nun busy at her escritoire.

"Mother," the nun kept her attention on her ink and quill. The Abbess looked over her shoulder at the copying of the Proverbs.

Who hath woe? Whose father hath woe? Who hath contentions? Who falls into pits? Who hath wounds without cause? Who hath redness of eyes?

Surely they that pass their time in wine and study the drink in their cups.

The spacing between words was critical. The last and first letters were as bookends to a gate of exacting size for the breath of the mind to pass through.

Look not upon the wine when it is yellow, when the colour thereof shineth in the glass: it goeth in pleasantly. But in the end, it will bite like a snake, and will spread abroad poison like a basilisk.

d's lean more to the left. There. There.

Thy eyes shall behold strange women, and thy heart shall utter perverse things. And thou shalt be as one sleeping in the midst of the sea, and as a pilot fast asleep, when the stern is lost. And thou shalt say: They have beaten me, but I was not sensible of pain: they drew me, and I felt not: when shall I awake, and find wine again?

Gisela pulled up her smooth quill and turned to her mother, who was closer to the fireplace doing embroidery while the governor read.

"Why do we copy the Psalms and Proverbs, Mother? Do we intend to copy every single one?"

"Proverbs, Psalms, entire Bibles, and even more. Augustine's commentaries on the Psalms. Pope Gregory's commentaries and dialogues on missionary work."

"But why?"

"So we learn them," added the governor.

"Your brother says many Bretons are willing to accept Jesus Christ as Lord and Savior, but the few priests who are there lack the guidance and wisdom to help them beyond the baptism. They hear the first words but fall back into sinful ways without proper guidance," Bertrada answered, her attention not leaving her stitching.

Gisela got excited. "Have we heard from Charles? Did he send a letter?"

"No, ma douce. You know he can't. He told us these things before he returned to join the Margrave on the Breton Marche months ago."

Gisela returned to her writing but remembering her older brother only filled her imagination with more of the Brittany tales he had told her of people like King Gradlon and the fairy queen Malgven. She tried to concentrate as best she could, biting her lip.

What, O my beloved, what, O the beloved of my womb, what, O the beloved of my vows? Give not thy substance to women, and thy riches to destroy kings.

"Why don't we write verses for the Wascon and Aquitaine prisoners we go see in the village every day?"

"I doubt any of them can even read," the governor warned.

Bertrada stuck her needle in the cloth and slowly stood up stretching. She came over to her daughter and knelt down. "We are not priests, ma douce. We cannot preach the words to them. But we can sing them in Mass. We can show them Christ's mercy with food, and healing. We can care for the poor as if they were Christ, and from our example, they can learn of our Lord."

"Many of the prisoners are already Catholic, and attend Mass when the Bishop is here," Gisela noted. "Many of the Aquitaine attended Mass here before the rebellion."

"Yes, but these people need more than an occasional visiting Bishop and more commitment in their hearts than a chained ear."

"Then why can't we read the Bible to them, or recite Bible verses?"

"You are good to wish such things, but it's not our place as women. It is too easy to make mistakes, too easy to misjudge or misguide someone into incorrect Christian thinking, and commit heresy," Bertrada answered her, standing up slowly with the governor's and Gisela's help.

Gisela looked suddenly serious. Even young children knew better than to meddle with heresy.

The old governor helped Bertrada back up. "It is best to quietly repeat your Bible verses amongst yourselves to face your daily trials as women."

"And when evil presents itself before us," Bertrada waltz-stepped back over to her cushioned chair and embroidery. "Saint Patrick and Saint Ninian left our blessed Saint Martin's Marmoutier Abbey to evangelize the Irish. Now Irish priests leave their land to evangelize the Saxons and Frisians closer to our home in Aachen and Soissons. What we hope to do is offer our support to priests heading for Armorica and Brittany and Saxony."

"Many of the Wascon prisoners from His Majesty's victories were already sent north. Did priests go with them?"

"I don't think so. Just soldiers."

Give not to kings, O Lamuel, give not wine to kings: because there is no secret where drunkenness reigneth: And lest they drink and forget judgments, and pervert the cause of the children of the poor.

"Some of the Aquitaine families amongst the prisoners are wine crafters. Does that make them evil to God?"

"No. Our Lord himself made wine. The priests transform wine into Christ's blood for communion. Making wine for this purpose is holy. A cup of wine with a meal, with the roasts and bitters, helps the digestion of the body. Making extra wine to sell is for the tenants and pagani. Only drinking wine to simply get drunk is considered sinful."

Give strong drink to them that are sad: and wine to them that are grieved in mind: Let them drink, and forget their want, and remember their sorrow no more.

"We don't drink wine during meals, because we are of the Royal Court and His Majesty does not approve of wine, but it is fitting for the poor to drink it," Gisela said aloud, trying to figure the proverbs out. "Some of the prison families plan to make wine again next year, and sell some to the church in Tours."

"How do you know that?"

"The nursery in the new church to St John."

"She talks with the other children there when you go to evangelize," the governor quickly added. "I thought you were aware and approved, your Majesty."

"It's alright," Bertrada claimed. "I knew she played with the young children there, I just didn't know they spoke our Latin."

Open thy mouth for the dumb, and for the causes of all the children that pass.

Open thy mouth, decree that which is just, and do justice to the needy and poor.

"The Aquitaine children do, at least d'oil close enough to understand. The Wascon don't. They were trying to teach me Wascon. Does His Majesty know Wasconian?"

"His Majesty has many wise men, soldiers, and servants to help him talk with all our people."

"That seems smart."

"But I've never heard him speak Wascon. Perhaps you can teach him a few words when he returns."

Who shall find a valiant woman? Far and from the uttermost coasts is the price of her. The heart of her husband trusteth in her, and he shall have no need of spoils. She will render him good, and not evil, all the days of her life.

She hath sought wool and flax, and hath wrought by the counsel of her hands.

She is like the merchant's ship, she bringeth her bread from afar.

"Will His Majesty be back this winter?"

"No, ma douce. You know full well he had to

pursue King Waiofar to Wasconia. He has to put an end to the rebels for our country to be whole for your brothers."

"I miss Charles."

"As do I."

And she hath risen in the night, and given a prey to her household, and victuals to her maidens. She hath considered a field, and bought it: with the fruit of her hands she hath planted a vineyard.

She stopped writing and studied both the copy and what she had written, and thought a long moment before continuing.

She hath girded her loins with strength, and hath strengthened her arm.

She hath tasted and seen that her traffic is good: her lamp shall not be put out in the night. She hath put out her hand to strong things, and her fingers have taken hold of the spindle. She hath opened her hand to the needy, and stretched out her hands to the poor. She shall not fear for her house in the cold of snow: for all her domestics are clothed with double garments. She hath made for herself clothing of tapestry: fine linen, and purple is her covering.

The nun stopped writing and put the quill down, massaging her hand as the Abbess came into her room unannounced.

"It's getting onto Vespers, Eusebia, and the snow is piling up into the narthex," the Abbess warned.

"I'm almost finished with thirty-one, Mother."

The Abbess tilted her head and looked over the nun's shoulder at her work. "Bishop Remigius was right! Your work is simply beautiful!" She took up the vellum off the escritoire to inspect it closer. "Your letters are still broad, but that was your upbringing in Chur, I suppose. Very nice Eusebia. You are a gem."

"Thank you, Mother. I am humbled to be able to serve the Lord.".

"May we all be."

"May I ask, Mother, where these pages are destined to go?"

"Bretons, Saxons, Frisians, Jutes, Danes. His Majesty understands we must armor our priests just as surely as we armor our warriors if we are to gain victory for Christendom. Oh, what a time to be a woman in the service of the Lord, Eusebia! When the apostles of Christ walked among us, women sang and prayed and preached as the men did. Then for hundreds of years, women were silenced. We supported our fathers, our husbands and our sons in the work of the Church. We became unnamed bricks in the foundation of the Christian ministry. But that was as the Lord intended, for now, our bricks are numerous beyond count, and have risen up to be churches, doms, temples, and monasteries. The praise and pondering for the Lord is no longer the province of hermits in caves. Now women can join covenants to seek a life with Christ, and our voices to fill his temples. We can minister to the sick and poor, for they are always with us, as Christ says, and so is he! Women can learn to read, write, and think, in the safe embrace of Christ. We can grow with God! Abbesses from great families can become lords of monasteries and lands, even rule over men now, and they say some Abbesses are even hearing confessions and granting absolution."

"We still do not do mission work to the pagans." Eusebia motioned to the Bible verses she was copying.

"Mission work amidst pagan warlords accomplishes us little but rape and bondage in this evil world. Men are still wicked! We cannot as yet inspire enough pagan women to the point of turning their men against heathen idols. But that time may yet come!" the Abbess declared. "For now women all over Austrasia, Neustria, Lombardy, Iberia...Bavaria..," the Abbess said, kneeling and taking up Eusebia's hands and squeezing them for a moment. "...Are taking up more than bread and water into packs, and doing more than waiting in doorways and windows for returns!" She stood back up.

Other nuns came around the hallway from their quiet alcoves as the unusual tone and excitement of her voice caught their attention.

"We can take up the habit, take up the hoe and rake, take up the plow, take up the quill, take up the song, take up the praise with all our might! With the houses and wealth God grants us in our lives, we can now endow priests with sacraments and ships, fund warriors girded in mail and sword to protect them, buy horses and wagons for farms and donate art and relics for churches. We may not be capable of being the spearhead, but we can be the mighty shaft following it in!" the Abbess declared, her hands sweeping many of the nun's hands together like a bird trying to take flight.

"Take up the word of God, into your hearts Sisters, and let it flow back out on these pages. Let it flow with this script of Marmoutier, so we speak with many voices as one. Let it flow with your passion...and your love...and your hopes," she said, emphasizing the emotions to the Sisters, who seemed to be feeding on it like starved castaways. She lifted up Eusebia's page of the Proverb. "Know this; somewhere, in Saxony, or amongst the Slavs, amongst the Danes, amongst the Saracens, by the seasides, under forest trees, in huts and hovels and caves and foreign palaces, a priest will be reading your copied Proverbs and singing the Psalms to the bowed heads of God's newest converts, as if from your very lips. They will ponder the wisdom of the Church fathers from our copied letters and their learned opinions, and your hands will have helped them show new Christians the correct paths, paths your feet could not have treaded before this time. Oh Sisters, let us away to Vespers and give praise to our Lord!"

Put in the sickle, for the harvest is ripe. Come, tread, for the winepress is full; The vats overflow, for their wickedness is great. The sun and moon grow dark, and the stars lose their brightness. The LORD roars from Zion And utters His voice from Jerusalem, And the heavens and the earth tremble. But the LORD is a refuge for His people And a stronghold to the sons of Israel. Then you will know that I am the LORD your God, Dwelling in Zion, My holy mountain. So Jerusalem will be holy, And strangers will pass through it no more. And it shall come to pass in that day, that the mountains shall drop down sweet wine,

"Very good! Your Roman cursive practice has glyphed the et into a ligature &!" chuckled the governor.

"Was I wrong?" Gisela asked, worried.

"No. It shows your mind is speeding up your handwriting."

and the hills shall flow with milk: and waters shall flow through all the rivers of Juda: and a fountain shall come

forth of the house of the Lord, and shall water the torrent of
thorns.

"Make your capitols longer. And thicker. Don't be
afraid to historiate the E in Egypt into some animal,"
the governor pointedly instructed.

Egypt shall be a desolation, and Edom a wilderness
destroyed: because they have done unjustly against the
children of Juda, and have shed innocent blood in their land.
And Judea shall be inhabited forever, and Jerusalem to
generation and generation. And I will cleanse their blood
which I had not cleansed: and the Lord will dwell in Zion.

Bérénice entered the room with a divinely smelling
covered tray, and Gisela put the quill down and lost
all attention on ink and words.

"Thought with all the heavy snow, perhaps, your
Highness, it might be alright," Bénénice meekly
offered with a curtsey to the Queen.

Bertrada hid her smile from Gisela, but only
hesitated her embroidery stitches. "With All Saint's
Day, All Soul's Day not so long ago?" she tisked.
"Hum. What do you say, Ma Douce?"

Bérénice removed the towel covering the tray, and
the honey and raisin palmiers steamed.

"I think God gets angry when people don't listen to
him," Gisela blurted out.

The governor raised his eyebrows in surprise, and
Bertrada's lips stretched before she nodded in
agreement. "Yes, with the stubborn, God can be
angry. He offers forgiveness first, but eventually, his
patience runs out with those who are true sinners."

"Then, let us say the Lord's Prayer all together, to
thank him for such a treat when so many outside in
the cold might be hungry," Gisela offered. Bérénice
winked at her.

"Alright," Bertrada relented, and they formed a circle and prayed before digging into the treats.

Run Away

"Now, don't think I didn't see you sneaking some of those palmiers into your kirtle pockets!" Bérénice scolded Gisela as she combed her hair out and put it in a simple sleeping veil.

"I want the snood!" Gisela begged. "It matches my kirtle!" she pointed at them both on the dresser.

"You'll sleep in your veil and your chemise with *no pocket full of palmiers!*" she emphasized with a stroke of the brush on every word. "There's no need to ruin good silver snoods with pillow hair," Bérénice insisted. "There. Done"

Gisela yawned, and Bérénice slid the sheets and blanket over Gisela's legs.

"You best be off to sleep early, ma princesse!" Bérénice tucked Gisela in under the tapet. The empty bed next to hers was starched and quilted, a pair of little slippers on them, and the empty crib on the opposite side stood quietly waiting its turn again later this winter. Bérénice stoked up the coals in the fireplace, closed the thick curtains to the Queen's adjoining bedroom and then closed the nursery door behind her.

Gisela popped up almost as soon as the door was closed. Casting off the tapet, she made her way over to the dresser by red coal light from the fireplace. First, she put on her blue sendal kirtle, then slipped the silver snood into her pocket and tiptoed over to the nearby bed, carefully grabbing one of the slippers. She took it to the covered window, setting it beside the trunk on the floor. She opened the lid of the trunk quietly and took out a dried grape leaf, placing it on the slipper. Climbing up on the trunk, in a surprisingly practiced fashion, she was able to reach the ties of the tapestry covering the window, and she loosened them. She climbed down and scooted up under the tapestry, against the shuttered window. She removed a familiar loose plank, and the outside cold and dim torchlight from the courtyard below covered her soft face.

"Little Father?!" she quietly whispered out. "We had palmiers tonight!"

She reached back under the tapestry for her slipper and leaf on the floor, then set them on the sill. She took her silver jeweled snood out and carefully opened it up on her palm, the glittering edges draping over her fingers and wrist. She one-handedly worked an ear-shaped palmier treat out of her kirtle pocket, then put it right in the middle of her snood. She leaned out the hole in the window shutter, shaking the slipper and leaf in her other hand, so one of the slipper's tassel bells quietly tinkled in the cold. In the other, she held out the treat in the snood. The thin silver and tiny sapphires of the snood glowed like a fine spider-web in the snow-light.

The nursery window, when the weather was pleasant, overlooked a pergola over the castle's bailey courtyard garden, and a huge old grapevine came from far below, almost up to her window, before twining out along the roof frames and Jove's beards of the pergola. The few torches by the gate and bailey walls below cast enough dim light to see the outlines of the vine, and the deep snow reflected more light than usual.

Gisela looked up. The castle seemed to be blocking the wind of the falling snow, for it caught the light of higher room windows and crenelated guard posts as it came drifting around the top and sides to land softly on the vine and her window frame. She brushed off some of the snow on the sill and leaned over to look down.

"Féer? Good People?" she called out quietly, still gently ringing the little slipper bells. She held a palmier in the snood out into the snow, watching for odd eddies or footprints along the sill. She began to sing a rhyming song of féer and the Tylwyth Teg and continued until her extended arms grew cold. She drew it back in and started eating the offered treat herself.

"Little Father," she addressed the grapevine lovingly, catching flakes on her dried grape leaf. "Birinus says your wine will be ready soon. Maybe by the feast of St John. Charles is still in the north, with the Bretons, in whose great halls the tales of Taliesin are retold every night. Tales of people like Math and Gwydion. They made a woman out of flowers, and Gwydion made an army of trees to fight as his soldiers. Gradlon and Dahut. Illtud teaching Paol and Samson and Gildas," she took another bite. "Keban was an evil sorceress who trapped Saint Ronan's daughter in a tree. We've talked about her before, you remember. He freed her and brought her back to life with the Lord's help. Ronan knew all about hamadryads. So did Saint Gildas. He brought a woman back to life, along with her unborn child! Saint Samson brought people back to life too, as well as

Saint Maclou. Only the saints can break the spell."

Gisela stopped both chewing and talking, snowflakes making the only sounds, singing with the wind.

"The Bretons make pilgrimages to the saints for pardons. Church pardons that grant indulgences from Heaven. They have small pilgrimages at certain times of the year. Near Saint Paol is a pilgrimage for Saint Guénolé. He was the priest for King Gradlon, you know. And Saint Corentin. Saint Ronan's pardon is supposed to be every six years, and this is the very year according to Charles. He has said we might make a pilgrimage to Jerusalem one day. Wouldn't it be grand?"

Gisela looked sad again.

"I'd miss you, Little Father, but it would be worth it." She finished the palmier. Gisela tapped the snow off the grape leaf.

"Charles is in the deep forests of the Breton Marches. What if he can go make the pilgrimage to Saint Maclou and Saint Samson? If he could go, he might earn a pardon...and maybe a miracle. We must go ask Mother if we can send him a message!" Gisela's eyes widened, her arms shaking, and she stuffed the snood in her pocket. She slipped her head and arms back inside and dug her way out from under the tapestry. She put the slipper back on the bed with its mate and ran to the door. She stepped outside along the balcony railing over the Queen's common room below, and looking down she remembered she was back in her dress and would get Bérénice scolded for it.

"Marching the prisoners north, in this early snow?" the governor asked, still reading as the Queen worked her needles by firelight. His long gray hair was no longer staying tucked under his cap.

"It seems so cruel," Bérénice agreed.

"But the rumors of an impending rebellion in the area come from several sources now, and with Duke Tassilo's odd withdrawal from His Majesty's war camp and subsequent disappearance, we cannot take any chances. We don't have enough food to keep feeding them all winter anyway. All my Captains agreed and urged me to do this. Hungry, bored, rebellious prison soldiers can be stirred up with hardly a switch and twig; much more so by a rich commander. The prisoners will have to be moved out. I've already given the order to have them taken to Andecavus immediately, and then up north to the Marches to help build the new fortresses." Bertrada resumed her embroidery.

"The little Miss won't like hearing this. She's grown close to the Aquitaine children she met in the new church," Bérénice lamented. "Break her heart again, it will."

"They are just poor children." Bertrada turned from her embroidery to look at the governor. She extended her arm out to him, and the older man looked surprised by the gesture. "Uncle, you've done a fine job with Gisela's courtly skills. Her dancing is wonderful, and her manners are superb," Bertrada told him with softer eyes than usual. "I was most unsure when the governess died you could take over her duties and still be her tutor. Prüm Abey would be proud of you. As would Mother."

The governor looked touched. "My good sister would have been proud of her daughter *and* her granddaughter. There are scribes who can copy, and then there are scriveners like Gisela. She can read to herself, without speaking it out loud. Most unusual. Her exegesis and understanding are remarkable for a child her age. I know monks as old as I who are still not as enlightened as she is. You know when she read Boethius' *Consolation* she understood parts of it?!"

"His pictures help."

"She surely loves the ancient stories," Bérénice added.

"She seemed to enjoy Homer's *Odyssey* last winter," the governor agreed.

Bertrada laughed. "Oh my, it was all Ulysses and Telemachus fighting cyclopes and sorceresses over the spring."

"Not no more, not since Charles visited over the last summer. Now it's all the poems of Taliesin with cities in the sea and King Gradlon and wizards and walking trees. Not good Bible stories like she should follow."

"Oh, Bérénice! Even Saint Augustine tells us the ancient tales are important, if filtered through the Christian faith! Gisela needs to see all men as they truly are. Strong, proud, valiant, yes, but stubborn and foolish! If she's going to be an Empress she will have to learn to navigate the world of great men and their constant folly and concupiscence." The Queen reached up, stretching her back.

"Gisela follows the Bible stories rather well, I think," the governor stated, at an elder age where common wisdom let him acquiesce to the attack on his gender. "She really tries to see things as the Apostles did, as the Israelites did, as Solomon might have."

As Bérénice tucked another pillow between the Queen's back and the chair, Bertrada's head was nodding in agreement. "Gisela's language skills amaze me."

"Her poetry is quite nice," Bérénice offered.

"Poems help in both speaking and writing," the governor explained.

"Speaking of Homer, you're going to have to start her on more Greek, and soon," Bertrada insisted.

"Yes, your Majesty, we will indeed."

"Your Highness, is there any chance I might have to go with Gisela to Constantinople?" Bérénice asked sheepishly.

"No Bérénice, I'll need you and your sister here for the new baby. Your proven value as midwives far exceeds your skill at dressing Gisela for dinners."

"Constantinople? Already?" Gisela whispered as she listened from the balcony, and suddenly forgetting all about Saint Samson.

"Oh, thank you, your Highness. I don't think I would be no good to her, and I can't bring myself to seeing our Gisela married off to that Leon boy. His mother's a Khazar, God save our girl's soul. No telling what she'll do as a mother-in-law."

"His Majesty and the Bishop say the Eastern Empire has been prosecuting people for venerating the Holy Mother Mary," the governor reported sadly.

"It's His Majesty's wish that she is to be married into the Eastern Roman Empire. We'll have to leave by late winter, to get her there by next summer."

Tears ran down Gisela's face. It was all too much. She made her way silently back into the nursery and quietly closed the door behind her, resting her sobbing head against it briefly.

Married, before her first Eve's curse had even started. She thought she'd marry the Prince of the far away Eastern Empire years from now. She adored

Christ's Holy Mother, looked up to her, and she would have to stop?

She left the door and walked around the room slowly in the red coal light. They had been keeping everything from her. No one would be left to comfort Little Father, and what if the féer wanted the new baby? When His Majesty came back, he would dig up ALL the vines. Little Father was the biggest grapevine at Mur; it would be the first to go when he came home. She would never be able to save Little Father if she were sent away. She thought of her friend's fathers and families being sent away against their will too. Being sent north. North to the Breton Marches.

Charles is in the Breton Marches! Saint Maclou's and Saint Samson's Pardons are there! She would go find Charles, and they would go make a pilgrimage to Aleth and Dol.

Determined, Gisela put on her over-sized boots. There were still palmiers in the kirtle pockets to eat on the way, and she put on her beautiful velvet gloves. She stole Bérénice's old cloak off the wall and wrapped herself well in it, hood and all. It was big but warm. She looked at her velvet gloves, and like a flock of golden plovers they stood out. She rubbed them in the fireplace ashes until they were a sooty gray.

Drying her teary cheeks, she became doubtful and confused. She loved her mother, so much. But, if she was going to be sent away anyways, what would be the difference? This way, she might impress her mother, enough to let her stay perhaps, or her mother might argue with His Majesty to let Gisela stay, or at least demand to go with her to the Eastern Empire. Yes, this was the better choice. It would be her choice.

Gisela found herself at the open hole of the

shuttered window all too suddenly. The cold on her face was sharply real. She tried to squeeze out the hole, but now in all her clothes, it was too tight. She reached up and undid the latch on the shutters, opening the one with the hole in it enough to squeeze through. The heavy tapestry behind her seemed to be trying to push her out. The vine was covered in snow, and the ground was a long way down in the shadows.

"Little Father, what do I do?" she begged, balanced on the sill. "You had the féer to lead you."

She looked at the quiet vine. Snowflakes drifted slowly past her face.

"God will lead me. Christ led me to the children at the church. Their prison families in the village will lead me north to Charles, and Charles will lead me to Saint Maclou and Saint Samson, and I will pray for a Pardon there. Praise be to God."

The tapestry settled gently against the inside of the shuttered window, closing it again, and the grand old gnarled grapevine barely even quivered.

Horses huffed at getting pulled from warm barns and hitched. Guards with tall spears and cold mail hurried past servants bringing and loading jugs and baskets. The courtyard was terribly busy given the late evening, and Gisela was confused until she saw Sister Rosine by a wagon. The chubby nun had been helping them feed and evangelize the prisoners in the village outside the castle. Gisela decided to take a chance. She pulled her hood back and unwrapped the cloak, pinning it to her shoulders so the blue kirtle showed, and boldly stepped around the woodpile from the garden.

"Put the oil there. Yes, come on Birinus, place those

woolen horse blankets right there. Child?" Rosine noticed Gisela unexpectedly climbing up onto the seat of the wagon beside her. "I thought your Mother had decided not to travel to the village tonight."

"She changed her mind," Gisela answered as if she were the Queen herself.

"Potzblitz. Make yourself useful then, and hold those salt bags out of the snow."

Gisela did as she was told, wrapping them in her cloak on her lap. The ruse worked, but only because of the haste in which the carts were being loaded. The half dozen carts rolled out under the barbican gate and across the drawbridge as servants ran alongside with torches.

She tried to peek through the snow down into the village, but it was blinding. She pulled her hood up again, dying to look back but afraid to glance and make Rosine suspicious. The train of supplies trundled into the village, all now awakened.

The castle blacksmiths were busy with the men and even some women, one metal wristband each, alternating on a long chain. Every chain seemed to link ten to a dozen prisoners, and every chain had a mailed soldier holding one end, guarding it. Other soldiers were rousting the huts to empty, their families and handfuls of possessions now tumbled out in the cold.

Gisela left the salt under the cart seat and slipped off towards the church when Rosine was busy loading more supplies on the carts. She drew the cloak back around herself, hiding her blue kirtle. No one stopped her or even seemed to notice her passing. The children did not seem to be a threat worth the cold hammer.

The church to St John was still only half built, with

no real roof to speak of except a temporary thatch ciborium over the altar area. Two deacons looked unbelievably busy and seemed about as useful as the nonexistent roof; both in keeping the altar sacred and reclining soldiers away as well as trying to pray with the many fractured families, and they seemed to have absolutely no power against the onslaught of soldiers, snow and weeping, pleading faces. Gisela had basked in the warmth of her mother's affections for years, now she was seeing her cold edge. She passed women she had seen her mother pray with, bring food to, even hold their babies. Now hard men used steel to enforce her iron will. The snowfall made it even more bitter. It was like being cast out of Heaven into Purgatory.

Gisela spied the old wide-hipped nun who watched over the orphans and nursery. There were twice as many children in the back of the choir as usual, and more arriving. A big fluffy white mastiff was barking at the bustling soldiers near the nun, and several of the children were huddling together. Wispy snow fell like momentarily floured stalactites amongst the boys, girls, and commotion. She finally spied her friend, Eulalie, hugging a small boy, and slid over into them with an extra hug around both.

Gisela's friend was a typical child of the rustics of the Loire, a mix of older Aquitaine and Orlèans bloodlines giving people a sinew more like stubborn goats than the enduring Wascon oxen temperament. Eulalie herself was shorter than most, with a narrow nose bridge like a plowshare between two soft eyes. She had a small mouth over the kind of sharp chin grandmothers could not resist pinching, and hair of a color Gisela felt was more like a bay horse in daylight, and of profound beauty if Gisela could only convince

Eulalie to let it grown out and comb it on the odd Saint's day.

"Eulalie. It's going to be alright," she offered. Eulalie's tears did not seem to agree.

"How will it be alright? We're going to be drowned in the river as spies!" she cried, the boy with her crying even harder.

"Don't be silly. You're being moved north, not killed," Gisela offered back, but as she followed the boy's strange eyes, she saw the men who would, until now, die protecting her, in a brand new light. One that sent shivers down her back, for she saw them as he did, and she had to admit they looked as if they would drop a rebel child into the icy water of the Loire without regret. This was not going as she had thought.

"Where are all these children coming from? You're supposed to be keeping a nursery, not an orphanage," a broad-shouldered soldier with chalk stick demanded of the old nun.

"People abandon their children here now because they frightened they be used against them. Your soldiers scaring everyone! They panicking!"

"Who is this one?" the soldier demanded. Gisela looked up to see one of the soldiers from Mur she knew, Julien, but there was no recognition in his eyes, at least not of her soot wiped face and wrapped in her nanny's old cloak. He was pointing the chalk at Eulalie.

"That be Eulalie. You have her father over there," Sister Amona answered. The old nun seemed as tough as Julien and just as ready for a fight.

Julien raked his chalk across Eulalie's shoulder as he was already asking about the next. "Who's the little boy in blue with her?"

"I don know his name, but he been here a couple of weeks now."

~Save me.~

Gisela looked at the boy again, swearing he had begged her to save him, yet no one else seemed to have heard or seen it, and the boy's eyes were clenched tightly shut in weeping fear.

"Take the boy outside," Julien ordered one of his men.

"He's my brother...Alesander." Gisela stood up in front of the approaching soldier's arms.

"Who is she?" Julien demanded with the chalk as a pointer.

"I don know," Sister Amona said in an odd voice. "She been here before...at Mass, I think."

"Where's your family?" demanded Julien.

"My father escaped at Bordeaux. He is either recaptured, dead, or still fighting in Wasconia."

"Where's your mother then?"

"You tell me. Four of your soldiers carried her away one night at Egolisma, and she never returned," Gisela answered coldly.

Julien's face showed a brief glimpse of compassion.

"Why you here child?" Sister Amona asked.

"We have an uncle already taken up to Bayeux."

Julien marked both her shoulder and the boy's and then moved on with Sister Amona to the next children. Gisela hugged Eulalie and the boy again, as much for warmth as to let a shudder of her nervous fear dissipate through them.

"His name is Sacha," an older girl called out, loud enough for Julien to have heard if he had been listening. The boy opened his eyes and glared past the girls at the older girl. "An he in't your brother," the older girl added.

"Hush!" whispered Gisela.

"Why?" replied the older girl. "His parents are dead. He's eating our food. Let somebody else take him."

"Maylis, you are pure evil!" Eulalie hissed.

The older girl beamed.

"Knowing that whatsoever good thing any man shall do, the same shall he receive from the Lord, whether he be bond, or free," Gisela responded, and Maylis' smile disappeared, accompanied by a dismissive wave of her hand.

Eulalie pulled Gisela's ear to her lips. "What are you doing?"

"I have to go with you. North."

"Why?! You're the Queen's daughter! You told the soldier MY mother's story. You don't want to die with us."

Gisela pulled the shaking girl to her. "We're not going to die. I won't let you. I won't let them. I can stop them if they try. You'll see," she whispered, then pushed her back and looked at her face to face. When Eulalie eventually nodded she looked at the boy.

"Are you going to be able to move?"

He nodded through his tears, and the girls helped him up.

"Help us get the toddlers on the carts! Help us get the toddlers on the carts," Sister Amona came by asking the older children. Gisela and Eulalie began gathering up the smallest children and following the old nun. The girls glared at Maylis as they passed, who remained seated and didn't move to help anyone, but did try to trip Sacha. He caught himself on Gisela but didn't fall.

The church nave was filled with families with older members or the sick who wouldn't be able to make the trek north. It was a tearful departing that didn't strike Gisela hard until the torchlit Castle of Mur appeared like an imposing mountain once they left the church walls. The snow blew around the carts and people and the giant dark trunk of the castle as the rattle of chains began, and the soldiers began marching man and cart down to the docks.

Square ferry-barges, the Aquitaine called them *calones*, were basically leaky rafts used for hauling building stone and ferrying horses across the river and had been drawn up to the docks at Mur. It was bitter cold and snow seemed to cover everything, but the water was still warmer than the snow this late in fall, and the Loire, while chilly and damp, wasn't going to freeze anytime soon. Carts were loaded onto the ferry-barges by the chained men, and the horses were taken back to Mur. Women and families scrambled for the dry spots. Gisela kept Sister Amona close and as far away as possible from Sister Rosine as the ferry-barges set out.

The chained Aquitaine farmers; the most local of the prisoners and familiar with the Loire between Mur and Andecavus after a hard-working summer and fall's worth of barging, polled the ferry-barges by torchlight along the banks downriver. Gisela huddled with Eulalie, Sacha and the other children under one of the big wool blankets beside Sister Amona's cart the entire night, until the Mur donjon became a trunk, then became a stump and then a twig, and then disappeared into the swirling dark behind them.

The sky was still a bleak white at midday. The circle

of the sun could not even be glimpsed through the clouds yet, but the snow had tapered off to flurries now, and along the white banks the Loire cut a black swath, like a swan's eye-bill framed in white. No real swans graced the waters, but ducks and cormorants abounded. The nuns and women cooked on the shore for the prisoners and families, if the hasty pea frumenty could rightfully be called cooked, as the ferry-barges all sat tied off together along the north bank. The Frankish soldiers seemed ill at ease and kept most everyone on the ferry-barges under a watchful eye. Sister Amona had gone with the other nuns to divide up what little food and wine there was amongst the prisoners.

Gisela was counting the number of chains she could see. She guessed there were twenty-eight or twenty-nine, meaning they had moved three-hundred and fifty people from the informal prisons around the village last night. She didn't know what the rumors of rebellion had been, but they must have scared her mother dearly to create this. This journey was slower and taking longer than she expected.

"Who'd ya steal your clothes from?" Maylis asked Gisela once Sister Amona was no longer around to keep order.

"I didn't steal my clothes."

Maylis coughed in disgust. "Those aren't your big shoes."

Gisela pulled her legs and feet up under her. "My mother gave them to me."

"She give you a pocket full of jewelry too?"

Gisela looked uncomfortable. "It's sugar on palmiers, not jewelry." She took one of the treats out and showed it to prove her point.

"What's your name?"

Gisela remained quiet.

"Eulalie, tell me what her name is!" Maylis lazily tossed a chunk of snow at the girl.

Eulalie looked panicked.

"It's Duende," Gisela finally answered for Eulalie.

"Duende?"

"Duende," insisted Gisela, getting up as Sister Amona came back with a pot of yellow pea gruel and a wineskin. She and Eulalie began helping the younger children get spoonfuls and a shared hanop of white wine, interrupted by Maylis darting in and swiping her share when Sister Amona was busy. It wasn't much food or wine to go around, and the children finished their spoonfuls in mere moments, looking to Sister Amona with brief hope before clearly reading the regret on her face.

Sister Amona's big mastiff rose up from under the cart and began barking at the river. Calls and pointing from some of the families on the ferry-barges alerted everyone to the opposite bank.

More than half a dozen riders in Royal livery were slowly riding up the snowy road across the river on the south bank.

The crowds got decidedly more nervous, and cackling, as another group of Royal riders appeared making their way along the north bank road as well. The guards and Julien went to greet them, seemingly friendly enough, but a woman on Gisela's ferry began screaming when several of the soldiers dismounted and drew bows on the ferry-barges. Mild panic rippled through the prisoners, and Sister Amona quickly herded the younger children behind the cart on their barge.

"Quiet Atenea!" she begged her dog.

The Royal soldiers on the south shore paused opposite the ferry-barges and remained seated; too far away for any bowshot, but it did seem to punctuate the point.

Oddly, Julien and the other soldiers began to take up a formation. One of the new riders was a Lieutenant Gisela thought she might remember seeing at the castle, but they were too far away to be sure, and much too far away to hear what was being said.

Soon all the Frankish soldiers acting as prison guards left the ferry-barges for shore and took up formation with their comrades. The Lieutenant and Julian began going to each soldier and talking with them.

"What do they do?" Sister Amona asked.

"It looks like some type of military inspection," Gisela answered her before thinking.

"This is odd, no?" Amona asked, uncertain. Gisela certainly thought so.

"They're looking for *thieeeeves*," whispered Maylis to Gisela.

Then, as suddenly as they had shown up, the Royal soldiers remounted their horses and rode back upriver the way they had come. The guard soldiers broke formation as if nothing had happened and returned to the ferry-barges and their respective prison chains.

Atenea gave a few last barks and then curled back up under the cart.

Andecavus

The prison ferry-barges set back off downriver, and Gisela gathered Eulalie and Sacha under her big wool blanket and shared a palmier with them. She began to tell them the bible story of Moses. Some of the other children got under the blanket to listen to her, and she shared the tiny palmier with them too. They only got crumbs each, but it was a treat. She even slipped Atenea a few crumbs.

All Sister Amona ever learned from Julien about the event was the Royal soldiers were looking for missing or unaccounted for soldiers amongst his prison squad.

They arrived the next afternoon at the port of Castro-Seio, where they were ordered to leave the ferry-barges. No longer passengers, everyone but babies were forced to walk. With no horses, the imprisoned soldiers from Wasconia were given the task of pulling the carts while the Aquitaine helped roll the wheels through the snow. Some of the youngest children capable of walking were tied together by a thin rope, more to keep them together than for any punishment, and one such group followed Sister Amona, Gisela, Eulalie, Sacha, and Atenea.

At first, it was rough going, over ramshackle icy bridges or cold mud, and the ground rose and became more hilly, but as they drew nearer to the town of Andecavus the grand manors and their mansi passed like fat sows suckling litters of piglets. The road grew straighter, and the snow was trampled down, and this brought them up to the wooden walls and gate of the town.

Comes Ceufroy, the local lord, had received word a small army of chained prisoners was about to enter his town and had ordered the gates shut. He mustered his own soldiers as well as the town watch to forcibly keep the gates closed. Julien and Ceufroy, separated by the gate's height, first talked and then eventually argued before night fell and the prisoners and Frankish soldiers, exhausted from the long journey, just collapsed and set up camp outside the guarded gates of Andecavus. Even the nuns were denied entrance into the city for evening prayer at the church of Saint Maurice.

Gathering wood for fires is never easy around villages or towns picked clean long before winter, and this night was made worse by the snowy landscape. Each cart sent out a group to scavenge. Gisela, Eulalie, Maylis and several other bigger children were sent with soldiers and a chain of Aquitaine prisoners to gather wood for their 'soeur-cart', as the nun's divisions were becoming known. One of the prisoners frightened Eulalie terribly. He was a big, thick man whose black nose and cheeks made him look diseased. Sacha had dubbed him an Ogre, but he gently and silently took all the branches the children brought to him to carry.

The children were tasked with gathering kindling; the small dry twigs and sticks to help the bigger wood catch. Gisela had observed how to tend a fireplace and add wood, but she had never in her life gathered any before. She kept collecting wet sticks, making the prisoners annoyed, though the Ogre would smile and shake his head. Eulalie began to show her how to look for loose bark on tree trunks and branches under snow and piles of leaves.

As Ceufroy had summoned his warriors, the lords of the local manors, to the town to defend it, the coloni and servi who remained on the estates were not inclined to challenge royal soldiers and angry prisoners over firewood. Indeed, with so many children and women amidst the desperate gatherers, many locals took pity and donated wood and food to them, left like abandoned presents to avoid contradicting Ceufroy and invoking his wrath.

Returning to the camp outside the gates by the soeur-cart cook fires, the prisoners slept in communal circles under the big wool blankets, like so many nomad tents. It was a miserable soiled camp of torches more than fires; to Gisela's eyes, the kind of camp rats at a crumb-gamble might gather to drink and throw dice. Beside the tireless Sister Amona and her cart, gathered under their own big blanket, Gisela continued to tell the other children the stories of Moses and the Israelites. How Moses dealt with the Pharaoh to convince him to let them leave Egypt, how he chased them in anger and how God parted the sea for the Israelites to escape and how they wandered in the desert, looking for milk and honey. She shared another palmier amongst the youngest ones, swearing them to secrecy, and again Atenea got at least a few crumbs herself, her secrecy being more guaranteed.

In the clear twilight of early morning the priests of the church of Saint Serge, which lay outside the walls of the town to the north, came quietly, ministering and tending to the prisoners and guards. By dawn a great

commotion of drums from inside the town walls
began, awakening anyone left. The Bishop of Saint
Maurice arrived upon the wall right of the gate, in full
Catholic litanies, along with the Abbot of Saint Aubin,
and both with a procession of lectors, deacons, monks,
and followers carrying so many crosses and banners
and books that Gisela wondered what could be left in
the church. The Bishop's miter, cope's morse, and
crosier were so layered with gold in the morning light
that some mistook the Bishop to be a sunrise over the
wall to the west. Ceufroy did not.

"What are you doing here Bishop Sidus?!"
demanded Ceufroy from up on top of the wall, but
left, on the opposite side of the gate. "I have decreed
these Royal prisoners shall not enter our city, but
should pass Andecavus by on their journey."

Bishop Sidus seemed far more interested in the
prison camp than Ceufroy's decrees.

"The Bishop has come to offer the Prayer of the
Faithful upon these forsaken members of God's flock,"
Abbot Folmar announced in a booming voice, more
for the prisoners benefit, and backed away, leaving the
Bishop the obvious godly man to speak.

"It is my intention to lead the Penitential Rite for
any in this camp who know their place. If they are not
to be allowed into our Holy Church...then the Holy
Church shall come to them! Kyrie eleison!"

The guards and families, and almost every one of
the prisoners dropped to one knee or kneeled on both
immediately, asking the Lord to have mercy. Those
few who did not were chastised by the nuns or their
chained fellows until they did as well. Gisela noticed
an older boy in one of their prison chains seemed to
resent being scolded and kneeling and added a prayer

for him.

"Kyrie eleison, on us all! Do we intend to start holding Mass at the gates of towns now?" Ceufroy asked sarcastically. "We've no need to tithe for your new cathedral if mud shall suffice!"

"Then let the unwashed in, and let us cleanse them properly Comes!" the Bishop demanded, finally facing Ceufroy. The sheer number of kneeling sinners in the camp gave him a superior position morally, if not yet politically.

"We shall not!" insisted Ceufroy, his hand on his sword as determinedly as the Bishop's on his crosier. "The dirt of these unwashed will fill our gutters and alleys and minds, even after they have gone their filth will linger in our town like a stain!"

"No one will remain behind! I swear before the Bishop and Merciful God I shall ensure every man, woman, and child leaves as we came!" yelled up Julien from the bottom of the gates.

"There are sick before you Comes! Cold and hungry at your very gates, asking for your charity, yet you would send them away with tansy and madder! I am told by the priests of Saint Serge the Captain of the Guard here has offered you a Royal largesse as payment for supplies and passage. Cheminage, murage and pavage, in coin, yet you will still deny your Queen?"

"Look at this rabble! Men chained together, like so many snakes! I shall not let this nest of vipers into our midst! Minister to them as the Lord sees fit, upon the road, if you must!"

Sister Amona suddenly looked directly at Gisela.

~Be strong and take heart~

Gisela's sudden fright was replaced by Sacha's

words, only the boy's mouth had not moved, nor did anyone else seem to have heard him. She looked at Sister Amona again and summoned her strength in the Lord as the Psalm suggested.

Sister Amona disappeared through the crowd and appeared beside Julien. Eulalie reached out and grabbed Gisela's hand in silent support, for the last time, if the ruse was about to be revealed.

"Julien, the children tell the stories of Moses in Egypt and leading them out. His staff turned into a snake, and then came back."

"And Aaron's snake rod ate the Pharaoh's snake rods as well!" a Saint Serge priest added, coming up behind her.

Julien looked at them both. "And by what divine magic are we to do this?" Both pointed up to the Bishop. "I'm not certain comparing Ceufroy to the Pharaoh is the wisest advice," he whispered back to them before turning back to the imposing wall and imposing men on it and posing them a riddle.

"My Lord, your nuns and priests amongst us say that the snake of Moses and Aaron consumed the snakes of the Pharaoh," Julien called up, unsure, but not having any other options besides walking away.

"Exodus Seven!" the Bishop smiled. "Yes! Yes, indeed, good Captain! Not only do you lead your tribe in bondage, but in spirit as well!"

"What is this? Are you to turn sinners into saints now, before our very eyes?" Ceufroy joked. Many of his soldiers laughed. Even a few prisoners did.

"We're all sinners," the Bishop admitted and thought. "Ceufroy? What if we turn the snakes into a staff again? What if we put all the chains together, end to end, to make many snakes one long staff through our city? Then no one can be lost, no one can rebel against you!"

"My Brother monks will walk with them, take up the same chain with them, to ensure none break free and remain," the Abbot offered, stepping up.

"Abbot Folmar does not have enough brothers of Aubin to mind the children, much less the prisoners!" Ceufroy argued.

"Then my priests and choir and officers will join them! We shall form a sudarium amongst the staff of the prisoners!" the Bishop countered.

"My soldier guards shall tie themselves to the chains as well, for they are already bound to them for this journey," Julien offered.

"We tie the women and children on a rope on the end as well!" sister Amona offered up.

There was a great murmuring from the other side of the gate, and Gisela realized the inhabitants of the whole town must be gathered, unseen to them, on the other side of the gate, to Ceufroy and the Bishop's backs.

"What say you, Comes Ceufroy? A Royal payment, a Church guard, a Holy confiteor?" the Bishop demanded.

Ceufroy did not like where this was headed. "The villainy and rebellion of these men are already proven! Their treason is worn on their wrists! Nothing can guarantee the will of such men."

"The words of our Lord, Jesus Christ! The words that follow fast on the heels of our Lord's Prayer in Matthew!" the Bishop demanded in return. "For if you will forgive men their offenses, your heavenly Father will forgive you also your offenses. But if you will not forgive men, neither will your Father forgive you your offenses!"

An audible cheer went up from the town's people inside the wall, and many of the prisoners smiled and took heart. Julien looked at Amona in surprise and almost grinned before turning back to the Comes and Bishop.

Several of his warriors and local lords came to counsel the Comes in a whispered debate. None wished to make him appear weak, and Ceufroy wished to avoid any erosion of his authority at all costs, but he was clearly losing ground quickly.

When Abbot Folmar appeared beside Ceufroy, on his side of the gate, the crowd grew quieter. There was animated talk for some time before heads began nodding in agreement. Abbot Folmar signaled Bishop Sidus, and the Bishop and his procession briefly disappeared from the wall. He reappeared on Ceufroy's side, they spoke a moment, and finally, backed by the Bishop, Abbot and his own warriors, Ceufroy spoke for both sides of the gate.

"Let the prisoner's chains be wedded together with links to form one long line. Let the children and women, however, lead their way, tied off with the pew and bell ropes of the town churches. Let the Royal guards, the monks of Aubin, the priests of Maurice and all who feel so moved by our Lord to be tied to the same chain amongst them. We do this as well with a split of the Royal largesse, as I have been justly reminded of his military cloak shared with a beggar, in honor of the feast of Saint Martin today. We shall do as was said, and all agreed here this morning."

A cheer went up from both the town's folk and prisoners.

The gates were cracked open but still guarded.

Blacksmiths from the town were brought out to hammer the links between the prisoner chains, and an enormous boulder of black slate near the gates was chosen as the makeshift cold forge. Julien arranged the prisoner chains in some specific order only he understood, though it became more apparent when the sick were placed last. Horses were brought to tow the soeur-carts through the streets. Townsfolk, including many women and children, went to the churches and brought back pew and bell ropes, and the priests began symbolically tying off the guards and monks and volunteers along the chain. Stern Wasconian soldiers found themselves shoulder to shoulder with soft choir robes pinned with posies of southernwood and rue while tonsured monks joked and talked with rough, long-haired farmers of Aquitaine as the hammers' song rang out.

So many hammers, and the trodding of so many people, melted the ice and snow around the forge boulder, and people of the town tried to claim it was a miracle that water flowed from the stone. Bishop Sidus, while not willing to declare puddles as miraculous, did claim it showed the righteousness of Ceufroy in the decision to allow them inside.

So the gates of Andecavus were finally opened under the waving hand of Comes Ceufroy, and a long line of believers, both old and new, followed Bishop Sidus through the streets in a joyous procession. They came first to the Church of Saint John and his hospital, where several of the prisoners at the end of the chain, men who had fallen into the water and were now sick or needed toes or fingers removed were tended. Prayers were offered by the Abbot at the shrine of Saint Licinius until the sick were crowded, still chained, back onto one of the carts. Then past the Abbey of Saint Aubin, the line went, winding like a great river of chain and rope and faith through the town, and then, more solemnly, through the church of Saint Peter, paying their respects to the tomb of Aubin, a patron saint of prisoners. As Sidus was leading and the children followed him, there was little doubt it was a purposeful detour.

The sun of midday and devotion of Saint Aubin's could not warm the heart of Ceufroy enough to free the prisoners, but it did bring back the more typical fall weather to begin chasing away the early cold snowfall. The footsteps of the people were carpeted by melting ice and trickling water on every street and alley.

The long train made its way to the Bishop's church of Saint Maurice. There was no magic in heaven or of saints that would let all the townsfolk and prisoners fit into such a humble church at the same time, so the priests and monks snaked and coiled the prisoner's rope-chain down the stepped road west of the church's doors. The choir was set up at the church's narthex, and the Bishop held Mass outside for all under a bright afternoon sun, reminding Gisela of a sermon on the Mount. After the liturgy of the Eucharist Julien and Ceufroy brought the coins of the Royal largesse up together as the offering, the first two to make the Sign of Peace, and then the gathered people did as well. The handbells did not stop ringing as slowly the entire line fed through the church, each townsfolk, soldier or prisoner receiving communion in a steady procession until all had passed.

The ice melted with the afternoon, and the roofs of houses and gutters of the streets everywhere flowed with sparkling running water, almost in deference to Ceufroy's fears.

Ceufroy had an ox brought forth and slaughtered, and a great deal of firewood was gathered and brought, enough for many good fires. Two rundlets of d'Anjou wine were taped and shared with all. The Feast of Saint Martin took place just as the Mass had; outside the church on the streets. To say the Frankish prisoners were well-fed and supplied would be gross; it would be far more accurate to say a small town shared what little it had with fellow Christians because their Bishop convinced them it would help their cause in Heaven. To those who had nothing, it felt miraculous. To those who witnessed the day, it seemed miraculous. To the Bishop and the devout, it only glorified the Lord as indeed miraculous.

Along with the meat and wine, they ate lovaged cabbages and endive, and the street was turned into a semi-covered barn with whatever planks, rails, fence, and thatch could be found. As night fell the various cooking smells soothed spirits, the warm red coals making the warm red cheeks smile and eyes dance, and the warm feelings seemingly hugged the town and people together. Most of the townsfolk returned to their houses, but the monks and priests, and Ceufroy's watchful guards stayed with the prisoners all night as they had said, many praying and hearing confessions.

By their soeur-cart Gisela, Eulalie and Sacha were joined again by many of the smaller children who begged Gisela to tell them more stories. Using the big blankets to form a makeshift tent around the cart, Gisela told them Taliesin's tales of good King Gradlon and his magical city of Ys which kept back the ocean's tide with a great dike. She told them how King Gradlon took ships over the sea on adventures to many lands, following the Chemin d'Ahès, the great river of stars in the sky, and of the red-haired fairy-queen named Malgven who fell in love with him on one of his voyages. They had a daughter together, named Dahut, who the King took back to Ys with him. She grew as beautiful as her mother and as courageous as her father, and Malgven gave him a magical horse called Morvarc'h which could run over the waves of the sea so the King could visit all his lands and visit her whenever he wished. Dahut, however, took a lover who turned out to be the devil, and the devil had her get the King drunk on wine, stole the key to the dike from him so the lovers could escape and instead opened the dike at high tide to flood the city. Only the King on his magical horse and his Bishop Saint Gwenolé, who had tried to warn him of Dahut's evil nature, were able to escape the flood of Ys.

A mona's cart happened to have been left outside a wool maker's house along the street, and the odd little tailor named Fidele listened to the story Gisela told. He took pity on the children before his home, bringing out huge trunks and putting them and their lids in a circle out by the cart to act as dry cots and box-beds. In their trunks, the children laid down to sleep on puffy wool. Gisela, Eulalie, and Sacha were huddled in one, Sacha fast asleep, with Atenea beside the opening and Amona's fire casting its warmth and glow on them. The waters trickle as it passed them competed with the crackle of the fire.

"I think we were supposed to be here, Eulalie," Gisela whispered proudly to her.

"You are dear to me Duende, but your father is not a chained prisoner, and sleeping hungry in a box on a cold, wet street is no longer an adventure when you've been doing it for months," Eulalie whispered back.

Gisela had to rethink her thoughts a moment. " My apologies to you. I meant I've seen the Bishop here before."

"Where?"

"I believe he came to Tours, with the other bishops and the Archbishop when His Majesty and the Court was there last summer."

"Do you think he will suspect you?"

"Oh dear no. But I believe Mother met him there, and with so few supplies in Mur, I believe she chose this town for our path north because she knew the Bishop might help supply the prisoners. The largesse they talked about, the one she sent with us. I think she planned that and hoped this would happen."

"Your mother's as clever as her daughter."

Gisela dug one of her marzipan wafers out of her hidden pocket and broke it in two, Saint Martin style, to share with Eulalie.

"Hum. Almond. I remember almonds. I liked them," Eulalie opined, then pointed at Gisela's pocket. Gisela looked down. Her silver jeweled snood was hanging out. Gisela quickly tucked it back out of sight.

"At the Hospital today. Did you see the shrine for the tomb of Saint Licinius?" Gisela asked, sucking on her wafer slowly.

"So many shrines to so many saints today. I'm not as learned as you are, Duende."

"Saint Licinius was a nobleman here, a Comes, like the lord at the gate this morning. Licinius gave up all his land and titles here to follow God."

"Goodness!"
Gisela nodded in agreement. "Goodness."

The morning broke cold and misty, some of the ice
having refrozen overnight, as well as Ceufroy's
temperament. The Aubin monks came through before
the sun had even risen, urging folks to be awake and
get moving. The town guards noisily brought in
horses for the carts and extinguished the remains of
any coals in the street fires in hissing, steamy clouds,
apparently to limit morning laissez-faire and
adequately motivate the prisoners. Gisela and Sister
Amona returned all the children's trunks and wool to
the odd little tailor and thanked him. Slowly the chain
took up again behind the Bishop, this time the
children in the rear, and they wound their way out the
northern gate of the town.

At the church of Saint Serge, the priests were
waiting, along with blacksmiths and Comes Ceufroy.
The families were directed to the walled-off garden
and shrine to Saint Samson of Dol. Gisela and Eulalie
kept young Sacha with them. The lengthy prison
chain was first split in two, under Julien's directions.
The men were allowed to bathe and prepare
themselves when the women and children had
finished. The soeur-carts were unhitched from the
town's horses, and the nuns were given baskets of
radishes and carrots, which Sister Amona felt were
generous. Ceufroy donated two festival tents and their
baldaquins he had used as shade for the Tours market
faire every October in years past. The tents were in
poor shape but usable. It was quietly mumbled
donating them to the prisoners was an excuse to wring
new tents for next year out of the town populace for

their support of the Bishop with the prisoners against him.

The chains were unforged, back to their original lengths and numbers. When the Frankish guards and nuns began saying farewells to each other, Gisela wondered if they were being released, but soon realized the prisoners were being split up into two groups. Eulalie immediately began to panic, and Gisela tried to not panic with her. One group, mostly the soldiers of Wascon, were apparently being sent northeast to the Bishop of Le Mans. The other group of prisoners, mostly the Aquitaine farmers, were being sent northwest to the Bishop of Avranches, if Gisela understood them correctly, and the girl's prayers were fervent the Lord let them go to Avranches. Their prayers were swiftly answered.

Sipia, before & after

Nine chains of prisoners and two carts, including
Sister Amona, Eulalie and Sacha, were queued up by
Julien by the church gates. Again, two chains of
prisoners each pulled a soeur-cart in place of horses,
and one chain was around the wheels and back to roll
and push them. Sister Amona's cart was filled with all
the extra supplies the tent pushed off the other cart,
and with only one infant boy left in their group,
everyone was walking but him.

Gisela was relieved Sister Rosine's cart was going
with the Le Mans group, and Julien had even
remembered Duende and her little brother Sacha had
an uncle in Bayeux, though Julien had no idea how
they would get to Bayeux after they arrived at
Avranches.

They crossed the Maine river on calones ferries and
left Andecavus. It was not as sunny as the previous
day, and the ground was still covered in a few inches
of snow almost everywhere but the road. The tree
trunks all looked like tower watch guards; their snowy
load having fallen off the branches to form white
parapet walls encircling them. The big fields of the
manors and the smaller fields of the mansi passed by,
first steadily, with a clear road as they paralleled the
Mayenne river, then slowly fewer and farther apart as
they continued up the valley. By noon there was
almost no hut or field to be seen, and the woods had

crawled up to the edges of the old road and vaulted it, and them, with limbs and shadows.

Julien, armored in his mail and sword and Royal Frankish tabard, walked like the lord of the valley in the lead. Gisela noticed his eyes never stopped scanning the brush, trees, and snows. It was an odd mix of caution and haste. Four of his soldiers with spears and sword and shield followed him closely. Many of the guards also had a small handaxe called a francisca in their wide belts.

Nobody carried a bow, which Gisela found odd. The javelin-like spears, they called them angons, were the guard's preferred missiles. The angons had long iron shaft points the length of her arm and looked quite deadly. They had leather straps called amentums wound around them with finger holes in the end, that let the thrower spin the spear farther and faster. Gisela had never seen such angons in her father's army, as they harkened back to the old Roman days and country folk, but the guards put them to wonderous hunting use every time an edible creature came too close to the train, even if it was many paces away. It became obvious why they still held favor with the prison guards, for one weapon could be used against both a prisoner charging or running away, and each guard often carried two or three.

Behind Julien and his armored guards came the carts. The first cart was Sister Basina's. Three groups of prisoners pulled and shoved it through the snow and mud along the road. Three more chains of prisoners followed in between the carts, alternately resting from the duty by walking and taking their turns with the carts as hours passed. Every chain had two or three mailed Frankish guards with an angon spear and a falchion who watched over them. The wives of the prisoners walked amongst them, and sometimes the children did as well, now they were away from people. Eulalie rode upon her father's shoulder for part of the afternoon, the chains of love being stronger than chains of iron.

As Gisela walked holding Sacha's hand, she was struck by the subtle differences in the prisoners. The Wascons tended to be strong and thicker, many sporting scars and healing wounds, and Julien had probably mixed the fewer Wascons in with the others so they could not form plots and plans together. This also tended to make them quieter, for most did not seem to speak d'oc or d'oil well. Some of them wore thicker leathers and fur hats, but none were armored or armed. Sacha's bearded and black nosed Ogre was one of them.

The Aquitaine vineyard workers were much like the guards themselves in physical appearance and temperament, though the Aquitaine tended more to yellow clothes and long cloaks trimmed with rabbit and the Franks more red with shorter cloaks trimmed with fox. Many Aquitaine wore jacks with studs, though they all wore two sets of clothing and cloth caps or hats. They would often sing together, their strange song's meaning lost to Gisela, but the chorus of voices would carry it up and down the chains like a cresting wave along the seashore of her ears. The Aquitaine were also like busy ants. Male or female, young or old, everyone had packs or shoulder yokes suspended with clay pots on each side; the butteries and pantries of the train, water skins, wineskins, cooking pots, and the valueless invaluables and frippery families had managed to hang onto through their imprisonment. Some of the Aquitaine men and women even talked and joked with the guards. These were not the rebellious soldiers of Wasconia, hardened to battle the enemy. These were grape-growing farmers the old king had handed pitchforks and bills and told to fight the Royal Franks or die trying. They had obviously not done either well. Eulalie's father was amongst them, as was Maylis' father as well as her mother, following him with the small baby boy.

Interspersed amongst the prisoners but far fewer in number were captured Saxons in their brown braies and shirts and long liripiped hoods. Their lack of thick clothing and tattoos made them stand out, and the guards caution when near them warned Gisela to do the same. These were the ones who hesitated to kneel for prayers or resisted Communion. The guards and Aquitaine often called them lazzi, though Gisela was never sure if it was disparaging or descriptive. These shadowy men were mercenaries from the battles, thief like in their manners and, given their constant squabbles with all the others over crumbs and water and sleeping positions, they appeared untrustworthy. One of them was a young boy not too much older than Gisela.

Sister Amona's cart, along with the usual bulk of the dozen children followed next, with the mastiff Atenea padding along with them, as well as their cart's three chains of prisoners.

Four Frankish guards brought up the rear, angon spears and shield slung as the miles trudged on beneath the entwined and largely still leafed beech and oak limbs.

The old Roman path between Andecavus and Reenes followed the Mayenne until they passed a manor and farms known as Le Lion. Here the river split; the Mayenne went north, the Oudon river northwestward along with the road, and the locals kept their distance from a cohort of chained men and Royal soldiers. The old road split, one way heading to a manor known as Combrée, the other towards a village known as Craon. Julien did his best to determine the correct path in the snow.

The train of tired men, women, and children rumbled to a stop at the crossing of the river Oudon. Julien ordered everyone to cross the cold waters of the ford. The smallest children were put up on the carts, and every chain pulled and pushed, even Gisela and the middling children helping, to get across the stream before everyone rested.

Julien had the tent of Ceufroy setup between the carts as a cook and command tent, and the children, three guards, and one chain were sent out to gather firewood. Gisela asked for a knife from Sister Amona, and she and Eulalie helped gather wood, bringing branches and dry twigs back to match the limbs the chain were chopping.

Behind a good sized oak, amongst long fern leaves turned copper brown by fall and early snow, Eulalie helped Gisela take off her big shoes and fine kirtle. Standing in her linen chemise it was chilly, and she wrapped herself in Bérénice's old cloak again quickly and put her big boots back on. Carefully they began cutting the fine cloth of her kirtle into many rough rectangles; a lampas edged blue sendal dress fit for the Royal Court wintering in Mur, now soiled at the bottom from trodding through the mud. They worked as quickly as they could, hearing the chopping of the prisoners' ax nearby and keeping out a watch for the guards if they wandered close until only a short vest was left of the once beautiful kirtle. Stuffing the rag squares into the pockets and the folds of their cloaks, they gathered up what limbs and twigs they could and returned to the camp.

They were greeted first by the smell of roasting tarragon and then a loud argument going on under the big blue tent between Sister Amona and one of the women, over how to cook the radishes. They left the firewood and disagreement to find most of the other children behind a cart with Atenea laying down like a great sphinx amongst them. Quietly Gisela began handing out the fine cloth squares of her kirtle as socks to the children, tying them off or stuffing them inside their cloth sandals. Gisela went to Maylis's blanket tent to offer her a pair and found her talking with a reclining guard. Gisela stood puzzled for a moment until Julien, passing by her, noticed it too. He dragged the soldier out from under the blanket tent and struck him repeatedly all the way back to the cook tent. Sister Amona came over immediately to make sure everything was calm.

"What happen here? Duende? Maylis?" she insisted, still holding a wet cooking spoon as if it were a judge's gavel.

"Nothing," Maylis scowled, looking at Gisela then pointedly looking at Gisela's pocket. Sister Amona looked doubtful. "Duende, this true?"

"Yes, Sister. Nothing happened. The soldier was just trying to talk to her."

Sister Amona put her hand on the blanket flap and turned it back up so Maylis could no longer hide under it. "You better say your prayers and keep your mind off such things!" she scolded and returned to the cooking tent.

Gisela and Maylis looked at each other before Gisela turned and went back to the other children.

After a dinner of the meager spoonful of pea-frumenty, some tarragon roasted radishes and a shared hanop of the d'Anjou wine, the children huddled down for the night under their big blanket behind the cart. Gisela shared the last palmier, now well squashed, stale and beginning to mold on one edge. The children ate crumbs and Gisela got the children to tell her tales. Who they were, where they were from, what they had seen in the southern wars. Some talked. Some didn't, but eventually, they all begged Gisela to tell them one more story.

She told them of one of the King of Glamorgan's great warriors, Saint Illtud, as deft with spear and sword as he was with ink and quill, and how he became one of the greatest teachers in the land. The three saints Paol, Gildas and Samson all learned the Bible and the Holy rites in Illtud's monastery and came back to Brittany to start churches and monasteries of their own and save the people. Now people made pilgrimages to their shrines and churches to ask forgiveness. The legendary poet Taliesin was a student of Illtud's with Saint Samson and recorded many of their deeds. Eventually, everyone fell asleep, and Atenea didn't mind the mold on her piece at all. As the dog ate, Gisela slipped the silver snood out of her pocket and wound it around and through Atenea's spiked wolf collar. It disappeared into the thick white fur like magic.

The next morning came damp and misty as wisps danced off the Oudon stream. Fresh carrots and apples made the day's start more passable, and praise and prayers were heaped on Julien for making the crossing last night instead of first cold thing this morning.

"Captain Julien?" Gisela asked as he got another apple from Sister Amona's cart. "The Roman road here was like walking along the back of a woolly caterpillar, for the road seemed to run on a hump, and the trees sloped off both sides."

Julien smiled and bit his apple, looking around and talking between chews. "Roman roads were built of many layers, hundreds of years ago, and were straight as arrows and sloped to drain and stay dry so the legions could move about quickly upon them."

"They don't look Roman to me."

"Not anymore. The top layer was cut stone blocks, and those were stolen long, long ago, by everyone, to use in houses, castles and town walls. The layer below that was this packed crushed stone, and it too would be stolen by nearby farms and villages over the centuries to use as fill rock in new constructions. In the deep woods like we are now, the sloping road still exists, even if marginally, and there were no people around to steal the crushed rock."

Jays and squirrels now stole falling acorns from underneath tall branches along the road. The layer of snow seemed their biggest obstacle now.

By midday, the stream of the Oudon disappeared to the north as the Mayenne had done, and smaller, unbroken snow covered trails headed off south towards a manor called Châtelais. The road ran on like a sunbeam, crossing a low ridge and then downslope to a stream called the Chéren, which had carved the gentle valley they found themselves in. The oak trees here grew massive, and the Saxon lazzi grew bolder, talking to the trees as if there were clansmen ready to jump from limbs and root any moment. Spear tips from Julien and his guards kept their ghostly talk and boasting grins to a minimum and their minds on the task of pulling the carts with real threats right behind them.

They camped again, and again they had to search for firewood before resting. Eulalie worked with her father on his chain, bringing him branches, and Gisela was bringing him one when she felt a soft hand on her shoulder. She turned, startled to see the Ogre's giant fingers being so dainty. He motioned to take the branch from her in an odd, kindly gentle way, so she decided to put her trust in the Lord and gave him the branch. He broke it with his hands and started his stack, motioning for her to continue getting more.

"Foru," he kept saying and looking around at the trees.

Gisela wasn't sure what he was saying, but he seemed to be friendly in a harmless way, and she had to collect more firewood anyways.

She drug back bigger limbs, one end plowing the snow behind her, and the Ogre would smile with all ten of his teeth, break it into the right sizes and nod back at her.

Eulalie, bringing a limb to her father, shrugged at Gisela and kept working.

"Nire alaba...good. Duende...zuk...good," the Ogre said on her next trip, smiling.

"I don't understand."

"Nire alaba...ez ikusi berriro. Zuk gogorarazteko."

"Have another stick. I'll be right back."

They gathered wood until almost dark and then headed back to camp. Gisela noticed Maylis had been missing the whole time and was not back at camp either. They ate, the usual spoonfuls of pea-frumenty, roasted radishes and shared d'Anjou wine again. The journey was taking much longer than Gisela had imagined, and was much harder work than she ever imagined. She was growing tired.

Under the big wool blanket with the other children, they were anxious to hear new stories this evening. Even Atenea seemed ready to settle into the usual routine. Gisela began talking about the poet Taliesin, retelling the tales Charles had told her. Taliesin was a godly man, trained in prophecies by Saint Illtud granted by the Lord to witness many miracles. He learned and sang about Saint Samson of Dol, Saint Gildas, and Saint Poul.

To Gisela, under the blanket, in the semi-darkness, Sacha seemed to change, appearing sick perhaps, until a wind flapped the blanket and a peek of clear firelight struck Sacha for a moment. Gisela gasped, unable to speak again and continue her story. Sacha's skin was dead white and covered in dirt as if he had crawled out of a grave. She threw back the blanket entirely to let the air and light in again, and it was the normal Sacha asleep.

"What is the matter Duende?" Eulalie and the other children kept asking.

"I'm...I'm just tired." Gisela crawled out and folding the blanket back down over them. One of the guards by the cart looked her way and nodded, but seemed otherwise unconcerned. Most of the camp was settled in and wrapped up tight in the Mur blankets. Maylis was back, under her blanket and wrapped in a cloak now, and glared at her briefly before turning over away from her.

"You. Duende girl."

Gisela almost didn't turn to see who was speaking, her mind was so confused. She looked over. It was the younger Saxon lazzi boy, still chained, talking to her.

"You think you know about the stories of Taliesin?"

Gisela didn't realize her voice had carried outside the children's blanket. "Yes."

The lazzi boy laughed. "Taliesin is no saint. He's a sorcerer. Yes, he learned under Illtud. But he's no Christian."

"He is! He traveled with Samson in Brittany!"

"He was born in a lake in Gwynedd. There, deep in the woods, King Maelgwen founded a monastery on a lake, where every day the monks would build the walls higher, and every night the devil would knock them back down."

Gisela turned white. Taliesin was born in Gwynedd according to the Llyfr, and this lazzi knew the details. Details she hadn't told anyone or even shared with Eulalie. This boy surely did know the legends of Taliesin.

"In a Saxon temple in the middle of the lake, is a pagan irminsul as old as the mountains. It holds up the sky."

"It's...a tree...an oak tree."

"It's a Saxon irminsul! Your Catholic days start at sunrise. Our Saxon days start at sundown." Gisela could see from the flickering firelights the boy was looking around at the tree limbs above, almost expectantly. "The lake around the abandoned monastery is guarded by pagans. By day with the skins of black horses on sticks. When night falls, and the moon comes out, the witches drink blood wine and dance, and the stick horses come to life and run over the surface of the lake as a ghostly herd," the boy told her, showing his arm tattoo of a black horse to emphasize the point.

The boy leaned closer. "Taliesin IS evil, Duende," he whispered.

"NO!" she whispered. "Saint Samson was his companion!"

"Taliesin's father was the fisherman Elphin. He pulled him from the river."

Gisela shook her head in agreement and disbelief. Now, this boy was even repeating details Charles had told her, and she had forgotten herself. He had to be speaking the truth.

"But his mother was not a mortal! Taliesin's mother was a demon!"

"Not a fairy-queen?"

"No, a hag of the Nightwash!"

"No," Gisela whimpered.

"We are on the Hent Ahès, the earthly road of white you spoke of in the sky. It is this fairy road leading us straight to the Fions who will ensnare you all with their magic for disturbing them! We Saxons know their korrigan spells! On the night of a Wednesday, juice the blood of a crab-apple till it boils an egg. Fennel & Thyme, Mayweed & Nettle. Blend in the cockspur's grass and the Lamb's cress. Roll the flat leaves of the fleawort around the flowers of mugwort, picked when the butterflies have come to fancy it," the boy said, standing taller and growing closer to Gisela with every new incantation. "Now cast the runes of the nine herbs charm!" he said jumping at her. Gisela fell backward onto the snow as the awoken, and annoyed, Ogre yanked on the other end of the Saxon boy's chain, pulling him back away from her as well.

Scrambling to get up, Gisela broke into tears and ran away into the cold night, away from the laughing lazzi boy.

Sister Amona added more water to her hanop of wine and sank down onto a rundlet by the dying embers of the cookfire. The carts provided a windbreak from the cold breeze, and the fire a warm moment of respite. The old blue tent overhead felt like a palace to her, and the rundlet seemed a throne. She removed her veil and cap, her greying hair falling down in a tangled clump. Her veil was soiled, so she poured water from the hanging skin on it and began wringing it out, but not before wiping her brow and temples with it first. She laid it out on her dress-covered leg by the fire and began combing out her hair with a small comb with only four teeth. She turned slightly while brushing to look out into the cold when the snow crunched near her.

"What? Duende? What you doing out there, child? You freeze." She got up, catching the falling drying veil and still reaching out to Gisela. "Come here," she begged.

Gisela could not resist and came to her shivering. Sister Amona looked astonished but hugged her back.

"What got you wandering?"

"The Saxon boy scared me."

"Did he touch you?!" Sister Amona demanded, placing her veil and comb on the back of the cart to reach for a cutting knife.

"No," she answered meekly, taking Amona's arm back. "He said the poet Taliesin was a warlock, not a saint."

"Pooough!" spat Amona with a chuckle. "Don't pay that Saxon boy no viaticum. He's just the mean one."

"You don't think Taliesin is a devil worshiper, do you, Sister?" Gisela asked. "You know he's a good and godly saint of our dear Lord?"

Amona took back up her veil and comb and sat back down on her rundlet by the fire, taking Gisela up onto her leg. She hugged Gisela one good time, before going back to work on her own hair.

"You a good child of God. You know so much, so many things," she told her quietly, brushing her hair out between them like a confessional shryving curtain. "I hear you speak stories, good stories, grand stories, from the Bible and all about saints. I don know the saints you speak of, they not in my country. I know Apostles, God praise their souls, and our good Virgin Mary, but many saints you speak of to other children I don known before, and I feel guilty. I sorry Duende."

"My teachers taught me the Bible, and my brother told me about Taliesin. All the bards can sing of Taliesin!"

"I believe your brother over that lazzi boy," Amona joked, touching Gisela's nose with her comb for a moment before continuing to brush her own hair. "Maybe time for you and I to be honest, no?"

"What do you mean Amona?"

"I think I know your secret."

"You do?"

Amona nodded. "You not poor girl. You not Aquitaine."

Gisela lowered her eyes and then her head in resignation.

"Uh-hugh. I think so right. You are daughter of Wascon Lord. Bishop, maybe Archbishop. No farm girl."

Gisela looked up. "What?"

"No deny now! I see in your eyes! I see in your face! I hear in your stories! I see your kirtle hem under your cloak at town when praying of Eucharist. I see children now wear socks made of same dress, and your kirtle gone. I see you read choiry tapestry psalms in St Maurice to other children, no?!" Amona insisted, her hair forming long parallel lines, reminding Gisela of her mother's bed curtains. "You know the Bible too good for farm girl. You brought up in it. And I see you talk to the big Wascon they call Rhoger."

"Ogre."

Amona pointed a shaking finger at her for trying to change the subject. "He no speak d'oil or d'oc, only Wasconi, and you two talk. You know Wascon, but hide it. You go without food, but not water, like Wascon. You take cold like Wascon. It ok, it be our secret. No one will know you daughter of Wascon bishop." Amona whispered through her hair and pulled it back up behind her to begin braiding it again. Gisela helped her.

"More finer the flour and the linen, the more lordly, Duende," Amona warned, the edge of her eye barely able to see Gisela working behind her now. "Your galeta? Your chemise under dress?"

"Galeta?"

Amona put her fingers to her mouth like she was eating a little cookie. Gisela nodded in understanding Amona had seen the palmiers.

After her hair braiding was done, Amona turned and reached for her chamois vest hanging on the side of the cart.

"You take this, wear to be warm."

"Sister, I can't, you need it."

Amona put her arms out to show she was warm.

"Am I wearing vest? I near cart all day, near cookfire all night," she insisted. "I have my apron, which now seems a choir robe. You take the vest. Sundogs in sky say maybe colder tomorrow."

Gisela smiled and hugged Amona.

"Let's pray together for everyone's safety, Amona," Gisela whispered.

"Good Duende, of course," Sister Amona agreed, taking out her wooden cross with a vine twined around it.

"What is your cross made of?" Gisela asked.

"A vine from my homeland in south. They call woodbine."

"It's pretty."

"Where your cross, Duende?"

Gisela felt her bare neck for the thousandth time this week. "It got left behind." Her face sank for the hundredth time as she scolded herself for leaving something so important in her haste.

A huge drooling white dog head appeared under Gisela and Amona's locked arms as Atenea quietly pushed her way into the whispered conversation.

"Atenea good judge of people anyways. She likes you," Amona offered the giggling Gisela as she petted Atenea. "And she bites that lazzi boy for teasing her too," she added.

The next morning was cold, and everyone was slow to get moving but Julien and Gisela. Eulalie's father jokingly referred to the cheerful pair as the King and his court jester. Everyone got moving along the old road again before the sun was a hands height off the horizon.

As they walked Gisela passed the Ogre, giving him

half her carrot and then passed the Saxon boy.

"I see your precious oak trees didn't break your chains overnight, lazzi," she strutted as she passed him.

"Not those trees, and not last night!" he taunted back.

She looked at him harshly as they paced the steps together. "Judges nine. The trees went to anoint a new king over them, and the trees came to the grapevine and said: Come thou, and reign over us as King! And the grapevine answered them: Can I forsake my wine, that cheereth God and men, and be lofted higher than the other trees?" she stated, then walked on.

Sister Amona laughed to herself as the cart and prisoners and children and the unusual train marched on along the snow-covered remains of the Roman road.

They followed the road along the side of the valley, crossing streams before climbing up along a ridge and then crossing the breadth of the Tertre valley. Another broad ridge passed by noon, and then across yet another valley, like gentle steps up to the north. They passed a big hill known as Féages, and then a lake called Rincerie before the road turned more westward. The sky grew clear and the sun bright, but the snow and air seemed to sap all warmth from the day.

By afternoon the road followed low rolling hills, and decidedly more westward. According to Julien it eventually ran towards Rennes, though they were not going to that town. They made their way as the cold sun sank towards the west. The rolling hillsides reminded Gisela of the ocean. The constant rumble of the wheels of Sister Amona's soeur-cart in front of her and the continuous swishes of chains over snow added to the feeling for her.

Late afternoon brought Atenea's hackles up, and she frequently paced, stopping to bark at the forest and hop oddly on her front feet as if she were pushing down a rabbit's head into its hole.

Along with the rumbling wheels of the carts and the sounds of the chains, the Aquitaine began humming again in d'oc. Eulalie sang a song that sounded sad to Gisela, and the rest of the train had taken it up with her. When Gisela would recognize the chorus coming again, she would try to sing with them, even if she had no idea what words they were singing. The mix of a deeply-felt song, hard mailed feet and soft leather shoes, grunts and burps and the living sounds of the moving train had all become the normal, and often only, sounds in the snowy landscape over the last three days. So it was with piercing and other-worldly eruption that the wolves' howls in the distance to the north struck everyone to the heart. The first dying echoes were answered by the metallic song of Julien's sword being unsheathed, and as the distant howls multiplied, so too did the murmurings and concerns amongst the prisoners and guards. Spears pointed semantically at snowbanks; eyes peered suspiciously at shadows, and amongst the trees, mere squirrels became monsters of horse-sized proportions.

A laughing Saxon prisoner began calling out in a foreign tongue, some kind of chant that did not sit well with any. With two swift strokes, Julien silenced the man, removed all but his hand from the burden of the chain gang, and left a fresh kill in their tracks to appease the wanton hunger that seemed to be closing in around them. No other Saxons seemed eager to rejoin the chant again.

They came down into a gentle valley and the crossroads and old Roman fort of Sipia late in the day. The sun had set, and the bright white band of twilight already framed the west as the first stars of the east twinkled a warning to the train. The wolf howls had vanished far behind them.

The fort seemed to be empty. The guards seemed concerned, for Frankish soldiers should hold this fort of the Berton Marche day or night.

Slowly guards crept up and back, crossing the river Siche, till it appeared no man or beast claimed the fort. With darkness falling quickly Julien drove the chains across the river, up the road, up across the trench and up the hillside of the rampart, through the rough gate where the sudis stakes left a hole large enough for a cart to pass through into the interior. The Frankish prison army invaded and retook Sipia without loss or wound.

Whatever cartus and praetorium had once commanded this Roman fort had given way to an apparent eon of reworking. Chaotic wattle and daub huts with thatched roofs now formed the camp center. The stable, being the most open building, was situated near the gate opening. The missing gates were a mystery, though, as their remaining hinges testified to their recent existence.

One thing was certain, the snow had been trampled down everywhere in the fort, and by the footprints of mailed soldiers and horses. The Frankish soldiers holding the fort had left within the past week, if not within the previous days.

After a guard inspected each hut for food, weapons or supplies, Julien ordered a chain of prisoners each into the huts along with their wives, and the bigger hut for the supplies and children. A guard remained outside of each. The carts were unloaded and rolled to form a new gate, the tent being stretched out from the stable stalls. They had little wood for a fire, and with wolves possibly outside in the dark woods, little desire to look for more. All the spare furniture in the huts, save for one table, was brought to the stable at the gate, and Julien declared it to be the only fire allowed of the night, surrounded by uneasy guards.

Julien inspected the walls of the fort as Sister Amona and Sister Basina gathered the children into the hut. One big heavy wooden table was all that remained in the main hall after the soldier's sweep, and the women set up bunks with blankets for the smaller children on top of it as the bigger children set up underneath it. Radishes and apples were a cold and hard dinner, with the night cold and hard to match. Julien stationed four guards, all close along the trenched ramparts of the fort after his inspection.

Julien stuck his head into the bigger hut, pausing to look at the door frame as he did.

"You might have better chosen the table to be against the open doorway," he suggested to Amona and Basina. Amona shrugged.

"Too many rats in this place," Basina warned.

"They're the only things remaining then," Julien lamented, looking back out the doorway at the stable and camp beyond. "Two years ago this was a permanent camp at these crossroads. The Margrave must have altered that. It seems to be only a stop-over camp for traveling troops now. It's in poor shape." He shook his head. "There are half a dozen breaches in the old outer walls. No stocks of firewood or supplies. Every door and shutter is missing, even the main

gates. You'll have to use our stable fire to cook what
we have and then distribute to the huts. We've set up
that hut over there as the privy. Don't let the children
go alone."

"We found candles under chairs when you guards
took away," Amona offered.

Julien took them from her. "They looked half
eaten."

"Someone stay here very hungry."

"And from the tracks they haven't been gone long,"
Julien warned, stepping back over to the doorway.
"Keep a sharp eye on everyone tonight. Ill-at-ease will
be our night's feast, and rest a hard tack without a beer
or boil to soften its edges."

It seemed to take forever for the pea-frumenty to
cook in the meager fire. One of the babies on the table
was crying and fussy, his mother exhausted. Gisela,
Eulalie, and Sacha were huddled under the blankets,
under the table with several of the others, trying
unsuccessfully to rest.

~We're dying~

Her eyes flashed open, and she knew to look at
Sacha. He was asleep, shaking with cold, and Gisela
was worried he was sick, though Eulalie didn't think
so. With a linen chemise, her kirtle top, Bérénice's
cloak and now Amona's chamois vest, Gisela was too
warm under the blanket, so she and Eulalie carefully
stripped Gisela out of her top layers and Sacha out of
his thick blue shirt and put her fancy kirtle top on him,
then put his blue shirt back on him. The blues were so
close it looked natural. Gisela redressed, and they all
huddled together again, though Gisela became lost in
prayer.

"Duende. Please help," Sister Amona asked under

the table. Gisela didn't know if she had fallen asleep or was lost in prayer, but she crawled out into the hut and helped Amona hand out the spoonfuls of pea-frumenty to the children and women. The mother of the crying baby ate hers as she paced and hummed, trying to rock the baby to sleep. Gisela followed Amona back outside. Amona turned, surprised for a second, then shrugged and let her help.

As Amona filled another big bowl at the campfire, Gisela wondered why Julien's guards were cutting long thin strips off the edge of the tent, like slings or bandages. They took a bowl of pea-frumenty to each hut in turn, doling it out to each of the prisoners in turn. They were getting cup fulls, a lot compared to the children, but then they were working much harder. In the few paces between the huts Amona and Gisela sang Psalm 146 together, and in the huts, the prisoners seemed grateful and thanked them. Gisela tried to give Ogre an extra helping, but he would not take it and shared it with the lazzi boy's still unfilled cup. She put one of her pocket marzipan wafers in his hand, but that too he gave back, smiled and shook his hands, kindly, no thank you. The lazzi boy tried to steal the traded wafer from her as she backed up, but Amona's hip check knocked him back down, and Ogre's big leg plopped over and kept him there till everyone else in the hut was fed.

After feeding the guards, Gisela and Amona returned to the big hut. The baby was crying worse now, Sister Basina and the mother taking turns trying things, with concerned Atenea following the baby in whomever's arms. The children were all huddled together under the table but not sleeping, and Gisela handing out the last of her marzipan wafer to them in place of stories tonight. She made certain Sacha was alright, but she couldn't find Eulalie.

"She's in the privy with Maylis," Sister Basina told her over the cries of the baby. Amona nodded for her to go check.

Eulalie was outside the big hut doorway, staring back at the hut they were using as a privy.

"Where's Maylis?"

"She wouldn't come back with me."

"Is she alright?"

"I don't think so."

Gisela went to go check. The stars were incredibly bright in the black sky, one near the pretty Pleiades winked as white as the snow on the thatched rooftops of the huts. Where the ground was not dark with mud it was white with snow, and even the walls of the wattle huts glowed. It was dark inside the privy hut, but Julien had one of the half-eaten candles lit inside to give some light, and again Gisela thought everything tonight was either in the light or in the dark. No one was in the hut. Gisela wandered back out and around the side, peeking. It was dark in the hut's shadow, the stable fire not being visible around back, but its glow apparent on the farther huts facing them. Maylis was around the back in the hut's deep shadow, crouched down, watching another hut. Gisela could barely make out her silhouette against the snowy rampart glowing in the firelight.

"Maylis?"

Maylis' head shot around. Even in the dark, her disappointment was evident.

"What do you want?"

Gisela offered her the last of the marzipan wafers. "My last candy. I wanted you to have it."

Maylis scoffed. "Keep your stolen piety. Give Christ his cut back."

"I didn't steal it."

"Spare me the sermon, Thief. You, you're so damn righteous. You think I don't know? You're bathed in rosemary soaps, your friend Sister Rosine isn't here to hide you anymore. So now you play Sister Amona's passions. You are a runaway kitchen serf from Mur, stealing from the Royal family."

"What?"

"The kirtle, the boots, the palmiers, the candy. I still bet you have jewelry and coins tucked away as well. You've stolen it all from the Lords of Mur and are hiding amongst us to make your getaway."

"These things were all my mother's to give, and given to me, not stolen. You have become a Jezebel in your pain and loneliness, and so you cast your fears as lies upon others now."

Maylis slowly stood up, facing her in the dark.

"You're out here meeting Huebald again, and this time you don't deny it. That is him over there guarding that hut you were watching! You wear his cloak now, and you have been eating the soldiers jerky you got from him too," Gisela insisted, feeling a bit of the righteous strength of the bishop inside, then feeling compassion instead. She put the wafer away and came closer in the dark, trying to take Maylis' hand, but Maylis recoiled.

"That's not your parents in this train, not your mother at least," Gisela whispered. "Your father looks at you and talks to you from the prison chains, but she doesn't, and their infant son now cries back in the hut, and it does not move you as it should a sister. Where is your mother, Maylis?" she asked, trying to retake her hand.

The truth was striking its mark. Maylis began to crack. Gisela took her hand.

"Is she dead?"

"No," choked out Maylis, sobbing up one long gulp. "My father bought his own freedom by selling my mother and big sister away to the Muslims when they fought the Franks at Narbonne. He joined King Waiofar's army at the siege. I was small baggage even the Andalusians didn't want." She looked back at Huebald guarding his door. "I served my father every day to stay alive. Cooked, cleaned, stole for him, whatever it took. Until she came along. Then I became baggage again. We were all captured at Poitiers. Now I am a prisoner thrice over, and if you think your judgmental verses are going to make me give a share of my nothing away to people who care nothing about me, you are so mistaken. You want me to think about heaven while I'm trying to survive this march. Leave me alone, Christian thief, or I'll reveal who you really are," Maylis warned. Finally regrouping, Maylis took her hand away and became angry she had revealed secrets about herself. "I'll tell Julien you are a runaway thief from Mur, in front of everyone."

"And if you do, in front of everyone, I'll tell Julien you are trading your body with his guards for favors."

A dark flash between two far-off huts made them both turn, but nothing was there. Then another dark flash passed through the light between the distant huts, and this time as they were looking.

It was wolves.

Maylis ran screaming towards her guard-lover Huebald's hut as Gisela ran around the privy hut towards the stable and big hut. The baby was crying,

Atenea was barking, the guards were all yelling, and a pack of wolves appeared on the rampart by the stable gate. The campfire erupted in a dozen bright blazes as Julien's men lit their prepared torches, the stable and camp suddenly in bright light. The wolves eyes showed back red in the light and chilled Gisela to the bone. One of the wolves was a big monster, all the shades of grey and white and pearl of an opened oyster shell. Spears flew up from the guards at the pack as Gisela ran into the big hut.

Amona, Basina and the guard named Suger were inside. Suger had a torch in one hand, the wrapped strips of Ceufroy's tent blazing like a bright star in the dark. With his other hand, he was helping the Sisters turn the heavy table on its side to act as a great shield wall. Their fear and panic were too great, however, and the table flipped all the way over with its legs up. The children were all backed against the wall behind them, crying, screaming or struggling to keep Atenea on her leash. Her rope was now caught under the overturned table, and Gisela grabbed it, finding herself sprawled out on the floor, struggling beside Eulalie and Sacha. Atenea's teeth grazed Gisela's arm in her eagerness to break the leash and go fight, and they tried to loop the rope on the table leg to keep themselves from being dragged out behind Atenea into the fight.

Suger propped his spear on the wall and grabbed the table to lift it up behind his right side. Amona, a kitchen knife in one hand, grabbed up the blanket in the other and began snapping it at the wolves like a ragged whip, using it and her body to cover the children against the wall. The children and the mother with the baby turned into a churning pile of desperation against the wall. Basina threw her weight back on a table leg, and the table popped back up on its side like a big shield again, sending her and the spear sprawling onto the floor. Outside the doorway, at the stables, the guards fought back as the pack charged down into them. Suddenly two wolves who had snuck in behind the guards appeared in the doorway.

There was more than one pack.

If Gisela thought the Oyster shell wolf had been a big leader upon the rampart, by color and markings this was Oyster's bigger brother. A second wolf, a lighter grey, dove inside past Big Oyster at Suger.

Horrendous barking came from the open window to Gisela's right, and a third wolf appeared, having jumped up and now trying to claw its way over the icy sill and down into the screaming children.

Two more wolves struggled in through one of the many holes in the walls of the other room of the big hut, snapping and snarling with each other in anticipation of the fight and feast to come.

The pack outside on the rampart was merely the distraction for the pack going for the easy kills inside the nursery.

On the far side of the sideways table, Suger drew his falchion from his side with a schling as Big Oyster grabbed his mailed torch arm and the lighter grey bit at his leg.

On this side of the sideways table, Atenea growled in a fury, her fur suddenly inflated to twice her normal size and her leash snagged behind her. She began pulling the entire table forward in noisy little hops as she snapped at the light grey wolf by Suger's leg.

The children screamed as their protective table

shield began to pull away. Amona tried to grab it with her blanket hand. "Let go!" she yelled at the girls. Gisela and Eulalie let go of Atenea's leash rope and fell back against the pile of children again.

Behind the table, Basina got up to her knees and picked up Suger's spear like a broom handle, but the blade caught on the wall.

Amona used her kitchen knife to chop the window wolf's front leg as it tried to climb in. Blood spewed, and Amona punched the wolf so hard it fell backward, back outside, yelping.

The two new wolves from the next room turned the inside corner, and Gisela and the braver children let loose a hail of stones and ice and snowballs at them. One was pelted back, and Atenea met it with a terribly violent fight, but the other new wolf dove past Atenea, and into the children, its snapping jaws grabbing the little girl Gersvinda's arm. The girl screamed, grabbing onto Gisela in desperation.

Atenea quickly got the upper hand on one of the two new wolves, and it tried to escape from beneath the terrible white mastiff's wrath.

Gisela had Gersvinda's coat and chest tightly in her hands, and Eulalie grabbed the girl's legs, but the wolves angry teeth were mauling the poor girl's head and other arm only inches from Gisela' fingers. She could smell the wolf's spittle as it shook its head violently, it's black ears flapping in her face. Gersvinda's free hand was striking the muzzle of the wolf over and over, her flailing fist grazing Gisela's face on every swing. Gisela screamed out in anger and terror herself, thinking if she let go, Gersvinda would die, and if they didn't, the poor girl would be drawn and quartered.

Suger's falchion chopped the side of the light grey wolf at his leg, sending it sprawling, snapping and gushing a flood of blood. Big Oyster's jaw clamp on Suger's mailed arm finally won out, and in pain, Suger dropped the torch. He tried to stab at the big wolf as the torch rolled on the wet floor, casting surreal lighting.

Atenea, bloodied herself now, sent up a horrible noise from the crushed throat of her defeated wolf and, dropping it, immediately dove snarling for the side of the new black-eared wolf trying to drag off the screaming Gersvinda.

Basina stabbed at Big Oyster with the wrong end of the spear as Suger stepped back to regain his footing and protect his side of the table. Two more wolves from outside scrambled in through the door.

"Saint Emeterius take pity on us!" Amona yelled, unable to stab the black-eared wolf's head without hitting a child, and instead snapped the blanket at the wolf in the evil tug-of-war.

Black Ears dropped the girl in its mouth to take on Atenea, and Gisela and Eulalie drug her limp body back on a bloody trail into the screaming huddle of children.

Amona threw the big wool blanket over the children, managing to cover everyone but Gisela.

One new wolf joined Black Ears' fight with Atenea, and the three formed a whirling, snarling ball next to Gisela. The other new wolf jumped at Basina, slipping underneath the backward spear and hitting the table hard, snarling and tearing at her apron.

Suger's swings at Big Oyster were keeping it at bay, but the wolf was considerably faster than the older guardsman. Its head was the size of a horse, and the sword knicks only seemed to anger it more.

Gisela kicked at the snarling wolf trying to come around the sideways table at Basina as one of Atenea's wolves dove into the wool blanket, biting at whatever lumps under the wool-skin that moved. More wolves could be heard snarling and growling outside the window.

The doorway suddenly turned into a herse of red and steel. Julien's shield looked like a great swinging door entering the room, his bright mail and red tabard flowing behind, and his sword already arcing through the air.

Big Oyster let go of Suger and spun, and Julien's blade divided its big face into two.

The table wolf turned from the kicking feet to face the new threat coming in the door as Atenea's Black Eared wolf tried to escape into the next room.

Spears, with the blades at the proper end, appeared in the windows from outside, and they stabbed at the wolf biting at the rippling blanket. One struck the back of the table wolf as it pounced at Julien's approaching shield.

Julien's pace did not even hesitate after slaying Big Oyster, as his sword carved a figure eight, missing the table wolf on his shield but nearly cutting the blanket wolf in half with his end stroke. Gisela could have reached out and touched Julien's sword it passed so closely, and a spray of the blanket wolf's blood appeared on the side of her face. Suger's sword found the table wolf's hide a second before Julien's blade snapped back into it. With soldiers at the window and door now, Julien strode after Atenea in the next room to help her slay Black Ear and take on any others.

Suger tried unsuccessfully to pick up the torch.

Basina, still screaming in terror, let the spear drop over the table, and it clattered to the floor. Amona collapsed for a moment, weeping, the baby was still crying in his cowering mother's arms, and now every child under the blanket was as well. In the next room, the black-eared wolf snarled, and its yelp was cut short forever.

From under the blanket, Eulalie's hand slowly crept out and up Gisela's back. Gisela turned to Eulalie's touch, which was seemingly calm, but tears streamed from Eulalie's sad eyes, and poor young Gersvinda's body was in her arms. Gisela's jaw and cheeks shook in disbelief as she and Eulalie, and then Amona, hugged each other, and the girl, and cried uncontrollably.

Julien argued authoritatively with several of the angry prisoners as his injured guard's wounds were tended. They were refusing to go back to separate huts and leave their families unprotected if another fight was coming. Julien doubted the wolves would try again. He guessed the recent snow had driven two family packs together and having lost close to ten of the pack members and at least one of the leader males, they would stay away.

Still, terrified families, three injured guards, two wounded children, and one dead girl were about all the prisoners were going to take in one evening, and the big hut was much too wretched to use again.

Julien relented. Prisoners and guards working together piled a snow bank under the carts to keep any wolves from entering the way most of the pack had easily escaped, and Julien decided to let everyone stay in the stables as a big group. It was riskier for the guards, but with the Aquitani fears satisfied it seemed the wisest course.

The wolves were skinned and butchered by several of the prisoners, including the Ogre, who was obviously skilled. The Sisters were each given a wolf hide, though nobody wanted to see them again tonight. The meat of the pack, on the other hand, was eagerly devoured by an equally hungry and dangerous pack.

Julien ordered a hut put to the torch. It burned miserably, and once the snow-soaked thatch roof was finally consumed the mud walls simply baked like smoldering bricks. Slowly, one after the other, all night long, the huts of Sipia went up in flame. Sisters Amona and Basina wrapped Gersvinda's body in part of the tent. They lit the remaining gnawed candles around her body in the middle of the stable and led the families in prayers for Gersvinda and her grieving parents. Even the ordinarily callous and burley Saxons held their tongues the rest of the night.

With the first morning's light, the big hut was all that remained and, packed with the wolf bodies, they set it aflame as well. The train made their way out the gate, onto the snowy road, and turned north on a new road, towards Avranches.

PART TWO

AGITÉ MYSTÉRIEUX

Billé

The cloth held the moss snugly against the wound and wrapped around the horse's pastern, right above the coronary. The bleeding was not severe, but the cut was still costly. It would be a few days before the horse could be ridden again. His cold fingers tucked the bandage tightly much higher on the horse's leg, and he let the hoof down again into the cold Oudon stream to reduce the swelling. Picking up his thick leather gloves but still crouched down, he stared at the tracks in the snow.

The trail along the ford here held tracks of so many boots, so many shoes, but almost hidden off to one side, by a big oak and copper ferns, were children's size footprints, accompanied by boots too big for a child but too small for a woman. As if they had hidden here for a while. There were threads of blue sendal, terribly out of place amongst woodland snow and prisoners.

The Archer ran his thumb over his lips. His mail coif was topped with a black pill helmet, one side with a big bright red button and three grebe feathers sticking out from it backward; two of grey and one of gold. He gathered his big twill cloak around him as he stood up. At least they were following the right tracks now.

He turned back to Thëo.

"I'm sorry, vieil ami. I didn't know the ice was that

thin by Le Lion. I should not have pushed you so hard." He petted his jenet and removed the feed bag. Thëo let the last oats fall with his final few grinding chews and rubbed his neck against the Archer's hand.

The Captain of the Archers looked up the road, then back down. His gamble had thinned now.

For two days the Queen had everyone searching for Gisela, every room in Mur castle, down into the old bathhouse and winery that was under Mur, and then in the tuffeau caves that ran for many leagues along the Loire. With so many prisoners kept there over the past months, it was like searching through an abandoned city. The Queen was convinced Gisela had been kidnapped by agents of King Waiofar and Duke Tassilo to use as a bargaining pawn against His Majesty in their war. She made sense at the time.

Gisela's shutter was broken, and there were clear signs someone had been climbing on the pergola outside her window.

There was the persistent rumor of a mysterious rebellion.

There was tremendous commotion all evening as the prisoners were taken away, the perfect opportunity with so many comings and goings.

Gisela had been taken against her will, for her necklace and cross were still hanging on her bed, and her quirt, Lord help us, Bérénice and the Queen were adamant that Gisela wouldn't even go to the garderobe without her magical quirt, which was still in her dresser drawer. Gisela was a loving, attentive child. She had no reason whatsoever to run away.

The other Captains felt sure it was a royal soldier turned traitor, so they had accounted for every soldier and questioned every single one, and no one was missing.

The Queen was still convinced it was a kidnapping, so by the third day he and his archers were sent out to scout the snow-covered Brézé countryside for miles, looking for tracks of a soldier that might have snuck Gisela away and given her to someone else, then returned so as not to be missed. Another lost day of endless, dead-end leads. Unless someone had killed her and hidden her body during the blizzard, there seemed no place left unchecked.

Finally, withdrawn to her chambers, sullen and awaiting some ransom or the terrible wrath of His Majesty if Gisela were used against him as a shield by King Waiofar, the Queen had ordered him to search the city of Tours. He sent his best archers to Tours, but he had disregarded her orders and set out on the only obvious trail he could imagine. Almost four hundred people had been moved downriver the same night she vanished. She had playmates amongst them from the new church. She dreamed of Taliesin's adventure stories in Brittany and dearly loved her big brother Charles, who was along the Breton Marche. Somehow, for some reason, Gisela had *willingly* gone with the prisoners north.

At Andecavus, Ceufroy told him the prisoners had been split, and there he had made his first mistake. The monks of St Serge said the majority of the children and families went northeast to Le Mans and then on to Caen. When he caught up to them at Durtal, Sister Rosine put all the puzzle pieces in place for him. She confirmed that Gisela had willingly been in her cart, with her big boots and supposedly Her Majesty's permission, when they left Mur Castle for the new church. To say goodbye to her friends there, she thought, but she hadn't seen her amongst the prisoners since that night. One of the guards, however, swore there was an Aquitaine farm girl, the spitting image of Gisela, in the other group that went northwest. Of course, nobody amongst the prisoners or guards even knew Gisela was missing. The royal riders along the Loire that first day said they were looking for missing soldiers, and not a word about a runaway princess to a few hundred enemy prisoners. That was all he needed to know. Gisela had indeed run away to find Charles or the legends of Taliesin.

He sent one of the prison guards back to Andecavus with his report and, in his haste, cut west straight across country through the snow. He could have gone back to report the news himself, but that would lose precious time, and he was sure that alone, on horseback, he could overtake a slow-moving train of walking prisoners. And he would have too, if the ice by the marshy banks of the Mayenne hadn't been too thin and broke through, cutting Thëo's leg. Now Thëo was his pack horse; he could travel with that wound, but not long supporting the Archer's weight, and so they were going to have to go after Gisela on foot for a few days.

The Archer Captain checked his sword and bow and then looked up the old Roman road. He was from Nantes, and all the roads, from Vannes to Rennes, from Laval to Le Mans, he had ridden, walked or hunted. His helmet's feathers pointed back towards Andecavus and Mur, his red button on his pill helmet matched the anger in his eyes. His red, royal surcoat below his neck reminded him he'd lose his head if he failed now.

He kissed once and trotted up the snowy road. Thëo

followed him obediently on the invisible lead rope of bonded friendship.

With the solemn day, fall decided to return to its proper place and timing, and the temperature rose nicely as the morning passed. Late in the morning Julien and the prisoners were denied entrance into the village of Bais by armed men. They would not treat with Julien, saying they had seen the burnings the night before and feared the prisoners, wolves and early snow were a plague upon them.

As noon passed both prisoners and trees shed their second layers and snowy burdens, often in sudden dumping heaps. On the road melting snow gave way to a great deal of mud, and streams and rivulets ran every which way, yet all who walked agreed that the mild wet won over the bitter cold.

The village of Vitré was miles off the road to their east, and Julien felt it would be a pointless detour given the general population's fear of so many chained men. They continued straight on the old Roman roadbed till almost night, when they came to the manors known as d'Ize. The coloni opened the cow gates to the settlement for Royal guards without hesitation. At a cluster of buildings, there was a simple church, dedicated to Saint Stephen. The priest there not only offered to let the train stay there for the night, but he also took pity on the pleadings of Sister Amona and allowed Gersvinda's body to be buried in the church's graveyard. Many of the prisoners helped dig her grave. Her mother and her father, freed temporarily from his prison chain with Julien's permission, accompanied the priest into the church for a Mass for the girl. The prisoners remained outside, but prayed along with the Mass.

The priest talked to the steward of the manor, a reeve named Wibert, and the party was encouragingly treated to a great many apples to add to their supper and allowed to stay in his barn for the night. It was crowded, but warm and dry compared to their previous nights. Wibert shared a jug of wine with Julien by a campfire under the lychgate.

Wibert told Julien the Margrave had been concentrating the Royal soldiers of the Marche into stronger fortresses, such as Vitré and Fougères. He also warned that the Lord of Bais's family might be of questionable loyalties.

Returning to the barn after praying at Gersvinda's grave, Gisela found Eulalie fast asleep among many others in the hayloft. She looked happy for a change, even in sleep, and Gisela thought it most appropriate after her depressed and fearful past few days. Whether it was Gersvinda's Mass, or the wolves, or the warmer temperatures, Gisela felt wary, as if she and Eulalie had traded natures during the day. The Aquitani were at home amongst cows and goats and chickens, but Gisela found the smells and air bothered her. After trying to go to sleep for some time, she began to realize it was her conscience that was bothering her, not the barn's manure, and she went to find Sister Amona.

Amongst the cluster of buildings, the barn was close to the church, and Gisela wandered to it and found Sister Amona seated inside.

"Come to pray with me Duende?"

"I hope. Proverbs thirty is on my mind."

Amona waved her hand. "Remind please."

"If you have been foolish, exalting yourself, or if

you have been devising evil, put your hand on your mouth. For whipping milk produces butter, twisting the nose produces blood, and stirring up anger produces strife."

"Why do you think this is?"

Gisela clenched her fists and stuck her chin out. "I haven't been honest with you, Amona, and Maylis has been threatening to tell everyone my secret."

"Aw, she not worry you. I know already, and no one throw you out when they learn."

"That is just it, Sister. I'm not Wasconi, like you thought, or Aquitani, like Maylis thinks."

"Oh?" Amona's eyebrows arched up. "So, what you, a Frank?"

Gisela looked around to make certain they were alone in the little church. "I'm Princess Gisela, from Mur."

Amona laughed, but the look on Gisela's face stopped her. "You serious?" she asked, then suddenly remembered back to the nursery and Masses at the unfinished church in Mur. Her eyes grew huge under the suddenly flat eyebrows. "That why you familiar to me there! You come with Queen to pray! You are Frank. ROYAL Frank!" she blurted out in a barely contained whisper, then looked around herself and spoke quietly again. "Why are you here?"

"I have been foolish, and I am secretly trying to get to my brother Charles. He is with the Margrave, I think, somewhere along the Marche."

"A princess among prisoners. What you thinking? No place for you!"

"Nothing is as I thought it would be, Sister."

"So why tell me?" Amona asked.

"God wants me too, I think. So you hear the truth

from me, not Maylis."

"You still Duende to me then. I not tell," Amona promised. "You tell Julien?"

"No Amona. If he realizes I'm Gisela, he'll turn everyone around to take me straight back. It would be that important to him."

"A long way. How you know he won't take to you brother?"

"That's my butter. My nosebleed. My strife. I need to keep my hand on my mouth," Gisela sighed, and Amona hugged her.

"Never hug a princess before. Maybe we pray God help you find brother?"

"Alright," Gisela agreed, and they prayed together in the humble church of Saint Stephen for an even more humbling miracle. Afterward, they walked back to the barn together with their arms around each other for warmth.

They did not see that Maylis had followed Gisela to the church, and was hiding outside the church doors when they passed.

Wibert and several of his men waited with eager horses and bright spears outside the barn in the morning. After everyone had risen and cleaned, they escorted them up over the ridge north of town, skirting a big hill. They led them into the valley of Nöe and then onto the edge of the valley of Veuvry before waving farewell to Julien and the guards, and the escort turned back. Ize's cattle were numerous and plump, and the mansi that surrounded the manor looked attractive enough that some Aquitani suggested they wanted to go back and live under such a good and noble lord.

The train climbed the gentle slope up along the valley of Alibart to come to the next manor along the road, named Mecé, where the cows were as plentiful, but Wibert's warmth was sorely missed. The prisoners were allowed only to use the well and ushered along without sympathy.

A mild afternoon awaited them on the road that took them down into the broad valley of Changeon. As the three branches were crossed in succession the fall returned in full force. The early snow was now melted thin and only patchy here. Low pale turquoise clouds drifted by overhead amidst a higher whitewash against the blue sky. When the sun shone on Gisela, it felt warm, but when the sun was behind the low clouds, the chilly breeze returned. The leaves of the oaks and beech let go in blowing winds of red and gold that reminded Gisela of shimmering dragons taking flight, or some tremendous invisible efreet swirling in a dervish frenzy. They crossed a high ridge and came down the long road into the valley of Billé.

Here the Billé stream formed an ox-bow, curving back away to the left and right, like arms hugging the manor up at the top of the hill. The ford was slightly deeper than the other streams had been, and the children had to put up on the carts to get them over. Julien headed the train back up the hillside towards the next manor at the top of the hill.

In the rear, Atenea began barking behind them. Royal riders appeared on rounceys at a trot, spears up with long red banners trailing, following them down the same road. Word passed slowly up the line, stretching out the train till it stopped.

The Royal riders appeared to have a prisoner on a rope running to keep up with them. The rear guards suspiciously began counting the prisoners on their chains, lest it be one of theirs.

Julien, swatting at flies, looked at the mansi and manors ahead up the hill.

"Meadows. Pens. Stockyards. "Why are there no cattle here?" he asked no one in particular.

"The cow gates by those barns up to the right are wide open, Taulière," one of his guards noticed.

"Royal soldiers! With a Breton prisoner!" the rear guards called up. The children were laughing by the cart, the prisoners all talking, the carts squeaking as the prisoner chains got Amona's across the ford while they blocked Basina's from rolling back down the hill.

"What?" Julien insisted, unable to hear his rear guards report. "Quiet down, everyone!" his big voice boomed back down amongst the train.

The Royal riders splashed across the Billé, almost dragging a big stumbling Breton along in their haste. Gisela looked to see if she recognized any of the soldiers in their Royal livery, if they might be Charles or the Margrave or, furtively, if they might know her.

The Royal Riders lowered their spears into them. Gisela saw the friendly guard known as Fridolin skewered in complete surprise, right in front of her.

A Royal rider let go of the Breton prison rope, and it was no rope, but a whip and his hands were not tied. The Breton stopped running, laughing at their ruse, and let the whip crack across the stream at several prisoners and their scrambling guards.

Gisela realized these were not Royal soldiers that had ridden up. They were bandits wearing Royal livery and riding royal horses as a disguise. Further uphill, Julien saw this too, and also realized four mounted men were no match for a full train of guards.

Amidst screaming children, the half dozen guards around Amona's cart formed up, spears out. One of the Ruse riders tossed a seax blade to one of the chained Saxon prisoners as they passed the broken rear guard and began battling the Amona cart guards. Francisca hand axes and angon spears flew. One of the horses went down into a prison chain. Maylis' surrogate mother was screaming on the cart, with the baby still in her arms. Atenea was snarling alongside the road by Amona, who was trying desperately to get the children out of tramplings way.

The guards of the middle walking group began forming up to join the guards down at Amona's cart as prisoners dove off the road, dragging each other into each other and trees and brush and mayhem. Shoulder yokes were dropped, the urns and pots scattered like makeshift caltrops in the chaos.

Julien called the middle guards back to Basina's upper cart, where his forward guards and the prison guards were setting up a defensive line instead of charging down the hill to help the obviously decimated rearguards.

"MIND YOURSELVES!" Julien ordered out to his men calmly. "FLIP THE CARTS!"

Gisela grabbed Eulalie's hand, running into the trees along the road as the seax, swords, and falchions began flashing. In the woods to the right, she saw the trees come alive like some spell of the Sorcerer Gwydion in a Taliesin poem. They were men, not trees; in league with the Ruse riders. Apparently, soldiers who had been hiding along the ox-bowed stream as a trap, and now set upon the right side of the train like blown leaves.

Julien's soldiers flipped Basina's upper cart and

were prepared, the seasoned warrior being keen, but the guards at Amona's lower cart were suddenly caught between the mounted Ruse riders and the charging ambush from the side and could not obey.

Gisela's appearing woodland apparitions were Bretons, dressed all in green wool and brown cloth leg wrappings. Many had shields with a crude wheeled cross, and all carried a shorter spear than the Franks. Amona's soeur-cart rolled in a turn to one side a few feet as the skirmish went on, the pole shafts sweeping Bretons back in an arc, the wheels running over prison chains before stopping against one of the fallen prison guards. Beside it, the Saxon lazzi boy took up Fridolin's falchion and began chopping and hammering his prison chain. The great whip cracking the sky on the opposite side of the ford kept everyone away from the stream.

The Bretons were good fighters, Gisela could see that all the way up the road from one cart to the next, but the Frankish guards were heavily mailed and equally experienced. The Breton soldiers fell three to one, paying dearly, but when a prison guard was taken down, they were mercilessly punctured in any mail opening, much like her mother's pincushion.

One came around the overwhelmed guard mob above Amona's lower cart and spotted Amona and the children. Charging Atenea lept and hit him in the chest with so much force Gisela felt the blow as well as heard it. She saw spilled apples rolling down the road, and was shocked to see Bretons grabbing them up, even in the midst of the fight. It was not only apples but the radishes and soldier's jerky and wineskins as well. As Eulalie put her balled fists to her ears and cried with closed eyes, trying to block out the horror,

Gisela watched a pair of Bretons scamper back off the road with a pot and stuff mouthfuls of food into their cheeks before returning to the fight. It was as if the hungry wolves had returned on two legs; these lycanthropes from the ensorcelled trees.

The three remaining ruse riders backed their rounceys away from the Breton mob at Amona's lower cart. One of them tossed a seax to the big Ogre to get him to join the fight. The Saxon lazzi peeked out from under the cart. He used his shortened length of chain to wrap and tangle the guard's legs and then stab at their feet.

The Ogre caught the seax, a little hunting knife in his big hand, and promptly slung it back into the surprised ruse riders face. The rider slowly collapsed off the side of his horse as the Ogre clobbered a Breton with his fist, then reached down and helped the last shielded rearguard back up onto his own feet. The whip cracked overhead like thunder, but not close enough to the Ogre for him to seem concerned.

Julien's guards had easily repulsed the upper portion of the Breton's charge that came near them, but the lower cart seemed to be losing. Julien stepped over Basina's cart's contents. The big tent, blankets, baskets of apples, pots and pans, everything was now spilled all over the road. Basina hid in the tumbled cart, trying to save the pots of flour.

"STRING OUT THAT TENT!" Julien ordered, pointing at a tree about twenty feet away. "SPEARS BY TWO, FOR A STAG CHARGE!" he added pointing west while he kept facing east around the cart and the Breton's gathered down the road below him.

His guards obeyed, handing one end of the tent to Basina at the cart and another guard dragging the other end towards the tree as all the other guards formed two lines.

The Bretons downhill between the carts began searching the prisoners amidst chaos on the road and at the woods edge. The violence from without mixed pent up violence from within. A chained Saxon murdered a chained Aquitaine over some insult days past, and the other Aquitani then fell on him in vengeance. The Bretons tried to subdue or fight the angry men in chains.

It was the turn of the woods to the left to come alive, and a wave of Breton's came from the opposite side of the road, from the other arm of the ox-bowed stream. They formed a long broken picket line stretching along the road from one cart up to the next. One Breton knocked Gisela over as he passed her in haste, children apparently being of no consequence at this stage of the battle.

Back up the road the tent guard reached the tree, slinging a rope around it, braced his foot on the tree trunk and pulled it tight with all his might. The stretched tent rose up like a wall of lightning. Julien had accurately anticipated a second wave from the more distant oxbow stream on the other side and had not let the Ruse riders tempt him into getting his men blindsided trying to rush to the rear to help the other guards. Ceufroy's canvas tent wall caught, slowed or deflected the first wave of the new Breton's thrown spears, but not before two found the obedient tree guard in the back and leg, and his grip on the tent rope was lost. The tent wall settled back down, but oddly it formed a crenelated wall like a castle now. The canvas had settled upon the spear points and shield tops of the kneeling line of Julien's guards.

Basina was stretched out over the cart, trying to tie off her end of the suddenly slackened tent when a thrown Breton spear found her back. She spun screaming on the cart only to have another pierce her stomach, and Gisela saw her through the scrambling prisoners tumble off her cart up the road.

The first Bretons charging from the upper left found themselves skewered by the spear points of hidden kneeling guards as the second line of guards threw their angon spears into the charging wave. The tent fell in misshapen blobs of tangled, warring men, leaving the upper line of Bretons to still face a wall of shields.

Julien turned to face the remaining Breton charge with his men. Gisela saw a Saxon prisoner rise up from the woods edge behind Julien with a guard's falchion in his hand. A francesca ax appeared in the Saxon's head, and he fell, passing Julien's peripheral vision. The guard at the tent tree was not yet dead and had saved his captain.

The upper Bretons facing his guards above Basina's cart having been repulsed, Julien ordered his men to peel, turn and follow him back east around the overturned cart, past Basina and now down into the scattered prisoner chains and remaining Bretons between the carts.

Only three guards remained standing at Amona's lower cart. The prisoners fighting amongst themselves added to the confusion, but also helped. The attacking Breton's had obviously expected a train of Breton prisoners, eager to break free and join them. Instead, they managed to enumerate their opponents by freeing the few Saxon's and then angering the Wasconi and many Aquitani.

The Saxon lazzi boy screamed as Atenea drug him by his kicking leg out from under the cart. Already bloodied from killing her last prey and her thick fur ruffled in her own version of mail armor, Gisela guessed Atenea had the boy by a good two or three stone standing upon him and easily outmatched his quickness.

The Ogre, two prisoners and several of his chained inmates dead around him, coiled his cart-entrapped chain around his massive arms and began pulling to try to bend a link and get free. The other two prisoners helped in desperation, and Amona's cart finally obeyed orders and flipped over, luckily onto a Breton and not the remaining, now two, guards, as a link of the chain gave way. They fell back in a tumbled pile.

The two remaining Ruse riders worked their horses back even more, and Atenea, tearing at the Saxon lazzi boy, turned to face the bigger opponents as their spearheads grazed her side. She darted at one of the horse's legs, sending the rouncey up in a spinning turn on its rear legs, its rider merely hanging on. Two horses and two spears, however, were too many for Amona's brave mastiff from the Pyrenees. She yelped and bit at the second spear as it pierced her side, and the bloodied lazzi boy dug his seax into her haunches before back kicking away. The Ruse rider drove his spear down hard into the road beneath Atenea to ensure she would never get back up.

Of all the deaths around her, Gisela's heart broke hardest for Atenea, and her eyes swole with tears. Amona grabbed her by the hood and Eulalie by the arm and desperately drug them farther back into the woods off the road with the rest of the children. Gisela fell down next to Sacha.

The Ruse riders on the rounceys fell back across the stream to the crazed whipping Breton, then turned beside him with pointed spears to help hold the stream.

The lone remaining guard, Syagrius, backed around the cart, his shield pierced by half a dozen iron-tipped spears whose weight was dragging his agonizing arm down with every step back. His sword arm still held its strength though, and parried off the advancing Breton's knife stabs and spear points as they followed him, around both sides of the cart.

The back of the Ogre's hand passed against slain Atenea's fur as he got up, grunting. It was soft, and for the briefest second his still chained hand stroked back against the fur, as if in sympathy to leashes and loyalty.

The Ogre rose up, one of his chained, dead-weight comrades now over his shoulder like a human cloak. The former butcher now sported a falchion, his left hand now painted with Atenea's blood. One of the remaining Aquitani stood with spear beside him. Syagrius was surprised when the Ogre appeared beside him, and then the Aquitani on the opposite side, but then his eyes narrowed in angry determination. The meager three met the dozen Breton's from the wagon in their last charge.

Seeing the Ogre's head appear, Gisela slipped Amona's attention, and she crawled back towards the road and the edge of the fight. Eulalie grabbed her, terrified and crying, begging her not to risk it. Gisela sighed heavily and slipped Eulalie's hand off her leg with a gentle squeeze.

Julien strode past the middle prisoners, and any Saxon remaining on the chain was struck down, no matter if they faced him in defiance or cowered in submission. The majority of prisoners fighting the Bretons dropped their weapons as Julien and the guards passed, the Bretons fearing Julien wrapped in chain far more than the half-starved men bound in chain. The Bretons fell back, around the cart, a last wave to break upon the rocks of a giant.

Syagrius and the Aquitani were dead by his side, but the wounded Ogre fought with a veteran soldier's nerve and the skills of a trained killer. The Bretons seemed both terrified to face him and eager to earn the potential glory. The Ogre's chain finally came up tight, too many dead men for him to drag like a sad stringer of fish. The whip across the stream behind him cracked in warning. He spied Gisela's face in the snow-patched edge of the woods. He smiled to her, and turned to face the Breton charge.

Gisela's heart broke again. She was coming to think the wars of men a terrible waste of everything good in the world.

Julien and his guards came around Amona's cart to find the Ogre falling to his knees, finally failing to fight the Breton's off. Julien and his remaining guards fell into their backs and slew several, then chased the remaining Breton's back across the stream as the big Wascon fell back onto the road, his dead man cloak falling off his shoulder, tangled chains everywhere, like Samson at the tumbled temple. Gisela scrambled out, angrily shoving and pushing the dead prisoner off his arm and the chains away so that she could cradle the big man's head.

The whip and the ruse riders seemed incredibly defiant but simply held their ground across the Billé.

Gisela ran her fingers through the Ogre's hair and

over this black nose and cheeks. It had been frostbite, probably at Mur, that now turned his skin black. Not evil.

Amona and the children came closer to the road and the striking face-off at the ford.

"We outnumber them, yet they don't flee before us," a guard noted.

"No," Julien agreed, scraping the point of his sword on the rocks just below the surface of the water.

"Then why don't they charge?" one of his guards asked.

"Because they are simply keeping us here..," Julien surmised, his head turning, scouting the woods again, then settling on the road that rose up past Basina's cart.

A line of horsemen covered the road up by the manor.

"...Waiting on them."

"Farmers on drays?" asked a guard.

"Those horses are huge."

"They're plow horses."

"There must be thirty of them locals. Saints be praised."

"They are the drays of Le Mans," Julien stated, taking up one of the fallen rear guard's shields.

Several of the soldiers became nervous at this, and confusion replaced the praising of saints.

"Why do you arm yourself against friendly farmers, Taulière?" one guard asked, but followed suit. Cast spears, loose swords, and shields were picked up off the ground by the remaining guards in anticipated defense.

"They're not farmers, and they're not here to help." Julien quietly eyed the Bretons across the stream.

"How do you know they are from Le Mans?"

Julien turned back around. "Those red and white banners indicate a Royal city, and the three candles on the flag tell me it's Le Mans," he explained in a voice that struck Gisela as learned and tutorial. "It's said they've been breeding drays as big as oxen for some time, for the faster pulling of siege wagons. Those funny-hatted soldiers in so much blue, though, I don't know them."

"They're Frisians," Gisela offered from the ground, still cradling the Ogre's head.

Julien cast a look at Gisela, then at the horsemen, then a longer look back at Gisela, and then the horsemen again.

"How do you know this?" Julien asked Gisela.

"Because my nannies are Frisian, and I've seen those hats before."

Julien looked back at her again, tilted his head and narrowed his eyes.

The horsemen began to move forward, walking their horses down the road towards them and the ford of the Billé. Almost all the guards faced the coming horses rather than the ford.

"Will they treat with us?" a guard asked hopefully.

The approaching horses increased to a trot. Julien looked back and saw the Breton's across the stream wring their hands on their spears tighter.

"No."

"Run children!" Amona began to quietly beg.

"NO!" Julien commanded in a voice that stopped them all. "They'll be chased and cut down one by one like so many rabbits. They won't risk any one of them making it back to warn Wibert."

He looked directly at Amona and Gisela.

"Surrender as a group. You might be spared that way."

"Spare? Spare for what purpose? Be made slaves? Servants? Be made sport of and rape?" Amona demanded.

"For the Blessed Lord's Purpose, Sister, the wisdom of which we simple servants are humbly unaware," Julien advised, then went into a low whisper. "Across the stream, by threes, on my mark. Lul, you and I take the rounceys."

The Ogre opened his eyes again. Gisela smiled down at him.

"Now!"

Julien and the guards drove across the water in a great splash, the whip finding it harder to lash mail into submission and the Bretons being out of spears to cast. The Le Mans horsemen coming down the road quickened their mounts into canters.

The Bretons had little fight left in them, particularly against hardened mailed soldiers, and several ran into the woods to escape the Royal soldier's onslaught. Julien, fell and dire, had defeated both the Ruse horsemen and butchered the whipper by the time the Le Man's horses reached Basina's cart. Lul jumped upon a rouncey, and Julien elbowed its hindquarters as it took off south on the road.

Julien and his last four guards splashed back across the stream to Amona's cart just as the horsemen arrived. Several of the big drays and two soldiers on coursers did not stop, but gave chase to Lul who escaping father down the road. The remaining Bretons came out of the woods and splashed back across after them to join the Le Mans horsemen in the semi-circle.

"Surrender, soldier," one of the bearded old

Frisian's commanded in fluent d'oil.

Julien glared back at him, their backs against the soeur-carts.

The old Frisian nodded once, and the horsemen shot a guard dead with arrows. These Frisians, it seemed, did have bows.

"Spare yourself a needless death, Captain," a Le Mans officer offered as the guard crumpled onto the ground at Julien's feet. The officer betraying the Franks was in the same type of red livery Julien himself wore. "Duty has been served. These prisoners are not worth your life."

The Ogre moved, trying to take Gisela's hand. She looked in his eyes and took his hand. It was like trying to comfort a bear. They both looked at Atenea lying near them.

Eulalie screamed as Bretons began to pick up the children and get the prisoner chains standing. Amona cried out to the other children as they started to be herded up the road.

"Barkatu, Duende," the Ogre grumbled as a Breton fished her up from under his head. She held his big hand in both hers till the Breton pulled her too far away.

Julien suddenly dove out at one of the horsemen, slicing the dray's throat in a spray of blood and horse screams that rippled through the half circle facing him. The horse went down on its front legs, violently kicking its neighbor as it fell over. Julien and the two guards, shields up, pressed against the impossible.

Arrows flew. Spear's bit. Blood flowed.

The loose women and children were gathered together near Basina's cart. Bretons swarmed the spilled yokes on the road and the overturned carts like rats, looking for food and whatever until the Frisians chased them off like indolent cats, then wantonly picked through the goods themselves. The pecking order did not escape Gisela.

The prisoners had looked like royal soldiers to Gisela at one point, standing strong against the Breton ambush. Now they appeared more ragged and meager than at any point in the journey, even more defeated than the Mur ferry's in the blizzard. There would be no help forthcoming from them any longer. Any prisoner dead or unable to walk was cut from the prison chain, their hands and arms in sick waves of farewell as they accompanying their walking comrades onward up the road.

Basina laid dead by her cart, tossed aside as unimportant. Amona and the free women were bound and taken away with the prisoners. No comfort would be forthcoming from them any longer. Gisela glimpsed a sad Maylis amongst them instead of the children.

The children were pushed down off the roadside, Bretons guarding them as if sheep. The carts were righted and then clumsily hitched to some of the dray horses to be pulled along. They began binding the children's hands, and a greedy Breton stole Gisela's fine dirty gloves, stuffing them in his shirt before tying her hands. Gisela turned her head and saw Eulalie and Sacha were being tied behind her.

Farther back down by the stream, by fallen Atenea and the Ogre and brave Julien, she saw the Bretons stripping the dead guards. No help would be forthcoming from her protectors any longer. Soon the feet of the Bretons kicked the children up, and they were marched up the road behind the carts towards whatever fate now awaited.

For the first time, Gisela realized she was truly a prisoner just like the rest. Her spirit broke, and she cried and wept like the other children.

Whatever warmth the sun had offered this morning was now gone, as if the vapors of blood stole it away. High sheets of white were now the backdrop for pearl and gray, and the blowing leaves no longer gold and crimson, but the colors of offal and dried blood. The féer could be as cruel as beautiful.

They were marched down a long ridge, over the stream of Tourailles and into the long valleys of the Couesnon all afternoon, arriving at a camp named Villeneuve in evening's last light. Whatever manor had been here was gutted, and now roofless stone walls held great kitchens and corralled stables of horses. There were hundreds of men billeted here, yet few slept. Endless lines of torch-bearing men, many wearing great turtle shells upon their backs, came and went in all directions. It was as if great crossroads the likes of Reims, Metz or Orleans had been placed at the entrance to Hell.

They were herded into an old walled vineyard, one no vine would ever grow in again. There were so many women and children crowded in, Gisela wondered if all of the northern lands were at war. Gisela looked back at her line of children, friends, and companions that might give her some hope, but they only made her sadder. Eulalie was stark white and stared off into nothing as if entranced. Other children she knew as vibrant were curling into balls and eggs. Only Sacha matched her focus, leaning out of the line to stare back at her pleadingly, desperately. No disembodied words of his fell to her ears now; his whole being had become a sermon of sight. It disturbed her deeply inside.

Volcanoes of the Couesnon

"That one there. Yes, her."

A guard's rough hands and foul breath of roasted meat in her face awoke Gisela. She was still in the old walled vineyard, they all were, but were being moved. It took a moment for her to realize they were cutting her loose alone, and they lifted her like a piglet up to the waiting soldiers. Eulalie's blank stare and Sacha's sad eyes before she passed over the wall was her last view of the prison train from Mur.

It was still dark, and she was carried along like baggage for a time before finding herself put upon a Le Mans horse in front of one of the Royal soldiers. There were several men in the group, and they rode quickly, following along the Couesnon, lit up like a stream of lights, then splashing across it and up steeply to a camp upon a hilltop. Horses, soldiers, armed Royal guards, Breton spearmen and Saxon warriors were all crowded around an oddity of a noble lords tent. Great doors formed makeshift walls, the missing gates of Sipia were here, and Ceufroy's tent was now stretched out over a grand wooden table and padded chairs, sitting on a mere dirt road like a splendid feast in a barnyard. Gisela was placed on a small unhitched wagon filled with boxes and crates of supplies, her traitorous Royal cavalry soldier standing guard by it. It was windy and cold, too cold for her to fall asleep again even amongst boxes. Horses arrived, and several men approached, talking to each other. She could not see them.

"We need us to push onto Harcouët by tomorrow, Gundebold. The Margrave will not let himself stay bottled up in Avranches for long," she overheard a Frankish voice saying amidst fluffing noises.

"We could take Fougères more easily if you weren't so squeamish about using sunstones to attack through the smoke, or killing the local coloni," another deep voice answered. She knew that accent well. It was Frisian.

"As for your using witchcraft to divine directions, I forbid it! As for killing, you are given the freedom to kill enemy soldiers in whatever manner you wish, and to take whatever servi you wish, but I need these freemen. The Gaul of the plundering Merovingians is gone, my friend. The new Gaul of the Franks now fills itself on wheat, barley and apples; crops that need to be planted and tended, and the craftsmen who support that endeavor. Your pillaging will leave only a swath of wilderness behind."

There was a pause of silence. She could smell foods cooking, rich foods with spices. Rosemary?

"Fewer people to fight at my back in years to come is good." That was the Frisian again.

"The Margrave will be at our backs by December if we don't look to him first. When you control Aleth, you can fight all you like, but to control Aleth, we must first take Avranches. If the Bretons are truly going to turn on Budic and follow you, then we need to remove the Margrave's strength."

"Taking Aleth first would turn more Bretons to our side, in numbers great enough to defeat the Margrave, even sitting in his Avranches fort."

"Or leave you vulnerable and weak against the Margrave' counter-attack on Aleth before you can sufficiently turn the new Bretons to us! We drive the Margrave all the way back to Laval by taking Avranches first. The city of Avranches is his strength, his tree! And that means plucking his apples at Vitré..," there was a tink of glass "...Cormier..," another tink of glass, how odd thought Gisela "...Tremblay..," tink "...Coglès..," tink "...Harcouët..," tink "...and Fougères first."

"You are certain this ploy will draw the Margrave out?"

"Pshaw! The Margrave is so impulsive and prideful, baiting him is like a red cloth to a bull. He'll ride out to retake his useless forts. You sail in, take Avranches behind him, move in your supplies, burn the bridge and give him nowhere to return.

"Your advice and support have been...unexpected. Helpful, but unexpected. Your coinage bought a great many warriors away from Budic."

"STOLEN coinage, Gundebold. Stolen. The Romefeoh for my pilgrimage to see the Pope was sadly stolen by bandits before I even reached Italy. Shameful."

"Pity."

The men began discussing alternate ways across the Sélune River, and Gisela tried to think.

Gisela stood up. She was hardly taller than the stacked crates. She was in the makeshift camp, and besides the cavalry soldier right there at the edge of her wagon, there were many other guards outside it. The top of Ceufroy's tent was next to the wagon but lower than her height so she couldn't see under it. That was where the talking men were and, she guessed by the smells and scraping, eating. In the middle of the night.

The Villeneuve camp was in the distance behind her now; she had no idea which cardinal way it was. It was lit up by torches, and the Couesnon stream they had followed and then crossed over coming up here was still a road of torch lights. She looked up and realized why this camp was on a hillside. It was a general's war camp.

A thick layer of clouds covered the skies, no moon or stars, and yet the sky glowed red in spots all around them. Pillars of smoke rose like distant volcanoes, sparks and flame and lights from below casting their eerie glow up onto the columns of smoke and cloud bottoms. All around her, four of these volcanoes were closer, and two were on separate horizons. The one closest, right here in front of them, was the one the Couesnon of torch lights flowed to and from, and from their overheard table conversation, she guessed it was Fougères. The volcano she imagined here was the siege of the fortress castle of Fougères. Fires, battles, catapults, arrows. Fire-breathing dragons or Cerebus himself amongst the ruins would not have taken Gisela more by surprise. She looked around. The other volcanoes were not volcanoes, but sieges of other fortresses scattered around the Breton countryside. Gisela sat down again.

She had stumbled into a war. The rebellion! Her Mother's rumors of an uprising were true, only it wasn't at Mur or Tours. Her Mother had sent hundreds of prisoners she suspected of being part of a rebellion straight into one. It was a disloyal Royal lord amongst Bretons and...Frisians? Frisia was a land north of their home in Aachen, and that was all the way back across the kingdom of Neustria, and much too far away. Gisela tried to remember maps she had seen in Court and her tutoring, but she had never studied them enough to figure this out. What she did remember was that the Breton Marche was the western border of Neustria, and that was at least a hundred leagues along the coast, down west of the Frisians. She obviously had not walked a hundred leagues northeast in the last few days. Then again, nothing was as she imagined.

The gate of the wagon opened, and the cavalryman motioned for Gisela to come out. He helped her down, not roughly if not tenderly either, and escorted her around past the other guards into the general's hilltop war camp, where two men were indeed eating.

Triangular bonfires blazed around their open-sided tent, and Gisela was grateful they were standing near one. Other men were seated around the two men, but they were not eating. Gisela recognized one older Frisian man from the Le Mans horsemen as the one who ordered Julien slain earlier in the day. That Frisian was sitting in one of the side chairs. Nobody else seemed to care about or notice Gisela, besides the cavalryman at her side.

Spotting the Frisian of the two speakers was not hard. Big beard, big eyebrows, dressed in mail, he looked like he had just arrived from the siege. His sword and ax were on the chairs beside him, as if they were his favored children.

The other man was clearly a Frankish bishop or archbishop of the church. Gisela had seen so many bishops at the synod of Tours last summer that she knew what they dressed like, but she didn't have any idea who this man was. He was not as old as Gravien, but mature. Purple stripes on his tunic, purple on his hat, along with a gold cross. Around his neck was a jeweled cross with maybe a dozen rubies. Awfully proper and dapper for a midnight war camp outside a siege.

There were candles all over the table's centerpiece, and toys upon the table near their meal. It took a moment for Gisela to realize it was glass tabula stones, save there was no tavli board, with string and odd items making some kind of impromptu map.

The tent rustled in a breeze and several of the bonfires flared.

"Ah, here she is. Bring the boy here as well," the Bishop finally realized, motioning and sitting back in his chair, taking a sip of wine from a silver goblet as if the moment were a treat.

"What is this?" Gundebold asked, continuing to stuff his face.

"Something that may interest you, if it's true," the Bishop answered him with a mock toast nod of his goblet.

Guards came forth with a rough looking Saxon man and boy. It was the lazzi boy from the prison chains, his bitten arm wrapped in bandages now, his neck and shirt still bloody from Atenea. Gisela didn't recognize the older Saxon.

"This young fellow is Jarvik. He was a Saxon amongst the prisoners your men encountered at the Billé today."

Gundebold cast a quick glance at Jarvik and kept eating, waiting for it to become more interesting than his hunger.

"Tell the good King here what you told my men earlier, Jarvik. Come now, don't be shy, or he won't even believe you to begin with."

"Yes, your Eminence, um, your Highness," the lazzi boy nervously stuttered.

"Well, what is it?" Gundebold huffed, insisting without even looking up from his plate.

The Bishop didn't like the boy's delays. "He claims that girl right there is the Princess of the Franks, Gisela herself," the Bishop finally announced.

The pieces of Gisela's broken heart sank into her big boots.

Gundebold stopped eating and looked at Gisela, then began laughing. "Your humor is a rich as your table," he joked and returned to his meal.

"Yes, that is what we thought at first too, only we put a few of the other prisoners to that question and they seemed to confirm parts of this boy's story," the Bishop revealed, placing patches of fine blue sendal cloth on the table like napkins. "Tell me, do you encounter this type of cloth frequently?"

Gundebold stopped eating and took up one of the cloth patches in his fingers, rubbing it to make sure. "This is excellent silk," he realized, suddenly serious. He turned in his chair to look at the boy. "Where did you get this?"

Jarvik pointed to Gisela. "She cut up her dress for the other children to use as socks in the snow."

"Cut up a dress worth a castle for children's socks? Are you serious?"

"She wears the vest of that dress even now, um, your Highness."

Gundebold looked back at Gisela and sat back in his chair. The Bishop nodded. The cavalryman beside her helped her take off the chamois vest and then Bérénice's old cloak. Underneath she was wearing only the linen chemise, soiled after so many days on the trail. It was obvious she was naked under the chemise, and not wearing anything else. She began to shiver in the cold.

"I see no silk dress," Gundebold grunted, leaning back into his supper.

"She was wearing it! She has velvet gloves on too!" Jarvik insisted, obviously surprised by Gisela's missing vest.

Gundebold huffed again in fatigue and took a piece of bread to sop up the chicken grease. "I see no gloves on her either. What waste of my time is this?" he asked the Bishop.

The older Saxon man cuffed Jarvik on the back of the head.

The Bishop looked amused. "The other children from the prison train insisted a 'Princess of Mur' had given them all this cloth before they left that town," the Bishop related. "Several changed their story under duress, and instead claimed this girl here gave it to them while on the journey." He leaned back in his chair and produced another trinket. 'Then there's the matter of this..," the Bishop announced with an open hand. It was torn pieces of an elegant silver net, delicate jewelry set with tiny blue sapphires, resting on his palm like a spider's web.

Gundebold set down his bread to take the little jewelry. He had trouble seeing it in the dark and had to lean over towards a candle to see it clearly.

"Pieces of an expensive silver hairnet. Would you say that silver-smithing was local?"

"'Tis fine silverwork...from the south, it looks like," Gundebold admitted.

"I told you it was Moorish," whispered one of the

off-seated Royal Frank officers to his neighbor. Gisela was close enough to hear but did not want to look over at him.

Gundebold handed it back to the Bishop. "I see no silver snood on her veiled head. Did she also hand out jewelry with her rich socks?" he joked.

"It was off her dog's collar."

Gundebold chuckled and put his forehead in his hand momentarily before taking up the bread again. "A Frankish princess and her dog go for a long walk amongst the Bretons. This is the story you are entertaining me with tonight?"

"She is Princess Gisela, admitted from her own mouth to one of the sisters in our train!" Jarvik insisted strongly now, without stuttering. "She ran away looking for Saints in the forest. She is smart in the head. She can read, she knows her prayers and all the stories of Taliesin. Her pockets are filled with gold and jewels! Her boots are her mother's!"

The cavalryman searched Gisela's cloak pockets, finding no gold or gems, only a tiny wafer.

"Is that an opal?" the Bishop exclaimed, his eyes widening.

"Almond, your Eminence," the cavalryman said after a sniff.

"This?" Gundebold motioned with both hands to Jarvik while looking pointedly at the Bishop. "I've killed at least seventeen men today, by my own hand, and ordered a thousand more. We just undermined an enemy tower in a tunnel with wooden beams weighing hundreds of pounds balanced just over our heads, and I've bribed half of Budic's relatives east of Carhaix with a borrowed fortune. Couldn't you have just found me a pretty slave girl to bed instead of this silliness?"

"Bring the woman," the Bishop insisted, his eyes shifting uneasily now.

Sister Amona was brought out, her hands tied, her arms and tunic stained red. She fell to her knees at the sight of the Bishop.

"This monk-woman confirmed all his stories! The girl confessed all this to her in God Church. The boy tells the truth!" the rough Saxon man insisted.

"Good Sister, is this true?"

Amona looked up at the Bishop and began to cry. "I agree to anything. He was skin me... skinning me. I would agree to him I was the Princess myself to make him stop," she broke down, sobbing.

The Bishop looked bothered and looked back at Gisela. "Enough of this. Tell us who you are then Girl, and where you're from if you're not the Princess."

Gisela began telling the stories the children had told her. She described the places in Wascon, in Toulouse, Bordeaux, Egolisma, and Poitiers. The battles, the fights, the captures. Her details rang true again and again to the off-seated Royal Frankish men nodding in agreement around them. The other children had saved Duende this time, with their own real horror stories.

The Bishop rose and came to Amona, took her hand and raised his jeweled cross to her face. "Sister, do you understand what will happen to you if you bear false witness to us, sworn in the name of Holy God?"

"Go to Hell," she admitted, her head dropping.

Gundebold laughed over his chicken leg. "Now *that* was funny."

"Then Good Sister, by all Holy to God and our Lord Jesus Christ, do you swear before him this is not the Royal Princess Gisela?"

"I swear it. She is no Princess," Amona begged, her eyes not leaving the Bishop as she kissed the cross.

"The girl was pulled away from a big Wascon man that *could* have been her father," the old bearded Frisian from Billé offered into the conversation from his off chair.

"Bless you, Sister. We pray you'll forgive us all for this unfortunate ordeal," the Bishop offered, then turned to his guards. "Make certain her wounds are tended to." The Bishop motioned for Amona to be taken away, then he slowly walked over to Jarvik, pointedly staring at the boy's feet for a moment.

"I've met Queen Bertrada, boy, and she's a club-foot. Those girl's boots could not have fit the Queen any more than they could fit me."

He turned to the rough Saxon man who brought Jarvik to his attention.

"Well, Hartigast, your Saxon boy seems to have been lying to you to gain favor. It's disappointing his stories did not turn out to be true." He looked at the dismissed Amona being taken away and then back at him. "And unfortunate that you rendered the interrogation meaningless by obviously offering her information during the torture," he added before turning back to Gundebold. "Saxons. They hold nothing as Holy."

"That makes them useful in war."

"And thieves and murderers in peace. What punishment would you find fitting for the boy's lies?"

Gundebold shrugged his hand away. "Laughter. Somebody needs to find this meal amusing."

The men off-seated by the table broke out into a strange burst of laughter at Jarvik's expense. Chills were added to Gisela's chills, and she stepped closer to a bonfire.

"See to it he ends up in Fougères," the Bishop ordered under his breath to his guards, and the older Saxon man brutally drug Jarvik away by his hair.

"I'm not lying! Wait, find Maylis! Maylis is the one who told me, find Maylis!" Jarvik yelled back as he was drug off. No one but Gisela was listening.

The Bishop returned to the table, motioning to the cavalryman by Gisela as he did so.

"Put her back with the others," he ordered, and Gisela was handed her cloak and vest and taken away from the camp as if nothing unusual had ever happened.

She was taken as far as the Couesnon by the Frankish horsemen but was then just left in the hands of a few soldiers by the streambank. They were Frisian warriors, preparing to join the siege of Fougères. Barefoot, ill clothed, ill armored, ill supplied save in weapons, of which they seemed strangely overburdened. One of these men of death offered her some of their early breakfast, a piece of roast so undercooked she couldn't stomach a second bite, and then laughed and offered her dark beer as bitter and unpalatable as the roast. She drank what she could, and then to their amusement she kept drinking more, hoping it would dull the pain about to come. She expected the worst, being cast like this amongst them, but these fell men had no taste for little children this early in the dark morn of battle, and they left her laying down in the leaves beside them.

"Hear me, O Lord; for thy lovingkindness is good: turn unto me according to the multitude of thy tender mercies. And hide not thy face from thy servant; for I am in trouble: hear me speedily. Draw nigh unto my soul, and redeem it: deliver me because of mine enemies. Thou hast known my reproach, and my shame, and my dishonour: mine adversaries are all before thee. Reproach hath broken my heart; and I am full of heaviness: and I looked for some to take pity, but there was none; and for comforters, but I found none. They gave me poison for my meat; and in my thirst they gave me vinegar to drink," she recited in prayer, over and over, until she fell asleep curled up in a ball in the leaves like a tiny mouse.

The morning failed to bring any clarity to her. Gisela awoke alone, and the strong beer made her mind hazy. There was the smell of smoke drifting down the valley, from the siege she guessed. The misty valley stream, however, was filled with lily pads, with little men wading about, water fairies herding the pads like sheep. Other fairies came by, paddling a hollowed log upstream against the flow. Their swords were like daggers, their bows like reeds and arrows like needles. A long line of fairy women and children drug a vine down to the water's edge, and then one by one they began to go to sleep and take naps on the lily pads, which were then slowly released downstream.

A big Breton in his green woolens lifted Gisela up from her sleepy leaf bed and hazy dream and carried her down to the stream. She had been sleeping above it on the bank, and when taken closer, it was not lily pads floating but the mysterious turtle shells on the backs of all the soldiers she had seen the night before. Her lily pads were her turtle shells, and both turned out to really be round coracles; basically waterproof baskets made of willow wood and cowhide. They varied from three to four feet across and were simple in design, much like big floating bowls.

It was not fairy women and children, but real women and children being tied up and place on the coracles. She was roughly forced in line, and when her turn came, gagged with cloth, tied by the hands, then tied arms to legs fetally and placed in a passing coracle, already filled upstream with onions. It was released downstream. She was merely a helpless bundle on a raft. The tree limbs passed by overhead in slow circles and lazy spirals. With an effort, she was able to work her way up on the onions to see over the edge of the coracle, albeit still mostly sideways.

The bounty of fallen Fougères was floating downstream on the coracles. Food, wool, cloth, leathers, weapons, chickens, everything was forming an endless floating baggage train on the Couesnon. Big, now that she was near to them, dugout canoes, hewn from oak trees with a dozen men in them, would swiftly row past her, parting the coracles for only moments. Men were stationed at every rapid or set of rocks to push, lift or portage the coracles on further downstream. Green and brown and caps, then blue and white and hats. Bretons and Frisians were the waders and occasional river guides.

Gisela spun this way and that, unable to control the coracle except to rock the bowl of a boat. She was as Moses amongst the reeds. Would Pharaoh's daughter find her, or the Fairy Queen?

Breton men with lions on their shields held a paved road ford across the Couesnon as she twirled past. It looked like the old Roman roadbed. It was hard to tell with men when they were fighting others or when they were playing with each other. She suddenly understood binding wounds - their playful wounds, and perhaps the real ones too, bound them together. She was bound too, and bound with so many bobbing lily pads further downstream. How long did she have to float?

Crows in the tree limbs far above watched her pass into a valley, her lily pad pivoting to force her to look the way she had been, moving yet getting nowhere. They cawed, and the mists danced as the stream grew darker under the bent trees. She was invading the fairy kingdom of Annwfn now, and the crow watchmen had just alerted the féer champions.

Through mist and trees, the morning drew on sluggishly as she was drawn downstream. Screams of a woman in the woods ahead made her cringe, and the herd of lily pads bobbed past one empty lily pad, pulled up onto the shore, its cloth spilled. Grunting men and the woman's screams passed by behind the brush and dark woods of the bank. Was that poor woman fated that day? Would Gisela be? What fate awaited in the half-light of this fairy forest, and what sunstone sorcery would foretell it?

The valley became deep, the sides vaulted, the tree trunks an aisled nave, the branches overhead the church ceiling. Look up to God. A bear on a flag looked down. Please don't mistake us for your trout lunch. The lily pad spun under the big branching tree church. Spare me, Little Father; tell your kin the trees to spare this child of God.

The sounds as they bobbed, the water dripped here in reverent silence, splashed there in eagerness, roared there as it tumbled over a bank. The stream whirled her around and around, the tree branches clapping at the passing parade. So rare a sight for a tree to see, a grand parade of riches would be.

Curiosity, aroused by the tree's cheering, brought leopards to see what all the commotion was about. The men in green bowed and scraped before the leopards, lying upon the shore and telling them stories. The leopards listened attentively from their shields and flags perch.

A mountain rose beside the stream, reaching up to break into the sunlight. Tower upon tower, as Taliesin had said, and the bright sun overhead. The sun's vision and light were thwarted down on the stream, as leaves on the hands of the trees hid the Couesnon in the darkness of night here, and yet peeked blazing beams through over there, and shown the fallen dead upon the base of the towering walls of Annwfn. Lily pads, it seemed, could turn over, and the passing girl now floating drowned alongside the bank was no siren to call her back to the rocks and join her forever in the shadow of Annwfn's towers. The siren herself was tied to the mast here in this place, to hear the cry she could not make with a gag. Gisela slid down in the onions, her wax. Odysseus needed Christ, and couldn't yet know him before. She couldn't have known either of them, only books of their tales afterward. Men were always at the wrong time.

Rocks peeked over the sides at her. By snuggling down into the onions she had finally managed to keep the trees distant, but now the rocks intruded into her little lily pad kingdom. The rocks turned her this way and that way, what an unusual onion, they must think, then passed her to the next rock, who did the same. Nine rocks of cold stone inspected the passing baskets. Don't peel me; I'm so sorry Amona. Cut onions make you cry. So do fools of men.

The trees parted in celebration of the zenith, and the

noon sun shown down, godlike and warming. The Couesnon must have grown to be a lake, or a sea, or an ocean! No longer flowing anywhere, but baskets seemingly drifted upon the tide. In, out, in, out. Slowly circling by the same shore, the gyre in water matched by the gyre in the air that only the buzzards could see. The buzzards looked down from their whirling above, circling, thinking 'pitiful things, floating whirling below, for they circle in the wrong direction. Ah, Look! There are our comrades, our suppliers of meat and drink! Behold, the warriors have come with more death!'

With mail and armor and dark horses, the warriors moved along the shore, with wolves on their shields to scare the children. They out walked the baskets, no matter which way the baskets traveled on the eddies.

'Come now, pluck death from a wolf's jaws, and we'll share in your feast, oh Men, great creators of carrion,' sang the buzzards.

The lily pads began moving again. The tide must be going out. No, it had only been a lake, not an ocean. The trees marched by again, off to do Gwydion's bidding. The hills crowd the Couesnon now, and the water flowed again. Time to look. She shifted back and forth until she was back up onto the onions. The next basket held Sacha, tied, helpless, looking at her with each spin, both hating to break sight of each other one way and turning to eagerly await reconnection the next go round. A different basket, but still Sacha. The baskets all hold Sachas! Count them all! Thirteen Sachas! All waiting to see what I will do. Surely witches and kings revel in the secrets of Annwfn. Learning the féer's secrets always comes at a price. What's my price to save the boy? Boys are the extremes of men; bitter, fragile, hostile, loving, cold and warm. As different as the sun and moon, yet to me, they are both tracking across the same life sky, with the same rises and sets. Do moons grow up to become suns?

Gentle, like the low tide, as if crawling and stretching upon the sand had sapped all energy, and the sea merely wished to just rest a bit. A respite. The Couesnon was in a respite, and the trees moved gently, swaying. Waving to the Frisians passing underneath along the shore. Soldiers marching, wave to them. Hail, heroes, but put out a line we'll be drug along behind you swifter than this current can muster. Bump. Her pad bumped into another pad. Who is that girl? I know her.

"JJEEEHHHLLLL!"

No, no, you cannot be Gisela. Then I would not be.

The girl who would be me tried to wiggle up against the bags beneath her and looked her straight in the eye.

Eulalie?

"Wuuwhawie?"

Chickens pass between them. Eulalie is not a chicken. Actually, she is chicken. The currents purl and toss the lily pads, away from the marching men, away from the horses and bright weapons, into the quiet times. The sky floats by. The fish watch now, watch from below. What odd things have come into their fishy sky to pass by. Dozens of new moons, dark as night, ripply trails like comets, passed and gone like falling stars to the fish. The sky grows pale for both worlds.

Men return, the fish leave. No wish to be caught, not beneath pink clouds, this close to darkness, Yet not dark, for the torches are out again. Fish can't use torches, it must be the men. They are filling the Couesnon with more lily pads, more baskets, so many we are to be a bridge across the stream to squirrels and badgers. Barking dogs. Are they barking at us? Chase us down? Go away! Atenea feasts now with Pwyll's hounds upon your stag.

The sky fades, stars begin to pop. They wheel and wheel and roll about the sky like some lawn game of God. And I get to watch. Watch from my onion throne upon the Annwfn waters. Taliesin, come humor me while I watch. A poem, goodly man, indeed, speak us a good poem of yours, fitting for the occasion.

"Perfect is my chair in Caer Sidi. Plague and age hurt not him who's in it. They know, Manawyddan and Pryderi. Three harps around a fire sing before it, and about its points are ocean's streams. And the abundant well above it? Sweeter than white wine the drink in it!"

She had finally arrived at the great fairy city itself, with walls of treasure and houses of food and rooftops of cloth. The griffon rose up in the sky above her. The treasure city was guarded! It was time to pay the price! Menacing, terrorizing, it flew down, and the great golden claw that stole Pryderi's youth was come to steal hers now too. Gisela screamed into her gag.

The Frisian with a griffon emblem on his tabard herded the coracles towards the shore, dozens of men lifting and hoisting under torchlight, clearing the stream of all that the goods that made it down. Arm and leg bonds were cut, gags were removed. Hands were left bound. Women and children were put in the bigger boats pulled up onto the shore, a makeshift wooden prison. Supplies were gathered on shore or sent up to Antran.

From baskets on the water to boats on dry land, how odd. Meager leek soup and watered wine appeared, eagerly eaten and drunk with bound hands.

In the crowded boat, Eulalie found Gisela. She fell down and hugged her. Sacha and two others of the prison children crawled through legs to join them, and they all cried when they found each other. Together, the five lost children of Mur huddled inside the wooden boat; a prison whose bars were the cold stars above them, no longer circling, at least not as perceptibly, but warning them their prison was still quite mobile.

Her head finally clear from the Frisian drink, Gisela decided the fairy realm of Annwfn sure looked a lot like her old kingdom of Neustria.

Angels of Tombe

The Frisians worked hard, getting supplies loaded on the bigger boats. These were much bigger than the canoes, well over forty foot, and built of boards, not hewn from the same tree trunk. Some were pulled up on the point between the Loisance and the Couesnon, while the ones being filled were tied off on the water, loading ramp boards out to them like poor docks. A town of supplies has grown here in the past days; the looting of Fougères, of Vitré, of Cormier, of Coglès, of Tremblay; all had been floated downstream on these two streams to be gathered here. The Neustrian countryside, harvested and prepared for winter, had been gleaned by the Frisians and Bretons to become a stockpile fit for an army. From their travel on His Majesties campaign in the Loire, Gisela knew she had become part of a war depot for the rebellion.

And there the coracles went, back upriver on soldiers backs, like turtle shells again. Gisela didn't realize there were that many cows in the whole world.

The women and children were herded off the beached boats and piled on the floating boats amidst all the other goods. The stockpile was still on the move.

There were thirty rowers in their boat, all Frisian, and Gisela guessed there were half a dozen boats in their group. Other similar boats occasionally passed them, going back up the Couesnon in the opposite direction. The day grew more cloudy and certainly looked of rain, though none fell on them. The woods passed by in huge curling arcs and tight half circles until they came to a busy crossroads. Here boats and ferry rafts clogged the shorelines, and many Breton soldiers held the road on both sides, but the supply boats slipped past. The river smelled different, rotting and pungent.

Gisela was caught unprepared when the woods opened up to marshland, and with every stroke of the oars, they rowed further out into a salt marsh as far as the eye could see. That is, if the eye could see anything besides the giant island of rock looming in the distance before them. It stood like a lone mountain in the middle of the marsh, in the middle of the entire world. It was forested with thick trees, and there appeared to be a tiny house on top of the mountain.

The sun walked by, strolling through the marshlands on bright legs sticking through the clouds, and when they left glowing footprints on the mountain trees, the stone seemed to be golden. The smell of the salt sea grew, and the edge of the marshlands pulled back from the horizon. As they drew closer to the stone mountain, the roofs of many odd houses could be seen down under the trees, and the sea rose around the strange island city in gathering waves.

"Ys," Gisela whispered to Eulalie.

Eulalie looked again.

"We're being taken to the fabled city of Ys, Eulalie. King Gradlon lived here."

"But you said Ys was flooded away by his daughter and the devil."

"Maybe this is what's left."

The Frisian boats joined other boats already pulled up on the shoreline. So many, in fact, that Gisela realized the island's city was built entirely of beached boats. These were not city buildings, not odd houses; but simply overturned boats, waterproof hulls put to use as temporary roofs.

This all made perfect sense to Gisela. The Féer lived apart from the normal, in the betweens of things. A tall mountain of rock in a flat marsh on the edge of the sea, with a city in the trees made of upside-down boats, all seemed the perfect place for a fairy king and queen to reside.

How the Frisians had found it was another matter altogether. She hoped any fairy king was a prisoner like herself, bound and forced to watch the Frisian's take over their kingdom instead of leading the rebellion.

The sea was rough, the waves chaotic, and splashes frequently tossed water into the boat, causing the women and children to scream, but the Frisians seemed undaunted and fine sailors, and they made the island safe enough. More Frisian men came down to water's edge with hand carts and oxen-pulled wagons, and the arriving ships were pulled ashore. The women and children were forced to unload the goods from the boats themselves and put them on the carts or haul them up the path to the store under the boat-houses.

Amidst the longshoreman's work, Gisela unexpectedly found herself standing beside Sister Amona. They both broke into tears, hugging and trading friendly kisses. Gisela insisted on seeing the wounds, and Amona obliged, Gisela gently touching the scabby area of her arms and back. The Bishop's healers had used wine and water mint to ease her suffering, and Gisela was grateful Amona's wounds were not as big as she had feared. The other women seemed to leave the two in peace, given an obvious, joyous greeting that most understood and felt sympathy with, but the Frisian men seemed annoyed or perhaps bothered about life in general, and ushered them back to work after a few minutes respite.

Eulalie, Sacha, Amona, Gisela and the other two children, Fara and Vedast, clustered together amidst the prison throng to work and haul the supplies for the Frisians. On one trip back down, Gisela and Maylis passed each other in the long lines going up and down. Maylis quickly tried to hide her face, but Gisela was so obviously overjoyed Maylis was even alive that she reached out a hand towards her. Maylis saw it too late, her own reciprocal reaching hand catching only air, and the opposite lines of work drove them apart as quickly as it had brought them together.

As supplies made their way higher up the switchback trail through the boat-houses, Gisela noticed the lack of men here and the lack of people in general. This was no real city of man nor fairy. No wells, cooking fires, laundry. No women tending families, no old or young. These boats were hastily placed here, not permanent houses. Indeed, it would take very little effort to relaunch them all. The fabled city of Ys had turned out to be just a military camp.

As the boats slowly emptied, there was considerable animosity between the Frisian men over something. Some of the boats that had brought them had hurriedly relaunched, heading back towards shore and back up the Couesnon. The remaining boats were filling up with the men left here, and those few Frisians who were apparently to be the guards of the

ghostly island seemed resentful. Gisela knew enough
Frisian to understand that many of the soldiers that
were supposed to remain here as guards had gone
with the boats back up to the Antran camp to revel in
the food, wine, and treasure. His Majesty had often
spoken of the dangers of spoils in war, to both sides.

The women and children were herded together
under two of the boathouses for an extended period of
the late morning. The five clustered prison children
and Amona were joined by two of the mothers from
the prison train, only Vedast being reunited with his.
Gisela decided to find Maylis again, but she was not
under her boat-house, and the few Frisian guards
chased Gisela back when she tried to go to the other
one.

The crashing waves became more subdued with the
passing hours, and sandy beach around the island
began to grow. By afternoon several horses were
ridden down past them and out over the rippling tide
and waves, which surprised Gisela. The remaining
guards then moved all the prisoners up the steep hill
towards the top.

The house perched on the island's peak turned out
to be a humble monastery; a long stone building in
three sections. It explained the great trees on the
island. The monks here were tending planted trees for
the future monastery expansion. The view going up
was extensive, and it commanded the whole bay. The
waters of the sea were rushing out, just like the
legends of Ys had described. Sand already formed
bars surrounding the island, as if it was rising from the
sea and shedding the tide off its shoulders. The
horsemen who just left were clearly riding, not
swimming, across what had earlier been rough waves.

The horsemen were headed up alongside the Couesnon as well, into the marshlands and distant coast.

Gisela could not see any of the sieges to the south, where she had seen several at Fougères. She tried in vain to see rumored Dol or Aleth off to the west, but the sun was too bright. One turn, though, faced her east, and across the growing sand, she saw the smoke of a distant city on a hill by a river, radiant in the rays of the sun, and only a half dozen miles away.

The gatehouse outside was a simple courtyard and lean-to stable, the door to the monastery the most imposing wall of it. They were ushered in by Frisian guards with spears.

Inside the monastery, everything was darker. There were no windows. On her right was a small room piled high with stolen goods from the stockpiles below. To her left was the chapter hall. She could not see clearly past the other women into that meeting room of the monks, but she saw enough by candlelight to see shed armor, furniture, and blankets.

After passing the presbytery, they entered the cloister, like a big open-hall joining the chapel, gatehouse and monastery rooms together. The only light here came from the fireplace and candles of the refectory. The darkest shadows were not in the halls off the cloister, however, but in the souls of the guards. The Frisian men at the monastery were anything but monks. There were at least five in the main chapel nave, drinking and boisterous, and the younger women were immediately separated from the older women and children. The rest of the younger women were herded into the refectory to work the kitchen and await their turns. The unlucky few chosen first were dragged towards the chapter hall that had become the Frisian den, one Frisian not even making it that far, taking the woman right in the cloister by the chapel. Amona and the children were hustled down past the chapel and cloister and into the monk's dorter, and then locked in behind the door. The yelling and cursing and screams went on far too long as the children huddled together in the darkness of the dorter.

Amona, however, was not going to sit quietly.

'For all my wrinkles and grey, when all men return, be some who no wait for beauty. They take me, even you, in time," she warned.

"What do we do?"

"Don think many men left now. Most left on boats and coursiers. Men here, the wine will make drunk in time. We take chance to escape. Maybe." She found and patted Gisela's head. "We go find night stairs to chapel. You rest wait here."

"I'm not going to rest here," one of the other, unfamiliar women insisted through the darkness.

"She means wait quietly so that we don't have so many people running loose up the night stairs we all get caught right away," Gisela corrected.

"What are night stairs?" the woman asked in a whisper.

"Monk use for Compline."

"Night Prayers in the main chapel," Gisela explained further to the impatient woman in the dark.

"Let me follow you to these stairs you speak of then. In this dark we can at least hear what you are doing and send others up if it is clear," the woman suggested.

"Let see if night stair locked." Amona tapped them

in the dark, and Gisela followed with a hand on her.

Groping, they made their way cell door after cell door before finding one where incensed air was smelled, and curved steps were felt. Gisela squeezed the hand of the other woman and then followed Amona up as quietly as she could in her big boots.

Amona had guessed correct, and the door of the rounded night stairs to the chapel was unlocked.

"They evil men not monks, so they not know," Amona almost giggled.

They opened the wooden panel door into the chapel ever so quietly. It was dark in the side chapel and the altar area, but the main doors to the cloister were open on the left side of the chapel, and a dim glow from the cloister candles shown in. There were open doors to the chapter hall at the other end of the chapel though, and bright torch lights from the chapter hall poured out into the chapel, straight down the middle of the nave floor. Gisela turned her eyes away from the Frisian den in that room, for it was hurtful to see what her mother called the 'concupiscence of men'.

A naked Frisian man passed across the bright doorway of the chapter house, disappeared behind the chapel walls, then reappeared in the cloister moving past the dim main chapel doors. There came yells, laughter, a scream and the sound of falling pots from the kitchen refectory, and a chubby Frisian bowman from the outside gate suddenly passed by the main chapel doors, in the same direction the naked man had gone. There were more screams from the kitchen, then they stopped. The Frisians in the den remained occupied.

Strangely, several young women from the refectory began tiptoeing through the dim cloister past the chapel doors, followed by the chubby Frisian. They did not enter the bright chapter house den.

Amona looked to Gisela in the shadows of the altar nave. Gisela shrugged.

The chubby Frisian bowman suddenly came back, and he stopped by the main chapel doors again, being oddly cautious, and looking back through the dim chapel into the chapter house den before croodling across the open doorway back towards the refectory.

"Did he just let those women out?" Gisela whispered in Amona's ear.

Amona got a strange, surprised look on her face in unsure response. She pointed down to Gisela's feet.

Gisela took off her boots and held them in her hands, and they tiptoed across the cold nave by the altar to the far aisle and then to the main doors. Carefully Amona peeked around.

"He at door to dormitory," Amona worded almost silently to Gisela

Gisela peeked around under her. The chubby Frisian guard was at the door to the dormitory dorter where the rest of the women had been locked in to wait. He had a lit candle from the refectory tables in his fingers.

"What's this?" a naked Frisian grumbled behind them, startling Amona and Gisela out of their wits. He grabbed both by the hair, and he was drunk, dirty and smelled of wine and intercourse. "Anxious for love are we? Come on, back you go. Have no fear, old mother, some toothless old geezer will give you your turn in due time. Come on, back to the dorter you two!" he insisted, laughing and half-dragging them both down the cloister.

"You there! Open the door, let these two mice back

in!" the naked Frisian barked at his archer comrade as he drew closer.

The chubby guard with the candle at the dorter door obeyed, opening the door.

"Maybe this cute one can be next. I've never taken a child before!" the naked Frisian laughed, reaching down to slap Gisela on her butt and into the bowman.

The chubby bowman's eyes got huge. Gisela gasped herself as the candle lit the chubby Frisian's face.

The chubby bowman flicked his wrist, sending hot wax into the stooping naked Frisian's eyes. The naked Frisian dropped his hold on the two women and put his hands to his face, crying out. The candle fell to the floor, its last flicker glinting off the bowman's sword being drawn. There was a sick sound, and the man's cry was silenced, falling into the darkness of the dorter doorway.

The chubby bowman grabbed Gisela and pulled her back in the dark end of the cloister behind the open door. Amona knelt to make sure the naked Frisian was not going to get up.

"Princess Gisela?!" he whispered.

"Wido!" Gisela blurted out and threw her arms around the disguised Captain of the Archers. He wasn't chubby; he was wearing his chain hauberk under the Frisian shirt. She felt him sigh deeply, almost shaking.

"We've got to get you out of here. Avranches is not far to the east, if we can beat the tide."

"We're in the rebellion!"

"We're in a Breton war."

"Gunda, have them bring more roast...and something sweet too. I'm so damn tired of beef," another naked Frisian called out as he came into the cloister from the chapter house den, scratching his stomach. He stepped down the dim cloister hall towards the kitchen door, and stuck his head in the refectory, then pulled it back out, puzzled.

In the dark of the hallway outside the even darker dorter, Wido laid his sword down quietly and pulled his bow over his head.

The Frisian looked down the hall and saw Amona's shadowy form by the dormitory door. "Come on, Gunda! How many can you handle at once anyways?!"

There was the sound of running feet, and the impatient woman that was supposed to be waiting by the bottom of the night stairs suddenly ran out of the chapel into the cloister and towards the front gate, right behind the naked, scratching Frisian. Women and children began to stream out behind her like a mob. They had apparently all taken the night stairs up to the chapel.

The naked Frisian turned back up the hall towards the fleeing prizes, and Wido's arrow hit him square in the back of the neck. He pitched forward onto the floor as the other Frisians from the den appeared amidst the running women. There were claws and nails on the first man who tried to close the door and lock them inside. Then a moment later, a half-naked Frisian coming out of the den with an ax sucker-punched one woman brutally with its handle, and every woman and child who had not made it outside yet began screaming and running every which way like scattering mice.

"Hide!" Wido begged, and drew aim. Gisela grabbed his loose sword and stepped back around the open door where Amona dragged her back into the pitch black dormitory doorway.

His arrow drilled the naked Frisian by the door and drew the attention of the half-naked one with the ax, who stepped back smartly against the chapel door frame with a quick peek back down the dark hallway.

The naked Frisian who had been shot fell back into the den, arrow fletching barely protruding under his right ribs. "The women have armed themselves!" he yelled to his comrades.

It did not take long before a Frisian ran across the dim cloister, a bare-legged man in a hastily donned ringed leather jack, his lion emblazoned shield trying to cover his dash over the open cloister and to the kitchen area. A second man also tried, this one carrying a griffon shield, and Wido's arrow caught the side of his head, sending him spinning and tumbling across the hard court.

Snapping heads now bobbed out from both den and chapel door frames into the cloister to get a quick fix on this new Archer. Wido drew aim again, waiting.

A burning torch appeared, slung around the doorway at him. His arrow was not fast enough for the arm that slung it, and the shaft clinked off the stone wall and clattered into the presbytery of the gate while the torch flared and ricocheted blindly down the hall towards Wido. He stepped into the open dorter door, hoping to preclude them from knowing just how many they were facing.

Hands pulled him fully inside, and Amona pulled the door shut.

"This way!" Gisela begged, handing him his sword back, and Wido let himself be led through the dark dormitory and to the night stairs.

Amona had a finger to his lips as Wido came past

her on the rounded night steps into the side chapel, Gisela stopping behind Amona and grabbing her hand.

Wido peeked out the open panel door into the chapel just in time to see the half-naked axeman slip out the main chapel doors towards the dorter. Several naked women in the chapter den were being kept at bay and repeatedly being told to shut up by a naked, long-haired Frisian carrying a sword and a hand ax. He kept threatening and elbowing the women back, his attention clearly on the chapter house doors to the dim cloister.

~Samuel~

Gisela gulped. There was Sacha, behind the crying young raped women in the chapter house den, hidden amongst the armor and cushions, peeking out from the den, his eyes directly at her. There was no way she could have heard him.

"Rasmus! Keep them quiet or slay them!" came a deep Frisian voice from the dim cloister. The long-haired Frisian with sword and ax threatened them again, and the women only cried louder. Rasmus raised his sword.

"Shoot," Gisela begged Wido with a whisper. "Shoot, or they die."

Wido breathed out, and the arrow appeared in Rasmus's back. He screamed and fell forward, and the young women lost no time in turning from tears into retribution. They beat him with pots and broken plates, and took the ax from his own hand and began chopping him mercilessly like a butchered animal. Someone else was in the room, on the floor, trying to fend them off Rasmus' body.

"Einar!" came a yell from the other man on the floor

in the den. "The women are killing Rasmus! One's shooting from the chapel!"

They could not see who this yelling second man was, but Wido guessed.

"That's the one I shot by the front door, wounded but keeping the women at bay in that den."

"Let's see how many of your friends you're willing to sacrifice!" came the deep voice from the cloister again. Gisela guessed that was this Einar, the half-dressed one with the ax.

~Samuel~

The word was even stronger, and Gisela blinked back tears at its power.

A girl was thrust out into the chapel doorway from the cloister, her hair caught in Einar's big hand behind her head and his ax at her throat, though nothing else of him was visible. Wido tied to take aim, but the girl bobbed too much to take the chance shot.

"Fara." Amona's voice dropped and choked as she recognized the child.

"DRAWDOWN!" Einar commanded, his head and body still safe around the wall.

On the steps, Gisela put a hand on Amona's side.

"David and Goliath," whispered Gisela to herself, though Amona and Wido heard her.

Fara's face went white, then splattered red, and Einar let her fall limp on the church floor.

Amona bit into her cross as tears ran down Gisela's face.

~Samuel~

Gisela looked the other way in the church, away from the den and towards the altar. Christ on the cross looked upwards above them, but the side chapel they were in was dedicated to the Archangel Michael. The statue of the angel, banner flowing on his spear above him and sword at the ready, looked down upon them, right where they stood below it.

Gisela stepped up to Wido.

"Give me your bow and arrows," she whispered.

Wido looked at her, his eyes and cheeks wide in disbelief. "You can't even shoot a bow."

"They can kill all my friends one at a time like this until hundreds more of their friends show up again in the morning."

"Your dying won't help that."

"Fight well and I won't. They already think it's a woman. Let them think it's me. Take your sword, and go back through the dormitory. You'll have a chance if I can distract them long enough. And my friends will have a chance."

"Dear Lord, this is lunacy."

"Says the lone man dressed as a Frisian in the enemies camp."

"Good notion."

"We have so many to choose from. You have nothing!" Einar's voice called out from behind the cloister door frame to the chapel again.

"Saint Gildas, unarmed but for his faith, faced down a noxious dragon in a cave on his trip to Rome. Christ will help me against this monster in the same manner."

Another child appeared, her reddish brown hair caught behind her, soft eyes bulging, terrified of the ax at her throat. It was Eulalie. She looked down at the pool of blood forming under Fara and cried out.

Gisela softly took the bow from Wido's shaking hands. "It's alright, Eulalie," Gisela announced, loud enough for Einar to hear as well.

Eulalie stopped crying, her eyes still upset, and now confused.

The quiver settled over her shoulder in Amona's hands, and Wido quietly slipped back down the dark night steps.

Gisela stepped out into the side chapel, Amona's hands running down her back like a departing blessing. She wanted to wink at St Michael above her shoulder for good luck, but she felt it might be blasphemous.

"Behold, he has now hidden himself in one of the places; and it will be when he falls on them at the first attack, that whoever hears it will say, 'There has been a slaughter among the people who follow,'" Gisela quoted forcefully, in her strongest speaking voice, as her governor had taught her to recite, as she was walking slowly out into the church chapel by the altar.

Einar chanced a brief snap look inside.

"Come closer!" he demanded when safe again.

It was a big church. She had time. "And the most valiant man whose heart is as the heart of a lion shall melt for fear: for all the people of Israel know thy father to be a valiant man, and that all who are with him are valiant." She let the bow scrape the floor, as her bare feet were too quiet. She felt certain Amona was still in the stairs alcove behind her, watching.

"Ib? Who's in the church?" Einar demanded.

The shot Frisian in the den crawled over sideways to look, using his sword to chase back the women off his dead companion Rasmus. Ib's head was on the floor, in obvious pain from the arrow that stuck out both his front and back. He finally saw Gisela in the torchlight of the den doorway into the chapel as she crossed the dim nave. Gisela glared at him.

"I...it's..," Ib blinked repeatedly.

"IB?!" Einar demanded again, agitated. His grip on Eulalie tightened, and she cried out.

"The archer's...a girl. Thor protect us! She knows the Christ-speak, Einar!"

Einar came around, lifting Eulalie up to his chest like a shield, and saw little Gisela for himself, slowly walking across the chapel floor towards him. He couldn't help but smile.

"But I counsel that all Israel be surely gathered to you, from Dan even to Beersheba, as the sand that is by the sea in abundance, and that you personally go into battle," Gisela rattled off. She winked at Eulalie instead, and let the bow drop to the floor behind her. Both her words and the bow's clatter were like thunder echoing in the chapel.

Einar let out half a laugh, his ax coming down and his grip on Eulalie loosening to the point she was nothing but a rag-doll at his side.

"So we shall come to him in one of the places where he can be found, and we will fall on him as the dew falls on the ground; and of him and of all the men who are with him, *not even one* will be left." She stopped, dropping the quiver to stand alone, not five feet away from the big Frisian. The arrows scattered nosily.

There was a sudden bark of anger and the clash of weapons from back in the cloister.

"Steen!?" Einar's smile evaporated, and he dropped Eulalie aside, cursing, and ran into the cloister.

The naked women in the den fell on the injured Ib like bloodthirsty harpies with the Frisian's own spears. Their vengeful cries almost drowned out the sound of clashing swords from the dim cloister.

Gisela ran back for the bow and arrows as Amona

ran out, and they ran to Eulalie, scooping her up in Amona's arms before stepping over to Fara lying on the floor. Gisela closed the girl's eyes. Everything suddenly got quiet.

They stepped over to the doorway and looked in at the cloister.

Wido lay back against the refectory walls, breathing heavily, his bloody sword still in his hand. The lion-shielded Frisian in ringmail lay dead, slumped across his legs.

Einar lay crumpled dead against the door of the dorter, the nearby thrown torch sizzling and popping as Einar's hair went up in little wicks of smoke.

"I should have put on the mail leggings too," Wido sputtered out. "It looks like you were right, your Highness."

Women and children came out of their hiding spots and ran for the door to the front gate. One girl stopped and did not run out.

It was Maylis.

Gisela and Amona came to Wido, and Maylis and Eulalie helped them pull the dead Frisian off the Archer's legs. Wido wasn't going anywhere for now, his knees being cut badly just above the calves.

"You not spurting. Maybe live," Amona offered as she checked out his wounds. "Maybe."

"Brave Wido. However did you find us?"

"Lul, the prison guard from Billé," Wido gasped as Amona tended him. "When I found Lord Wibert I was only an hour or two behind you. He loaned me a horse, and they rode with me as an escort, till we encountered Lul being chased by Frisian archers on those big drays. Lul told me everyone had been captured by Frisians and Bretons."

"You were so close!"

Wido nodded. "We tracked your captured group up to their siege camp. I took a Frisian archer's clothes as a disguise and one of their horses to go in and find you in all that confusion."

"Archer, so brave! Why in heaven's didn't you bring more help?"

Wido looked blinking at Gisela. "Nobody else knew how to speak Frisian. Alone, I was just another warrior under orders to do something in the rebel's eyes. Wilbert went back to defend his lands and see to Vitré, and Lul went with an escort of Wilbert's men to warn Ceufroy and the Queen."

Gisela put her arms around him in a hug again.

"All the women and girls were sent downstream with the supplies. That made it easy to track your direction, if not you. The boatloads of women and children at Antrain were hard to miss."

"We've got to get you out of here."

"Listen to me Princess, you have to get out of here before the morning. Run, hide amongst the marshlands. The Frisians will return tomorrow or the next day, and this King of theirs is supposed to be coming with them in force. They'll kill everyone they find alive when they discover what's happened up here."

"I'm not leaving these women and children just to save myself."

"Then lead the women and get to the marshes, have them run for it."

"Where's your boat?"

"I rode one of the Le Mans here, across the sand at low tide."

"Then we'll go back the same way. Amona, help me

drag him to the altar."

"What? No, wait..."

Amona, Maylis, and Gisela dragged Wido into the chapel. Eulalie dragged his bow and quiver. They propped him on a cushioned bench and got him comfortable as Amona began lighting the chapel's candles so they could see his wounds better.

"Listen to me Princess, I could have missed sleeping soldiers getting up here. Frisians could appear at any moment. You have to get off the island now."

"You are right, Captain. I can ride to Avranches to get help. You can hold out in here from any stray guards."

"You can't be serious," Wido asked.

"Charles should be at Avranches. I can convince him to come back." Gisela caught his chin. "My turn to save you."

"Princess, you can maybe make the marsh before the tide, but never Avranches. There's no chance, the tide's already coming in. You'll never make it leading a train of women and children across the sand at night. The tide can get several feet deep out there quickly."

"Amona? Round up the others, get them back in here. Barricade the doors behind you."

"We die no matter what way we go, Duende," she predicted sadly.

"Not if you stay and I can go bring help back," Gisela stated firmly. "Eulalie?" she asked, taking her friend's hand and looking into her soft eyes.

"Yes?"

"Help Amona bind his wounds, get him some wine, and stay with him."

Eulalie took a deep breath and shook her head. "I'll try to be brave, like you Du...Gisela," she gulped, petting Wido's hair.

"We take care of him," Amona promised, then took off her simple woodbine cross and put it on Gisela. "You need more than me. Besides, I got the big one to pray to here." She pointed behind her to the huge cross at the altar.

"And what am *I* supposed to do, your Highness, in your absence? I won't be able to fight long at all."

Gisela kissed his cheek. "Simple, my Archer Captain. Pray."

Gisela stepped back, a hand on Eulalie and Amona, then ran out the chapel to the main gatehouse. Maylis paused in the chapel for a second and ran after her.

Outside the gate, the setting sun was just disappearing over the cloudy western horizon, and the wind was brisk. There was the big Le Mans horse and a rouncy pack horse with it. Gisela stepped back. The dray horse was the size of a soeur-cart all by itself.

"You're going to ride that?" Maylis asked in disbelief as she came up alongside Gisela.

"I have to. To save Wido and my friends." Gisela turned to look at Maylis. "Please help me get up on him."

The pack horse suddenly put it's head up over the big dray's back. It was Thëo. He had heard a familiar voice.

"Thëo!" cried Gisela, running around the dray's enormous legs to get the jenet.

Thëo put his head down to her, blowing with uncertainty.

Gisela smiled, and searched deep in her pocket, praying herself.

She pulled out the last marzipan wafer and offered it to Thëo. He sniffed once, ate it and began nuzzling her for more.

"I'm sorry Maylis."

"For what?"

"That was supposed to be yours."

Maylis helped Gisela untie the packs off Thëo, and they began dropping to the ground. Wido had left the saddle on, hidden under the supply packs. "The new stur rods are tucked up underneath. He must have anticipated needing a fast ride out of here, but they won't do my short legs any good. Take Wido his blanket and packs when I'm gone."

"It's still a big horse. Are you sure about this? Should I go get you your boots?" Maylis asked.

Gisela looked at Maylis. "The boots are about your size. Keep them warm for me, alright?"

"Gisela, I'm so sorry I...was cruel...to you."

Gisela looked at her. "I forgive you, Maylis, I honestly do. If you honestly feel what you are saying in your heart, then take my place and help Sister Amona save the other children. If the Frisians arrive before we do, surrender up that strong spirit of yours to Christ, by praying at the altar in there, so that you will come to know what true love is," Gisela almost begged. "It'll be the best trade for love you'll ever make."

"I'll try," Maylis said, teary-eyed.

The last pack on Thëo appeared to be another rolled blanket, but it was the Captain's Royal red caparison livery for Thëo, carefully hidden away.

Gisela grinned in surprise. "That will be as good as a flag to get me into the fortress! Leave this one tied on him. Here, help me up."

"Aren't you scared?"

"I'm terrified, but the only hope I can see is finding

help and bringing it back."

Maylis helped her up into the saddle. Gisela felt so small. She tucked her bare feet back behind her under the rolled livery. She leaned up to get Thëo's reins, and his head came back towards hers.

"You'll have to become my Morvarc'h, dear Thëo. Carry us across the waves now to my brother, to save Ys and our friends from the hands of the Devil!"

Thëo bobbed his head, and they trotted off, down and out the gate, then cantered on down the trail of boat houses towards the sinking sands and rising tide.

Maylis watched her disappear, and then quickly struggled to get the Archer's packs back inside the monastery.

Empress of the Sands

Thëo's hooves bit hard on the damp sand as they passed beyond the last rocky roots that thrust the island up from the sea. Avranches had been so clear from up at the monastery's gate, now in the pales of twilight, the edges of the salt marsh blocked her view. East became more difficult to discern with every stride. The wind was bitter cold, and Thëo rocked at a hard gallop that gave no moments to regain bearings.

A seawater wave washed up like a thin sheet under them, frightening Gisela, and she pulled Thëo up, lest they dive deep into the cold sea. Thëo pawed and paced in place, eager to run again, but suddenly began nickering oddly. Something did not feel quite right about Thëo to Gisela, and as soon as he started neighing in a mild panic, she was sure of it. When she urged him forward, she was almost thrown over his head. He came down to his knees, but he wasn't bucking. His back legs had sunk into the soupy sands of the rising tide as he had danced in place, and Gisela panicked. Thëo struggled up and then finally out, in great lurches, and Gisela regained her thoughts and urged him on across the thin sheet of waves at a gallop again.

She caught her breath, realizing for them to stop on the sand could mean becoming trapped and drowning as the tide rose.

"Don't stop Thëo! We can't stop till the shore! Oh,

Saint Michael, lend us your wings!" Gisela looked back towards the monastery. The island was still a huge domed mountain towering behind them, even against the darkening sky. Her tattered veil blew off, twirling away with the winds, dancing like a fairy above the hoof prints that would swell and grow smooth again, with both disappearing behind her.

Gisela turned and tried, with difficulty, to make out Avranches on the horizon again. How the bottoms of the clouds above had shined with brilliance only minutes ago! Now the night's graying shadows deceived her. She aimed Thëo more right, and he ran like he was born for this moment.

Water and sand splashed up from his efforts, a flying wake she could reach out and touch at times.

Thëo neighed and turned hard left as they came to a sand wall too high for him to jump. Gisela was able to hang on, but she slowed Thëo to a canter as they paralleled the sandbank wall back out into the salt flats. Seagrasses whizzed by on her right now, and the edge of the sandy cliff seemed to undulate up and down in rhythm to Thëo's bobbing head.

Marsh grass would not do, Thëo's legs would be cut to pieces. The path to Avranches that Gisela saw from the top of the monastery was straight across tidal flats, not marsh grass. She had drifted too far south, and she cantered him back out left into the growing darkness.

Thëo splashed across a river of water more than a foot deep, frightening her again. It was getting too dark. They would hit some rock or log or deep pool and die in the cold rising waters. She would have to trust Thëo's eyes more, for he could see better than she in this dark. She slowed Thëo to a trot. What had Cancellarius said about prayers? 'It is best to quietly repeat your Bible verses amongst yourselves to face your daily trials as women,' her governor had warned.

Psalm sixty-nine came to her mind again, as it had on the Couesnon. "But as for me, my prayer is to thee, O Lord; for the time of thy good pleasure, O God. In the multitude of thy mercy hear me, in the truth of thy salvation. Draw me out of the mire, that I may not stick fast: deliver me from them that hate me, and out of the deep waters. Let not the tempest of water drown me, nor the deep swallow me up: and let not the pit shut her mouth upon me."

The waters rose now in places, even minor waves occasionally washed underneath them. What was left of the sun was now a faint pearl string in the far west, beneath a layer of clouds. It was dark and cold as they trotted across the dimming black, into the darker black. She wished it had snowed again, that would have made the shore easier to spot.

Psalm sixty-one then sprang to her mind. "Hear my cry, O God; listen to my prayer! In despair and far from home I call to you! Take me to a safe refuge, for you are my protector, my strong defense against my enemies."

A point of light appeared in the distance, like an unwavering candle flame. She pointed Thëo towards it. The light grew taller, and it formed a tail. At times the tail would undulate like a slithering serpent, but always it pointed towards the light.

The light grew into a glow. The tail became a streak; a thin hair of reflected light, dancing out from the distant light across the water's surface towards her. It was almost nothing, an insubstantial wick, but log or wall would clearly show itself in that thin beam. Gisela decided to trust in Thëo's eyes, and she gave him his head. His legs raced back into a gallop, his body pumping like some blacksmith's bellows, superheating his soul.

And hers.

The tides washed past in slow waves, trying to slow the horse, grab his hooves, lure him back out to the darkness.

The glow seemed to rise up into the thin gap between horizon and clouds. It became a curved letter from her writing practice, then a curved sword, like her wedding kilij. It was a distant hill! The half-moon was breaking through a thin gap in the cloud layer above her, to paint the hillside ahead in moonbeams. The line of their wet path grew thicker, wider, brighter. It was the hillside of Avranches, with thin lines of smoke rising like poles, beneath it.

"Psalm 89 Thëo! And his throne as the sun before me: and as the moon perfect forever, and a faithful witness in heaven!"

The waters became shallower, then the sand firmer. She could feel it under Thëo's hooves, through him.

The bright reflected line on the water's surface wavered, then broke. Something was in front of them. She slowed Thëo, and they came up onto mowed marsh grass, like a carpet rolled out for royalty, and Thëo blew and breathed as if he had found his own heaven.

Three panicked sheep passed by. Then two more, racing away from the frightening centaurian sea monster that had just emerged from the dark flats to devour them whole.

Gisela stopped Thëo, who blew and breathed and trotted in place.

"You did it!" Gisela praised him over and over,

petting his neck. Where he wasn't soaked in frothy sweat was a dusting of wet sand. She looked back, pulling her loose hair from her eyes. Her hair was caked with sand too. The sea waves washed up against the marshland coast behind them. The monastery island was no longer to be clearly seen, a bump against stars on the dark western horizon. She walked Thëo forward slowly through the grass towards what looked like trees ahead. Sheep parted as they passed them, their dirty white taking the place of the snow she had missed.

The trees here were not the giants of the Couesnon she had passed beneath, nor even the good sized tended trees of the monastery island. These seemed shorter and stunted, like dwarvish trees that still clung to half their leaves. There was a fence or gully by the trees, she could make out the line of it by sheep, and Thëo stepped down into it. Some tiny stream from deeper in the forest fed out to sea here, only with the rising tide, the sea now crept up to suckle the forest instead. She stopped Thëo and slid off on the opposite bank, being careful by the crumbly edge. The initial rush now over, she felt the cold keenly again. She wasn't terribly good at judging such things, but she guessed they had run at least a league across the sands and tide.

The hillside of Avranches had been clear from the island, and then in the moonbeams, even from the tidal flats. She knew it was ahead, but now she did not know how far. When the trees had been a mile away, out on the tidal flats, they had not prevented her view of the Avranches hillside. Now that she was up against the trees they were taller than her and blocking her view, catching the half-moon up in their tangled, wind-blown branches, to toss it about in the sky like a ball.

After resting a few minutes, Gisela carefully untied and unrolled Thëo's Royal caparison. She had forgotten how big it was, expecting a blanket that hung down both his sides, but this one would have draped all the way to his neck and then still hung down to his hocks. There was no way she was going to get a caparison that big tied on him alone, so she piled and drew the material up like a horse cloak behind and around the saddle, and even gave herself a hood out of the petryl. Thëo nickered a bit at her until he settled down.

When she climbed back on from the sandy bank, she pulled and gathered the livery up around her. It felt warm, and she imagined it looked like a regal red gown of her mother's. Thëo followed the sand gully amongst the trees before stepping up and climbing out at a suitable place. The moon passed behind more roofs of thatch-like clouds, and softer lights appeared ahead. They carefully picked their way through the trees towards the lights. It seemed to be the campfires she had seen on the hillside from the island. There were men's loud voices, and she slowed to a walk, being cautious.

It was a farm, one of the smaller mansi. Two of the buildings had been burned down and still smoldered red, and a group of men were gathered in the dark by another unburned barn. Gisela hoped she was near some of the farms just outside the fortress.

The cloud thatch above drifted, and the moonlight caught the surface of a stream beyond and to the right and, still far away on her horizon, the hillside of Avranches rose up in a curved dome under the moonbeam. She was disappointed by its distance and felt cheated by such a wavering mirage. Then she realized the far hillside was glowing aflame in places, like this farm. The pillars of smoke she had seen were not welcoming chimney hearths but more warfare. Avranches was under siege, just like Fougères and the other castles. She was back in the war.

If the siege concerned her, then the stream confused her. From the soaring heights of the top of the island she had seen a river running by the hill fort of distant Avranches, but on it's right, and it had been a sizable river. This was a narrower stream and wound on the left of the hill fort. With the moon-dappled tide visibly chasing her in now, she was not going to chance another run across sand and marsh. She would have to get around this farm, then pick their way carefully upstream and hope for a way to cross over to the Avranches fort, perhaps if the flats got narrower. She shuddered, suddenly feeling both cold and fear keenly, and she closed her eyes to fight it off. What was she doing here? She started to panic, and her mind raced.

Out of the darkness, on her right, an arm appeared, reaching out to grab Thëo's reins in an almost casual way. The appearing man clucked softly to her, almost friendly. There were other men too, coming out of the woods behind him, carrying sacks over their shoulders or on poles suspended between them, and calling out.

Gisela spun Thëo to the left and hawed him to speed, obviously startling the man. In the dark, with Wido's big saddle and her half laying on Thëo's back under her livery blanket, they must have thought he was a loose or riderless pack horse.

In the fire-lit shadows, she barely glimpsed the

approaching fence posts, and that was because sheep were on the other side, but Thëo cleared both the rails and the wool as he leapt over. She managed to stay on Thëo only because of the weight of the livery blanket upon her back and head.

The men behind her were certainly Bretons, that was confirmed by their yells as they gave chase to her. Both their burdens and the fence slowed them considerably.

Gisela tried to think straight, to remember the siege of Fougères so that she might sneak around this siege here. Surely men fought like they danced, in repetitive patterns. The warfare pieces in shatranj all had predictable moves.

It wasn't far across the sheep fields that another house burst into flames. It was just one house of a sizable manor of homes, it's mansi clustered close, it's buildings squat and sturdy like the seaside trees. It was not quite a village, but there were low walls and fences everywhere. Gisela paused, only to hear the Breton voices behind her catching up. She urged Thëo on to trot around the manor, but more Breton men appeared by the burning house, momentarily clueless to her or Thëo's presence, but still a danger. With men on her left, a tidal stream on her right and men coming up from behind, she had Thëo canter and leap a fence to get into the manor grounds. They darted forward between the barns and main house, and she saw what looked like a church ahead.

Breton men with an odd assortment of sacks, torches, and depraved intentions crossed the manor fields around her. They were a disorganized mob, many at a dead run, streaming from the forests towards the tidal stream by Avranches, looting and pillaging on their flight. Like a cloud of locusts, devouring everything. She passed mere yards behind one group, so intent in their whooping and hollering and leaping about to get to the stream they did not even acknowledge a horse passing behind them.

More buildings burst into flame, and more enemy soldiers appeared coming into the farm fields on the direction she had chosen. She pulled up before a simple church whose roof was collapsing down into roaring flames, Thëo pogoing on his front hooves in protest.

"Think Gisela! Be smarter!" she scolded herself.

With men ahead and to her right she turned Thëo left around the church and ducked as they rode under the lychgate into the walled church graveyard. If these Bretons were anything like the Saxons, they'd be superstitious.

High cross gravestones instantly became both her guardians and prison guards, the tops lighted by bright flames, the bottoms and tombs in darkness, There was a stone ambulatory set facing the graveyard and away from the church, and Gisela slowly wound Thëo at a walk underneath its processional. Vague faces of revered saints she did not recognize, surrounded by phrases extolling their virtues, too dark for her to read, formed the ossuary wall beside her, and she begged them for protection.

Her Breton chasers came to the square, and the burning church, as well as more of the manor buildings, went up in flames. Having lost sight of the talking horse, their passing comrades, with their flaring torches and calls 'to the Sée! to the Sée!' drew her chasers away along with them, like smoke, away towards the stream. She petted Thëo's neck in the dark, and the reflected glistening off his eye clearly told her of his discomfort.

As suddenly as the raiders had appeared, they disappeared; a receding Breton tide, moving away towards the stream. She kissed Thëo out from their tomb and back out the lychgate, turning to head back into the woods towards Avranches even as the backs of some running Bretons in the fields were still lit by the fires of the manor buildings. A line of so many men with torches marked the stream-banks of the river for her that she was reminded of His Majesty's royal welcome along the Via del Corso. The raiders had small rowboats and the big hide canoes awaiting the sweeping parties arrival at the stream, and they immediately began launching out across the tidal waters. The fleeing Bretons painted a clearer picture of this new stream that ran between her and Avranches. Charles had spoken of the rivers around Avranches to the Court in Mur, and Gisela wished she had paid more attention.

Thatched moonlight only confused her vision in the thinned woods. The road through the forest from the manor to Avranches paralleled the stream, but dangerously closer than she cared to be. The occasional Breton straggler, almost all without torches and thus popping out of the dark brush like silent owls, crossed both in front and behind her. She walked Thëo now, letting the noise of the whooping Breton raiders cover his hoof clomps as her livery cloaked Thëo's form in the moon-dark.

The stream road drew past the last of the line of ferrying Bretons, and across the stream, the hillside of Avranches grew in height. She could see the timber and moat walls of the fortress better now, lit up by bonfires and torches and Royal banners. The fort had not fallen, the Margrave still held sway, and her brother Charles was now only a mile away. She kissed Thëo into a trot along the road.

The boats of the Bretons did not land on the Avranches shoreline, but came close enough for them to toss their torches ashore and onto the bank. The Breton raiding parties on the stream slowly retreated back into silent invisibility as the attack of the flames sputtered and smoldered in their false advance. From this side, she could see the Breton boats silhouetted against the flames on the opposite bank, and they began slipping down the stream, not attacking. The Bretons always fought by misdirection and confusing tactics, she sighed and looked back towards the town and fortress across the stream.

The first enemy warrior was upon her before she even realized it. She turned Thëo left, but the Saxon dodged the horse and came around her, behind Thëo. He smelled of roasted meat.

He was the first of what must have been two dozen Saxons charging at her.

Panicked, she drove Thëo into the woods. Limbs and branches raked them both as she tried desperately to get away.

The Saxons began passing by. Some obviously noticed her, like the first man, but they neither stopped nor spared a spear at her in their haste. She threaded the trunks with Thëo, trying to put more distance between them.

Gisela scolded herself again. Men didn't fight sieges like they danced or played shatranj. That had been a foolish notion. They lived and died by opportunity, whatever opportunity that fate and luck provided, and men in haste might find a horse very opportunistic.

The last of the running Saxons was followed by mounted men, but either riding with them or giving chase, Gisela couldn't tell. The Saxon lazzi boy's tale of conjuring witches on black skeletal horses made her heart shy, and she wound Thëo through the woods, further away from the stream, in fear.

Beams of dancing thatched moonlight stabbed down from the trees where the canopy was open, casting rays at an oblique angle on trunks, bark, and leaves. Every bush hid a waiting Saxon thief, every shadow a Saxon witch ready to ensnare Thëo's spirit.

She pulled the reins up as the trees thinned abruptly. Somehow the stream must have wound its way back over to her, for not only was it there in front of her again, but she was also on the side of an entire port of walls, docks, and buildings, lit by both moon and bonfire. A great lanterned ship was moored to a long pier out into the stream.

The ship was a balinger. She had seen several of His Majesty's ships like this at the wharves of Andoverpis and Quentavic. They could hold a hundred men at once, or a dozen horses. Its split masts were like some giant scissored crane, the enormous sailcloth rolled up along the angled spirit. Now the oars all stood straight upright on the gunwales of the ship, like thirty extra masts all along the ship's edge. Fish netting was strung between them, making a high wall of netting all around the ship to turn it into an odd kind of floating castle. Sailors climbed all over the net walls and ropes, apparently having put out the torches the Breton's threw during their raid. Her heart sank, as the long streamers from the ship were not Frankish, but clearly Breton.

She looked around the port, and her heart soared. The port was filled with Frankish soldiers in the Royal red livery, and these were no costumes on Saxon bandits, but real Royal soldiers in bearing and manner. They were along the port walls, on the dock and ship as well. The Breton ship must have been captured! A dozen soldiers rode out of the port gate across the fields and down the road after the Saxons she had passed. Not witches on black Saxon horses, but Royal riders! The tallest barked commands to patrol the banks of the Sée.

"No wonder the Saxons didn't attack us, Thëo! Charles' troops were giving them the chase!" she bragged to Thëo. "The Sée. One of the rivers by Avranches was called the Sée," she remembered.

She looked back to the port, and her heart soared even higher, enough that she gasped. That was a bridge the ship was moored to, not a wharf.

"It is our bridge across the stream!" Gisela laughed, sitting upright in the saddle as best she could and kicking Thëo into a trot. The grasses of the grazed fields whisked by her feet as she let Thëo break out into a canter, and she pulled back her hood and let the livery flap and fly from her legs like the wings of a pegasus.

Gisela passed the gate into the port at a gallop, yelling out "Alarm! Alarm!" She was fed up with anything standing between her and Charles one moment longer.

The astonished soldiers parted for the odd Royal messenger child.

The attack on Avranches was itself a Breton trick. The rebellious Bishop at Fougères had said so himself. There would be no lines of the enemy trenches attacking the Avranches castle. Their plan had progressed to the point they wanted to draw the Margrave out, not keep him bottled up longer. King Gundebold would be at the island monastery tomorrow perhaps, and here the days after, the Frisian fleet taking the castle from the water while the Margrave was away chasing retreating Bretons on land. Charles and the Margrave had to be warned of the rebellious Breton plans.

She angled Thëo up and onto the bridge, and liveried soldiers split like waves before Thëo's thundering hooves. She felt guided by Moses, parting the Red Sée. Surrounded by Royal soldiers, the town of Avranches rising two hundred feet on the hillside above her, the fortress clear, it's banner's high and beckoning in the night beneath the thatched moon, Gisela broke into an exhausted, crying laugh, and they galloped off the bridge.

The road up the hillside to the fortress was a switchback, zigging and zagging upwards in three great sweeps. There was a massive bonfire up on the hill, outside the gates of the castle. A burning bush to guide Moses's tribe through the town's houses and alleys to the castle gates.

"They don't advance," the young warrior wondered aloud, looking over the wall at the peninsula where the Sée and the Sélune rivers ran together.

"They hug the shoreline like seals," the enormous warrior observed, taking off his helmet. It was a golden and pearl helm surrounded by a thick wrapped coil of black and white feathers, giving it the appearance of a wrapped Mongol turban.

"What do you think, Margrave? Do we sweep the

men around to the west to engage them head on?" the tall warrior asked, hand on his sword.

The Margrave shook his head, his goatee like a dancing arrowhead. "No. Have the Third remain defensive in Grand Chien, to protect the bridge at Pont Aubaud if they attack there again. This..," the handsome older man declared, motioning down to the shoreline where the Breton's had cast their torches from their boats, "...This is a feint."

"Surely they will attack us again?" the young warrior questioned, looking to the big warrior and the Margrave repeatedly. "That was an awfully half-hearted attempt at these walls."

"Less than an afternoon," the big warrior agreed. "We didn't give them a sufficient beating yet tu drive uff a real, determined attack."

"What is going on with this attack..," the tall warrior wondered and asked aloud of the moon and shadows, stepping around the shielded scorpio and joining the young warrior to look over the wall. His eyes fluttered in a reflection of the great bonfire below as he tried to see into the dark distance. "You have any enemies amongst your clans that would try to kill you, King Budic?"

"Many!" the enormous warrior granted, almost proudly, puffing out his golden scaled chest to the point his huge belt squeaked in a complaint. "But they'd have attacked me at home before I left, ur taken my home in my absence, nut chased me all the way ut here."

A royal messenger on horseback bolted out of the town alleys, passing the bonfire and riding into the gate below them, yelling for the alarm to be raised as if they hadn't just fought off a weak-willed army. The tall warrior turned his head listening, then walked to the other side of the barbican tower to look down at the messenger's arrival in the well-lit courtyard.

The Margrave and King Budic joined him looking down.

"Who is that child raising such an alarm at the end of the battle?" the Margrave asked.

"CHARLES!" the messenger girl yelled as the soldiers tried to help her down. "CCCHHHAAARRRLLLEESSS!!!!" she screamed again as if she were dying and the soldiers torturing her instead of merely blocking her advance into the castle itself.

The tall warrior stumbled back in disbelief into King Budic, who half caught him. He ran his gloved hand on his mailed neck and stepped back up to the wall edge and looked down again.

"That, gentlemen, is the future Empress of the Eastern Roman Empire. My sister!" Charles fled the tower for the stairs down, pursued by his young squire.

King Budic looked pleased. "How grand! How did she come tu arrive here?" He and the Margrave went to follow Charles, at a much slower pace.

Gisela beat upon the mail coat of the soldier in front of her with her balled fists.

"You're a wildcat!" joked one of the guards.

"YOU THERE!" a voice came through the guards. "LET HER THROUGH!"

Gisela spun to the voice she knew so well, and the guards parted again like the heavens. Charles was striding across the courtyard directly over to her. Her feet left before she did; her legs carrying her so fast and hard that she nearly toppled her brother over when she jumped up and wrapped him in her arms.

Charles pushed her back slightly, biting off his chain mitten so that it hung like a bracelet for a moment. His squire, not much taller or older than Gisela, took it from him. Charles looked at her face, and then brushed her chin and hair.

"Gisela?!"

"Oh, Karl! Help me, brother! Help me, help me, help me!" Gisela was shaking.

Charles finally fully recognized her. She felt Charles gently hug her back in return, as if she were the most precious thing in the world.

Gisela burst; sobbing, crying, a guttural moan coming out of her so hard it brought the attention of two priests to Charles' side.

The Margrave and King Budic walked up behind him, followed by the third young warrior.

"The Empress seems a bit yung tu travel withut servants ur a guard." Budic petted her sweaty horse, rubbing the sand off and then smelling his fingers. "And by sea, nu less."

"That is indeed the Princess Gisela, His sister," the Margrave nodded in recognition as well.

"My sister, up from Mur." Charles pushed her out, shaking his head, and then hugged her again. "But where's Her Majesty? Is the True King with you?" Charles looked back out the gate, expecting to see the Royal Army marching in behind her.

One of the priests kneeled with his silver cross. He was wearing a mail robe and an old Roman sword but carried his silver crosier like a quarterstaff. "Look at her clothing, Prince." He let the cross drop and dangle from its chain around his neck and switched hands with his crosier to put a gentle hand on Gisela. "Calm, my child. Calm." The older priest stroked her head.

Gisela buried her face in Charles orange silk surcoat, still sobbing.

"Moruuan." King Budic motioned for the young warrior. "Have them see tu her horse. Check *everything* on that jenet," he ordered, chin down and forehead bouncing with his eyebrows. "Then find ut from the guards in town which way she came and *ask questions*."

Moruuan looked at the girl again carefully, then nodded to Budic and led the horse away.

Charles swept her up in his arms and carried her inside the castle.

A commanding woman in a black and gold dress, a veil of thick hair that hung to her waist and a bright silver headband across her bow, came quickly to the Margrave's side as he entered the castle hall. The host of curious women followed behind her in an obedient train, all deeply veiled like ghostly spirits. Each sported a single jeweled ring that matched its mate on the Margrave's wife's eight fingers, which now clamped like talons on the Margrave's arm and shoulder.

The Margrave stepped on into the hall, removing his gloves and stuffing them in his belt. "Ogiva my love, the Breton have fallen back across the river."

"Oh, thank the Lord!" The woman nodded with a deep sigh, then looked at Gisela and Charles. "And this?"

"This, is apparently Charles' sister, the Royal Princess Gisela, just arrived."

"Arrived? Is the Que..."

"Alone, we believe," the Margrave interrupted the

obvious next question, taking off his black fur cloak and tossing it on a table. Two servants fell upon it before it had even fully landed and took it to be hung.

"Gisa, what are you doing here?" Charles asked her as they crossed the great hall.

"I discovered how to save Little Father, Karl," she coughed out between tears as Charles sat down on a bench near the great fireplace. He sat her down next to him. "You have to help me before Father comes home to kill him and they send me away!

"Little...? Gisa, tell me you just didn't..."

"They are going to cut Little Father down when His Majesty returns! I couldn't let that happen!"

Charles took off his other mailed glove and pulled the coif back off his head. He gently held each of Gisela's smaller hands in his.

"Gisa, Little Father is just an old grapevine."

"NO! A margot fairy from the Loire loved Pepin's hair and stole him, leaving a changeling!"

"Gisa, those were just stories told by the poets."

"No! The fairies stole our real brother, and when I discovered the changeling, the fairies tynged him and trapped him in our grapevine! We must get the changeling free to trade the river fairy for our Pepin!"

"Gisa, Pepin is dead." Charles pulled her closer. "He was my little brother too, Gisa. I was at Mur too when it happened, remember? Bérénice said he was chasing white plume moths when he fell out the nursery window into the courtyard, not fairies."

"They were to fairies. He was taken by a margot of the Tylwyth Teg."

"Gisa..."

"Margot? Is she speaking uf the Korrigane?" Budic quietly asked the others around him.

"Teuz," his male servant behind him quietly replied.

One of the priests looked uncomfortable.

"It was a margot, a groac'h, a water fairy! She stole Pepin last summer, and trapped the changeling in Little Father when I exposed him!"

"Gisela, LISTEN!" Charles had a booming voice that sufficiently commanded the rest of the room, if not his little sister. "We buried Pepin under the garden stones of the courtyard at Mur. He's not trapped in that grapevine, he was buried as a Christian near it, to keep his body from being desecrated. You're getting it all confused."

"The changeling *IS* trapped! Saint Rowan's daughter was trapped in a tree just like it!"

"Saint Rowan? Him I've heard uf." Budic took out one of the many crosses he kept tucked in his belt and shook it at the Margrave as if it proved his point.

"Oh Karl, I have to make a pilgrimage to Brittany for a Pardon, so that the saints will grant me a blessing to free the changeling. They brought so many people back to life! You have to help me!"

"Ah, a pilgrimage for an Indulgence; the Tro Breizh," the older priest realized. King Budic agreed with him.

"You?" Charles asked.

"Me." Gisela's tears started again.

"Why you, Gisa?" Charles touched her chin up so he could see her eyes. His were big and brown, and she melted.

"I...I put foxglove blossoms...on the changeling's fingers to prove it. When I did, I broke the charm. The fairies appeared and lured the changeling out the window, and the margot cursed him with a tynge to be trapped in the grapevine so she wouldn't have to return Pepin," she confessed.

"Oh, Gisa. You didn't do anything wrong. There was no curse, and no changeling. You didn't kill Pepin. It was a cruel accident that took our brother from us, not fairies or foxgloves."

"But the pilgrimage for a Pardon..."

"The Saints can't return Pepin. Fairies and changelings were just tales told to you by our court poets, like the Taliesin stories."

"Poets? The cler lisant, Princess Gisela?" Ogiva came over to touch the Princess on the head. Gisela silently looked up at the noblewoman. Her eyes were red, and her soul laid bare. Ogiva shook her head. "Where is Daev? Where is that bardd of yours, Budic?"

"Here, Lady Ogiva," Budic's male servant called out from the group of gathered servants in the hall. He was an older Breton man, clean-shaven, but dressed simply like the rest of the staff. "What do you wish, my Brenin?" King Budic waved him over to Charles' bench and Lady Ogiva.

Charles kept looking at Gisela. "This is King Budic's poet," he explained to Gisela. "Daev, do you know the stories of Taliesin?"

"Aye, I know the Llyfr, an' the Logres stories that Taliesin told Childebert. The tales of th' fairies an' curses you been speaking of as well."

"Are they true?" Lady Ogiva asked pointedly.

Daev smiled, and half laughed, but the serious tone of his King and company focused on one little girl's sad face seemed to strike him like an arrow. He knelt down beside Lady Ogiva and leaned close to the faces of Charles and tearful Gisela so their eyes met.

"We poets are tasked with rememberin' what came

'afore, tha lines of kings an' great families an' such. We come to tell ya tales of tha past, both true an' fanciful histories. If tha kings an' queens don't listen, we don't get our meals. If we want ta stay around a while, become bardds, your court poets...your Frankish cler lisants, as Lady Ogiva's sayin', then we weave your castles an' kingdoms an' your lives into our stories, so you keeps us in your halls," Daev revealed with disarming honesty.

"They tell us the stories we want to hear, mon cher," Lady Ogiva added, her ringed hand softly laying upon Gisela's shoulder.

"Particularly...ta entertain Royal children," Daev looked almost ashamed, and dropped his eyes.

"Then Taliesin's stories were not real?" Gisela begged Daev.

He shrugged and looked back up at her. "Maybe. We like ta think so Girl, but we don't really know."

"But fairies and changelings HAVE to be real!" Gisela insisted, her lips and chin jutting, her hands balling into fists.

"Fanciful legends can't bring Pepin back," Charles warned, and Daev stood up and stepped back towards Budic.

"Why can't the saints help Pepin?!"

"The saints surely can, Gisa. Just not the way you think."

"Was Pepin baptized?" the older priest came closer again, his friendly hand brushing supportively on Daev as he passed.

Charles nodded.

"Good." The older priest kneeled. "Then Princess, Prince Pepin was protected from all this witchcraft you speak of. He is with the Saints now. He knows their love and piety."

"We *will* see Pepin again, before the Lord's Throne in Heaven!" Charles offered hopefully.

"Nut in a grapevine." Budic gave an understanding nod in sympathy and rested a hand on Daev's shoulder with an affectionate, if overly strong, shake of the poet.

"You won't, though, unless you let go of these wicked notions!" the older priest warned. "You've got to give up this witchcraft first!" his tone and voice made Gisela quiver.

The Margrave crossed his arms, having difficulty summoning patience.

"I believe in our Lord Jesus Christ with all my heart!" Gisela pleaded in defense, her watering eyes returning.

"This witchcraft nonsense will keep you from him, and from your baby brother! You've got to give them up!"

"Then, what can she do, Bishop?" Ogiva asked.

The old Bishop looked at Charles and then back at Gisela. "I think that's obvious."

"What is?" Gisela begged.

"Break tha tynge," Daev realized out loud.

Gisela drew back at the command, but Charles' strong hands and Ogiva behind her kept her from recoiling too far.

"...but Pepin will die..."

"He's already dead my child. He lives in Christ, our Lord and Savior, now."

"Come on, Gisa. You can do it. Have faith." Charles' face beamed at her.

Lady Ogiva put her hand over her mouth, her eyes welling up above her ringed fingers.

The old Bishop began praying. The fat priest kneeled and began to pray. King Budic pulled a cross made of schorl from his belt of many, kneeled and prayed with them. Heads went down all over the great hall. Even the Margraves'.

"Break it," Charles begged. "Break the tynge. Say there was no changeling, and there were no fairies."

Tears streamed down Gisela's face.

"I...can't...save...you...Pepin...I...can't...catch...you..."

Tears began streaming down Charles' face as well.

"...fairies...aren't real....the changeling...isn't real...Pepin is...dead..." Gisela's cries trailed into wailing, and the room erupted in blessings and praise.

PART THREE

ALLEGRO BOND

High Tides

There were enough servants coming into the great hall to host a feast. The fireplace was banked up by more and more logs until it began to roar, and banners dropped down from the balcony rail as if the Pentecost itself had just arrived. Enough food for a dozen children began appearing on the table from down in the kitchen and buttery in a continuously snaking line of servers.

Gisela's sobbing was now significantly reduced, and Lady Ogiva managed to gently pry loose Gisela's locked embrace on Charles. After wiping away tears and hugging away nervous shakes, they checked her for injuries and, finding none visible, got her to stand up on the bench. With a few mouthfuls of michette bread the rose water and fresh milk worked its usual charms, and after a few minutes, it even calmed her enough for them to get a half smile out of Gisela.

Pepin's fall and perceived entrapment had been her world for months, and together with what had been her quest for the past days, everything now suddenly seemed utterly lost in the past. Her young brain was struggling to let go and catch up. She had run away for nothing, and now, despite the sweet bread, a bowl of myths and lies was her bitter breakfast.

Mother was going to be furious. Bérénice's favorite winter cloak was ruined. She had interrupted her brother's war. She missed her toys. She missed

Atenea.

She was a royal. The here and now was a rebellion, and she knew things that they might not.

Pepin.

Three of Ogiva's ring maidens surrounded Gisela in a female circle and sister screen. Gisela felt like they were the Graeae and she their one eye. First Amona's borrowed, ragged chamois vest, then Bérénice's old cloak, and finally her soiled linen chemise disappeared out over their shoulders. Gisela cried a rebuke only when one of them removed Sister Amona's woodbine cross.

"I am the Catholic Bishop of the Diocese of Poutrocoët, your Highness. I assure you your cross won't go astray." He took the necklace from one of the women's hands and smiled at its simplicity as he turned it over in his fingers.

Water, towels, oils, and herbs all entered the women's ring in gentle hands and working elbows as they cleaned up the Princess.

"Gisela?" Charles began to insist, unbuckling his curved Turkish kilij and placing it on a table next to the pile. He ran his hands over Gisela's discarded clothing in wonder. "You must tell me how you got here!"

"Mother heard rumors of a revolt being stirred up by someone named Tassilo and sent Father's prisoners away, thinking it might be them." Gisela stepped up on tiptoes to peek over one of the woman's shoulders like a shower curtain as she was bathed inside the woman's ring. "Some of the prisoners were Wascon soldiers, a few were Saxon mercenaries, but most were Aquitani local farmers and their families from Mur. I hid amongst the children, I knew them well, and ran away with them."

The Margrave barked out a disbelieving laugh.

Lady Ogiva folded her arms. "You can't be serious, mon cher?!"

"I was disguised!" she pleaded as a fine new linen chemise parachuted over her arms and head. She stepped back up to peek over shoulders. "You saw me for yourself, My Lord. If Charles had not been here to recognize me, I'd still be arguing with your gatemen."

King Budic began nodding in amused agreement.

"So you pretended to be a child of a prisoner?" Charles sat down backward and reclined back against the table.

"Yes," she replied from inside another linen smock being pulled over her head as if linen also made a bandage for the soul.

"And when you arrived in the wilderness marche, through a blizzard, you escaped, stole a horse and conveniently came here?" the Margrave shook his head and held up his hand.

"I wish it had been that easy, My Lord."

Lady Ogiva was offered four different beautiful dresses to choose from by her staff, and she looked back and forth a moment before touching the gold nacré velvet.

Charles motioned for the Margrave to settle down. "So, where are these prisoners?"

"Can I explain it backwards?" Gisela asked her brother as they untangled her hair. He seemed agreeable, and Budic took a seat across the table, slathering honey butter on the michette bread and dipping it in wine as he listened.

"I just escaped, this very night, from the island of Ys a few miles west along the coast...OW!"

"Ys? Do you mean Tombe?" Charles' forehead wrinkled.

"I don't know...OW...there were no abbots or priests to ask, just the monastery and a tiny chapel to Saint Michael. It's on a giant heap of rock in the middle of marshlands and sea."

"Tombe," the Margrave and Bishop both agreed.

The ring maidens continued to comb her hair. "Many of the prison train's women and children captured by the Breton rebellion were taken there, along with a lot more. My horse is Thëo, he's from the Captain of the Queen's Archers from Mur. The Captain was the only person to figure out where I had gone, and using a disguise he craftily managed to track me there through the rebellion."

Charles relaxed back against the table and crossed his legs. "That Archer Captain would be...Wido of Nantes?"

"Yes, but he got hurt fighting off the Frisian soldiers in the monastery to free us."

"Frisian?" the Margrave came close enough to peek over and see her face at least.

Gisela met his eyes and nodded. "Frisian. Their Frisian King is named Gundebold, and he's attacking forts all over the Marche to lure you out into a trap."

"How in the name of all the Apostles in heaven could you come to know that?" the Margrave demanded.

"Because I met him. He seemed focused. Reminded me of Father."

The Margrave sat down on the bench next to Charles, in disbelief.

Budic raised an eyebrow as he ate another slice.

Charles started to say something but stopped.

"How did you get to meet their King, mon cher?" Lady Ogiva asked as they handed over the hastily pinned dress.

"Well, first, the Frisian invaders have a fleet of big boats on Ys...the island...Tombe, as you call it."

"We haven't seen any ships there," Charles interrupted.

"Not ships, at least not like the balinger down there at your port. Boats, but big, thin and long like eels, made up from wood planks like steps. They don't have any sails, they row them everywhere like madmen. There must be at least a dozen boats on the island. They pulled them up into the trees and turned them over to make house roofs of them while most of the soldiers went to fight in the rebellion. It looks like they did it just before the blizzard. Your snow didn't seem quite as bad as it did in Mur and Andecavus."

King Budic perked up in his chair "Did yu ever see how many Frisians were un each boat?"

"Maybe a score, but they were loaded with supplies and us as prisoners. They could fit double that, I suppose."

The Margrave looked up for a moment, then a King Budic. "That's easily five hundred Frisian soldiers."

Lady Ogiva chose a snood, a silk charmeuse veil, several bracelets, two pins, and a necklace from jewel boxes that were brought to her, and handed them over to the ringing ladies.

King Budic chewed his tongue slightly, looking back at the Margrave. "How many Frisians are still un Tombe?"

"I didn't see any when I rode away a few hours ago. Maybe none. Most of them left the island and went upstream to get fresh supplies. Wido said he killed all he came across when he came up to free us, but he couldn't be certain there were not more drunk or missed. The Breton rebellion has its main supply depot set up in a town called Antrain, a couple of hours upstream from Tombe. Well, at least downstream. All the supplies they have raided from all the forts and cities are sent floating downstream in coracles to Antrain," she explained, her fingers doing an animated dance of lilypads downstream. "Even prisoners like me. I don't think there is a cow left in the Marches they had so many..."

The shocked Margrave looked to Charles and Budic like he was listening to a scouting report instead of a sobbing little girl only twenty minutes past. Charles just smiled and shook his head, still paying attention.

"...Some of the soldiers that were supposed to be guarding us on Tombe got eager and rowed off to get to the supplies, then more rode out on the horses with the outgoing tide. Otherwise, there would have been dozens to guard us. You wouldn't believe how hungry some of the rebellion soldiers are. Half cooked meat, eating stolen food even as they fought, it was disturbing. Like they were famished."

Lady Ogiva's three ring maidens backed up, and Gisela stood there on the bench, a far different young girl.

"From a crying child to a charming Empress," the Bishop uttered, surprised and pleased at the transformation. "My Lady is to be commended," he nodded to Lady Ogiva, who nodded back.

Gisela curtsied to him, then the Margrave and Lady Ogiva and then King Budic.

"Princess Gisela de Laon, a pleasure, My Lords." She stuck her chin out properly.

The still shocked Margrave stood up. "All mine, Highness," was all he could bring himself to say. King Budic and a bemused Charles stood up, as Lady Ogiva's seamstresses sat on the floor and kept pinning the too tall dress hem at Gisela's feet.

"Princess, these are our hosts. The Margrave de la Marche, de Lionrouge, you know, and the Lady Ogiva de Boos," Charles introduced their hosts.

"Thank you for all you have done for my brother, Margrave and Mistress, and now myself too. I am extremely grateful."

"And this is Budic the Great, de Poher, Comes de Cornuaille, and King of the Bretons."

"Yur Highness, a pleasure." King Budic bowed.

"A pleasure, your Majesty. I adore your nickname, but aren't these your Bretons in revolt?"

"Regrettably, but it is unly a small faction uf malcontents. The peuple uf Brittany have nut gone tu war against the Franks, in fact, that is the reasun I am here."

"This is Bishop Cadocanan of Aleth."

"Your Highness." He stepped up with a bow to hand her cross back to her.

She took it, smiling at him. "Your Eminence. You'll need to get home quick."

"Really? Bishop Jumael, Curé Leufred, and I are on pilgrimage with good King Budic here to St Amandus. We're going to visit Archbishop Remigius in Rouen and then attend an assembly in Attigny this spring."

"Probably not, your Grace. The Frisian invaders and Breton rebellion are taking the Marche forts..," she swayed one way "...so that they can take Avranches..," she swayed the other "...so that the Margrave is stuck too far away in Laval when they finally come to take your town of Aleth, which is their main goal."

"Oh my!" the Bishop clutched his crosier against his shoulder in his folded arms.

"Your Highness, rebellious soldiers made war upon us all evening, almost to the instant you arrived. You wished to talk backward, so please tell me how you know their plans so well before I die in a fit!" the Margrave begged.

"Yes, My Lord. Our prison train turned north off the Roman road before Rennes and accidentally marched into the middle of the rebellion, where we were ambushed by Breton militia. Helping the Bretons are Frisian soldiers, and I mean stout, trained Frisian soldiers, not militia, and they are being helped by professional Saxon mercenaries. All of it is being heavily funded by an underhanded Frankish Bishop."

"Uh dear."

"Good heavens."

"Dear Lord."

"Mon ami!"

"One of the older children had overheard my secret confession to a nun about who I was. When we were captured, one of the Saxon prisoner boys tried to trade that information to King Gundebold and this Frankish Bishop. They didn't believe him, but I was at their war tent long enough to overhear some things."

The Margrave shuffled his feet, and his lips pressed together. "And they just let you go?"

"Sister Amona and I had to lie to them. It was terrifying. They had tortured Amona. Afterward, we were all made slaves, just like the rest of the spoils of the rebellion."

"Mon cher, you must have been terribly

frightened!" Lady Ogiva realized and stepped around the seamstresses to hug Gisela.

"What a stroke of unbelievable luck." Charles looked between the Margrave, Bishop and King Budic.

"Princess? Do you know who this Frankish Bishop was?" Bishop Cadocanan begged.

"They never said his name like they did King Gundebold's. He was shorter than you, he had a wide purple hat with a gold cross on it, and a big gold cross with red rubies around his neck. His robes had purple trim, and it was like he was running things in a way, or both he and the Frisian King were. It was hard to tell just who was the one in charge."

"That ruby cross sounds like Bishop Gauciolenus of Le Mans," Bishop Cadocanan suggested. Charles and the Margrave nodded slowly in agreement.

"Oh! The Captain of our prison guards said something about the big drays we saw them riding being from Le Mans! There were Frank officers seated at the war tent too, the filthy traitors."

"I thought Bishop Gauciolenus was on a pilgrimage to Rome?" the fatter, younger priest asked.

"This Bishop used a Romefeoh for a pilgrimage to Rome to bribe off Saxons, Franks, and Bretons into helping the Frisians. They bribed some relatives of yours to their side of the rebellion, King Budic."

"Did they ever say whu?"

"Not that I heard, but it seemed to be quite a few."

"Budic, I must apologize to you for my comments today," Charles stepped over to him. "It would appear we all have traitors to be ashamed off in our lands. My regrets to you, Roi."

"Regrettably for us buth, Prince."

The Margrave lifted his head from his hands. "I've been here in the Marche for years now, and this girl is schooling me as if I were wet behind the ears!"

"This *Princess*, mon amour," Lady Ogiva corrected, adjusting Gisela's veil.

"Any ideas who these relatives could be?" the Margrave asked Budic.

"Several," half-joked Budic. "Were there any Bretons at this war tent?"

"Yes, there were."

"Did anything stand ut abut them?"

"At the war tent, they were all obviously captains or officers seated around."

"Any distinctive clothing, hats, armor un the Bretons?"

"Besides all the swords, axes and so much mail?. A lot of green wool and brown leather. One had a wheeled cross on his shield."

Charles and the Margrave looked to Budic, who frowned and tilted his head back and forth.

"Did yu see a blue axe, or perhaps a hunnish bow?"

"No *blue* axes. Some had bows, but I don't know what a hunnish bow is."

"It's got bone in the center grip..," Charles described for Gisela.

"...and made of horn..."

"...and it curves back at the string ends, unlike our longbows."

Gisela's eyes widened. "Yes, an older Breton with long brown hair had a bow like that, I thought he was Greek."

"Who is this bowman?" the Margrave asked Budic.

"If the Princess is right, it sunds like a Breton Lord named Tortulfe."

"I chased Comes Tortulfe out of the Rennes area over two years ago," the Margrave recalled.

"He is a Frankish sun uf yur Ragenfrid. After the Neustrian rebellion years ago he was traded tu my wife's Bru Erech husehold as a child hostage during the peace talks with your grandfather, Charles Martel."

Charles nodded.

"Tortulfe was a loyal follower and companion of your rebellious half-uncle Grifo," the Margrave reminded Charles.

Budic turned to his men and staff. "Have we any word un Tortulfe?"

"Only rumors, Sire," Moruuan offered.

"It's whispered he's been hidin' up in tha hills behind Dinan. He leads a motley clan calling themselves Bagaudae, causing trouble fur Franks an' Bretons alike with petty theft...piracy..," Daev added.

"There wuld be many friendly ears tu a Breton rebellion in the Mené."

"Dear Lord. We've got a rebellious Breton thief and a small army tromping around the woods, a traitorous Frank Bishop coining and lardering the war party, and a Frisian King and his cohort making up the spear-point and back-bone. I don't know Frisians well, they live so far away. Who is this Frisian King Gundebold?" the Margrave demanded of the room.

"He's an ex-king, actually," Charles quickly answered before anyone else could speak. "His son, King Radboud the Second, kicked him out of Frisia. Radboud's been ruling the Frisian east Laubach for, well, over a year now, is my understanding. Gundebold got upset at our Father years ago when the True King denied his request to marry our Aunt

Landrada." He winked at Gisela. "Gundebold wouldn't take no for an answer. Claimed lineage back to Clotharius as a pretense. He sent the same two ambassadors back again and again so many times Father began yelling at them when they merely appeared in Court."

"Apparently he can't take no for an answer about his sovereignty either," the Margrave calculated and turned to Budic and Cadocanan. "Would an invading ex-king of the Frisians find any kind of welcome in Aleth to even bother with such a distant campaign?"

"Desperate men huld unto power desperately. He obviusly still has a loyal cohort willing tu follow him, if he can find someone tu set him up in a fortified place." Budic then looked to his men again. "What bed wuld this evil man find in Aleth?"

"A cold one," Moruuan spat.

"I have to agree with Moruuan, Brenin. You could convince me Alethians might follow one of their own in some revolt, but not a foreigner such as this," the Bishop advised.

"Two centuries ago a Frisian chieftain named Corsold of Gouët resisted Saint Brieuc, about the same time as Saints Illtud, Samson, Maclou..," Daev recalled.

The Margrave sneered and pulled his sleeves. "That was two-hundred years ago."

"Tortulfe in Dinan, Frisians in Brieuc. I'm guing tu have tu pay the lords uf Tregerieg much greater attention after this," lamented Budic.

"My Lords, the tides do not wait, if you please? King Gundebold is bringing his army and all those stolen supplies secretly down from Antrain to Tombe, and then they plan to launch an all-out attack and take, well, *here*," Gisela opened her arms to the hall.

"Here? Avranches?" Charles asked to make sure.

Gisela nodded. "The Frank Bishop was assuredly certain that he could bait our good Margrave out of Avranches by attacking all the Marche forts. His plan was so simple they used tabula playing stones and string to make a map! Even I understood it! They took the forts in quick surprise raids, feeling certain you will predictably come out to take them all back. They have already emptied the forts of supplies, sending it down to Antrain. As you ride out, they abandon the forts back to you freely as you arrive. They spoke as if they *want you* to play the hero taking them back, and are counting on your renowned pride for their plan to work. While you are away to the south retaking the forts, they attack Avranches from Tombe and Antrain with the main army. " Gisela pointed at the Margrave. "You've retaken empty forts, but I've seen what is left of the abandoned fort at Sipia. You can't leave hungry men in cold forts for the winter. They think you've nowhere close to go to resupply them but Laval. They are planning to loot Avranches fort and castle and attack Aleth. With the King and Royal troops away in Bordeaux and your supplies limited, they think from Aleth and Avranches they can fight you back for every Marche fort from here to Nantes."

"They can't have taken all the forts. Tonight they broke upon us and ran away like a neap tide. Even now they still struggle to take Harcouët!" The Margrave's face tightened, and his voice raised, irritated by both her facts and insinuations.

Gisela seemed shocked. "I *admire* you, Margrave! The True King speaks only in glowing terms and familial bonds of your service to Him and our

kingdom...and our family!" she blurted out. "Karl here
told us without you in the Marche there would be no
dialog or even hope with the Bretons!"

Charles looked at the Margrave unapologetically,
and King Budic was nodding in agreement.

"Oh, mon cher ami!" Gisela turned awkwardly to
face Lady Ogiva but unable to move from the
seamstresses. "How can I tell him to beware of certain
danger if this man closes his ears to me!?"

"Mon amour! How can you not believe the Princess
as she tells us these things?" Lady Ogiva agreed,
stepping over and hugging her like a little sister.

"How? HOW?!" The Margrave grimaced and
pointed his index finger at her, seemingly frustrated at
anyone's advice. He stopped and breathed deeply to
calm himself down. "Budic, you have heard the
legends of the sunken city of Ys?" he asked, still
staring at Gisela.

Budic broke into a big smile. "Indeed! I know them
well! By Cruzan, in the Bay uf Duarnenez, they say. I
uften looked upon those waters as a boy and dreamed
uf seeing Ys rise up again!"

The Margrave's stare at Gisela intensified, his wife
no shield for her against his indignation. "You called
the rock of Tombe the legendary city of *Ys*. You
thought your dead little brother *a changeling*! You
believed so strongly that *fairies* had cursed him into a
grapevine that you *argued* you were right. You arrive
like a wisp on my doorstep, on an injured horse over
the wild tide, with a tale just as unimaginable, and
then wonder *how* a Lord *can even consider* the
possibility a runaway child might be wrong about
battle tactics that could put our very lives and the
entire kingdom at risk?!"

Gisela recoiled under the Margrave's unrelenting attack.

Lady Ogiva hugged Gisela tighter but nodded at the Margrave to reassure him. "All you have seen mon cheri, is helpful to them," she tried to comfort the scolded princess.

Charles stood up. "I, for one, believe you, Gisa." He touched his forehead to his sisters.

The Margrave unfolded his arms and huffed in closing. "Your Highness." He nodded, then stepped away to his messenger guards. "Assemble the rest of my Captains immediately." He turned and left the hall.

"Karl?" Gisela begged, her head resting on Lady Ogiva's breast as the rest of the men began to depart as well. Gisela thought the Margrave would not have spoken to Charles like that. Charles, however, stepped back to her, smiling.

"Wido was upriver in Antrain with the supplies, just yesterday. He said Gundebold was coming to Antrain and would be coming back down to Tombe, maybe even by this coming morning. There will at least be more Frisian soldiers with the tide in the morning."

Charles put his hand to her arm in sympathy.

"Wido is an injured and a lone soldier, hurt finding and defending *me*. His legs can't walk enough to fight, and there are two dozen women and children, *my friends*, to defend. They might lock the monastery doors against some Frisian soldiers, but not against their army. If we don't go help them now, they will all die."

Charles thought and then nodded in understanding as he grabbed up his curved sword and stepped after the Margrave to join the war council.

"Karl?" Gisela added, and he turned yet again. "I would not be here to tell you any of these things without my friends on Tombe."

Charles smiled again. "Gisa, are you telling me I need to lock up the horses?"

"No. I can walk all the way back there at low tide," she warned him with a serious stare.

Lady Ogiva recognized both Charles and Gisela had the same mischievous family grin when they were determined.

"Are you entirely certain this is wise right now?"

"No, Margrave. I am not at all."

The door to the Margrave's chamber cracked open further. The strong scent of mastic and frankincense was a vaporous wall in the air and pushed Charles' head back like a surly house guard when they peeked into the room.

Lady Ogiva's eyes did not rise to their intrusion, and the notes of her soft singing did not acknowledge any disturbance. She was half sitting, half laying, as if expecting them in her bed, draped upon all the animals of the forest, from thick bear to the softest minks. In her black and gold dress, her hair cascading around her, she herself had become one of the many soft animals making the bed a cushion of luxury, all paying homage to the sleeping litte Noah's head on her lap. Her finger's dipped gently, almost in time to her song, in the offered gold cup, and then let the drops of chrism trace down Gisela's sleeping face. The drops glistened in the many candles like the snood and necklace gems, yet gone were all veils here, save perhaps Gisela's illusions. Like an adopted mother, Lady Ogiva was a living pillow, and Gisela's new gold nacré was splayed out like a gift-wrapped pillowcase. Every ring maiden was awake and attending, from holding the oil urn to hemming Gisela's dress to slowly feeding shavings to the fire to bank the heat of the room far beyond the bite of blizzards and sharp ice.

Charles pulled the door back closed again.

"My Liege, I urge you, we don't have all night to decide this matter." The Margrave wrung his hands together with such force they squeaked.

"Let's give her a pause to sigh, and a slow breath more. Dear thing, she's earned that moment tonight, at least. Let her chase moths with Pepin in her dreams while she can."

"Chasing fairy dreams may be *all* this is."

"Then dawn will awaken the truths for us. Have Budic make ready his offer." Charles' eyes had forceful intent until the order was clearly understood, then they left the Margrave and darted about the outer chamber and out into the busier hall. "Are your Captain's gathered?"

"The last gather in the courtyard now."

"Then for the moment, our place is with them."

After the hasty war council and full patrol of Avranches, Charles reentered the dining hall and did a double-take. He had obviously not expected a feast before dawn, yet clearly, the room was filled with people in their best finery, some dancing, and the smell of fresh raspberry tarts was overwhelming. They seemed to be celebrating the routed Breton attack. He seemed to catch his breath and stepped inside quite carefully.

A flung baton whizzed by his legs, and he managed not to knock over more skittle quilles with his feet than the baton did. He realized the people dancing were mostly youngsters, and that Gisela wasn't amongst them. There were two children playing hopscotch with gold coins, a table with a nine-man's morris board and a ring toss, all apparently awaiting their turn at play. Charles, incongruous in his gilt armor and great weapons, passed through a crowd of adults; the more important people in the village it appeared. They were all watching Daev and two others playing the flute, a lyra and a drum as several blindfolded children groped and tried to catch Gisela, who was wearing bells on her wrists and clapping every so often in rhythm to the music. She smiled at him as she dodged a passing child's hand that tried to tag her.

Amused, he stopped by the ring of blindfolded children and waited for the song to finish. His sister was inextricably both innocent child and cultured royal.

"You look puzzled, your Highness," said Lady Ogiva as she slid up beside him like some mystical hostess.

Charles went to speak, then stopped himself for a moment. He breathed in deeply as the tarts passed by his nose. "Miam. Your breakfast is delightful. Here I recognize my sister fully."

"Once she awoke, there was to be no idleness. I thought it might take her mind off her trials of the past days. I'm honestly quite déconcerté as to why she isn't still fast asleep, the poor child."

"Come to be seen," Charles mumbled. Lady Ogiva

tilted her head at him, and his face suddenly apologized for his mind's wandering. "I have watched several men die in the past day, though none so close as to be by my own sword, but still. Raiders have caused much trouble in our countryside and the edges of town, the sun isn't even up, and yet here the court society is in full bloom. Come to see, and be seen by, the Royal Princess."

"For some here, it may be their only chance to ever look upon her, and that child could charm a bald old ass into a ride." Lady Ogiva chewed on the edge of a fingernail.

Gisela came closer to them, clapping and dodging hands.

"Yet?" Gisela asked as she passed, betraying the real focus of her thoughts.

"Yes."

Gisela nodded and clapped enough to get caught by several laughing children at once. Daev and the musicians stopped playing.

"Get her ready for the ship. We're sailing for Tombe."

"You can't take her!" Ogiva blurted out, her eyes suddenly creeping up her forehead. "No, no, you can't take her Highness back out into that!"

Charles looked at Gisela as she graciously thanked the many adults who were watching, one after the other, to eventually come to stand by him. "Ready."

"Your Highness, you could find your death out there. I beg you not to go!" Lady Ogiva pleaded with a loud voice and clasped hands. All the children and several of the adults also joined in the dismay that Gisela might be leaving the safety of the castle.

"If Avranches is truly a target, then she could find

death just as easily in here. We must be away to the docks," Charles insisted, taking Gisela's hand. The incredulity only grew louder and more animated as they passed through the crowd.

Gisela felt the tug on both arms as Lady Ogiva grabbed the other.

"I beg you two not to do this!" her face seeming distorted in some melange of uncertainty and fear. "I can't help ensure your safety if you don't stay."

Gisela turned to look at Lady Ogiva, and her head tilted in wonder for a moment.

"Then please come with us," Gisela suggested, and she and Charles left the dining hall for the main hall and courtyard.

Lady Ogiva bit her nails hard as townsfolk consoled her, and then she fled from the room like a running doe.

Gisela had not forgotten just how cold it was outside and wrapped herself in a frock of more fox furs than she ever remembered seeing before, much less owning. She wiggled her toes in her fitting leather shoes as she walked. The Margrave's main hall was not as busy as she might have guessed, and he was nowhere to be seen.

They passed out the main doors into the courtyard, and there, prominently in control like a courtyard general, was a priest Gisela had not met before. He was a sturdy fellow in thick blue robes and a golden crosier, and the Frankish troops with him stepped up as well. This priest's sturdiness turned out to be a heavy, sleeveless chainmail vest and baldrics, and the maces that hung from his belt did not look like they contained holy water.

"Præfectus, the Second and Fourth have been made ready," the priest reported, before looking down. The hard face of stone suddenly glowed. "Aha! Is this..?"

Charles nodded. "Princess Gisela, meet Joshua Jumael, the Bishop of Avranches."

The Bishop kneeled with his head down and scrapped as assuredly as if she were the Queen Mother herself. "Your Highness, if this humble servant could beseech thee for thy blessing err this day comes?"

Gisela almost laughed, and rubbed her mittened hand on the bare tonsured crown of the Bishop. He looked up, smiling.

"My child. Your brother has told me much about you. I can't tell you how thankful we are you arrived safely from your wandering in the wilderness."

"Thank you, your Eminence."

"Your brother says you're a good Christian child. Will you pray with me to our dear Lord and Savior?"

"Of course!"

"What would you suggest?"

"What day is it?"

"Bless you child; you have been in the wilderness. It's the 19th of November."

"Then Psalm 107, is that good?"

"Good?! The Lord does shine from within you, child! Indeed."

Gisela, Jumael, Charles and several of the Royal soldiers all took a knee like rocks in the passing sea of soldiers and citizens.

"The LORD changed rivers into deserts, and water-springs into thirsty ground, A fruitful land into salt flats, because of the wickedness of those who dwell there. He changed deserts into pools of water and dry land into water-springs. He settled the hungry there, and they founded a city to dwell in. They sowed fields, and planted vineyards, and brought in a fruitful harvest. He blessed them, so that they increased greatly; he did not let their herds decrease. Yet when they were diminished and brought low, through the stress of adversity and sorrow, He pours contempt on princes and makes them wander in trackless wastes. He lifted up the poor out of misery and multiplied their families like flocks of sheep. The upright will see this and rejoice, but all wickedness will shut its mouth. Whoever is wise will ponder these things. Amen."

"Amen," Gisela repeated.

"May God keep and protect you on your journey, child."

"You as well, Bishop."

Charles hugged the beaming Bishop and clasped hands warmly with his troops before they moved to young Squire William and the waiting liveried royal horses.

"That Bishop has his own light about him," Gisela whispered.

Charles laughed in agreement. "We have charged Bishop Jumael with the defense of Avranches in our absence. He'll be at the center of whatever happens here."

"Well, there won't be any heathens here, that's a certainty," Gisela noted, a look back at the priest. "What's that chain baldric he wears?"

"That's the pallium of Dol."

"I'm sorry, I didn't know Bishop Cadocanan and Aleth were suffragan to Dol," she said, looking back again. "And I thought pallium were made of wool."

"They aren't, and they are. Dol is a...complicated

diocese for the Church."

"Our ship must be going to Tombe, but what is the plan after that?"

"Not here, Gisa." Charles lifted her up onto an older bay gelding. "We'll talk on the ship."

Four of Charles' armored bodyguards took the horse leads, and they proceeded out of the warm stone of Avranches castle and through the cold soil of its fortress motte to enter the torch-lit village. It was still dark, the coming sunrise did not yet brighten the air beyond a wash of milk sky to the east, but man and child and beast were all in preparation with comings and goings around them.

Gisela became intrigued with her brother's young squire who walked with them along the ground. He was a Goth boy her age and kept looking up at her.

"Who are you?" she finally asked him when their eyes met for the fifth time.

"William of Gellone, your Highness, in the Præfectus' service."

Gisela thought the little soldier was so different than the dirty and laughing children of the prison train. She looked back behind them, expecting to see the Ogre and Fridolin trailing behind. Instead, there was a fancy two-wheeled carriage with a gray horse in silver livery trailing them, along with a throng of people. She was surprised to recognize so many of the villagers from inside the hall, who were now following them down to the port. They even waved to her when they saw she was looking their way. She was familiar enough with her parent's fame in public, but not accustomed to this kind of personal resplendence. The anonymity of the prison train seemed a dream.

As they came down the switch-backs to the port, she

looked west towards Tombe and saw the half-moon, playing peek-a-boo with her in the many clouds as it set. Gisela realized she was the moon, and her mother was the sun. She was so used to being in her mother's brilliant light of court society, she had not expected to glow this bright on her own. She had been right not to tell Julien who she was; he would have marched every single prisoner back to Mur itself because of her. Now here she was instead, her own entourage in train. Her mother was still the sun; only its reflection upon her, and Charles, was the reason she glowed royally at all.

The Breton ship had been prepared, the great netting walls down, the oars at the ready. She could see King Budic, and that tall soldier Moruuan with him in the fur cloak, and the Margrave on board. She hadn't expected that.

"The Margrave must be coming to verify my story," Gisela whispered to Charles.

"He's not coming," Charles shook his head with silent lips as they clomped across the wooden beams of the bridge of the Sée.

The ship was riding low alongside the pier and was all lit up by oil lamps. The Royal soldiers helped Gisela down off the horse and passed her across the gangplank like a precious treasure.

The balinger ship was huge to her, as big as the dining hall. There was a big open deck with high sides and one big quadrilateral sail, still furled on its spirit up on the mast. Another sail in front that was rolled up like a carpet. The front deck of the ship was covered over by blackened hides to make a small tent-like room. Great wooden fins, like flukes on a whale, were tied to both sides, half out of the water. Beside and behind the mast were the oar racks in the center.

About two-thirds of the way back were oval ribs across the entire deck that held up another rounded roof tent-like room of blackened hides. Behind it was what looked like a pergola where all manner of ropes were tied off, and the big steering oar.

The sturdy ship was filled with a score of Breton sailors in their sealskin limestras and violet caps, each seated along the sides on their footlockers that doubled as their benches. The round tented room had the sides tied up like a rain fly, and she could see Bishop Cadocanan, King Budic and several of his bodyguards, the tall soldier Moruuan, who seemed to be Budic's younger brother or ally, and now Charles and his bodyguards. A pair of Ogiva's ring maidens were packing supplies in a huge chest under the bow-tarp of the ship. Budic, Cadocanan and the Margrave were all talking to the ship's Captain, probably the oldest living Breton Gisela has seen so far, and quite possibly the oldest living person who could still move.

"How do yu like my ship?" Budic asked them, his shoulder out and his eye gleaming, but he was already nodding in enough self-approval to drown out any negative observations. "Its heart is a frame uf Biscay oak, but it's planks are uf legendary iroko wood; the plank's spirits talk tu the Captain!"

"You Breton's build fine ships," Charles granted him, looking up at the tall spirit mast above their heads.

"Bah! We didn't build it! My brother Daniel stole this ship from the Wascon!"

"Have it your way then; you Bretons *steal* fine ships."

Budic laughed heartily.

The silvered carriage that had been following them

stopped on the Sée bridge by the ship, and Lady Ogiva herself was helped down, resplendent in a mink-lined hooded cloak and accompanied by a third ring maiden.

"You'll have few options after Tombe," the Margrave stated as the men all came together under the round tarp in the center of the ship.

"Assuming the Frisians aren't landing with this tide," Budic stated.

Moruuan shook his head slowly. "Brenin, I suggest we give it a wide berth if they are."

Bishop Cadocanan was storing his crosier under the deck as they talked. "We've sent Curé Leufred with an escort to Caen, to beg for assistance."

The Margrave looked up for a moment, thinking. "That would be about a week before we could see soldiers from Caen."

The bishop nodded and exhaled deeply. "Assuming they'll even come."

Lady Ogiva stomped onto the boat with half a dozen sailors' assistance and promptly took a bear cloak from her maiden and tossed it around Gisela as if her teeth had been chattering.

Gisela felt Ogiva planned to force her to stay by rooting her in place with a mountain of clothing. She was beginning to sweat under all the furs, but after the past week of chills, she suddenly favored not saying anything about being too hot. She wondered if that they would get help from Caen, and if Bishop Jumael could hold out until they did.

"What about the Lenuri?" Charles asked.

The Bishop looked white, even under the lamplight. "The sinking isles?"

"Yu might find help in Augia, but yu are just as

likely tu find they're helping the Frisians and the revolt," Budic warned. "The Lenuri Bretons there have been losing farmlands tu the sea fur years."

Moruuan nodded again with Budic's words. "They'll have a number of swift little boats to try to capture this ship, if that's true."

The Margrave shrugged and crossed his arms. "That leaves you Roque de Lihou."

The old Breton Captain made public complaints and noises at the mention of the town of Lihou.

Charles just shook his head and looked at Budic. "What did he say?"

"He says Lihu is un oyster village. They have dikes from hundreds uf years uf shell dumping that makes treacherus tides into their harbor."

The Margrave uncrossed his arms and held onto one of the roof ribs. "It's only a long day's walk to Avranches though if you get trapped. Reasonable."

"We'll leave such a decision as that tu the needs uf the moment," Budic agreed, calming the Captain with a few words and hand motions. Gisela was reasonably certain the Captain was back talking, even though she couldn't understand many of the words.

Lady Ogiva stomped into the middle of the round-tent, crossed her arms much like her husband and stared everyone but her husband down. "All are no places for a Princess to be taken! Why can't you just fill Tombe with your troops and jump down upon them when they return?"

"We can't get men everywhere," Charles argued.

Lady Ogiva pointing west. "You could march there in a half day!"

"The paumelles, Tombe's tidal sands, are tricky. Columns of men, horses, and wagons make the sand there softer," Charles warned.

Ogiva put her hands on her hips. "Yet you would have us believe this girl rode across those same sands, in the dark?"

Gisela was not going to speak, but Ogiva had included her. "Thëo almost got stuck at one point when we stopped. The sand out there acts like cheese on soup!"

Charles put an arm down around her shoulder in support.

"Tombe is a place where you could wait out a siege for a very long time," the Margrave warned. "If the rebellious Bretons and Frisians are there with a countryside's worth of supplies, all they have to do is keep us along the shoreline, and the tide will do their work for them, washing us away every few hours."

"This is true uf many villages all along the Domnonée coast," Budic agreed. 'It is why they were chosen as our towns."

Ogiva pointed down at the deck. "Then use this ship to ferry soldiers there." Gisela decided the Lady was not going to take no for an answer any more than Gundebold. Then she wondered why.

"Mon Amour, even if I got enough of my soldiers there by boat, the Frisians have no reason to siege *us* there. They will simply come here, or go elsewhere."

"Then my original suggestion, and my presence, still stands. Aleth!" the Bishop offered as if it were the only logical choice for sane men.

Charles tilted his head, and one eyebrow went up. "Aleth could soon be under attack."

The Margrave nodded. "Or in league with the rebellion."

Budic shook his fist at the sea. "I tell yu, Aleth will

nut surrender itself up tu this Frisian King unless
there are a lot uf dead bodies un the tide first!"

The Margrave looked at him pointedly. "How can
you be so certain?"

"Because the Comes of Aleth is Hoel mab Ernoch, a
descendant of Alain Hir himself! Moruuan here is
Hoel's son!! I've his cousin in Carhaix, and wuld take
Hoel's lands in Quimperlé, Vannes...he's a bright
fellow; he'd nut risk such foolery in Aleth, and nut fur
what minor monies this Le Mans traitor might be
offering abut!"

"Præfectus, I beg you as a good Christian. Let us
see to the defenses of Aleth, warn the Comes and his
people, let them prepare." The Bishop clasped his
hands together.

"And tip our plans away?" the Margrave argued
back.

"Not if the Princess is right! If they plan to take
Avranches first, we will have time tu reach Aleth and
come back with a fleet of troops to challenge them
long before any of Caen's soldiers can arrive. The
church of St Maclou will ring with prayers, and the
town will rally to defend itself. Avranches is also a
place where you could weather a siege for days. Trust
in the LORD with all your heart, and do not lean on
your own understanding. In all your ways
acknowledge him, and he will make straight your
paths."

"Proverbs 3," nodded Gisela, looking at the
Margrave. The old Bishop nearly giggled.

The Margrave turned and looked out over the stern
at the clouds in the sky. "The sky says rain today. The
weather of late November can delay you for weeks if it
turns nasty. Your Aleth fleet may not be able to return

as quickly as you think if the seas are rough."

"My Captain feels after the rain we're in fur clear, culd weather in the coming days. I'd certainly take a gamble un his uld seafaring skills being right."

"Margrave, let us see to the prisoners we know are on Tombe, and rescue my sister's rescuers. If the Frisians are there, or her friends are not there, we will return to stand with you here at Avranches. If they are there, and corroborate her story, then we will sail to Aleth, raise the warning, *and* a fleet, and return to come stand with you here...providing the weather stays agreeable. We can return to Avranches across land through Dol with them easily enough if the Captain is wrong."

"Any rebellious army at the ford of Couesnon could stop you from reaching Avranches on horseback," the Margrave warned.

"If they are still there, if we are delayed, and if the weather turns. Many ifs for a tertiary plan to begin with."

The Margrave looked at Charles and Gisela and Budic for a long pause.

"You're really so certain these Aleth Bretons will help you fight those Bretons?"

Charles looked at King Budic and Cadocanan. "I am."

King Budic put a heavy arm on Charles' shoulder. "Saint Melanii taught us Peace must be made between Christians."

The Margrave scratched his goateed chin, shook his head and looked at Gisela again. "Alright. Show her the map."

King Budic and the Captain left for the bow as squire William handed Charles a rolled map of their area of Neustria. He tapped it on his other hand a moment as he looked at her, then handed it to the Margrave instead. They stood under the round-tent by one of the ship's lanterns.

"Now Princess, we are here at Avranches, on the Gallicus coast. Tombe is here, just to the west, where the Couesnon river enters the sea. Now, down here, your prison chain left the old road from Andecavus to Rennes...where?"

"A Frankish fort called Sipia."

"Sipia, so you said. I've been there myself, last September," he said with a pat. The Margrave pointed to it on the map. "That would be about right here."

Charles nodded. "You were at a war camp when they questioned you. You said it was...?"

"Fougères. They called the fort by name."

The Margrave pointed to it on the map.

"Alright, and these other sieges they talked about, the ones with tabula stones on their makeshift map, can you tell me anything about where they were?"

"They were just scattered on the tabletop around the string."

"What about the fires in the distance you spoke of, Gisa? Can you remember any of those?"

"The fires made the low clouds passing overhead glow red like volcanoes."

"Can you remember any general directions?"

Gisela closed her eyes and put out an arm straight in front of her. "The siege was right in front of the camp, and the river flowed from that town away that way before turning up that way."

The Margrave studied his map carefully, running his finger across it as if he were drawing in the sand. "You were facing east-northeast, the Couesnon river runs west before turning north."

Gisela, her eyes still closed, turned 45° left. "There was a red glow beyond the horizon," She was pointing at the mast, though with closed eyes she did not know it.

She turned almost 45° left again. "Just a few miles away, the fires and smoke columns were clear." She turned another 45° and pointed her arm down again. "At the horizon, a red glow."

Bishop Cadocanan moved slightly and stood on the boat where she had just pointed. Charles ushered young squire William to where she had pointed to just before.

She turned left almost 90° again. "At the horizon, red glow and clear smoke columns."

Moruuan stepped over near the stern and stood there.

She turned left about 45° again. "Very distant, red glow beyond the horizon."

She happened to be pointing at Lady Ogiva. King Budic returned with more of the Breton sealskin limestra coats and looked around at the oddly standing men and Gisela with her eyes closed tightly. "Are we tu play Hoodsmen's Blind urselves nuw?"

Charles moved Budic over a few steps as if they were about to dance, and the big king tucked the coats away under his arms and obeyed.

Gisela opened her eyes.

The Margrave twirled in place a few times, holding the map out. Then he began pointing at the standing men.

"Fougères," he said, pointing to himself.

"Harcouët," he said, pointing to the mast.

"Châtellier," pointing at squire William.

"Tremblay," pointing at the Bishop.

"Cormier," pointing at Moruuan.

"And Vitré," Charles announced as the Margrave went to point at Lady Ogiva.

"Yeesss!" Gisela bubbled out excitedly. "They had glass tabula stones and a string on a blank map and said those names! They jokingly called them the Margrave's apples.

He lowered the map, looking off into the dim morning. "They are the fortresses of the Breton Marche," the Margrave rubbed the fingers of his left hand on his throat, and his eyes narrowed in the lamplight.

"All of them?" Gisela asked.

The Margrave sighed so deeply that his breath formed a cloud amongst them. "All but one. Avranches."

"The Couesnun river flows frum Fougères past Cormier and Tremblay," Budic pointed out.

"And the Loisance flows from Châtellier down through Coglès to join the Couesnon at..," the Margrave drew out on the map with his finger again.

"Antrain," Charles admitted, his head dropping as the Margrave's finger came to rest on the town.

"I should have known. Gisela's string amongst the glass tabula were the rivers," Charles deduced.

The Bishop rubbed his forehead in his hand. "I forgot the Bishop of Le Mans is illiterate."

"What?" Charles asked, swallowing.

"How can a Bishop preach the Bible if he can't read it?" Gisela asked.

"He can't," the Bishop agreed. "And it's becoming clearer he doesn't."

"That still leaves that fortress at Harcouët, out here

by itself, away from Antrain. It seemed terribly important to them to get there two days ago. What river flows from Harcouët?" Gisela asked.

Charles pointed to the river that flowed just on the other side of the Avranches fortress. "The Sélune."

"The Bretons attacked us yesterday from the Sélune River. As if they had crawled out of it," Moruuan insisted.

"Maybe they came down on lilypads," Gisela quietly said to herself.

"Lilypads," the Margrave huffed. "Our scouts reported they found dozens of odd little hide raft coracles."

"Good Margrave? Good Prince? How can we not believe her story at this point?" the Bishop asked as he came to stand by Charles. Budic came over, handed the sealskin coats to Moruuan and picked up Gisela like a baby onto his hip.

"Whoa!" she gasped.

"This King believes this Princess tells us the truth," he stated emphatically. She smiled and teased his beard.

"You have a lot of crosses in your pretty belt. King," Gisela whispered.

"I have a lot uf faith," he whispered back.

"That's good, but some of your faith is hurting my leg."

Charles and the Bishop walked over to the others as Budic apologetically shifted Gisela on his hip.

"Gisela's truth is not what has the Margrave worried, your Eminence," Charles admitted with a nod to the Bishop, coming to stand beside Gisela in Budic's arms. She reached out and pinched Charles' nose.

"Oh? Then what does worry you?" the Bishop asked.

The Margrave handed Charles the map and kneeled before Budic, or, more correctly, Gisela's temporary Kingly throne.

"I have and do again pledge you my sword and faith and life, your Highness," the Margrave took her hand. "I believe you saw everything you have told us and are truthful beyond argument."

"Then what is the problem, my excellent Margrave?" Gisela asked.

The Margrave stood back up and crossed his arms.

"I don't believe you saw it all by accident."

Low Tides

"You believe the Princess was...was...shown these things...on purpose?" the Bishop asked, baffled.

The Margrave nodded, slowly at first, then more sternly.

Charles's arms fell in acquiescence, and he stared up from the map in his lowering hands. "Everything about the Breton rebellion so far has been about trickery, deception, and surprise."

"They show us one hand to hide the other's strike," the Margrave insisted.

"The Breton are skilled at deception?" Gisela asked Budic. He grinned broadly and shrugged his shoulders, then went to pinch her nose and tickled her side with his other hand instead. Gisela's giggled in his arm, but then her eyes got big.

"In the Breton ambush on our prison train, they played a trick of mounted Frankish soldiers with a Breton prisoner to get in close enough to us to surprise the guards. They were Breton and Saxon soldiers in stolen Frankish armor and horses, and the Breton prisoner's rope was a whip! Then the other Bretons charged in from a hidden ambush from the sides as the mounted Frisian and Frankish traitors came in last to clean up the survivors," Gisela realized. The Margrave beamed as if she were admitting he was right.

"Then yu think they knew they had the real

Princess, and let her gu?" Budic asked, tickling her chin as she stood up taller on his hip.

"That might have been more of a chance, a rolling of their tabula dice perhaps, but this Bishop of Le Mans has been a tricky one in politics since his father set him up as bishop," Charles admitted.

"Bishop Gauciolenus of Le Mans may be illiterate, but he's fiendishly clever at manipulating people," the Margrave stated. "Dux Robert has been an ardent supporter of the Bishop of Le Mans for the past few years."

Gisela's nose crinkled and her brow wrinkled decades beyond her youth. "Dux Robert? I've met him in court, he's a charming man!"

"That he is, and the Dux controls all the lands behind the Breton Marche, including Le Mans," Charles agreed.

"But why would he like this evil Bishop and allow him to rebel?" Gisela asked, her nose still out of joint.

"Courtly politics, Gisa."

"He's kept his Bishopric and diocese through...unusual...arrangements and finagling," Bishop Cadocanan agreed.

The Margrave crossed his arms. "Plus Dux Robert is away in the south, fighting alongside the King in Bordeaux."

"While the cat's away..," Moruuan shook his head.

Gisela's face returned to normal, and she crawled her hand up Budic's arm and under his beard like a scurrying mouse.

Lady Ogiva stepped up into the close circle. "You men speak of this child as though they could arrange such an elaborate deception on the whim, and on the off chance she escapes a Tombe tide with her life to reveal it to you?" she argued.

"The runaway daughter of King Pepin stumbling into the rebellion has no immediate value on a battlefield," the Margrave corrected his wife.

"She wuld be a fine hostage against the two uf yu," Budic pointed out.

"No, I wouldn't King."

"Yes, yuu wuld, l'ange."

"Gisela is only useful as a hostage if they want to pursue for terms and want to meet us face to face. If the rebels had a bold leader, and a real army to conquer Neustria or Brittany and face the Franks on the field, perhaps, but not as these raiders," the Margrave insisted. "They only way they want to meet us face to face is at *our* surrender, by then she would be of little leverage."

Charles swept his arms out at the dark banks of the Sée where the fleeing Bretons threw their torches. "These invading rebels are more locusts than occupiers."

"If they had delivered Gisela into our hands, mon amour, this might seem sensible, but the poor creature nearly died to reach us!" Ogiva tried awkwardly to angle herself behind Budic and Charles to be nearer to Gisela on Budic's hip.

"Did she?" the Margrave asked. "Was she molested? Despoiled? Tortured? Injured in the slightest? Did you find a mark upon her anywhere?"

"But what of this Archer who saved her?" Ogiva asked.

"The Præfectus here tells me this Archer Captain, Wido of Nantes, is a charismatic young man," the Margrave insisted. "What if his clever disguise as a Frisian was more clever than Gisela realizes?"

"What do you mean, mon amour?"

"A lone Archer from Mur? Passing through the entire rebellion battlefield with a liveried horse to a rock where the number of guards was conveniently diminished?" the Margrave spelled it out, the pointed fingers of his hand tapping out his points in the air before his wife.

Gisela grew angry, banging her fist upon Budic's scaled shoulder, making a sound like a tambourine. "Wido is bleeding real blood, and Sister Amona wasn't certain he'll survive it. I *SAW* him fighting and killing the Frisians, not acting. Tell him, Karl!"

Charles looked oddly quiet. "Gisa, I've met Wido. I know Mother trusts him, and I know you like him. But do you know who Wido's parents are?"

Gisela suddenly got quiet and put her head softly down on Budic's shoulder instead of her banging fist. "Please don't tell me..."

The Margrave did not hesitate for her sake. "Your Highness, the tide does not wait, if you please," he threw back at her. Gisela's arms came up closer under her, and she dug deeper into Budic. "Wido's grandparents were the Comes of Hesbaye, near the Royal court in Aachen. Their cousin is Dux Robert; he also the *current* Comes of Hesbaye. As we just said, Dux Robert is also the Dux of Neustria, the Lord of all the Frankish the lands behind these Marche forts."

"And at least a tacit supporter of the Bishop of Le Mans, Gisa."

"Do you know how Dux Robert serves your father's army in Bordeaux this winter?" the Margrave asked. Gisela nodded no, but with her head down on Budic's shoulder, it looked like a yes.

"Dux Robert had to leave his troops in Neustria to

deter the Bretons, but he became the aide-de-camp to Dux Tassilo of Bavaria, fighting with our True King in Wasconia," Charles answered. "Only that's not where Dux Tassilo is anymore, is he Gisa?"

She shook her head no again in yes-like fashion. "Mother said she was worried since Dux Tassilo had vanished mysteriously from Father's war-camp in Wasconia."

"Dux Tassilo may not be slipping home to Bavaria. If Dux Robert has brought Dux Tassilo into the Breton Marche, this may be more than a Breton rebellion and Dux Robert's distant cousin Captain Wido may well be a traitor working for them," the Margrave explained.

"Dux of Bavaria, Comes of Hesbaye, Dux of Neustria. Our brother Carloman in Aachen could be quickly surrounded by these Dux and their three armies, with Father too far away to save him. I don't like the thought of it either, but we've got to admit it *is* possible."

"So you think Dux Robert and Dux Tassilo are the real leaders behind this rebellion, not King Gundabold or the Bishop of Le Mans?" Gisela asked.

The Margrave gave a rare smile. "We're too far away from Frisia for Gundabold to have plotted all this, and frankly the Bishop of Le Mans isn't brave enough to stand up to me in public, at least by himself. He *must* be being supported by someone with more authority."

Charles put his hand on Gisela's back. "Gundebold, the Bishop of Le Mans, the Captain of the Archers, they may be just the elephants, chariots or even footmen on this shatranj board, Gisa. Dux Robert and Tassilo are perhaps the king and adviser of the board."

"Shatranj?" Budic asked. Bishop Cadocanan shrugged.

"It's a Persian game of war strategy, one army against another. It was one of the many gifts of Emperor Constantine to the Frank court that accompanied my kilij sword when the marriage between his son and Gisela were arranged."

"Royal games and curtly politics incite rebellion." King Budic shook his head, a consoling hand on Gisela's veil. "Yu Franks certainly dream in elaborate schemes."

"Grand, elaborate schemes, I'll grant you, but they don't normally involve little girls in snowstorms." Lady Ogiva wasn't backing down yet. "Mon Princess claims this Wido fought and killed for her. Was that her imagination too? And why go to this grand a ruse for a girl, who you say *yourself* would be of no value to them? What good or evil purpose does it serve? Tell me!"

The Margrave came over closer, such that everyone was under the fly and close at hand.

"That puzzled me greatly at first." He put his arm around his wife. "If you are trying to take the Marche forts to lure me out, what do you need her to bait us for? The Bishop of Le Mans and Dux Robert seemingly know me well enough. Why not just let me fall into their well-planned trap?"

Budic and Gisela both shrugged like some two-headed ettin.

"Why not?" the Bishop asked.

"Me," Charles stated simply, tilting his head. The Margrave pointed at Charles with a wiggling hand.

"Prince Charles came *back* with me this fall. He was supposed to go south with his father the True King, but instead, he unexpectedly came back to the Marche and Avranches, at my request."

"Tu met with me," King Budic stood tall and jutted his chin out to Gisela.

"Because Saint Melanii said peace must be made between Christians," Gisela repeated, finally raising up her head and patting Budic.

The Margrave pulled his wife around to the front of Budic by her ringed, soft hand and kept his arm around her waist.

"Now tell me, My Love," he whispered to her, though all under the fly could hear him clearly enough. "In the midst of a rebellion, I would leave Prince Charles in charge of important Avranches while I retook the Marche forts...can you think of a more opportune cheese to bait our good Prince Charles here out of Avranches than his wayward sister dragging him away?"

"An unexpected solution..," Bishop Cadocanan pointed to Gisela "...For an unexpected problem?" he pointed to Charles and began smiling broadly.

"And YU wuld make a FINE hostage against the Margrave," Budic realized, also pointing at Charles. "Yu are the only one here whu outranks him, and he culd nut in good conscience draw sword against those whu held you."

"Lure me onto Tombe, where we can't bring our army to bear. Trap me on a rock that cannot be easily besieged by the Margrave. Use me to break open the gates of Avranches in a single day instead of weeks. Threaten Gisela and me to gain the Margrave's withdrawal or surrender when he returns with a fresh army from Laval," Charles rattled off the possibilities.

Lady Ogiva whispered back to her husband behind

her. "So the Princess is coming back to the castle?"

"I wish," the Margrave shook his head sadly. Ogiva shot a look at Charles.

"You see, for all the sense the Margrave makes to me, I believe Gisa," Charles offered, stroking his sister's veiled head, and Gisela fell from Budic into his arms instead. Budic laughed as he helped her pass to Charles.

"Yu'd make a good Breton, L'Ange."

"We'll take all the precautions we can to see if the Margrave might be right," Charles announced. "I've had our sharpest eyes on Tombe since the high tide during the night. We sent scouts ahead on this incoming tide on small rowboats, to see if the Frisians have walked or landed with a trap in the past few hours since Gisela left. We'll go find out if Gisa's rescuer is real or not. If she's right, we'll light a signal fire on top of Tombe and sail to Aleth to raise the warning. At the first hint that something is not right, we'll come back here instead." He let Gisela climb back down.

"And yu?" Budic asked the Margrave with a thump on his breastplate.

"I've apparently got a reputation to catch up too. I'll leave a strong force in Avranches under Bishop Jumael, but march my knights and army to siege and liberate Harcouët. I want to see for myself, first hand if the Princess is right about these rebels falling back before me."

"Mon Amour, what if they come to our gates while you are in Harcouët?"

The Margrave smiled. "Jumael and I have got a few tricks of our own to try on these crafty rebels. Avranches will not really be defenseless, and if the rebellious Bretons fall back before me at Harcouët, I'll return to Avranches instead of pursuing them."

"Maybe, send enough troops to fool them into thinking you're pursuing them?" Charles asked, and the Margrave smiled at the idea.

Lady Ogive drummed her fingers on the Margrave's encircling arm and clenched her jaw. Finally nodding, she drew her husband's arm away and, kneeling, took off one of her eight rings and put it on Gisela. "As you suggested to me, Your Highness. One of my maidens at least will accompany you, then, to Tombe and Aleth, or wherever your brother's winds take you."

Gisela looked at the ring on her finger. "It is beautiful. Merci."

Ogiva looked at Gisela and put her hand on her shoulder lovingly. "The maiden is the real gem, Princess. The ring can be replaced."

"It's decided then?" Charles asked the Margrave.

"It's decided then, Prince." The Margrave hugged him strongly, then knelt beside his wife before Gisela herself. "Forgive me, Your Highness. No matter who may have played you, or for whatever reason, I am heartily impressed you made it from Mur, through snow and war and tide, on your own, under these conditions. You are indeed Charles's sister...and both your Pepins would be proud of you."

Gisela kissed the Margrave on both cheeks. "Make us even prouder of you, Red Lion."

After Bishop Cadocanan offered a prayer for them all for the day about to come, the Margrave left the ship. Lady Ogiva did indeed send one of her ring maidens to tend to Gisela while she returned, still pouting, to Avranches in her carriage with the other two. The sailors cast off the lines as the sky to the east washed ever brighter, and the clouds above ever darker.

The rowers pushed off from the bridge, and the twenty oars began to dip into the Sée in rhythm.

The old Breton Captain became cheerful and kept pointing towards the slightly less black Tombe in the distance against the pale western sky.

"Does he see Frisians?" Gisela asked Budic.

"Nu! He says Saturn sets over Tombe, an auspicius sign fur ur voyage!"

"Let us hope we can offer Lua as much praise afterward," Charles joked.

"Let's hope you all remember our God and Father in Heaven instead of all this heathen talk," the Bishop scolded.

Budic shrugged and laughed. "My Captain has crossed the Mor Breizh several times in his long lucky life. He takes his superstitions as seriusly as he dues his Gospels."

The eastern sky grew brighter, and the western sky pinker as the dawn came closer. The Sée river meandered through the tidal flats, and the Captain was way up in the top of the mast to judge the shoals and tides. The Captain had with him a great whip, not terribly unlike the Breton at the Billé ambush, Gisela thought. He would use it to crack and point and punctuate his orders, which he kept barking down to his sailors, who in turn steered and rowed to his whims.

Gisela found it funny when Budic referred to him captaining from the top of the mast as 'crowing'.

Avranches' hillside town came to life as it passed by

to their left. Squads of soldiers scoured the burned banks and barns looking for dead, or perhaps hiding, injured Bretons. They passed numerous small fishing boats the guards were using to cross and check the Sée, and Gisela was ever so happy to be on a ship headed for the bay's waves rather than one of those little rowboats.

She saw the way the Sée did indeed curve around a thick woods, something that only a few hours ago confused her. The woods looked less frightening in the growing light than they had in the moon-shadowed darkness.

Finally, the banks of the grazed sheep fields passed by, and Gisela wondered if any were the ones she and Thëo had met in passing. She waved at the sheep, though none of them seemed to remember her.

As the clouds above them began to glow brighter, they joined up with the much stronger flow of the Sèlune, and the changing tide seemed to push every wave and ripple into its own vortex. Gisela remembered her coracle floating uncontrollably and was glad for the rowers around her now.

Moruuan handed out the extra sealskin coats, Budic called them limestras, as the waves picked up in the bay. Gisela was already hot under so many furs, and Charles politely refused one, but the others took them against the sea spray. Avranches fortress was now difficult to see, though the hillside and town were still visible enough. All eyes turned to the great rock in the distance. Tombe stood like a giant frog on the water's edge; still and slick, rough and seemingly ready to jump away from them at the slightest spooking.

It did not jump, but the old Captain became spooked and animated up on the mast, cracking his whip so that no matter what language you spoke not a soul on board could possibly misunderstand that he wanted their attention on the island.

"He says the Teuz are trying tu wreck us un the rocks!" Budic translated.

"Tuez?" Charles asked. "More of Gisela's fairies?"

"Tuez. Tuez," Budic repeated, trying to explain them.

"Wisps," Daev interpreted the translation.

"Yes, wisps! The Captain says he sees wisps un Tombe."

"Are they blue?" Charles suddenly asked.

Budic shrugged but asked. Daev smiled as the Captain apparently agreed.

"Yes," Budic told him.

It was Charlie's turn to laugh. "Those are my scouts. We gave them blue lanterns to signal us the safe parts of Tombe."

Budic relayed the good news to the old Captain, who seemed happy to hear it was scouts and not evil spirits.

Soon enough everyone began to see the steady march of blue lanterns up the hillsides, and the little Avranches rowboats pulled up in spots along the shoreline.

"Tell him to stay to the north side," Charles instructed Budic.

"He says the anchorage is better un the suthwest," Budic relayed.

"So are the odds of getting caught by Frisian boats coming out the Couesnon on this high tide."

"I see yur notion."

The sun struck the top of Tombe, and it seemed like light pulled it even higher up out of the water. The shadow it cast, however, made the north cliffside shoreline even less inviting. The sun made its way down the white and black granite of the opposite side of Tombe as the ship made its way closer to anchor just offshore. Gisela looked over the sides of the ship at the waves and gulped as she realized she had ridden over sand where now the sea would easily be over the horse's back. Wido had not been wrong in his warnings that the tides were deep here.

Two of the scout's rowboats came out from the dark shore to meet them.

Charles came to Gisela's side on the deck. "I'm going ashore. Our scouts are at the top now and have not signaled any alarm. So far it seems safe enough for you to come as well. If your friends are still inside, you might open a door faster than we can. I'm not certain I could stop you anyways, save your smock and furs might keep you from swimming ashore."

The ring maiden stepped up quietly behind Gisela. Charles was going to argue but decided to let Gisela decide.

"I'm coming with yu," Budic demanded.

Gisela turned to the Bishop. "Please come too, Eminence."

"Then I shall as well, if only to assess the condition of the monastery and chapel."

Four of Budic's bodyguards, two with bows, went back on the one boat, and Charles' four heavily mailed soldiers went ashore on the other.

"Prince?" Budic asked Charles as they awaited their turn on the rowboats. He handed him a beautiful wooden box carved and gilded with silver waves. "I was tu present this tu yur Father, the True King, at the assembly in Attigny next year. I wuld prefer tu offer it tu yu now, instead."

"What is it?" Charles asked as Gisela helped him open the box. "It's a great ivory tusk. It must be three feet long!" Charles laughed. "Look at the scrollwork, this is most impressive. Is it an elephant tusk?"

"Nu, a walrus tusk, hollowed ut and made intu a Breton warhorn. It is the Horn of Finistère, a heirlum uf Amorica, of old. It was tu be a symbol of ur people, yurs and mine, being called together in Christ."

Charles held it up and turned it over in his hands. He put it to his lips and tried to blow it, but it only made a squawking noise that made Gisela and a few sailors laugh. Budic motioned for Daev to come over to blow it.

Daev looked about the rocks of Tombe and up to the top with some trepidation.

"I want whu's ever up there tu know we are here, so nu need tu blow it soft. Nu secrets this morning."

Daev nodded his head, then put the horn up to his lips and let out a blast that made Gisela scream and clasp her ears, shook the sailors, scared the rowboat soldiers and echoed off the rocks of Tombe, sending seabirds into flight off the cliffs. The old Captain cackled and laughed up on the mast.

"King Budic, what a gift! I'm certain they heard that back in Avranches!"

"It is yurs, Prince. Daev, carry it fur him up the hill."

"Perhaps you can still give it to my father in Attigny," Charles offered.

"Perhaps yu can give it tu him. Fur now, I give it tu yu, my Prince," Budic offered, then turned to Moruuan. "If yu hear that horn again frum up there, then we see the Frisian's are coming down the river.

Prepare accordingly."

"Yes, Brenin."

Budic looked to Charles. "As yu Franks are fond uf saying this morning, the tide does nut wait, if yu please."

So it was that Charles, Gisela and her ring maiden, Daev, Bishop Cadocanan, and King Budic came ashore on the two rowboats to join their soldiers and bodyguards, and they began to climb up the trails of Tombe from the shore.

The rocks were far too steep and craggy to climb the north side without assistance, and the wind was sharp. They made their way along the shore east, towards the Avranches facing side and into the sunlight. It was steep here as well, but two of Charles' scouts came down to meet them and show them the way up to the trees and overturned Frisian boats.

Already several women and children had come out of hiding, and they fell at Budic and Charles' feet in praise when the group got to the Frisian camp.

"Beds, cook fires, oxen, supplies, overturned boats hidden and acting as roofs, prisoners," Charles observed.

"*Slain* Frisian soldiers." Budic and his guards pulled one back over into the camp.

"There's a giant plow horse tied up down here, and more of these boats upright and pulled up beyond the tide," the Bishop pointed out.

"So far Gisa, you are being vindicated."

Gisela looked pleased, until none of the children recognized her. She had to pull off her veil and show her hair, and then sit with them before they slowly began to recognize her. When she offered hidden raspberry tarts from her pockets, several suddenly broke into tears and hugged her and each other.

"You serve the Royal Princess of Austrasia and the future Empress of Byzantium, ring maiden," Charles instructed as they watched the reunion together. The veiled maiden kept her head down and nodded, seeming to understand. "If any evil is to get through me, you are to be her shield, no matter what strikes at her, do I make myself clear?"

"Yes, Præfectus," the maiden quietly replied and drew her golden dagger.

Charles put a calming hand out to hers. "I don't believe you have to protect her from hugs and kisses this minute," Charles laughed quietly, shaking his head.

The maiden looked humiliated and slightly disheveled, bobbing her head in silly apology and anxiously sheathing her dagger.

"Yu were close, Gisela. There are furteen Frisian boats here."

"I've never seen anything like them."

"These culd cross the Mor Breizh, if manned by brave men."

"Scouts! I want constant eyes on the coast and the Couesnon. If you see anything bigger than a seagull coming this way, I want to know about it."

The Frankish scouts nodded and set off into the treetops and cliff tops.

"King. Bishop," Charles motioned up the hill. "Gisa, let's go find your friends."

The sun was briefly bright as it rose higher, coming up over the marshlands and Marche forts to the southeast. Charles tried to peer into the distance to see any sign of the sieges, but nothing in the distance was clear in this weather. Quickly the sun rose up into the clouds, and the brief warming rays were lost to a dull gray.

Charles's soldiers went before and after them in twos. Of the soldiers in front of her, Gisela recognized one of her brother's men with an ax; it was the baron Ebrulf of Woensel. His shield with a red circle and silver swans on his shoulders not only reminded her of him from last summer in Mur, but she remembered dancing with him all the way back in Aachen court last year. She smiled knowing Frisians weren't the only ones in the Marche with strong, professional soldiers.

The trail wound back and then up steeply before approaching the outer gate of the monastery. Gisela gulped yet again as she realized she had ridden Thëo down this steep path.

Scouts stood by rubbled wall blocks away from the gate.

"There are people in there, but they've got the doors jammed tight, Præfectus."

Gisela whispered to him, and Charles decided to try a gentler approach, and he began calling out in d'oïl and vulgate he was with the Frankish army of Avranches, come to look for the friends of Duende. They heard a lot of obvious commotion going inside, but the doors did not open.

There came repeated whip cracks and hammering sounds and noise from the ship down below, still in the morning shadow of Tombe, but what they were signaling was unclear till a girl's and a woman's heads popped out around the cliff edge side of the monastery. From some crack in the cliff wall, they had emerged from the monastery onto the perilous cliff edge.

"AMONA?" Gisela called out, and the wide-hipped nun came out around the edge to the gate as if she had found her lost fortune.

"DUENDE!!" Amona yelled, over and over till they embraced. The girl followed her.

"MAYLIS!" Gisela yelled, and the three fell down hugging each other by the gate. The ring maiden knelt with a hand on Gisela as if in sympathy of the love, and the Bishop knelt in prayers of thanks to the Lord.

"We can't get in Sister!" Gisela pointed to the door.

"You can't! We pile all tables and chairs against door to keep out any soldiers who come!

Maylis looked at Gisela as if she were dressed in a dream. "Not stolen."

"You really are Princess. You Charles?" Amona asked Budic.

Budic just smiled and pointed to Charles.

"I am Gisela's brother, Prince Charles. If we can't get in, how did you get out?"

"There's a ledge on that side, you have to shimmy along it the whole length of the monastery to get to other side." Maylis got up to go back to the edge of the cliff and point.

Budic and several of the guards went to look and then looked back at Amona and Maylis as if they deserved medals.

"Can you hack the door down?" Gisela asked.

"That monastery door is thick sea-petrified wood designed to keep people out. It would take a while. We're fighting a tide, or we might be fighting an army," Charles advised.

The ring maiden made a squeal as Gisela jumped up and disappeared around the cliff ledge, followed quickly by Maylis.

"Yu'll nut make that with shields and weapons," Budic insisted and began shedding clothes. "I'm nut certain I'll make it naked."

"I'll go," Charles said, taking off his sword.

"No, Prince. I'll go with them," Daev offered, handing Charles the huge Breton horn. "We'll clear th' door."

Daev disappeared in his clothing around the edge, but it took Budic a minute to get enough armor off to keep his balance on the ledge.

He waved at Charles and the Bishop. "I want a Mass a day fur a month if I fall," he said, then looked back and laughed. "and twu a day if I make it!"

They peeked around the edge and realized why the ship had been signaling them. Gisela, Maylis, Daev, and Budic stood out moving along the ledge, and stark as the seagulls against the shadowed rock wall of the monastery.

"No wonder this is a chapel to Saint Michael. You need wings to get here." Charles watched them creep along the ledge.

"You, really Charles?" Amona asked, watching from below him.

"I am. You are Sister Amona, I take it?"

"Yes. Pleasure, Prince?" she caught her breath as Budic swayed once. "You got a sister who loves you much."

"I know."

"You should maybe beat her for running away from Mur, then maybe hug her for loving you so much."

Charles looked down at Amona.

"Maybe not beat. She help me, help all the everyones, no matter child or prisoner. She face off a real killer with Bible verse, even pull a dying girl from a vicious wolf's mouth. Christ in that girl. Maybe you just hug," Amona suggested, catching another breath and only breathing again when Gisela cleared the ledge on the other side and disappeared around the monastery. Amona disappeared when Maylis did, and Charles lived vicariously for a few long moments until Daev and Budic finally did as well.

Charles looked down at the ship, then turned back towards the main gates of the monastery.

"Anything to shore?" Charles came over and asked the scouts along the wall of the gate.

"Nothing yet, Præfectus."

There was a great deal of noise from the other side of the gate; Budic's unmistakable barking of commands and the equally distinct tossing of heavy objects.

In moments the monastery doors swung open to reveal a beaming Silenus; a half-dressed Budic with a dozen women around him, hugging him, giving him kisses and escorting him out the door with children streaming after them.

"Cassyon, get them down the hill. And take this," Charles commanded one of his soldiers and handed him the great horn. "This is too many people for rowboats and this tide, and I'm not risking them swimming in this cold. Get one of those Frisian boats into the water. Use the oxen if you have to. Hurry!"

"We'll give them a hand, Prince," offered Budic, getting dressed again, albeit with a great deal of help this time. "See tu L'Ange and that fellow in there. He's in a bad way," Budic advised, a serious tone to his voice that gave Charles pause.

Charles ordered the scouts to move the barricade piles of furniture from inside to outside the gate in the courtyard. It faced east towards Avranches, and would make the ideal spot for a signal fire with such ready firewood.

Charles put his hand on his sword hilt and stepped inside as the scouts began dragging the tossed benches and tables and pews outside. The women and children had piled anything and everything up against the doors in a defensive effort to delay any attackers. Budic and Daev had hastily tossed everything to the sides, now blocking the two rooms off the gatehouse foyer. He stepped over things, past the unreachable door to the infirmary on one side and the chapter house on the other, into the warmer cloister.

To his right was a refectory with a roaring fireplace, and then the kitchen and a ransacked storage room.

There seemed to be candles lit everywhere, for he could see all over the refectory easily. There was a good deal of blood on the floors, fresh from the smell, but no bodies.

When he came to the doors of the glowing chapel on the left, he heard voices, and he stepped inside.

An altar and a cross made up the far end, a statue of St Michael looking up in a side apse. There were enough candles lit to not only illuminate the whole room but heat it as well. He stopped to look at the wrapped bodies lined up in place of pew benches. Foremost and prominent was a child's, wrapped carefully and placed on a table and surrounded by candles, but there were half a dozen others as well, dead bodies, men it appeared, with crosses drawn in ash upon their wrappings.

"Præfectus?" Daev's calling voice echoed sweetly in the chapel, but the name struck Charles as if he were being called to task for what had happened here by the angels themselves.

There, below the altar, was Gisela, Amona, the ring maiden, Daev, and Bishop Cadocanan, along with the girl from outside, and another young girl Gisela's age that he didn't recognize. They were all around the Archer Wido, who was lying on pillows, his legs cut severely enough to still be bleeding through bandages and wrapped up below the knee. He looked unhealthily pale.

"Præfectus," Wido croaked out and smiled, not even attempting to get up. "You did it, Princess. You saved us, or I'm in Heaven, and that's just as good."

"Hush Captain. Save your strength," Gisela urged, holding his hand tightly.

"She's yours now, Prince. Get her back home for me," Wido reported, relieved.

"No, you stay with us Wido!" Gisela begged. The ring maiden drew her into a hug, and she hugged her back in dismay.

Charles realized right there before God, Jesus and St Michael that Wido of Nantes was no rebel, and falling to his knees he begged God's forgiveness for failing to see this man for who he really was and for ever doubting him.

"We've got to get him out too! We can't leave him, Karl!" Gisela's begging brought him back.

"We've got to get those dead priests out too," Charles pointed back to the dead bodies of the men. He was still a bit choked up.

Amona looked at the wrapped bodies. "Them no priests. They be the Frisians who captured us and Wido and the young women killed."

Charles turned to look again. Obviously, Amona had them treated in death with more respect than they deserved.

"We made Wido a litter from a bench to move him, but he say he stay here in Chapel and die with pretty angels."

"I'll get the litter. Show me where, Sister," Daev asked, and they went to fetch it.

"Captain Wido?" Charles asked, kneeling beside the Bishop. The Archer refocused his eyes and looked over again. "Prince?"

"My thanks to you Captain," Charles gripped his shoulder. "My family is ever in your debt."

"It might help my petition at the gates if you mention that to Saint Peter, my Lord."

The Bishop put a hand on Wido as well. "But he said to me, 'My grace is sufficient for you, for my power is made perfect in weakness. Therefore I will boast all the more gladly of my weaknesses, so that the power of Christ may rest upon me. For the sake of Christ, then, I am content with weaknesses, insults, hardships, persecutions, and calamities. For when I am weak, then I am strong'."

"I don't know that one, Bishop," Gisela confessed, tearful.

"It be Corinthians. Ha! I finally know one you not!" Amona cackled coming back with Daev and the litter.

"You've added a Prince, a Princess, and a Bishop to the angels praying for me Amona. You are one powerful nun."

"Well then, LORD give me strength to carry you down hill," she prayed as they began to slide him over onto the litter. Daev picked up the front, but Charles unbuckled and handed his sword to Gisela and took Amona's hands off the back of the litter to carry it himself.

"You've done enough, good Sister," he praised Amona, "And I must do more." The ring maiden broke into tears.

As they passed the last few scouts clearing the gate and building the pile outside, Charles ordered two to bring the girls body down with them, and leave the rest.

They passed out of the monastery into the cold breeze. Amona led the way, checking every corner and pointing out every rock that might catch a foot. Gisela walked beside Wido's pew litter, holding his hand and Charles' great sword with the ring maiden right behind her helping. Eulalie was on the other side, carrying his bow and quiver. Maylis came after, carrying Wido's sword and pack, and then the Bishop, deep in prayers over the whole affair.

The last scout came out, trailing behind the two carrying Fara's body, and he tossed a lit torch onto the barricade furniture pile out in the courtyard before heading down after them. The wind fanned the flames into a blaze quickly. Avranches several miles away would have to be blind to miss the signal from on top of Tombe.

Mulling

"The tide's going ut fast." Budic was up to his knees in waves. They had harnessed the dray and working together had drug one of the Frisian boats out onto the tidal washed sand. The scouts leaving on the rowboats had informed the Captain of the new plan, and he had sent over several of his sailors on the rowboats to help. The ship had moved to the southwest side and now laid off a few hundred feet, trying desperately not to run aground, as the tides had shifted.

"Everyone in!" Budic ordered in the only voice that could compete with the waves. Soldier and sailor alike took to an oar after they lifted Wido into the long Frisian boat.

"I want to scuttle the other boats first," Charles tried to command them. Budic lifted him up and put him in the boat.

"Nu time, Prince, ur yu can walk ut tu a beached ship!"

"Sacha?" Gisela suddenly asked, looking around. "Sacha?" she called out again.

It was not that big a boat. Sacha wasn't on board.

"Wait! We have to go back for Sacha!"

"Wait! We have to cripple their fleet!"

Along with the scouts off their rowboats, Budic put his shoulder into the stern of the boat and was amazed how easily it slid out to deeper water. Soldiers and Amona and children held Gisela and Charles in the boat as they helped Budic climb in. The oars dropped in and began rowing.

Bishop Cadocanan was in the bow, his silver crosier high, praying with all the authority due a Captain, in a sermon voice that might have rivaled Budic's. "So Joshua fought the Amalekites as Moses had ordered, and Moses, Aaron, and Hur went to the top of the hill. As long as Moses held up his hands, the Israelites were winning, but whenever he lowered his hands, the Amalekites were winning. When Moses' hands grew tired, they took a stone and put it under him, and he sat on it. Aaron and Hur held his hands up—one on one side, one on the other—so that his hands remained steady till sunset. So Joshua overcame the Amalekite army with the sword."

Budic's ship ahead grew closer at an agonizingly slow pace, the island of Tombe behind grew smaller frighteningly fast, and the waves only grew bigger. It was a terrifying race to Gisela, who couldn't understand why the ship Captain didn't slow and wait for them.

"My ship is fast, but if this Frisian eel-boat were handled by worthy seamen, it wuld catch it easily," Budic warned Charles.

Another island, a seeming miniature of Tombe, passed by just off to their right by a mile or so.

They could see into the green water as the waves rose and fell around them, and at first, the eel-boat stayed dry, but as the time passed the wind and waves frequency increased and the eel-boat began to take on water from splashing waves. There was a great deal of crying out and fear, and the Bishop tried to lead prayers for the children at least. Budic on the tiller oar and Charles beside him didn't limit the old Bishop's attempt to the young and prayed right along with him.

The sun climbed lower behind the many thick blobs of clouds as the afternoon wore on. The cold was biting, and sheets of high white clouds began to join the floating gray mountains above them.

The swells abruptly lessened, the rolls farther apart, and finally, the Captain turned his ship into the wind and gave up the race. The eel-boat quickly caught up. They came up alongside each other, oars on one side each retracting and suddenly overcrowding both decks. The ship's sailors tried to tie off the two vessels, and over-zealous soldiers and children tried to scramble over the higher rails into the ship. One woman, Gisela remembered her from Andecavus, tried to jump up to the ship and mistimed it, falling into the water between them. A sailor on the eel-boat attempted to reach down to her, but the waves dropped and then slammed the two vessels together, crushing them both to death. Amona screamed, and many fell back. It took all of Charles and Budic's commanding presence on the eel-boat to calm the rush of panic and avoid losing more people.

The Captain came down from his mast perch and ordered the Frisian boat's oars strapped into a gangplank shape and passed over the side. The sailors hastily built a makeshift ramp from the ship down into the eel-boat, and lifeline ropes and outstretched arms came across to help the women and children up and over.

If the passing waves had been fearful, then this rough crossing between vessels was terrifying. Wido went over with the soldiers and the body of Fara with three Royal scouts who hadn't left on their rowboats.

"I want to keep this Frisian boat!" Charles yelled over to Budic as he made it across the ramp.

"The sea's are tuu heavy tu pull it!" Budic yelled back.

The Captain came to the gunwale beside Charles and looked down at Budic and the eel-boat. He emphatically said something Charles didn't understand and Budic couldn't hear.

Daev came up. "Th' Captain tis warning us we'll have ta cut th' boat loose, or we'll never make th' coast by night, if we make it at all."

Charles sighed deeply, and he and Daev outstretched their hands over the ramp to Budic. He grabbed them both and leaped up into the ship.

Instantly the Captain had the sailors cut the lines, and the prized Frisian eel-boat went adrift behind them. It did not take long before it was swamped by waves, and less than half an hour later they even saw one end pitch up like a tumbling whale in a passing curl.

The sailors rowed the ship west as the Captain had the round-tent sides lowered to make at least a spray-proof den for the women and children in the middle of the ship.

By mid-afternoon the Captain had the mainsail unfurled and turned the boat more south-west. The wind that had fought the rowers all the way out from Tombe was now at their side, and the Captain ordered the big rolled carpet-sail put up, in front of the mast.

Gisela marveled at the great triangle of canvas; liver red, but spotted by white tics at the top, perhaps from weathering or sun-bleaching. She had seen sails, even been on a ship, but she had never seen a sail in front of a mast before, and the ship sailed even faster once it was up. She wandered forward on the deck to look up at it, then stumbled on Fara's wrapped feet sticking out of the bow-tent. Next to her was Wido, tucked up under the bow-tent asleep, an white as the sea foam. The joy sank, and anger at the Frisian welled up in its place. Exhausted, she slowly collapsed down the gunwale to Fara's feet, and the tears began. She rested her head on the departed girl's wrapped legs in apology and sobbed, and that is how later Eulalie and the ring maiden found her asleep.

The passing marshlands of the Dol coast slowly reached out at low tide, beckoning, trying and lure them back into the sandy shallows.

The racks for the oars made an excellent second deck, and the sailors covered the oars with tarps to make it more of a makeshift hold, at least for those who wanted to lie down. The oars overhead like roof beams worked for light cargo and children, but an adult could not even sit up fully. Still, it made for a safer berth for many.

Fast asleep under the warmer round-tent, under the bear cloak in the arms of the ring maiden and hugging Eulalie, Gisela dreamed of how the Margrave was doing in his battle for Harcouët.

Gisela awoke to the unusual sounds of a wooden ship at sea. Buried amongst children and blankets under the round-tent that arched over her from one side to the other, she sat in the huddled warmth for a time, putting her thoughts together with her memories and dreams and trying to sort out the story she was going to have to tell her Mother at some point, in infinite detail. Her own Odyssey. Eventually, her stomach began to turn her mind away from fancies to food, and she slipped out from under the cradling arms, blankets, and round-tent to quickly remember just how cold November was.

It was late in the afternoon, the sun was hidden by clouds, but it had not set. The old Captain was steering in the back, which she had quickly learned meant they were not in the shallows. Her brother and King Budic and all their guards were in the bow, reclined and relaxing as best they could in the crowded space. The sailors were as sailors always were, either incredibly busy at something critically important to the eminent survival of the ship, asleep or watching the sea go by.

The waves rolled slowly underneath. She found the motion slightly disturbing, but not as queasy as it made Eulalie or Amona. Tombe island was merely a tiny spot on the horizon behind them when it could be seen at all. One of the waves to the south did not move, and she asked a nearby sailor why. When the Breton sailor didn't understand her, Daev, seated slightly aside to the conversation and playing his flute while tapping out some slow tune on his knee, stopped and asked him again for her. The sailor shrugged but asked his Captain, who called out a word she did recognize, 'Dol'.

"They say tha' be Mont Dol," Daev translated, looking back over his shoulder without getting up, and took up his quiet dirge again.

Gisela wondered at a coastline of salt marshlands that seemed to go on forever, tidal flats that could rise up from the seafloor and briefly extend beyond the eye's sight, and both containing giant boulders of rock dropped like half-sunk marbles in pudding.

The coast turned north in front of them, and soon

enough everyone else was awoken by the sails being furled, the round-tent sides being rolled up and the oars coming out again. The sailors stretched the hides back over the empty oar racks to keep the children and women below it somewhat dry and warmer. As the sun set, the ship was rowed north into a series of broad bays that Budic called Kankaven. Amongst the rocky islands and jagged points, the Captain returned to his mast post and whip cracking against the twilight. The seas were rough, and the waves seemed angry.

With twilight slipping away, the ship finally came gently into a quieter beach, crawling sideways like slow crab at one point with an odd, playful tidal current. Great barnacled pilings stuck out of the water here and there in the shallows, and the Captain had the ship moored between two of them for a disturbingly long time. As the tide slipped back out the waves diminished rapidly, and they moored closely to only one, after it had been first wrapped in some of the stolen Frisian oars. More of the oars were used to brace the ship upright on the sand as Charles, Budic, and their various soldiers dropped into the cold, shallow water and waded ashore with camp supplies. The ship settled down tremendously once the keel found firmer sand. Amona and the ship's cook tended to the supper and needs of the children, and the Bishop tended to Wido, greatly assisted now by Daev. The round-tent went back up, and the hides were stretched out over the racks of oars again to provide as much covered deck as possible. As secure as could be, everyone settled into a restless sleep as the tide began draining back out, leaving the ship completely beached along the cold shore.

Sailors trading watch accidentally awakened Eulalie yet again, and she and a sleepy Gisela left from under the round-tent to take care of nature on the damp sand below the boat. Gisela couldn't miss the fire amongst the rocks on shore where Charles had made a camp on higher, drier ground. Picking her way through seaweed piles with sleepy Eulalie in tow, they made their way over to Charles' beach camp. Budic, Charles, and Daev were reclining, talking around a small but warm campfire, hidden from the bay, wind and open sea by the jumbled rocks that rose up around them. Gisela noticed one of Budic's watchful bodyguards up on the rocks above them. All three of the fireside gentlemen stood up when Gisela dragged a stumbling Eulalie into the firelight.

"Pleasant eve to you, may we join you Brother?" Gisela asked politely of her brother, now Royal Prince of sand and shells and the only warmth in sight. Charles had pulled a blanket off his legs to stand, and with it, he made room for them next to him. Behind him one of his soldiers slept under a makeshift tent, Cassyon, she thought, from the boots and great Breton horn.

"Wido's resting now. Even took a bit of broth before he fell asleep. My thanks unto you Daev for helping the Bishop sew up his legs. Amona said you were a great help in keeping him calm during the process." Gisela sat down, dragging Eulalie down and the men sat down again.

"Time an' travel teaches many a thing," Daev replied. "I hope yur archer friend lives."

"Gentlemen, I'd like to introduce you to Eulalie of Bordeaux. Eulalie, this is my brother Prince Charles, Budic the Great King of All Brittany, and the poet

Daev of..?"

"Gwynedd, my ladies, thou now o' th' good King's court."

"I don't know where that is, but it sounds dreamy."

"I dream of it a' times, but I don't know if you would. It lay across th' Mor Briezh," he mused, looking out over the water then back at the girls. "Do you treasure being freed, Eulalie?"

Gisela translated his question into d'oc for her.

"Yes, Lord," she meekly answered in her broken Latin.

"I'm no lord, love, just a singer a' tales. No' much different from you on a night li' this. Where are yur parents?"

"Her father was on the prison chains from Mur. He's disappeared as slave labor in the Marche forts, at least we suppose. Her mother disappeared on their prison march from Bordeaux." Gisela put a comforting arm around her.

"What did yur parents do fur their living in Bordeaux, sweet-voiced young Eulalie?"

Gisela translated it again for her.

"Vignerons. Grapes," she muttered, putting her head down on Gisela's lap as if she had become the princess and Gisela the ring maiden.

Budic and Daev shared some of their mulled wine with the two girls. Eulalie was far too struck shy to even look upon such great men, even though Gisela tried to include her in the talk frequently.

"Where are all your men? I see but two sleeping, and one on watch," Gisela asked.

Charles pointed her to down the beach. It took her a while to spot the dim blue lantern glow. Once she did, he pointed up the beach, then inland across the dunes towards the stunted woods.

"They stand watch with the scouts," Charles finally spoke. He seemed to be preoccupied in thought, and Gisela wondered if she had intruded lightly on a deeper conversation.

"Did you manage to get your swim?"

"No, I settled for a cold sea bath instead."

Gisela decided to change the conversation. She may have intruded, but the ship was cramped, and the little fire here was delightfully warm, as was Budic's vin chaud.

"Where is the baron Moruuan? I thought we saw him go a-hunting before dark."

"I've sent him tu Aleth tu warn them we arrive tomorrow." Budic had his arms behind his head and swayed slightly. He reached down and picked up his cup again. Gisela wondered how much mulled wine the big man had consumed.

"You sent him to Aleth? How close are we?"

Budic set down his cup and put one hand up towards her and the fire, pointing at his wrist below his thumb. "Kankaven is a great cape that sticks ut intu the sea," he explained, moving his pointing finger around his thumb and extended fingers and back to the other side of his wrist. "We sail arund. I gave Moruuan and twu of my men ship's lanterns and sent them across tu Aleth by night."

"I wondered why the ship was darker than this morning. Isn't it dangerous for them to try that at night?"

Budic picked up his cup again and laughed. "Moruuan is a brave enugh man, and there is a sentier tu follow."

"A path? To Aleth? From where?"

"Kankaven. Long ago Saint Meen set up a church north uf here, and a village grew up arund it fur the fishing of belon. That is what those pilings are fur, when the belon boats come in the season."

"Why aren't we in that village, instead of hiding out here on the beach?"

"Most uf the fishermen live in Aleth fur winter, so there is nut anyone in the village, and any whu might be..."

'Those who remain might well be our enemy," Charles finished, his voice and eyes far clearer than Budic's.

"What are belon?"

"Oysters," Charles answered with a snap.

"The BEST oysters in Brittany!" Budic toasted.

Gisela felt she was angering her brother. "Charles, what weighs upon your mind so this eve?"

"So?" Charles asked with a sad laugh. "Affairs of state, Gisela. Dux, comes, bishops, bandits, wars, thieves, empty forts. Full ones. Tomorrow. Next week."

"I dreamed about the Margrave this afternoon."

Charles looked up at her with some focus and poked at the fire with a stick. "I'm concerned about him too."

"Why? His prowess at war is renowned."

"Because you turned out to be right."

"Because I told the truth?"

"Because that makes the Margrave wrong. He is almost certainly stepping into a Breton trap at Harcouët."

"But he knows tu expect this!" Budic stated.

"Gisela overheard this Bishop of Le Mans tell

Gundebold that the Margrave could be baited like a bull to a red cloth." He shook his head and clenched his fists around his stick before poking at the fire again. "They're absolutely right! The Lionrouge can be as reckless and terrifying as a bull if you stir him up, and let me assure you, my dear sister, they have stirred him up sufficiently to see red! If they try even more trickery, more goading, I'm concerned the Margrave's fascination with facing the death blow is exactly what this Le Mans matador wants in this case. If these Dux have become traitorous and also shown up, he may discover he faces three matadors!" Charles exclaimed angrily, breaking his stick and tossing it into the fire before standing up. "Oh, he'd just adore that. That's the kind of dire fighting the Margrave lives for!"

"And could die from," Gisela noticed she had been twirling a lock of Eulalie's hair the same way Charles had nervously taken out his frustration on the stick.

"And instead uf fighting by his side, we sit un a cold beach, with nu one tu fight."

"No one to fight but ourselves, apparently," Gisela rebuked her brother. "Have I caused all this?"

"No," Charles replied childishly, then breathed in, calmer. "No, Gisa, you have not."

"Did King Budic?"

"In a way."

Gisela was taken aback.

"I'm going to check the watch." Charles kicked at Cassyon, who had already stirred with all the loud talk of his Prince. "I'll go do something useful in place of worry." He paced off, Cassyon chasing away after him, pulling up his coif and putting on his helm and shouldering the great Breton horn.

Gisela looked at Budic, who smiled and toasted his cup to her.

"Tu brothers!"

"To brothers," she broke a half-smile and toasted, taking another sip. "Miam! Your mulled wine is simply delicious! It's sweeter than our Christmas vin chaud, and has some other flavor as well."

Budic nodded and looked at Daev's little kettle as he took a long gulp.

"Bretons add honey an' cider ta' their mulled wine," Daev admitted.

Gisela also thought it was a good bit stronger as well.

"Here, Gisela. I want yu tu have this."

"What is it?"

"A fork."

"It looks like a little silver fork for fairies."

"Well, yes. It is a Bretagne charm against kerrigan...fairies. Get it ut the next time yu think yu see one. Now, tell me abut yur brother Gisela! Tell me his story!" Budic requested as Daev refilled the King's cup.

Gisela looked away into the dark in the direction Charles had gone. "Charles is much like His Majesty. He loves to hunt, loves eating..."

"Nann, nann," Budic waved an arm like it was broken. "Tell me abut yur *other* brother."

"Carolman? He's younger than Charles, and remains in Aachen..."

"Nann, digarezit ac'hanun," Budic interrupted again, looking angry at himself. He crawled around the campfire with effort, full cup still in one hand, to be nearer Gisela and managed not to trample Eulalie's legs, spill hot wine or fall in the fire in the process. He finally sat back beside her with a big huff. "Nu, mun L'Ange. I have a brother with the Lord now tuu. Tell me abut this little brother uf yurs."

Gisela suddenly wasn't sure she was ready to talk about Pepin yet.

"Your Majesty requests a hurtful tale," she hid and bided time behind a long sip of mulled wine.

"Maybe we trade hurts and bandage une another. I gu first."

Gisela put her cup down, her other hand stroking Eulalie's red-brown hair softly.

"I had a great brother, his name was David de Poher. Uh, he was a gem uf Cornuaille and Vannetais and Dumnunée, a hero in the splendor uf all the Osimi, the Veneti and the Curiosolites. The deeds uf ur pius father had garnered the support uf the Holy Church and many uf the Kings uf the clans uf Brittany as well. These were the princely gifts the family bestowed upun David, since he was old enough tu ride a horse and slay a thief. Nut as tall as I, but he was thick, like me, with strong arms that culd wrestle a belon from it's piling. He culd eat his weight in biscuits and drink yur weight in ale and still dance. He had hair so lung he kept his loveliest maidens in it tu amuse him when bored un his travels. He's just take them ut, and let them sing and dance fur him, then stuff them back in quick-like when bears ur mermaids attacked!"

Daev laughed, and so did Gisela.

"He was destined tu be the Great King uf all Brittany, the King amongst all the uther clan Kings."

"How did he die?"

Budic, gently swaying, looked at the fire. The wrinkles beside his eyes suddenly grew deeper, his grinning cheeks flattening like a sheep gutted by a butcher.

"Fighting infidels. Heathens," he said in a guttural tone that added far more syllables than the word owned. "I watched him die, right in front of me. Helpless tu stop it. Unable tu hold ur comfort him ur lessen his pain. His every gasping last breaths made me, his brother, more and more the King, and I'd' have gladly traded everything I've ever own ur known tu take his place and let him live on."

Uncontrollable tears ran down Gisela's face, and she put a hand on Budic's arm.

"Somewhere amongst the firmament, God needed a mighty warrior angel in some grand battle against the Evil One tu take David as he did."

The campfire crackled. The brew pot puffed little clouds of aromatic steam out like an escaping genie.

"Whu was Pepin, L'Ange?"

Gisela paused and gathered her strength, aided by the mulled wine.

"Somewhere in the firmament, God needed a wondrous cherub to make him smile and remember the good things in the world. Pepin was a golden summer sunrise. His laughter was like the ducks on the Loire. He had eyes *so* blue. He could run like the wind in the trees and yet stumble over his own feet like a newborn calf in the fields, only to repeat both over and over all afternoon. He ran so fast...so fast I could not catch up to him."

Gisela paused, her eyes lost in some memory.

"That's the second time yu said yu culd nut catch Pepin."

Gisela's face broke.

"In Mur castle...our nursery...he ran towards the

window...after the fai...moths...chasing them...I saw him against the open window jumping for them...his feet going over the sill...inches from my fingers...those slippers..," she gulped out. Budic leaned over and gave her a hug.

"He had hated those belled slippers, oh, he hated them with a passion all spring long, then suddenly, they became his favorites. Mother had to forbid him to wear the slippers outside. His change in his love for those tinkling slipper bells was one of the clues....to my mistake." She leaned hard into Budic.

"The last look in your brother's eyes. Yu saw it in yur Pepin tuu, didn't yu?"

"He caught a grape cane as he fell out the window...a little nothing of a twig, a cruel thread of a hope...now I remember...seeing it peeling back...white and pretty off the vine branch..," she sobbed.

Even Daev had sat up by now, tears running down the poet's face in dual sympathies.

"...his arm was reaching out to mine as he fell further down...and away...and there was nothing...I...could...do...his blue eyes...I wanted to follow down after him...I caught my shoulder on the pergola..." She rubbed her shoulder's ghost.

The fire continued its pops, and the pot its wisps of steam. Gisela and Budic holding each other shook in mutual tears. Daev dropped his head. The fires' smoke rose and rose and twisted and danced and disappeared from the light against the gray clouds of night above.

Daev played a soft, melancholy tune on his flute as Budic and Gisela tapped their cups together in a toast to lost brothers for the fifth time.

"Budic! You said your brother David died fighting heathens? Was he no martyr? Why is he no saint? He deserves a whole day to honor him!"

"That he does! Have you heard uf the great Saint Turiaf?, L'Ange?"

Gisela blinked and then shook her head hard. "No! Was your brother Saint Turiaf?"

"Nu, nu, nu, nu!" Budic waved his free hand. "Saint Turiaf, nuw, HE was a great Bishop. Born in Vannes. A Bishop of Dol...right uver there, that way," Budic pointed back south in the night.

"To Dol!"

"Tu Dol," Budic toasted but didn't drink. "Well, yu see, Bishop Turiaf hears uf a lord amongst the Rennais people, a lord whose fame stories du tell terrible things abut, and he goes there tu chastise this lord into God's way. But when they hear the stories abut this lord, the Rennais say, nu! The pagan lord you seek is living amongst the Eux. Su Turiaf goes there. And when the Eux hear the stories, they say nu! It is amongst the Retz this wretched pagan lord dwells, and su Turiaf goes there. There are wretched pagan men indeed amongst the Retz, but nune such as in these tales, su the Retz say Nu! Gu find this evil, wretched pagan lord amongst the Nantais! *SU* Bishop Turiaf gues there. The Nantais hear the stories, and say, We've heard them tuu, but nut uf a Nantais lord but uf a lord uf the Vannetais! Gu there tu find this accursed, evil, wretched pagan lord. Su Turiaf goes tu the Vannetais. And he tells the tales, and the Vannetais say Nu!"

"NO!"

"Nu! This cruel, accursed, evil, wretched pagan lord lives nut amongst us, but amongst the Domnonée! Su

Bishop Turiaf goes tu the Domnonée. Now the wood's women of Domnonée can birth some vile children uf the Devil himself, it is said, but nune such as told in these tales, su the Domnonée say Nu!"

"NO!"

"It is nut amongst the Domnonée yu will find this vile, cruel, accursed, evil, wretched pagan man as a lord, but in Cornuaille! So yu know what good Bishop Turiaf does?"

"He goes to Cornouaille?"

"He goes tu Cornouaille! And yu know why?"

"Why?"

"Because tu root ut the Devil, there is nu place Bishop Turiaf will nut gu! Su he gues tu Cornuaille, and he finds this disreputable, cruel, accursed, evil, wretched pagan Lord in his castle, and he enters and steps right up tu his throne and pif! Strikes him square in the forehead with his crosier! Ut pops a demon and Turiaf banishes it in a flash of light! Right there before everyone, because such a trail uf believers had followed Turiaf there tu find this lord that nune could turn away from the sight."

"Goodness!"

"So this Cornuaille lord's name was Riwallon, after his grandfather, and he knew he had done great evil while under the spells uf this demon, su he fell down at the feet uf Bishop Turiaf and kissed the hem uf his cloak and begged forgiveness fur all his sins. But Bishop Turiaf was nut convinced that this lord would nut call the demon back after he left and return tu his old wicked ways, and he told lord Riwallon - fur seven weeks I have chased the stories uf thee, through seven kingdoms! If yu wish tu du just penance for yur evils, then I command yu, fur seven years yu must be

faithful tu God and the LORD and du good things!
And yu must du seven times the good as yu have
done evil tu erase the memory uf those in this land
who called Lord Riwallon the Wicked, such that they
call yu Lord Riwallon the Pious instead! If yu du this,
then and only then shall yu be forgiven uf yur evil
ways and receive the blessings uf the LORD! And
Riwallon did it! With God's help and by the Grace uf
our LORD for seven years he was moral,
compassionate, laudable, great pious Lord. And the
people saw him changed and called him a Great King,
and the stories uf his piety and the generosity uf his
deeds came even back tu Turiaf's ears in Dol, and after
seven years he came and forgave King Riwallon uf his
past and welcomed him intu the church of our
LORD."

"Oh, how wonderful a Christian tale!"

"And du yu know whu King Riwallon was? UR
father, David and I's." Budic thumped his chest and
then hammered his hand on the sand several times.
"He united the kingdoms uf Brittany under ur Lord
and Savior Jesus Christ, and passed that legacy down
tu King David, and then tu I."

"But how could your brother King David not be a
martyr if he passed from this earth fighting infidels?"

Budic sighed, his head and shoulders drooping, and
put his cup down. "Nuw it is yur turn tu ask fur a
hurtful tale. I dun't know uf I have the heart tu tell
this tale yet again this night," he said slowly.

"Sire?!" Daev exclaimed. "It is forbidden to speak of
it."

"Save royalty. She is a Princess. Frankish royalty.
An Empress to be. I shall nut hide my crimes frum her
any more than I wuld frum the LORD, and ask her

forgiveness in the same due measure. I grant yu the right tu hear frum my voice this tale."

Daev looked uncomfortable briefly, but sat upright as Budic began his tale.

"Du you know uf Archbishop Winfrid Boniface?"

"Well yes, of course. Everyone knows of Boniface. A good Christian missionary in Germany, well schooled in East Angles. He worked with my grandfather, coronated my father and my brothers Charles and Carloman..."

"The same...the same. Pope Gregory conferred upon him a pallium tu help him convert the Germans, Frisians, and Saxons over tu the Lord, and the Archbishop was a fearless campaigner against the heathens uf those lands."

"I've heard many the tale, with the Archbishop himself in our court to confirm them. His travels with Saint Willibrord, the felling of the Jupiter's Oak, the missions of the Irish priests in Frisia and Saxony."

"Then yu have the same memories as we," Budic fumblingly motioned to Gisela then himself. "Nuw Boniface discovered, through one of his new chieftan converts, the location uf a great pagan Irminsul in Bretagne, below Rennes, near Essé, in the Theil forest...*very near* yur Sipia fort!. The Irminsul, it is the symbol uf their pagan beliefs."

Gisela recoiled slightly when he mentioned the Irminsul. The Saxon boy had spoken of it. Saints spoke of it. Taliesin spoke of its magic. Her own fears about Pepin in the vine had been touched by it. The Saxon seemed to grow bolder in that area by Sipia, and then there were those vicious wolves.

"Su. More than a dozen years ago, King Adgillis uf the Frisians had died..."

"King Adgillis? He was a fierce opponent of Grandfather Martel's," Gisela remembered hearing the stories in Aachen.

"Indeed. Well, his son, Adgillis III was of a different mind, and a different soul as a convert tu the Lord. He helped Boniface convert many uf his Frisian clansmen tu the Lord, and he happened tu know the secret location uf varius Saxon Irminsul. Adgillis wished tu help Boniface find and destroy this pagan Irminsul in Brittany tu prove his new faith. Nuw naturally, Boniface considered it critical tu destroy this legendary pagan tree. Boniface's cutting down of the Jupiter Oak was a legendary inspiration. Everyone knew about it, and it had broken the Germanic people's hold un paganism. Archbishop Boniface thought he culd use that to help him do the same tu the Breton pagans that had plagued Saint Armel, and su bring more Bretons intu the Catholic church. Su Boniface proposed what he called a Croisière pilgrimage into the Theil Forest after this Irminsul, a strike into a pagan stronghold where they were said tu be sacrificing missionaries," he explained, taking another sip from his cup.

"Boniface was trained just across the Mor Breizh, your Gallicus Sea, in Exeter and Winchester, and was well-known tu ur father, who had donated more than once tu his monasteries. *Bishop Turiaf*, whom I just told yu uf saving my father, had been a student of Boniface before he came tu Dol. He answered Boniface's call fur a Croisière against the Bretagne pagan Irminsul. Many other great Bishops came tu Boniface's secret call fur a Croisière. The Bishops of Tréguier, Rennes and Saint Brieuc. Good Christian souls such as Bishop Eoban, Archbishop Lullus of

East Angles, back then just a Curé under Boniface,
Bishop Heardred uf the Angles, Abbot Gregory, all of
them joined Boniface's Croisière. With the Bishops
came strong men of Christ tu protect them. King
Aelfwald uf the Kingdom of the East Angles, his
comites Alberht and Beonna, and then uf curse my
brother David, King of Bretagne."

Gisela listened with intense focus. The mulled wine
was strong. "Why were Bretons working together
with Angles?"

Budic smiled for the first time in his story.
"Boniface was schooled in Angles! At the time, my
brother David was curting Miriam de Framling for
marriage. Her father is from the South Folk near
Gipeswic in Angle! Ah, David thught it perfect tu win
her father's favor and Angle lands in the process."

"But Daev told me Miriam is the Queen of Brittany.
Your Queen."

Budic nodded in agreement. "The secret Croisière
set ut tu the pagan Irminsul in Theil in the summer of
the year 749. After crossing the Mor Briezh they came
from Dol down tu Rennes and then entered the
forest."

"Why were there no Franks on this Croisière?"

"The Franks knew nothing uf this! Yur father was
Mayor uf King Childeric's palace and nut yet King
himself, and there wuld have been much argument
over things between your father and Archbishop
Boniface. The uld pagan Saxon King Theoderic had
been repeatedly captured AND released by yur
Franks. He was considered tuu friendly uf an enemy
for such secrets. Boniface had tu choose which side
wuld accomplish God's goal, and secrecy was needed
tu catch the pagan Saxons there."

"Now living in the greenwood of Theil was a future Saxon king named Widukind, a duke uf the forest, hidden away in Brittany frum yu Franks by the noble Saxons opposed to their own King Theoderic. And this Widukind enjoyed the support uf the Swedish and Danish Kings too. He and they didn't like these Irish Catholic priests stirring up truble, and oh how they hated Archbishop Boniface and yur father's campaign against their sacred sites. Widukind turned ut tu be only a yung man, preparing tu rule in uld Saxon King Theodreric's stead."

Gisela thought of the Saxon boy about that young age.

"Tu ur unfortunate surprise, Archbishop Boniface had been cleverly deceived. Frisian King Adgillis whu set all this up was nu true convert! The Frisians had been plotting with yur escaped uncle Grifo and his companion Tortulfe, tu lure yur father ut into the wilds with Boniface. They built a false Irminsul in Essé in the Theil forest, erected just tu fool Boniface's spies and lure him, yur father and Widukind there. Can yu believe that?! Adgillis had created a devilish plan tu have his Christian irritants and the yung Saxon leader all kill each other uff, leaving him tu rule both the Frisian and Saxon lands afterward. When the Croisière warriors arrived in Essé, the Frisians turned un all sides and simply retreated. The Saxon pagan's fught bitterly against us and the Frisians. Their arrows were as deadly bee's frum every side uf the forest. Bishop Turiaf was struck, as was King Aelfwald, as well as Miriam's father. My humble self, I was my brother's page and was ordered by my brother David tu gu with the Comties and protect Boniface. We fell back with the Archbishop and Bishop Heardred all the way tu Rennes, and once they were safe, then we returned tu help my brother."

Budic drank a sip himself and made the sign of the cross. Gisela and Daev did the same.

"What we found when we returned..," Budic started, and stopped, and drank again before surrendering to his tears and laid back on the sand, looking up at the smoke.

"What the' found..," Daev continued for his King, "...was th' Saxon pagans had captured all those who weren' slain, an taken them ta tha' false Irminsul. There th' surviving Croisière members had been sacrificed. Burned alive on crosses they were. Kings, priests, soldiers. It must ha' been a terrible sight ta behold, but it was even worse for Budic. His brother ha' lingered, not dying. He was a charred corpse that spoke still, else Budic would not have even recognized his burned body. Poor Budic could not get him down, for when he even touched his poor brother, his body fell ta pieces instead, yet neither would the poor man die. Finally, after begging him fer an eternity, Budic gave into his brother's request an' relieved his brother's pain."

"With the same stroke, I ended my brother's reign and sadly began mine. I was all of nine years old," Budic confessed, still laying down and looking up.

"Why is this great martyrdom not revered in every Mass?" Gisela begged, teary-eyed.

"Pride. Pope Zachary issued a rescript tu Boniface's petition tu have the failed Croisière sanctified," Budic replied. "It was an ignominious defeat fur Archbishop Boniface. And the Pope. And the fledgling church presence in Brittany. We had all offended God somehow, fur despite ur fervent prayers HE was nut with us in the forest that day. Nuthing was gained, the Christians had been made tu appear as fools, and the young Saxon king as well, while new King Adgillis wuld become the popular symbol uf the pagan tribes. Nu one wanted it known, such a loss tu the pagans, such a failure uf a sweeping Croisière un the name of the LORD, the deaths uf su many good men. The Danes, the Swedes, the Jutes, Saracens, the Magyar, even Byzantium itself would relish exactly such a failure that revealed weakness at a time when the church and the Franks and the Angles did nut need more enemies, ur stronger ones. They became simply missionaries whu died in Brittany. Great men, reduced tu nameless martyrs."

Budic and Daev both made the sign of the cross again. Gisela did so slowly.

"Your uncle Grifo escaped, as did the Young Saxon Widukind. Yur father, the Franks, never knew till afterward. Boniface told us the Pope declared in a rescript that the failed Croisière nut tu ever be mentioned, and fur all uf us tu pray un ur part in the failure."

"Why tell me this? I sorrow with you for your brother David as I do my own brother Pepin, good Budic, but why tell me of this?"

Budic sat up. "Because yu need tu know everything, Empress. The evil King Adgillis uf the Frisians? False convert whu tricked Boniface and my uwn brother?" Budic asked. "After his victory, he changed his name tu became known as King Gundebold."

"My...our..," Gisela tried hard to understand. "Are you saying our invading Frisian King Gundebold right now is this same false convert King Adgillis from your story? They are the same?"

"King Gundebold uf the rebellion right here and right nuw was King Adgillis that tricked us intu fighting the Saxons at Essé twelve years agu. The same man yu saw, returned here after all the years. He, tu, won't just die."

"Gundebold's not just looking for a new home. He's looking for retribution," said Charles, walking back into the camp out of the dark with scouts and soldiers. "Gundebold chose the Marche because he can drive a wedge between the Franks and Bretons in the same stroke. What power he lost in Frisia to his own son, the old kook now seeks to regain at the site of his greatest unheralded victory."

"He's still playing everyone, I swear it. I'd wager a new monastery his eel-boat fleet was funded by Jutes and that he raided along the Angle coast un their way tu Tombe," Budic insisted.

"Brother, you cannot be angry at King Budic for this," Gisela demanded, standing up to him.

Charles's men began quickly packing up the camp.

"I'd have preferred to know this before we left Avranches. We already feared the Margrave was walking into a trap. Knowing the Frisians were proven to be willing to sacrifice their own Breton and Frank allies to do their battles for them and gain an upper hand in the end, would have been timely advice. Something the Margrave should have been told."

Budic looked hurt, and struggled to get up with the breaking camp.

"Father kept this failed Croisière from you for a dozen years. Budic kept it from you for a dozen hours, and has taken every risky step right alongside you. Make certain your anger isn't misplaced, Karl!"

Charles looked hard at his sister. The mulled wine had given her a royal courage.

"du Du," Budic said as Daev and Gisela helped him up onto his feet.

"What?" Charles demanded.

"Du Du," Budic repeated again, staggering a bit.

"Black November," Daev translated for his King.

Charles sighed. "Rains are coming from the north. Get everyone on the ship."

Shipwrecked

Charles and his scouts and soldiers made their way across the sand by blue lantern-light, Budic followed, carrying Gisela, and Daev beside him, carrying the sleeping Eulalie. Onboard, the Captain was awake, and the sailors had been anticipating the coming rain as well, for the round-tent and hide covered oars had grown larger over the deck.

Budic cut himself several strips off a corned beef and handed some to Daev and Gisela as well.

"Roast?" Gisela asked as Daev began eating.

"Eat meat ur be beat un the 'morrow, L'Ange. It is the way after drinking."

The round-tent began popping gently here and there, and an odd dull silence crept across the rocks and sand towards them, sounding like one long low wave that never broke. The popping on the tent became a teasing patter, and the smell of the sea air was fresh and crisp. The harder rain came like an advancing wall, and the noise of it fell above them and plopped beside them in cold drops and thin streams.

They ate in verbal silence and fell asleep in a jumbled pile on the ship; seventy cramped bodies attempting to remain warm and dry on the ship as the tide slowly crept its way in.

The sky over the ocean was a dull glow on the east, and dull was the way Gisela felt. Gisela was tired, and sick, but not. Amona's big bicep was on her ear, she was against the ring maiden's bosom, and Eulalie's foot was in her ribs, and all of them were covered by Lady Ogiva's bearskin cloak. She pulled it off her face, almost painfully. There was a booming in her ears, growing louder, and the noise made her head spin.

The sound of breakers growing closer had already awoken many. Now, with the oar-hides coming down everywhere but the round-tent on the ship, the wet and cold added itself to the sea breakers and busy sailors to awaken any who remained asleep.

Gisela got up with Amona and looked about. The tide was already washing over the sands she had crossed last night, but it was not yet floating the ship. She looked over the side, the rain dripping, the seaweed a watery tumble to wash the belly of the wooden ship like a morning sponge.

She thought she might throw up onto the sand and thin waves below.

"How are you Gisa?" Charles asked, coming to pull her farther from the gunwale and farther out of the sailors way as they prepared to remove the bracing oars.

"Like the bear that is missing my cloak. Cold and grumpy. My mouth tastes like I've been eating raw fish."

Charles let out a half chuckle as the Captain lit the remaining ship's lanterns. "This is the morning trouble with drinking."

Sister Amona got busy cooking again at the edge of the bow-tent, and even the old Captain was growing hesitant to get in her way. Gisela looked at the last sleeping man and realized it was Wido. His eyes were closed, and he was breathing.

"He got back color, a little maybe. Best let him be," Amona advised.

The ring maiden was bringing pumpkin seed oatcakes from the chest Lady Ogiva had them prepare in the bow. Gisela wanted water, but the maiden wouldn't give her any yet.

"Trust me, your Highness. Eat the oats first," the maid urged, and returned to the bow. Gisela sat down next to Charles.

"I was told...interesting stories last night. You seem to have been told them too, am I remembering that correctly?"

"Yes," Charles nodded, eating some kind of cabbage pottage in the half-light with her.

"Are you still angry?"

Charles chewed and thought for a moment. "Gisa, you'll need to understand that wars are either fought by men who conduct themselves as gentlemen, or by men who conduct themselves as brutal tyrants."

"What difference does it make to those they fight?"

"All the difference. This Frisian is a brute."

"So we don't trust him. How has King Budic conducted himself?"

"As a gentleman."

"Yet you still don't trust him?"

Charles shrugged. "I'm not certain I trust his people."

"You can still put trust in the man, if not his people."

"That is risky."

Gisela looked over at the bow and King Budic. "He trusts his people, and his people trust him enough to let him talk to us. He is putting himself at risk and starting to bleed followers just for talking to Franks about all of us coming together for the good of Christ. He's trusting his family and the church and his father and brother's history to make the right choices."

"Many of his people won't like that idea. Enough to fight."

Gisela shrugged herself after another bite. "So will some Franks. We can build on the faith and trust we have together in the Lord to start something besides a war."

Charles wiped the crumbs off her cheek. "You're getting quite full of yourself, Empress."

Gisela wiped her already clean cheek with the back of her fingers after Charles had and looked at Budic again. "He was thrust from dreams and playing games to being a King as a child. So have I been, grown different, closer to God from this experience."

"It's not as pleasant and carefree as childhood, is it?"

"No, but ask Paul. The Lord's way is rarely a smooth sea."

Charles sighed and rubbed her head before standing up and stepping away.

The ring maiden brought her a cup of liquid that didn't look or smell like water.

"And they gave me gall for my meat and vinegar to drink," Gisela mumbled.

"It's a bryndon, and it's not that bad," the ring maiden replied, going back to the bow chest.

Gisela drank the cup down, the wet cake and all. It reminded her of the taste of last night. The ring-maid returned with a Flemish box under her arm and sat down behind Gisela, pulling the bearskin blanket up behind her as well.

Eulalie came and sat down beside Gisela and the

maiden.

"What's your name?" Eulalie asked the maiden.

The maiden reached over Gisela's shoulder to put her ring against Gisela's ring from Lady Ogiva; the rings that bound them together in some trivial way that seemed to please the great Lady.

"My name is Copar," she answered, then shifted Gisela around in front of her to tend to her hair and veil.

"How long have you been a maiden of Gisela's?"

Copar laughed under her veil. "Let's see...one day. I was sent by My Lady to tend Her Highness on this voyage."

Gisela turned to ask Copar a question, but the maid scoldingly turned her back around by her hair. Gisela asked anyways. "How long have you been a servant of Lady Ogiva?"

"Oh, since before I was your age. I was a child in Boos when the Lady was still a maid herself."

"My Duende!" Amona came and sat with them, hugging Gisela with one arm and then finally eating for herself. "You save us all yesterday."

"God saved us, Sister."

"Well, you good messenger for God then."

"I like your dress," Eulalie said.

Gisela beamed. "It is pretty." She showed more of it from under her bear cloak. "I adore nacré." Then she looked up again and realized Eulalie was stroking the exposed hem of the ring maiden's linen dress.

Copar stopped working Gisela's hair and looked long at Eulalie. "You are most gracious, Eulalie."

The boat shifted slightly on the first big wave of the incoming tide, and everybody caught themselves with a mix of fear and giggles.

"Hard to eat boats," Amona observed, scooping her pottage in her mouth faster.

Eulalie was looking in the Flemish box, it's small lid open like a miniature treasure chest to her. Gisela touched Copar's knee to share in the sight.

"What is that?" Eulalie asked.

"That is a hair stick," Copar answered.

"They look like magic wands."

"Can you hand that barrette to me? The one with the cloth horses on it."

Eulalie picked it out carefully from the box of combs and leather strings and tassels and pins like she was playing pixie sticks.

"Do you want to help me?" Copar asked, opening up the bear blanket with one arm for her to join them. Eulalie grinned and crawled under.

"Amona?" Gisela asked.

"Yes?"

"Where is Sacha?"

Amona stopped her eating and put the bowl down. "We hope he was with you."

"What?"

Amona sighed. "Maylis..."

"Comb that lock there for me Eulalie. Careful, it's got a tangle."

Maylis got up and came over to them as if she'd just been invited into a Royal court.

"Tell Duende about Sacha."

The happy smile on Maylis' face disappeared. Her courtly invite suddenly became a court, and she looked like she felt was being judged. She sighed and kneeled beside Gisela, who offered the open bearskin in comfort and sympathy.

Maylis pulled it up around her to join them. "After

you rode off, we got everyone who would come back up to the monastery. We couldn't find him. Then several of the women who had fled to the bottom of the island said they saw a young boy run out into the sands after you rode by."

"Clip that twist there, dear...there. Perfect. We want to lift it up."

Amona slid in under the bearskin court as well. "We check, Duende. Footprint follow hoofprint out into the rising tide."

Gisela looked sick again.

"I sorry Duende. No one know he did it."

"I don't remember a boy following you into the castle," Copar asked from behind her.

"He didn't. He couldn't have, not on foot, with that tide coming in." Gisela's eyes began watering. Eulalie hugged her back and Maylis her front. Copar hugged her as well when she realized this Sacha was obviously important to her.

"Oh Sacha, why did you follow me?"

Copar lifted the veil around Gisela's head again and crowned her with an obsidian gemmed ferronnière.

"Maybe he along shore there now."

"Do you think?"

Everyone agreed and seemed hopeful, and Gisela decided it might be more for her benefit than any real hope.

The boat shifted again, catching fewer people off guard this time. Several sailors began working the braces off the sand and sides. Properly veiled, Gisela moved with the shifting ship to turn under the blanket to face Eulalie. After a momentary eyebrow of disbelief at Gisela, Copar turned Eulalie around, and they began brushing and braiding Eulalie's hair.

Gisela reached into the box and handed a few bows to Amona. Maylis turned to face opposite of Eulalie, and Amona started braiding Maylis' hair.

As the tide rose the ship and the sailors got it underway, they all chatted under one edge of the round-tent, out of the rain, tucked into bear skins and blankets. The women talked of the prison chain, and Eulalie's father, and where he might be, and how they might find him again, and how much Eulalie missed him. They talked of Maylis' father and step-mother, and how she had not seen her or her baby half-brother since the Fougères vineyard prison.

Gisela sighed. She was becoming a Royal. These were *her* women, and she felt a responsibility growing in her for them and their families that had never existed in her life before.

The Captain was atop the mast, sporting a straw hat with a brim so wide Gisela thought it could keep two or three people dry in a pinch. His whip cracked more infrequently now as the oars dipped and swept in a steady unison. In the rain, the sunrise left little to see or feel, and the passing roof of the village church off the opposite side of the ship seemed just as cold-natured. They passed between a promontory of the Kankaven and two small rocky islands and turned north, and the wind and cold grew in direct proportion to their distance along the Grouin Pointe.

The Pointe consisted of long, thin gray islands of rock, and the ship passed between them with seeming practiced precision. The rocks themselves looked like city walls to Gisela, the tidal lines as distinct in color as if painted. White on the lower cliff edge, yellow middle, darker gray-brown higher up. Long rocky fingers of the hand of Kankaven digging through the sand out into the sea.

Gisela showed her flat hand to Budic, as he had done last night, and pointed to her thumb and the rocky point. Budic smiled and tapped his index finger instead of his thumb, and Gisela seemed pleased in her understanding and their progress.

The ship rounded the Pointe a good distance and turned a hard left, a maneuver both the Captain and the waves seemed to take quite seriously, and almost immediately the oars rose up and were stored again on the oar-deck and recovered by the black hides. Irrespective of tired arms and backs, the sailors unfurled the sail down off the yard as the Captain came back down himself. They hoisted up the livered triangle foresail with great abandon and energy, the multitude of ropes strung about plucking and singing in response. The cold wind they had fought so hard for an hour now drove the ship west south-west along the coast at a speed that pleased everyone, though the more frequent sprays off the bow did not. Under the round-tent Gisela looked back and forth from the Captain on the rudder board behind her, the old man almost motionless save for a slight swaying, to the Breton sailors in front of her, who all crab-walked left and right in unison across the whole deck and oar-deck like some formal court dance with every changing wave side. They seemed to steer the boat on the tops of waves more with subtle pulls on tight ropes than the old Captain ever did with the steering oar, and Gisela decided the mysteries of ships was both wondrous and terribly confusing.

With the increasing cold, the rain began to freeze, and flakes flew, washing the sky darker and making the shoreline a mix of green and gray watercolors. The period of the waves grew longer, and the sway of the ship running oblique along them took a decidedly horse-like if slow, canter. It was an enjoyable sensation to Gisela, though Eulalie and Amona did not find it as agreeable. Gisela tried to get Budic to dance amongst the sailors, and the two tried their best to snake and spin on the rocking boat in the table-sized space they had to move. Daev began singing to their impromptu dance, and several sailors joined him.

"Ha! A kan ha diskan!" Budic called out and began singing with the sailors, trading off lyrics with Daev, lyrics going back and forth between them and then all voices joining together every few lines, only to separate and do it again. Several sailors danced together with Gisela and Budic, but none of the rescued women would try to dance with them save Maylis. Gisela danced, not knowing the words they were singing, but picking up on the repeated ones enough to sing along to her own satisfaction. It was a similar song, yet a far different feel, to the prison songs she had tried to learn. The festivities only stopped when the Captain sent his whip cracking to get his crew's attention back on sailing and not, what he was calling, a 'fest-noz'.

The sailors returned to their crab walking vigil over the waves, but Daev, not being part of his crew, began singing a Breton gwerz, and instead of dancing, everyone else just listened to his enchanting voice. He had a knack for timing the waves to be some base rhythm to his song, and with the snow and the ship drifting along with the wind the flakes seemed to occasionally hover around them. Gisela then begged for a hymn, and Bishop Cadocanan finally relented, and he, Budic and Daev sang a hymn that made Gisela teary-eyed, and she didn't even know all the Breton words.

Finally, Amona asked for a Psalm that everyone could sing. Gisela and the Bishop decided on Psalm 128, and as they sang the first tones and motioned with their hands to indicate pitch and rhythm, something the Bishop referred to as chironomy, almost everyone on board joined in. Even Charles in his ill mood sang with them.

"Blessed are all they that fear the Lord: that walk in his ways.

For thou shalt eat the labours of thy hands: blessed art thou, and it shall be well with thee.

Thy wife as a fruitful vine, on the sides of thy house. Thy children as olive plants, round about thy table.

Behold, thus shall the man be blessed that feareth the Lord.

May the Lord bless thee out of Zion: and mayest thou see the good things of Jerusalem all the days of thy life.

And mayest thou see thy children's children, peace upon Israel."

Daev asked Charles for the Breton horn, and Charles agreed. Daev put it to his lips and let out a huge blast that seemed to call up the snow furiously. Twice more he blew the great horn, and before he put it down the echos off the distant coastline fought back against the wind and subtly returned one, after the other, after the other.

Charles moved to the stern and seemed fixed on the echoes of the passing rocks and islands, as if they were sirens to him alone.

The ship began making odd noises, and Gisela asked Budic if it was the iroko wood spirits he had talked about. It was like birds with crickets and purring kittens. It grew louder until no one had trouble hearing it on deck, and then the sea around them erupted with whitecaps and dark forms.

Charles called them dolphins, some of the sailors called them blackfish, but the Captain told Budic they were pilot whales. It was a massive herd to Gisela, with hundreds around them chasing some fish or shrimp she couldn't see. For many minutes the ship floated along amidst the whale herd, wrapped in the odd noises and the wash of the waves, the quiet snowflakes and the creaking of the ship's timbers in the wind, and Amona swore Daev was the greatest water-shepherd calling in the flock that she had ever met.

The whales went their separate ways, and the ship continued on, passing a point called Meinga. The snow began to decrease and the skies to lighten, and the cold became sharper. Wido had awoken with the horn blasts and was able to lift himself to his elbows. Gisela helped Amona feed him more broth, and had Copar and Eulalie bath him and comb his hair.

They passed more rocky islands and turned southwest, the sail and foresail now stretched out on both opposite sides of the mast, the ship running along in the same direction as the waves in a pause and slide motion, and to Gisela, it felt like the wind had died, though the sails stayed full.

The snow flurries lessened, and the Captain alerted Budic to approaching ships ahead. Budic and Charles took an interest in what could be seen, and went to the bow to get a better view. The sailors told Budic it was two galleys being rowed, and the scouts told Charles the galleys flew Breton banners.

On the bow gunwale, Budic held onto the forestay to maintain his balance in the waves. "It is Moruuan's father, Comes Hoel, ut tu greet us frum Aleth! I'm sure uf it!"

Bishop Cadocanan came in staggers and stood on his tiptoes, clinging to Budic over the tops of the rolls to try to see as much as the big king. "I recognize those as our berlin galleys of Aleth! They did not come patrolling out this far on their own. Moruuan must have arrived and let them know to expect us."

"If this is a trap of rebellious Bretons, will we be able to outmaneuver their liburnas?" Charles asked Budic.

"One yes, two..," Budic shrugged his shoulders. "...they can rake ur oars. With this wind and the waves we can keep them frum boarding us easily enough, but uf they have arrows they can rain them un us till we are all dead ur swimming."

"There's no place to hide!" Charles yelled at the ship deck, racing from nook to cranny, looking around and shoving aside anything in his way such that the sailors had to both avoid running into him and repack their carefully stowed ship's gear. "My inheritance for a pavesade! Can we use the oars and hides to make a hasty wall here in oar racks of the middle of the ship? Can we make a run for the beach?"

The Bishop swapped his grip over to Charles as he left the bow, a firm hand on his shoulders. "Prince, have faith. I am convinced that is Abax Maguno, of my own church, there on the prow's corvus!"

The Bishop's priest's presence on the approaching galleys notwithstanding, Charles made his soldier bodyguards and scouts ready and cleared more places underneath the oar rack where the women and children could hide if he were right.

The Aleth galleys stayed together instead of splitting up, and they were on a parallel course to pass on their downwind side, tactics Budic and the Captain both seemed to regard as friendly. In the distance, the sun peeked a weak eye through the many layers of clouds and snow showers for a moment to cast a bright glow upon a patch of the distant sands and water of the shoreline.

As they passed to the leeward, the galleys turned together, and the priest on the closest galley began waving as the ship approached. No soldiers looked armed, no bows were being drawn. The large number of rowers still disturbed Charles, but the Captain ordered the foresail lowered to reduce their speed. Gisela found it odd that Charles' bodyguards and scouts were hunched down behind the sides and cover while everybody else on all three ships were standing up and calm. Finally, the closest galley came over a wave close enough yell back and forth, or shoot accurate arrows.

"Bishop! We are overjoyed to have you return early, and saddened by the news of our rebellious brethren and your abandoned pilgrimage!" yelled out the priest from the galley. Daev translated the Breton calls for Charles and Gisela, and whomever else might be close and listening.

"Abax! The needs of the Lord make clear our path!" the Bishop yelled back over the water and his face beamed in relief. "See, Prince?"

"I see your welcoming. I see no ambassadors for me."

"Because you already have me on board," Budic's voice was flat and matter of fact.

"Brenin Budic! I bring welcoming from the Comes of Aleth! Pemmaeth Moruuan arrived at this dawn with news of your coming and the woes in your wake!" one of the galley captains called out.

"We must make haste! Already the battle may be at hand!" Budic called back.

"The Pemmaeth anticipated your need for haste. We've extra rowers aboard to make your dockage more swift. Will you allow them to board and row with you?"

Budic looked at Charles as Daev translated the request, and he recognized Charles unease. "If they remain unarmed, then yes!" Budic responded back before Charles could deny the request.

"I wanted to be consulted, Budic!" Charles spat out, almost at a panic.

"All this past month, were your words and ur common trust fur naught? Did we nut hunt and dine and talk together as allies? Did I nut sign yur charter?" Budic retorted. "I cannot swear what other men shall do, but I will swear before God and his Bishop here un this very deck that I will face whatever you face, alongside you!"

The Captain ordered the sailors to turn the ship into the wind, and the mainsail sheets were let out to be reefed. They slowed, drifting into a turn and one of the galleys rowed to come alongside.

The corvus dropped onto the gunwale of the balinger and, despite the waves, a score of unarmed sailors made their way smartly across. All knelt and scraped in honor and reverence past Budic, the Bishop and Charles before helping extend the oars and taking a place beside the ship's sailors to row.

"The boarding dock rises, Karl," Gisela advised

quietly to her brother, trying to be helpful now that the danger was passed.

The galley and the ship separated again, and the rowing began in earnest for all three vessels. They turned back with the wind, and the snow spotted coastline leading to Aleth drifted past and grew larger ahead.

The Captain once again climbed up into the masthead. The green tide of the Rance Bay was increasing, slowly hiding yet more rocky islands off yet another gray bouldered promontory. The teeth of this Breton coast seemed as endless as a shark's mouth. Gisela tugged on Budic's arm and pointed to her pinkie finger. He laughed, nodding, and pointed to his pinkie finger in agreement. They had come all the way around the hand of Kankaven.

"Are one of those islands the Monastery of Saint Aaron?" Gisela asked.

"No, those are the Bè. There, the monastery of Saint Aaron is on Cézembre!" pointed the Bishop to a huge island a couple of miles away to the north over the sea.

The turbulence of the driving waves diminished significantly once they rounded the promontory and entered the quieter bay. The strong tide still looked as dangerous as the tall waves had been to Gisela.

Safely behind the barrier of rocks and promontory along the sea, tucked up in the estuary of the Rance, was a peninsula with a fortress with banners flying and a village flanked by beaches filled with tiny fishing boats pulled up far from the surf.

"Aleth!" introduced Budic with wide open arms.

The galleys flanked the ship as they came around the fortress. They had to stay farther apart, for the tidal eddies grew strong, and the shallows rose and fell in the same treacherous way they did by Tombe.

The Captain yelled down, and Budic nodded.

"We're going arund tu the uld Roman port. There are nausts there that will allow us tu get closer to shore," Budic advised.

Gisela's face scrunched up. "Nausts?"

"Um," Budic bit his tongue. "Ah, boat-huses."

"Dry docks," Daev added.

Gisela nodded in understanding. "Look, Brother! People are gathering on the point there!"

"And troops," Charles noted.

"They seem welcoming, Brother."

"So was Brutus."

"Brutus was accidentally stabbed himself by his fellow conspirators in the assassination uf Caesar. Su shall it be with me if this gues ill," Budic pledged.

Gisela laughed. "I didn't know you knew such history."

"Rome is both a shoal and a sail of the Breton's past."

A paved road flowed all the way down from the village and fort out onto the sands like a sinking stone quay. Several boats were obviously ready on the sands of the tide, and four more ships, not as big as their balinger, seemed to be waiting at moorings in the deeper water of Aleth's sheltered bay.

"There, there is Moruuan!" Budic called out, obviously relaxing more himself at the sight.

"He is with a military escort," noticed Charles. "Is that his father with him?"

"I think so."

They drew closer to the edge of the shallow sands, and the Captain had them moor the balinger to two great columns as rowboats came out across the water.

Charles, his soldiers, Budic and his guards, Gisela, Copar and the Bishop all entered the boats and were rowed the short distance ashore. The snowflakes drifted by in the lightest of flurries, like ashes.

"That's not the Comes," the Bishop told Gisela in their rowboat. "That is Moruuan's half-uncle, Dominus Arastang, sent down to greet your brother. I didn't know he had come up to join his brother. Moruuan's father Hoel must be as suspicious of a trap as Prince Charles."

The soldiers at the water's edge came to attention in unison as the rowboats ground up onto the sand. Sailors and dockhands drew them up entirely and helped the passengers off onto the wet sand and smooth paving stones.

Budic walked beside Charles, their soldiers and bodyguards surrounding them. Bishop Cadocanan picked up Gisela in his arms and carried her to the paving stones of the quay himself.

Budic nodded to Moruuan, who nodded back.

"Aleth welcomes you home, Bishop Cadocanan," the man the Bishop had called Arastang announced. "We regret your pilgrimage will be delayed."

Gisela thought the man didn't look like Moruuan. He was far older, and far shorter, and far more richly dressed.

"Servants of the Lord and Aleth have to remain loyal and ever at the ready," the Bishop answered.

"Brenin Budic, we are honored by your unexpected return. The fortress of Aleth is at your service, and already prepares itself against this rebellion, with our thanks to you for the fair warning."

"Arastang," Budic replied. "I'd have thought Comes Hoel himself wuld have come down tu greet the

Prince uf the Franks."

"My brother is across the Mor Breizh with Brenin Cawrdolli, helping fight the Mercian Bretwalda Offa along the Tamar."

"Oh?" Budic's head twisted, and his shoulders flinched back, his eyes narrowing. "I had nut heard that."

"So, my nephew Moruuan spoke truthfully." Arastang took a step up and looked over Charles carefully. "A Frank without an army, and the Prince himself no less. I am Hoel's brother Arastang, Dominus of Aleth in his absence." The rich uncle bowed nicely.

"Prince Charles of the Franks, good Mayor." Charles stepped forward himself, only his head bowing.

"Very good. Put the Prince and his soldiers under house arrest, and escort them to Oreigle Tower," Arastang ordered in a voice that sounded final. "Shoot anyone who resists."

The sound of swords being drawn and shields coming up almost drowned out the various cries of dismay. Not only from the suspicious Charles, but Budic himself, the women back on the boat, and even the crowd of villagers come to receive the Prince of the Franks, all voiced surprise. The sound of Arastang's archer's drawn bowstrings in response punctuated the tension.

"Uncle!" Moruuan angrily drew his sword against his uncle only to have Aleth soldier's bill blades on their long poles arrayed against him as well.

"Arastang! How dare yu!" Budic yelled, pointing his huge sword at the unflinching man.

"How dare *you* bring a Frank overlord to Aleth on

the lips of such news as a war against their Margrave!!! But you are not under arrest here, Budic, only the Franks."

"What you do tu Charles you du tu all Bretons, and thus me, little man."

"So be it. Take Brenin Budic as well," Arastang commanded with a wave of his fingers.

"Dominus! I beg of you, in the name of the Lord, think about what you are doing!" the Bishop begged, his arms back around Gisela protectively. Copar stepped in front of them both.

"I am thinking, your Eminence, in the scant few hours I've been given to react. I intend to get to the bottom of all these rumors of war and rebellion, for the good of Aleth, before I decide what is the best course of action. I'll first question the crew of this ship, and then question the Prince until I'm satisfied I know the whole truth that arrives upon my brother's city like a sudden storm," Arastang demanded, and the sheer number of soldiers around them guaranteed he would have his way or their many deaths. He looked past Copar and directly at Gisela, then back at Moruuan.

"Is that the little girl you spoke of, woven through all these tales?"

Moruuan, bills so near his throat his breath left vapors ghosting across the shiny blades, would not back down in spirit, even if he had to surrender in body. "I claim the Princes Gisela under my protection and the house of my father, the Comes, Uncle. You will have to slay me in front of all Aleth before you touch her!"

Groans and calls from the crowd created a palpable dissent against Arastang if he drew their favorite son's blood, particularly over protecting an innocent young girl.

"Very well. If she leaves the fortress, both your freedoms are forfeit. Take them all away." He walked past Budic and Charles towards their ship as if they were jesters and not armed, dangerous men.

The wind blowing past them, Charles resheathed his kilij and ordered his men to do the same. Budic was of a far different temperament, their fear and patience seemingly exchanged.

"BRENIN!" yelled out Moruuan, and that was the only thing that stopped Budic in his tracks. "There'll be a bloodbath of innocents over these stones if you do," Moruuan warned his King, and the closing Aleth soldiers eclipsed the moment.

Gisela saw them escort her brother and Budic up the ramp to an odd little turret tower right by the harbor, but she, under the protective arm of the Bishop and along with a bitterly complaining Moruuan, was escorted up the hillside to the motte walled fortress.

The main gate was locked tight, but the soldiers took them through a postern gate into the fortress and the protected portion of the Aleth village. Away from his uncle Arastang, Moruuan was once again treated like the royalty he was. He seemed to make certain soldiers, guards and staff realize his great displeasure, and they got out of his way. Many, but not all the harbor's crowd, followed them up the narrow village streets. Buildings of random stone blocks, each wall straight but out of parallel with every other house, were decorated with blue shutters and doors. As they passed a church, a number of the priests gathered outside on the porch made a hasty retreat inside while two began following the soldiers and praying aloud.

The parade passed up alleys and roads still draining wet from the morning's rain; the air may have grown cold enough for flurries, but the ground had not yet refrozen. Past cedar and yew trees they came to the donjon tower of the fortress, gated and walled off along with the stable and forge. Walls within walls.

An older woman came running out of the donjon into the soldiers and threw her arms around Moruuan.

"Mother, what is going on? Has my uncle lost his mind?"

They were escorted inside but then left alone by the guards. Moruuan introduced his mother Janig and little brother Enoch, and the poor woman nearly hemorrhaged when she discovered Gisela was a Princess of the Franks under house arrest. Moruuan came to Gisela and knelt, almost apologetically.

"Princess, you must *stay here*. My Uncle is serious about his threats if you try to leave. There are bigger forces at work here, that much I understand since our arrival this morning, but this, this arresting and questioning business, I must talk to my father's Captains. They remain loyal to my house, and they can perhaps explain his mood. For now, though, remain safe here in our house."

Janig, Moruuan's mother, showed Gisela and Copar to the sewing tables in the main hall where they were given relative freedom. Copar consoled Gisela as the Bishop tried to talk to her.

"Listen to me, Your Highness. I must go to my church and try to decipher what is going on here. Don't do anything foolish or make a deadly mistake."

"You could play a melody on the bowstrings here, everyone is so uptight," Moruuan added, standing up.

"Will they hurt Charles?"

The Bishop lowered his head to look at her. "I pray to God they don't, Your Highness."

"They might, and will, if he provokes them," Moruuan replied before stepping away.

"Charles, provoke a fight? Have you met my brother?"

"Yes, and well enough to know he will be smartly patient till an opportunity arises, and so should you be! Trust in God!" The Bishop put his hand on her shoulder and left the warm hall and donjon after Moruuan.

So Gisela sat amongst the looms, on a bench where her feet could not touch the floor, under the arm and reassurances of a maiden she had known for a day, overlooked by the wife of her new prison warden, who brought yet more food Gisela didn't want to eat, and yet more milk Gisela didn't want to drink, while she worried about the Margrave and Avranches.

It was over an hour before the Bishop returned with swift steps, and two priests trailing. Gisela hopped off the loom bench.

"Your Highness, where to begin?" Cadocanan blurted out.

"Is Charles injured?"

"No, Your Highness..."

"Praise be to the Lord," one of the priests mumbled.

"Then begin with the ship, your Eminence."

Bishop Cadocanan nodded and caught his thoughts with a breath. He talked with his hands in such a bold way that Gisela wanted to see him at the lectern in a sermon.

"Arastang questioned everyone on the boat; the Captain, the women and children, the sailors, and

Wido."

"Did he mistreat Wido?"

"No, he was able to see Wido was clearly in a bad way, and listened to our pleas not to put him in the tower with the others..."

"Praise be to the Lord," the other priest exclaimed.

"...but if Wido leaves the ship, he'll be hung. Arastang talked to him almost the longest. He even respectfully put the bear blanket over Wido himself by the end of their conversation. Wido's fluent Frisian and story were terribly convincing."

"Almost? Then who'd he talk to the longest?"

"The Nun Amona. When he discovered she had been in the General's Camp at the Fougères siege with you, and again at Tombe, he absorbed her whole story like a sponge."

"Did he believe her?"

"Apparently. His personal physician is treating her skinned arms even now."

"But even if you should suffer for what is right, you are blessed - do not fear their intimidation; do not be shaken," One of the priests fell to a knee as if he had witnessed a miracle.

"Peter," Gisela answered the kneeling priest autonomically without looking away from the Bishop. "How are the other women and children?"

"Arastang is a clever host, if mistrustful. They remain on the ship, stuffing themselves on minted cod, roast duck and ale, God bless them."

"Merciful God, we thank thee," The other priest exclaimed to heaven and the rafters.

Moruuan came back into the donjon hall with half a dozen soldiers and left them in the main hall to come join Gisela and the Bishop by the looms.

"Where is Charles now?" Gisela asked Cadocanan.

"In the Oreigle Tower, and now Arastang and his guards as well."

"And King Budic?"

"In the Tower with Charles and the old Captain."

"The old ship Captain? Why him? He's Breton!"

"Because the old coot threatened to take his whip to Arastang's soldiers if they touched a line of his ship," half-joked Moruuan as he stepped up. "Don't worry yourself about Captain C'hreac'h."

"You said his name. No sailor or king has spoken it to me before."

"We're on land now. Besides, nobody on this coast would dare harm that old fool out of pure superstition and genuine respect."

"You joke at a time like this?"

"My apologies, Your Highness. Here's what I can now piece together of my uncle Arastang's thinking. My father indeed sailed over to Cornwall after the feast of Saint Ignatius, assisting in the fight against the Saxon Offa there, so my Uncle is within his rights to rule Aleth in his stead, as my father would have wished."

"True rights have not seemed to give him clarity," Gisela noted.

"Moruuan was away, I, as Bishop, was away. Arastang's advisers were much reduced," Cadocanan pointed out.

"Now, for the war rumors here. The city has been on alert for days but has had little news. Aleth scouts reported *Franks* had raided the outskirts of Dol and farms in the Tressé some three days ago. With the Margrave and Prince Charles at Avranches, everyone was suspicious it was a Frankish push into Brittany, so my uncle sent his scouts to the hill-camps of Bonaban and Châteauneuf. My uncle only learned of King Gundebold and the corrupt Le Mans Bishop this morning, from my own lips. He is suspicious Budic has sold out the Breton nations to the Franks, and this is some kind of trap."

"He does not believe his own nephew?" Gisela asked, her jaw still hanging open. There was an uncomfortable pause from the two men.

"He believes his nephew Moruuan is blinded by what he calls 'Brenin Budic's martyring campaign and fervent orthopraxy'," Cadocanan answered the difficult question for Moruuan, but proved Arastang's very point in the process, thought Gisela.

"Surely Arastang believes you, Bishop?" Gisela asked Cadocanan.

"Like many of my struggling people, Dominus Arastang pays far more credence to worldly politics than righteous belief, I'm afraid."

"Show me the right path, O LORD; point out the road for me to follow..," one of Cadocanan's priests beseeched.

"Twenty-five," she responded to the imploring priest. "What are we to do? How can we convince your Uncle Arastang that this city is not under threat from the Prince of the Franks but instead from a Frisian band of cutthroats and rebels on both sides?"

"Short of Gundebold standing on a hill outside of besieged Aleth, I don't know," Moruuan answered, plopping down on a loom bench, shaking his head and running his fingers through his hair.

"Aleth seems a village, not a great city. I can't see why you two wished Charles to come here to raise an army to help at Tombe and Avranches. You'd have trouble filling the ships with bakers and farmers, much less soldiers."

"Bakers and farmers?" Cadocanan scratched his cheek. "The farmers and sharecroppers. Tithes and corvèe," he said to the looms, thinking out loud, then turned back to Gisela.

"Your Highness, this peninsula is just the fortress, you see but the head of Aleth. The manors, orchards, wheat fields, and pig farms; the body of Aleth, they are inland and stretch down the shoreline of the River Rance," he described, pacing past a loom, his fingers playing the strings like a silent harp. "What if Gundebold sees but the head as well?" he asked Moruuan as he came back by his bench.

"That's why he wants the eel-boats again. No need to fight through every manor and mansi farm in a long drawn out siege over farmlands. Attack Aleth directly by boat, be at the very walls in moments," Moruuan followed his thinking.

"Overwhelm the fortress in one swift battle," Cadocanan agreed.

"And control Aleth's head?" Gisela struggled to understand. "The body of farms will follow the head?"

"I can assure you, my Uncle is thinking precisely this, and it explains his thinking to me," Moruuan realized, standing up as if he had seen the answer amongst the woven cloth and spindles. "He knows Aleth Fortress is the head of this land."

"What do you mean?" Gisela asked again.

"Oh my," Cadocanan realized as well.

"What?!" Gisela begged.

"What was it my Uncle said to Brenin Budic when he greeted him on the shore?"

"That the fortress was at his service," Gisela distinctly remembered the words.

"And being prepared!" Moruuan continued and laughed at himself. "Your brother Charles and Budic and their bodyguards are not just prisoners of Aleth. They are kenneled like hunting dogs before the chase. My uncle wants Charles and Budic as guardians against the impending attack on Aleth!"

"Why, with their soldier bodyguards they would be a small army to defend this fortress," Gisela finally understood.

"Particularly against such skirmishing raids as these rebels have shown," Moruuan pointed out.

"Arastang wanted me in the fortress as well!"

"Charles would fight his way to you if he had to," Cadocanan added with a pointed finger.

"Plus Frankish troops would come to help save the city if we were telling the truth all along about the Frisians."

"Your Highness, the body of Aleth, in the fields and woods around us, is large but slumberous to awaken. I must go to the lords of these manors. Comes Hoel is a magnificent war-chief, but he appointed me tax procurator of Aleth, mostly because he can't read or count to one-hundred."

"What is your plan?"

"The coloni and slaves of the manors pay their taxes in goods and supplies to the manor lords. The manor lords pay a share of these goods to the Comes of Aleth as a lease tax, and also send their workers to Aleth for the corvèe; public projects like roads, walls, timber cutting. Between the tithes to the church, the lease taxes and the corvèe, I can sway a lot of manor lords to our side, and they can send willing farmer militia in their place if they wish, staying safe at home to defend the town and farms."

Gisela's brow wrinkled, and one eye narrowed. "You are going to recruit farmers to fight in Avranches?" Having traveled along with humbled grape farmers who had weapons thrust into their hands and ordered to fight a war for someone else, she had not been particularly impressed by the outcome.

"Many of these Breton farmers are quite capable, and include retired soldiers," Moruuan mentioned with a gleam in his eye that almost reassured her.

"Be aware, however, what I propose could put you at risk of being imprisoned with your brother," Cadocanan asked.

"Be it looms of thread or bars of iron, I can but look out through them nonetheless. I'd rather be at Charles' side than the seamstresses."

"My Lord, will you accompany me to the farms?"

Moruuan thought. "They won't hurt Gisela if they want Charles and Budic to fight for them when the time comes." He scratched his nose and beard. "Yes, your Eminence, and I know a way we can leave my father's fortress without undue notice."

"Then we ask you to remain here, your Highness. Be a distraction. Be a *Princess*. Make yourself known. Inspect the soldiers and meet the staff. Ask to tour the grounds, get a feel for the place. If we fail, you may be Charles's scout for defense in the end."

"If we fail, we'll all join Charles and Budic in Oreigle, I can assure you," Moruuan predicted.

Copar came up behind Gisela and put her hands on the Princess' shoulders in support.

"May God be with you," Gisela wished.

"May God be with all of us!" Cadocanan beamed,

and they left each other to weave their plots without the still looms.

"Lady Janig? Lady Janig?!" Gisela insisted loudly, pushing past servants as if they were insubstantial ghosts. The white veiled lacy caps of so many women in one room made Gisela wonder if she had entered a convent.

The rattled Lady came out of the Housekeeper's office in the kitchen. Military strategy was not Gisele's forte, but she had been immersed in courtly strategy her whole life. She had seen the very best at it, her own mother, up close and hard at work.

Gisela guessed Lady Janig was a woman in her forties. From appearances, she was a rich Breton or Welsh daughter, whom Aleth had entirely consumed into a world that revolved around her husband the Comes and this fortified city as if God and the world as a whole were within the town walls. Gisela knew well the shape of the bowl that formed the souls of such Lord's women. Every moment of the day was a play to be scripted and directed, every room a frame to display the Comes like a beautiful painting, every meal a flawless execution of grace and plenty to woo the inevitable guests into seeing the Lord as distortedly grand as the rest of the household did. Reality often dismounted for perception's pleasure on the ride in such grand houses, and here indeed was the noble Lady, coming out of a kitchen office that served up the fantasy in such heaping proportions that Lady Janig was the veritable master of the atelier of this craftswoman's house guild.

But Gisela understood fantasy on a royal scale and the infinite subtleties of courtly behavior.

"Yes, Princess Gisela? What may we do for you?" the Lady asked, a towel still in her hand, obviously preoccupied with other things as if Gisela were about to ask for a cookie and could be easily dismissed with the jar.

Gisela decided on less finesse, and that perhaps a battering ram was needed to break down the walls of this Lady's donjon.

"Empress of Constantinople, to be, dear Lady. Between the squill and stale tarragon stench of the sewing room, I have grown faint, and require fresh air."

"Good Princess, the mice are terrible with the sewing hereabouts if we don't. Come, let us show you to the library to change your airs."

"I wish fresh air, or you can garderobe the house if you prefer."

The cost of showering the halls in expensive southernwood showed clearly upon Lady Janig's face, and suddenly all the woman's focus was on this comet of a child that had burst into her little celestial night sky.

"Empress, I was commanded to not let you out of the hall..."

"You were commanded not to let me out of the fortress, good Lady. No Lord has ordered my imprisonment in this clemping stench."

"Let me get an escort from the Captain, it won't take long," Janig begged, grabbing the house steward as if he were a broom.

"Oh! Intolerable!" Gisela over dramatized. "You there, Moruuan's little brother?" Gisela called softly, a silky contrast to her knife's attitude to the lady. The boy got up from the hall floor where he was playing and ran over to Gisela like an accustomed playmate. "Enoch mag Hoel, Great Lady," the little boy bubbled out, taking her offered hand.

"Master Enoch! Come, be my escort and show me around this fortress of yours!" she said charmingly. Enoch beamed. Lady Janig turned pale.

"I beg of you, Empress, await my Captain."

Gisela made her eyes water and waved her one free hand by her nose. "I think not. I shall not leave hold of Enoch's hand then, and we shall hold hands outside to await your Captain's arrival. You have my word, good Lady." And she pulled Enoch through the gathered staff and scullery maids like mice fleeing the smell that created the situation in the first place. Copar and Lady Janig fought their way through after them.

The courtyard was quiet and uncrowded, save for an odd tent over a rowboat and the soldiers on the encompassing walls. She and Enoch swung hands as they walked in the crisp cold. Gisela took in the two-storied tower behind her that stretched out in wings like open arms, its heart pierced with the only visible gate; the donjon a great triumphal arch around it. The ovens and hot kitchen to one side of the gate, the stables and foundry to the other, and three rounded watchtowers at corners that made up the yard's encircling walls.

She and Enoch walked together, into stalls, up stairs, along walls, amidst the workings of the fortress. A smart looking officer appeared with two guards, and after a word, Lady Janig left them to shadow Gisela in her place. Copar now strolled behind the Princess as the obedient abigail, quickly coming to understand the ploy. Gisela stopped and asked names of watchful soldiers, and after the affairs of craftsmen, and while she charmed answers out of them, her thoughts were always of Avranches, and the possible war there. Bishop Joshua Jumael might be fighting for his life as she casually strolled in this parade. Joshua was a good nickname for any priest.

Gisela wondered about priests and bishops like Joshua. She had known the royal almoners well enough, and the chapelle du roi was its own walking church to her royal courtly life, but this recent journey outside of the rarefied courtly air into the cold reality had shown her bishops that were far different than the ones she had known. In family discussions and courtly debates, her father and wise priests had talked of Christendom often, and Gisela had come to recognize two particular types of bishops.

There were the martyrious, ill-tempered judges; the ones looking to remind every soul of the death and misery, indeed to often personify that misery, that was man's portion in life. Her mother had called these 'Old Testament' bishops; at the ready to bring down God's wrath in an effort to win a convert or save a soul. These bishops achieved great things and performed Godly miracles. Often, Gisela thought, they sought to stamp out the 'mice of sin' with a catapult that destroyed the entire house to exterminate the rodent.

Then there were what her brother Carolman called the 'New Testament' bishops. Men of hope and reason, they walked as if the charm of their Lord Jesus Christ himself were within them. They exuded the love and hope of God instead of the terror. These men were warm, compassionate, and their works built both souls and churches from the ground up.

Sacrilegious as it sounded, Gisela wondered why

they didn't just nickname them Hell and Heaven bishops; for the division was that clear, and the message that plain. Gisela knew this before ever she ran away, but until now the two different styles of Christ's priests starkly bookended her religious reading and writing.

Gisela looked at the sky up as she climbed stairs to a bigger watchtower. The low snowy clouds, still showering beggarly flurries beneath them, were retreating from the sun like sheep before a shepherd's dog. Long ribbons of high clouds, thin and razor-edged, stretched off into the distance over the bay as if God had made a pass overhead with an enormous sky rake, revealing the blue beyond.

Gisela looked out over the sea. The rocks of Saint Maclou stuck out from the promontory further downriver along the shore, and out on the horizon the gray line that defined the island of Saint Aaron, and its mystical monastery. Minor Bishops became ossuaries, and great Bishops became saints in time, but Gisela was now becoming keenly aware, for the first time in her life, there was a third type of bishop. They held the titles, ran the churches, spoke the same words and performed the same rights, yet these men were petty, evil sinners. It was confusing to Gisela. Why did God let them be bishops? Why didn't saints prove them liars? Why didn't deacons and good followers of Jesus Christ recognize them and toss them out the door of the church like the thieves they were?

She felt Enoch's hand squeeze hers as he looked upon her with an admiration due much greater women than her. Enoch. She remembered a last summer's eve debate the King had with visiting bishops about fallen angels and a controversial book of

Enoch. It was a Jewish book that been considered for the Bible and rejected, but Enoch was still in the Bible and had been taken alive up into Heaven, a scarce thing indeed. Enoch spoke of fallen angels, the giants, taking mortal women to have children and spread their evil before the Flood. It would take that kind of satanic power to fool Popes and saints and deacons and bishops. She tried to remember what they called Enoch's giants. Was it Nephilim? Yes, that was it. Nephilim. The bloodline of fallen angels of old, the cruel Nephilim, becoming an evil vein amidst our modern priests and bishops to rob and agonize mankind. Sin, hidden amongst grace.

Gisela thought of the questionable Archbishop Gravien of Tours that caused so many problems for her mother, and then this corrupt Bishop of Le Mans, paying bandits with church money and starting traitorous wars amongst his own people.

"Dear Saint Raphael, help us to see them, to reveal them, for how are we mortals to ever know?" Gisela prayed under her breath, and she took comfort in the heavenly feelings that had surrounded her under Saint Michael's chapel on Tombe only nights before. Copar standing behind her rubbed her shoulder in encouragement.

"You didn't gawk at the howdah. Most everyone wants to see my uncle's howdah," Enoch stated, his face smushed up as if he were smelling something foul. "Besides, it's cold up here," he shivered in the sea wind as they stood on the wall. Gisela looked down and realized the boy could not even see over the wall to enjoy her view.

"I'm sorry, Sacha. Yes, you can show me...whatever this thing is."

Copar, a brushing hand on Gisela's shoulder, lifted the boy into her hands, and quietly whispered "Let's get you out of this cold *Enoch*," to both he and corrected Gisela. The boy snuggled into Copar's arms and pointed the way back down. Gisela felt an odd mix of feelings at her mistake as they climbed back down the steps to the courtyard.

Gisela, Copar holding the little boy Enoch, the Lieutenant of the Comes Chambers, and his two guards, and now a handful of servants and domestics as well, all stood on the paving stones of the block-walled courtyard, looking at the odd little tent over a rowboat.

"What did you call this again?" Gisela asked Enoch. "A hoodah?"

"A howdah," Enoch said, giggling and teasing Copar's veil playfully.

"It is Dominus Arastang's prize sella," the Lieutenant behind her added respectfully. "He brought it with him from Vannes."

"It is quite old, isn't it? It's nicely carved, indeed those...lions? Perhaps?...on the sides look fearsome, but I don't think it would float on water anymore," Gisela noted.

"It doesn't float on water!" Enoch giggled.

Gisela looked harder. The rowboat was squarish like a tiny ferry and had cushioned seats facing each other as well as a seat facing behind on the stern. The canvas top had once been painted brightly but had long since faded in the sun, and the whole thing had been placed on an old carpet of embroidered canvas or aida cloth with four flaps sticking out, like some odd bearskin rug or animal skin with its legs all sticking out from under the squashing rowboat.

"A howdah," Gisela repeated again, unimpressed, looking at Enoch, who was too busy playing with Copar's veil to reply.

"It is an elephant carriage, a litter once owned by the great Roman General Belisarius," quipped Arastang as he stalked through the gate into the courtyard behind them, followed by dozens of guards, scribes and several of the town's wealthy lords. He stepped right up beside Gisela and admired his own howdah despite her derisive smirk.

She looked at him and was reminded of her father. Arastang was as old and short as the True King, and as overdressed as one in his black wool and mink and his silk-lined jack underneath it. His furred boots came all the way up beside her to her waist. Looking up, Arastang sported a clean-shaven jutting chin surrounded by a long mustache and short beard that disappeared back under dark brown hair, all three of which rippled with gray streaks. He looked down at her.

"I've spoken to the rest of the pieces in this shatranj game today. Kings and miles and chariots and pawns. Now, at last, I come to the white vazir. It is our turn to talk," his voice was curt, snappy.

"I am surprised you even know of shatranj. Few do."

"The whole world passes through Vannes and Aleth."

He left about as much room to maneuver in conversation as the coracle had left her while spinning down the river. She suddenly better understood the Pil, the elephant piece in shatranj.

"Your eyes are not angry, yet they focus on me like

an archer," Gisela finally summoned her courage. "I find it is odd you describe this imprisonment as a shatranj game. Do you see yourself as the black king?"

Arastang, thinking, rubbed his fingers together as if sprinkling salt.

"In this game of rebellion, I'm trying to determine exactly who's playing the black king, for it is not I," he finally answered, then his hand shot out openly to the howdah. "We shall have our talk over a meal on my howdah," he insisted.

"It is cold out here, Dominus," Gisela responded.

"Then may it flavor your stories and answers with brevity," he snapped as servants were already racing back into the donjon hall to fulfill his request. A footman placed a step stool by the howdah, and the Lieutenant offered Gisela a hand as she stepped up into it. Copar lowered Enoch into his chambermaid's care and stood next to the howdah attentively. Arastang followed Gisela up into the howdah, and there the two sat, across from each other in the un-elephanted carriage, as food and drink were brought out. Gisela decided the plain truth of her journey would serve her imprisoned brother more than any guarded truths, and was a more natural Christian defense against the rapid-volley questions of Arastang'.

They dined and talked together as she told him the whole, abbreviated, tale of her journey from Mur to his howdah. Arastang would not let a nagging detail or confusing point pass for a single moment, but as the story wound on his interruptions grew less and his listening even more intent. Gisela noticed his fingers ground the invisible salt even more incessantly, and he spun a ring around on his pointing finger just before he asked another question.

As they talked, a number of people entered the courtyard. First Bishop Cadocannan and so many priests they crowded the donjon doors, then Moruuan and so many manor lords they filled the stone pavers from the gate to the howdah, yet Arastang's focus never left Gisela and her tale.

"And this is how I come to be before you, Dominus," Gisela finally breathed out.

"I have one more question for you, your highness. The Prince carries a curved Thracian falx with a gold crystal in the hilt. To say he would part with it without dying first has become evident. What relic or treasure does it hold for you Franks?"

"It is a Turkish kilij called the *Enduring Petros*," Gisela answered, then smirked. "As for what measure it holds for Franks..," she said and shrugged. "As for what measure it holds for Emperor Constantine and the Eastern Roman Empire, it is part of their bridewealth to our house for my arranged marriage to the Emperor's son Leo this coming spring," she spoke cloyingly. "I'm certain you would not try to break that unbreakable arrangement."

"I'll take my chances the Emperor isn't coming from Byzantium to rescue his future daughter-in-law anytime soon," Arastang retorted. "My thanks to you, Your Highness, for your refreshing candor." He stood up. "Now let me tend to *my* house," he whispered and winked to her, and faced the Bishop and his nephew and their many followers.

Cadocanan with his old Roman styled sword stood like a statue, his silver crosier and his robe with a cross and circle of thorns leaving no doubt about the wishes of the diocese of Poutrocoët. Behind him were his vicars, priests, deacons, monks and lectors.

Moruuan stood nervously kicking at the paving stones and whispering with one of his Captains and several other important looking, unarmed men. Behind them were a dozen wealthy manor lords, and their pages and staffs as well, along with a large hog. What opinions and leverage they held were still a mystery to Gisela, though the pig with them she thought she understood.

"Bishop, Nephew. My apologies, you've just missed our lunch." Arastang lowered a firm hand on the shoulder of the still seated Gisela. Even she realized she was being used as a pawn for the moment, though these men did not look angry or violent.

Another of Arastang's armed Captains joined the Lieutenant of the Chambers and his house soldiers, and three of the armed town lords also joined Arastang beside his grounded howdah, each offering quick praises and fine boxes of trinkets to Arastang before taking a supporting position beside the howdah and their leader.

"Uncle," Moruuan spoke in an official sounding tone. "The Aleth assembly of manor lords has come to petition you for the release of the Prince of the Franks and Brenin Budic and grant them leave to sail back to their battles."

"Your concern is Prince Charles of the Franks. Budic imprisons himself."

"Granted, then, Dominus." There was a murmur of support for Moruuan.

"I could have you arrested for calling an assembly of the manors without my permission, Nephew."

"If it is your intent to stop every good man from trying to defend their farms before war arrives upon

Aleth's doorstep, then so be it." Moruuan motioned, and the pig was brought forth and offered by a farmer to Arastang for the aggrievement. Arastang nodded in approval, and one of his servants took it behind the howdah. Gisela had guessed correctly; the pig was a sacrifice in Moruuan's place for doing something behind Arastang's back. Court favors took so many forms.

"Dominus. The Franks are not planning an attack on Aleth. I have fought amongst them, been amongst their council, as was my father's wish, and I will swear before family, and my fellow Aleth citymen, that the Franks are fighting a rebellion of many peoples. These three Aleth lords all claim that friends of theirs and distant relations were recruited..."

"...Or attempted too..," one lord corrected.

"...By our own Breton Bagaudae, for unsanctioned skirmishes against Frankish forts and lands," Moruuan continued. The three men stepped forward.

"Nephew, most of the people along the River Rance, and probably this pig too, know someone's *friend* who's dabbling in the piracy of the Bagaudae," Arastang observed, amidst the chuckling of his followers.

"We've scouts in Bonaban who claim no army of any kind approaches as of this morning. The scouts in Châteauneuf say the same. You yourself sent scouts to Dol, and they were turned away by the Dol defenders, claiming they did not know friend from foe anymore, but they were not being sieged!"

'I do believe he has left the town to know such things," Arastang suggested to Gisela.

"But being in the wrong has made him right," Gisela offered. "Will being in the right make you

311

wrong, I wonder?"

Arastang looked at her for a long moment before looking back at the gathered men.

"We know you have sent messengers to both Rennes and Avranches."

"Neither have yet to return, though they are not overdue as of yet."

"Dominus! Uncle! There is no army marching upon Aleth yet! There is no fleet advancing along the coast towards Aleth yet! Once Avranches falls, there will be."

"And Aleth will be prepared when they do!" There was murmuring of support for both sides of this argument.

"If we can strike this Frisian raiding fleet first at Tombe, there never will be a battle at either town!"

"I will not spare the soldiers of Aleth on such a gamble for the Franks benefit."

"You have two-hundred soldiers here. The manors of the Rance can muster ten times that! The ships are at the ready, the sailors and warriors are willing!"

Arastang looked to Cadocanan.

"I see you have used the tithe and taxes to raise a navy of farmers."

"Comes Hoel saw fit for the Diocese to be granted the authority to collect the tribute as procurator."

"All gratitude to the town's Christian patrons, no doubt, and conveniently, your parishioners."

"A generous person will prosper; whomever refreshes others will be refreshed."

"And the Catholic Church feels we should let the Frank Prince and Princess go, and even fight their war for them?"

"What's righteous does not bend a knee to any but

almighty God. The ships will contain only those who choose to go, not those sent."

"You've raised a militia in an afternoon?"

"No. You did, Uncle, with your preparations of the last three days."

"We've simply gathered some of them together for the task."

"And used their due tribute to Aleth as a soldiers payment for your Frankish war!"

"Only a third, Dominus. The corvèe and punera. No one in Aleth will starve unless we wait like belon oysters to be sieged."

"Such talk from my Nephew and Bishop! I should have you all locked up for being treasonous. You must stop all these efforts behind my back immediately."

There was a great deal of murmuring and pleads to fight, as well as quite a few calls to bolster Aleth's defenses no matter what was decided.

"My Dominus, if seeking to sail back to Tombe to take on this foreign fleet is treasonous in your eyes, then you shall need to lock me up with Brenin Budic, for I will return to Tombe and Avranches, crawling upon my knees if I must."

"As you ask. Captain. Escort our good Bishop to the Oreigle Tower."

Several of the priests demanded it be taken back, and a deacon drew a sword on two soldiers, facing off in the tension before Cadocanan lifted his crosier and hand to quiet them. Many soldiers made a racket with their weapons in support of Arastang.

"All the oysters in one pot?" the Bishop asked, stepping obediently over to the Captain. "Be careful, Dominus. The whole town will not fit in Oreigle."

"And one pearl," Gisela announced, standing and

gently pushing aside Arastang's hand from her soldiers. "My deepest thanks for the lunch, Dominus. Your hospitality has been remarkable, and I shall remember our conversation fondly, but I must ask to accompany the Bishop to join my brother and King Budic."

"I ask you not to do this, Princess."

"Dominus, you are my Circe on this Homeric adventure, for while I may be trapped by you, you are trapped indeed between Helios and Perse."

Arastang thought long, then nodded in agreement for her to be taken as well.

Copar helped her down and followed her over to the Captain and the Bishop, who put his arm around her.

"Uncle!" Moruuan argued once more.

"I gave you fair enough warning, nephew. You will accompany them," Arastang commanded. It was impossible to tell exactly which side supported whom any longer, but Arastang was winning with the soldiers. Moruuan, Cadocanan, Gisela, and Copar were escorted out of the donjon gate and into the city amidst a wash of people following them.

Gisela heard the donjon gate close behind them. Arastang was not a man easily swayed from his opinions. She wondered if the Margrave had changed his yet.

The town streets seemed narrower with so many people, the random block buildings closing in like a rabbit warren. Blue shutters were open now, and people draped themselves out window and balcony to call down to the guards for gentle treatment for Cadocanan and Moruuan. As they passed the church of St Maclou, the calls for the guards to release the Bishop became more vocal. Gisela noticed the guards grew nervous when they saw fresh piles of rocks had been placed along alleys and doorways.

The main city gate was still down and closed, but the smaller postern side gate was still open, and they proceeded out of the city and across the port towards the Oreigle tower. Gisela could not see anyone in the windows of the tower, but plenty of guards by the gate outside it.

The Captain nervously ordered the guards to open the tower for the new prisoners, and the guard captain looked at Moruuan in disbelief.

"I said open the tower, now!" the Captain ordered the guard captain again. The crack in his voice was like a cold river's plunge.

The guard opened the gate, and Gisela ran inside, followed by the others.

"Gisa!" Charles beamed and hugged her, then frowned as the gate door closed behind them.

Oreigle was a simple two-story tower overlooking the port, with a desk and supplies and benches in the bottom and stairs around the walls leading up to the third-floor parapets. Barns beside the tower held the supplies, and the windows might allow Gisela to escape, but not Charles and certainly not Budic.

Gisela noticed a feast and wine had been provided, a great deal of both, it appeared.

"Moruuan! What did yu du tu get yurselves locked up with us?" Budic asked, hugging the tall warrior.

"Listen, Prince Charles," the Bishop begged. "by nightfall a crowd..."

There was the noise of the shutters being pelted by hail, and then the door as well.

"Your crowd has obviously gathered faster than you anticipated, good Bishop," Charles replied.

The rooftop hatch opened, with the guard on top showing swords and spears to those down below.

"You up there? Rigund?" Moruuan demanded from down below.

"Moruuan? Moruuan, there are crowds threatening to storm the tower!" the soldiers from the top warned.

"And it will not go well for you if you come down!"

"It won't go well for us none if you escape neither!" Rigund yelled back down over a shield to protect him from Budic's archer's potential arrows.

The gate behind them opened, the guard with his arm up behind him to stop the beating he was receiving from the townsfolk.

"Here's our chance. We must make it to the ship before the guards rally," Moruuan advised.

The rocks against the door stopped, and the old Captain and Copar made it out the door to obvious cheers.

"Nata." Charles strapped on his kilij and pulled up his coif.

"What?" Budic asked, turning part way out the door of the tower.

"I'll not run. This levereter Arastang will have to negotiate with me, or his battle for Aleth will come sooner than he imagines."

The Bishop broke into a broad grin.

"Nata," Gisela repeated to Charles, smiling, as they left the tower. "There's an elephant saddle I wanted you to see in the fort anyways."

"A howdah? Here??"

Over a thousand people cheered when the Bishop appeared outside. He raised his crosier to a cheer, and then they cheered again when Moruuan stepped out.

"To the Fortress!" Moruuan yelled, and the crowd cheered even more and lurched backward like a rebounding wave.

Women, men, children running amidst everyone, old and young alike half-pushed and half-carried the freed Frankish party along towards the closed main gate. Moruuan and the Bishop tried to explain what had transpired to Charles and Budic as they crossed the port.

"The many rabbits seem to have found their courage in numbers," Gisela remarked.

"This nest of rabbits, as you call them, can get ugly quickly," Budic told Gisela. He sheathed his great sword and picked up Gisela in his arms for her own safety.

Soldiers scrambled along the walls and battlements of Aleth, reluctant to shoot friends and neighbors. Poles the length of masts came up from the port and were placed against the gate as nimble young men scampered up them to get on top. Soldiers tried to fend them off, but a hail of stones from both sides of the gate drove the soldiers to seek the safety of cover atop the wall. The side gate flew open, and before Charles had even passed through it, the main gate began to creak and raise under the combined lifting of so many people with no one to stop them.

Once in the town, people had already begun to clog the streets. The church bells rang away in glee, and Budic and Moruuan had to bark commands to get the townsfolk to part enough for them to squeeze through to reach the donjon gate of the fort. Every angry yell of Budic's was taken up by the crowd, such that he began to amuse himself as he struggled through the human quicksand by giving them odd things to yell back.

Archers lined the walls above the donjon gate, but they did not draw bow or notch arrow.

Gisela saw a woman in front of the gate of the donjon.

"That's Lady Janig! How's she holding back this crowd?" she whispered in Budic's ear.

"Guts," Budic replied.

Lady Janig sported a few scrapes and a bruise, but she was a veritable dragon guarding the gate of her house. The crowd would have pushed aside any gate guard but her.

"The crowd will have to break them both down," Gisela observed.

"Mother!" Moruuan cried out, struggling to finally get up to help her.

"I'm not hurt bad! Tell this mob to turn around and go home!" she insisted.

"They won't, Mother, you know that." He put a protective arm around her. "You have got to order them to open the gate."

"No! I've built our home here my entire life, and these hooligans will ransack and plunder it in mere minutes. We'll lose everything!" She was crying, but tough as nails through the tears.

"Don't hurt her!" Budic called out, but now that he had seemingly joined Lady Janig the crowd had decided to no longer echo the King.

"Let me see what I can do..," Cadocanan squeezed up against them. "Brenin, can you help me up?"

Budic passed Gisela to Charles next to him and then helped lift the Bishop up.

"O LORD, thou art my God, I will exalt thee, and give glory to thy name: for thou hast done wonderful things, thy designs of old faithful, amen," the Bishop exclaimed, his crosier up, his hands extending it over above the crowd, his eyes closed.

"For thou hast reduced the city to a heap, the strong city to ruin, the house of strangers, to be no city, and to be no more built up forever," he yelled even louder. Priests and monks and the more religious folks began to take knees, and the crowd pressure on the gate began to lessen.

"Therefore shall a strong people praise thee, the city of mighty nations shall fear thee. Because thou hast been a strength to the poor, a strength to the needy in his distress: a refuge from the whirlwind, a shadow from the heat."

"Job?" Budic asked Gisela in a whisper.

"Isaiah. I think," she whispered back.

"For the blast of the mighty is like a whirlwind beating against a wall," Bishop Cadocanan called out, and the crowd had subsided in its frenzy enough for him to speak without yelling so hard. He took a deep breath.

"And it came to pass on a certain day that Jesus went into a little ship with his disciples, and he said to them: Let us go over to the other side of the lake. And they launched forth. And when they were sailing, he slept; and there came down a storm of wind upon the lake, and they were filled with fear, and were in danger."

"Luke," Budic and Gisela both whispered and nodded together in recognition.

"And they came and awakened him, saying: Master, we perish. But he, arising, rebuked the wind and the rage of the water; and it ceased, and there was a calm," the Bishop exclaimed, moved to tears by the spirit.

"And he said to them: Where is your faith? Who being afraid, wondered, saying one to another: Who is this, that he commandeth both the winds and the sea, and they obey him?"

"Praise be to the Lord!" Budic yelled.

"Praise be to the Lord!" the entire crowd echoed to him this time.

"Are you certain of this my son?" the Bishop whispered. Moruuan nodded and started trying to climb up the gate and Budic.

"People of Aleth! Hear us! Hear your favored son!" The Bishop commanded, opening his eyes again and helping Moruuan up.

"My people! You now enter my house!" Moruuan yelled out, hanging from the gate beside the Bishop. "What theft you do would be against me! What rage you embody would hurt me! What destruction you would bring would be upon ourselves!" he yelled. "Now that the will of the people of Aleth is known to my Uncle, let myself and the Bishop talk to him once again!"

"Embody the patience of the Lord!" the Bishop added and began singing Psalm fifty-five. The crowd, being mostly good church-going, God-fearing folk, quieted down and joined him in singing.

Lady Janig hugged her son, her forehead to his in gratitude and respect, and then turned, nodding to the guards on the other side.

The donjon gate slowly rose up, as did the volume of the singing.

Lady Janig and Moruuan, Bishop Cadocanan and now King Budic, Charles and Gisela and their guards entered the courtyard. Three lines of spearmen stretched across the paving stones between them and

Arastang. Stout men with swords and shields flanked them, and all along the walls were archers by the dozen. There, on his howdah, as proud and old and worn thin as his magnificent litter, sat Arastang, sipping wine.

"Offer him terms for his surrender," whispered Budic under his breath as he took Gisela back. Charles almost laughed. People began pressing in behind them, backfilling the courtyard.

"As I feared, Franks have invaded the fortress of Aleth!" Arastang toasted Charles.

People began relaying what was being said back through the crowd.

"This time we are free, and you are behind the bars, Dominus," Charles motioned to the spears between them.

"Any attack would be a death sentence for both of us, good Prince."

Bishop Cadocanan stepped forward. "Dominus. Can you now see the will of God as it moves in his people? Aleth wishes to drive off these foreign invaders before they lay waste to our lives."

"I will keep the Franks out with my dying breath, and false kings of Bretagne, and any other foreigners who come to lay claim to my brother's Aleth."

"You are but a steward in my father's absence, Uncle."

"And you are still a boy shield-bearer for a Catholic church-anointed puppet king, Nephew."

"It is only a matter of time before either the Frisian rebellion arrives here by fleet, or the Margrave arrives here by land, and you do not have enough men to fight either off, with no hope of reinforcements," Charles warned.

"If the Frisians arrive, you can fight your way out and assist me by having the Margrave come save you from them. If the Margrave arrives, I can negotiate to be made the King instead of Budic. What is it you Franks call them, Dux? Yes, Dux Arastang will do nicely. Are you willing to do that Prince?"

"The Frankish Court rewards loyalty. Arresting us to use as a shield is treachery."

"How will your Dux Tassilo or Dux Robert be rewarded for their dis-loyalty, I wonder? Has anything I have done not been in the best interest of Aleth? Have any of you or your people been mistreated?" Arastang demanded, standing up and setting his cup down. "Your sister shows up in a whirlwind on your doorstep, and you want to believe her, but you have to make certain. The Margrave also wants to be sure. She's prone to imagining things, and her tale is almost risible. So you go check, but remain cautious! How am I different? I ask you, Prince, how is this any different? The Merovingian's of *Ducatus Cenomannicus* were often outright insane, prone to greed and deception with each other, and the Bretons. The Mayors of the Franks are not always forthright, as your own brother Grifo showed in Le Mans. Indeed, a slice of Bretagne is carved off like a roast, an overlord is appointed to Marche over us and subdue us to Frank Neustrian will, and then, what have we here?! Suddenly Frankish Neustria can't keep its own house in order, with traitors from Le Mans *again* joining foreigners to overthrow the Frankish overlord, and now *the brother* of *the whirlwind sister* arrives on my doorstep *in a snow flurry* with his mymmerkin King *and an unbelievable tale*! Empty your fortress of Aleth to save the Frankish Overlord! So that we can carve deeper yet another ripe slice of Bretagne into Neustria and bring Aleth under the Frankish Marche?" Arastang demanded, stepping off the howdah, and stepping through his parting soldiers to come to face Charles more directly, though they were still a fair distance apart. His words resonated with Alethians, soldier and commoner alike. The town may have wanted Moruuan and the Bishop freed, but Arastang was speaking directly to their very hearts and fears.

Charles looked suspicious, and Gisela wasn't entirely certain he wasn't going to draw sword and take Arastang on.

"I should have your head for this selfishness in Bretagne' time of need," Budic warned.

Arastang's face contorted. "You are just another king of Cornuaille, but you call yourself the King of all Bretagne because the Church adores you and coronates you, Budic. So many Bretons do not follow you that you actually feed this rebellion yourself. You speak for the Church of Bretagne, not its people, Budic the Great Disappointment."

Bishop Cadocanan stepped forward between them and kneeled, his head bowed.

"For behold, darkness will cover the earth And deep darkness the peoples; But the LORD will rise upon you and His glory will appear upon you. Nations will come to your light, and kings to the brightness of your rising. Lift up your eyes round about and see; they all gather together, they come to you. Your sons will come from afar, and your daughters will be carried in the arms."

Arastang chuckled. "Cadocanan will be the savior of Aleth, it seems."

"The Lord will be the Savior of Aleth," Budic

corrected, obviously irritated.

"You are a lucky man, Cousin Budic. Your father mends his wicked ways and inherits a Kingly title from my grandfather King Iahan, mere months before our father is conceived. My brother Hoel should be King of Bretagne and carry the Horn of Finistère, instead of fighting Offa in Wales. You should be a mere Dominus of Carhaix."

"Is that what this is honestly abut? Yu wish tu be Prince Arastang? DUX Arastang, yu said it yurself," Budic realized, laughing to himself. The 'good uf Aleth' is a prud ship tu sail upon, but yu use it as a mere ferry tu reach the opposite shore of ambition," Budic handed off Gisela from his hip to Charles' hip again. Gisela put her arm around her brother's neck and watched. Some of the crowd gasped as Budic went for his sword, but he unbuckled the great steel on his side and dropped it to the ground with a clatter and drew a cross studded with aqua quartz instead.

"What are you doing?" Charles asked as Budic took a step over to Daev to take the great ivory horn back from him.

"Saving my people."

"Arastang will not save Breton in the coming battle," Charles argued.

Budic looked at Charles and then Gisela and smiled as he stepped back over to the Bishop.

"I'm nut warring tu save the lives uf my dear people, Prince. I'm battling tu save their everlasting suls."

Budic stepped forward again, holding the cross out. He showed the horn.

"This is my cross frum Aleth." He put the cross in his hand with the strap of the horn. "These are the crosses of Vannes, Auray, Lorient, Quimper..," his hand swiping across his wide pearl studded belt of crosses. "...Faou, Breast, Lèon, and yes, Carhaix," his voice was loud and rumbly. Arastang swept his hands in the air as if it were trivial. Budic reached under his collar and pulled forth a necklace with dozens of tiny silver and gold crosses like charms. "These are every Bretagne village church I have prayed in and felt the will uf God fill me," Budic insisted. "Dun't speak tu me uf the will uf the men uf Bretagne. The will uf God fur Bretagne comes first."

"And God wishes you to make us Franks?" Arastang asked. "That would set your title in church mortar."

"If making yur brother Hoel King uf the Bretagne in my place wuld change yur mind and allow us tu launch a fleet against the Frisian's un Tombe, then I will renunce my title as Brenin of Bretagne and return it tu yur side uf the family."

There was a rush of disbelief, and many heads in the crowd popped up higher to hear or see what was transpiring.

Arastang spun the ring on his finger and thought.

"You can't give up your title, Brenin," Moruuan begged.

Budic laughed. "I'll still be King uf Cornouaille, just nut Bretagne."

"I don't understand Hoel's right to succeed Budic," Gisela asked Charles.

"A King named Hoel, in'a far older time, had two sons, Judicael and Rhiwallon," Daev whispered to her, though in a louder whisper than necessary. "Tha' be the common ancestor of a distant split of the two family lines of today's Comes Hoel..," he pointed to

Hoel's half brother Arastang, "...and King Budic," he pointed to the king.

"Hoel has the blood right," Budic agreed with Daev.

"Convenient, given my dear half-brother is across the Mor Breizh, and thus unable to take the Title in a proper ceremony."

"Neustria, nor any Frankish kingdom I honor, will not recognize any renouncement that elevates you beyond dominus of Aleth, Arastang. Your treachery against me has seen to that. You're but half-brother to Hoel, yet if he falls in Wales fighting the Saxon Offa, you would be made King of the Bretons. Intolerable," Charles insisted.

"Then we seem to be at a bloody stalemate once again," Arastang surmised, backing up slightly, and he ground the invisible salt with his fingers again.

"He's thinking," Gisela whispered to Charles' ear.

"What?" Charles asked, and Cadocanan and Budic leaned into them to form a tight conversation.

"He's being swayed. I saw the same thing in Andecavus, but *you've* got to offer him something that lets him save face in front of his people. Give the Dominus a way out. He sees the crowd, he reads the mood. Stop being vengeful, Karl, and be more like Budic. Be magnanimous. Win the greater war by surrendering this petty battle."

The Bishop put a hand on Gisela's back and bowed his head in gleeful prayers as they all thought.

"Moruuan," Budic stated the answer.

"His nephew?" Charles asked.

"Comes Hoel's son. Miriam and I've no sons. Moruuan is like a son to me. He would make a good Breton King.

"Arastang could not deny Aleth's favorite son the honor. It fails to elevate Moruuan's father Hoel though," the Bishop pointed out.

"I can honor Aleth for what they have shown here today, and help Arastang elevate both Moruuan and Aleth, if not himself. He'll look petty if he refuses." Charles turned his head to look at Gisela and rub her chin. "You've grown up on your odyssey, Gisa."

Gisela pinched his nose in disagreement, and they both smiled.

"ALETH! HEAR MY WORDS!" Charles yelled out, more to the soldiers and crowd than Arastang.

"King Budic will renounce his title as King of the Bretons, and pass it onto his distant cousin, and rightful heir, Moruuan mab Hoel mab Ernoch mab Iahan."

Lady Janig hugged her surprised son, and tears came to Moruuan's eyes as clear agreement rippled through the soldiers and crowd.

"Bishop Cadocanan will sanctify the coronation this day in his church."

"You are The Great," Gisela quietly praised Budic.

"To the people of Aleth who have shone their heart and spirit this day. I do not ask for you to leave Aleth defenseless, nor rob you of your future. As Prince of the Franks, I will one day inherit Neustria and the Breton Marche. I shall elevate King Moruuan as Comes of Brittany today, as had been negotiated for Budic this fall, until I have the authority to appoint him a Duke. This, I can do for you!" Charles announced to a great many cheers, but he spun, looking at everyone.

"What can you do for yourselves?" he asked. "If you will send a fleet with me to fight these foreign invaders today, I will grant a sacramenta, a pact in writing before the Bishop and King Moruuan and Dominus Arastang, that Aleth will be a free city in the Frankish realm, for as many days as my life might last. I do this in the example of our Lord and Savior Jesus Christ, shown wisely by your Bishop Cadocanan, shown selflessly by your King Budic, shown by the sacrifice of your Lady Janig at her gates, and so aptly shown by you good people at Oreigle!"

The crowd erupted in wild cheers.

"...And exemplified in His spirit, flowing from the heart of my dear sister," Charles twirled his sister on his hip around amidst the cheers.

Many eyes looked to Arastang, and many of his spears wavered in uncertainty.

"Then in the name of my Brother, Comes Hoel, and his household, I, Arastang, the Dominus of Aleth, will acquiesce to the will of King Moruuan."

The crowd and soldiers erupted into cheers again, and intermingled almost immediately. Gisela noticed soldiers were embracing families that had been in uncomfortable opposite sides, and Lady Janig and Moruuan embraced Arastang.

"I will arrange a Mass for the coronation," the Bishop beamed.

"We shall prepare a grand ceremony!" Lady Janig spouted.

"We've no time for feasts," Charles corrected. "My sister and the Bishop can write the scramentia, and the Bishop and his priests perform the Ceremony during Mass, but the ships must sail this afternoon."

"We'll not get far with the remaining light after all this," Moruuan warned.

"Yes, we can," Charles grinned. "Dominus

Arastang?"

Arastang stepped up, and from Charles' hip, he suddenly looked shorter to Gisela.

"I wish to thank you for seeing the will of your people done so wisely."

"I still don't trust your people to validate all this."

"They shall. We have the King's ear." Charles glanced at Gisela. "I have a favor to ask of you, though."

"Yes?"

"I need you to wreck us along the Kankaven."

"What?"

"Let us do away with pretense, Dominus. The Bretons are fabled for wrecking ships along the shore at night by setting false signal fires on shoals and rocks, the kind that haunts the abers of the Breton coastline of Gallicus. The signal fires fool captains into thinking them safe ports, and they run their ships aground instead, to be plundered by Breton pirates. You cannot deny it to me; I saw the burn marks of bonfires and even stockpiles of wood on many rocks and islands we passed this morning."

"I wondered what you were looking at," Gisela realized.

"And why should you wreck your own fleet?"

"Because we can take advantage of tonight's high tide if you wreck the many dangerous shoals with your bonfires. Our old Breton Captain can safely sail through them in the dark, and lead the fleet well past sundown."

"You have already sent scouts ahead along the Kankaven to lookout for the Frisian fleet, Uncle," Moruuan remembered.

"Tombe will see fires clearly along the Dol coast.

Our advance will be heralded," Budic warned.

"We'll not sail past Grouin Pointe. That should keep us hidden from Tombe's eyes," Charles advised.

Arastang looked to Moruuan. "I am but a Dominus, Your Highness. If this is your first royal command, we shall see it done."

Moruuan suddenly grinned, then he looked at Budic and his grin faded.

"I did not wish your reign to end on my account, brother," Moruuan decried, and they hugged. "I will lead the people of Bretagne to victory."

"Lead them to the Lord, Brenin. It is the only real victory for Bretagne that will sustain time," Budic offered and handed Moruuan the great ivory horn.

"Then I will lead them in your example, for that will be the path of the Lord."

"The path of the Lord goes through the church of Saint Maclou first, Brenin," the Bishop advised, a hand on each King's back.

"May I ask a favor of you, Good Dominus?" Gisela interrupted.

Arastang looked at Gisela, and a warm smile crossed his face for the first time.

"What can this simple mayor do for the Empress of the Eastern Empire?"

"Let the women and children of my prisoner train leave our ship and stay here in Aleth in safety. They have seen enough of war, and their husbands are pawns lost within the battles of it. It will take time to find the men, if we can find them at all."

Budic chuckled. "She's a true Empress." He patted Charles.

"I shall do as you ask," Arastang agreed with a bow.

"From what I saw, Oreigle Tower would be perfect for keeping them together, warm and safe, and out of trouble, I should think."

"Then so it shall be," Arastang confirmed her wishes. "I understand the children of the prisoners can be quite unpredictable."

The Mass at Saint Maclou Church was a remarkable event. It was decided only the sailors and soldiers of the embarking fleet and the women and children of the prison train could fit inside for the Mass and Eucharist, but the people of the town and a sizable portion of the surrounding manors clogged the streets around it.

With the first liturgy Cadocanan read from One Chronicles 12; *All these, being men of war who could draw up in battle formation, came to Hebron with a perfect heart to make David king over all Israel; and all the rest also of Israel were of one mind to make David king.* And with the second liturgy Revelations 17; *These will wage war against the Lamb, and the Lamb will overcome them, because He is Lord of lords and King of kings, and those who are with Him are the called and chosen and faithful.*

Cadocanan used the homily as a funeral liturgy for the child Fara, slain on Tombe, but held her as the example for all on the prison train that had faced death, and then all in the town who faced trials. The prayer of the faithful was emotional for Gisela and the refugees of the prison chain. One by one, Cadocanan read out the names of all the missing prisoners, wives, and children, all who could be remembered by them, and they asked the Lord to watch over them. After Mass, Fara's body went to Oreigle for the vigil before the burial the next day.

Budic and Moruuan exchanged through the Bishop the Crown of Brittany, which Budic had long ago made into yet another gold cross carried on his belt, as well as the ivory horn. Thus Budic, Comes of Cornouaille first kneeled to King Moruuan in the Church of St Maclou in the diocese of Poutrocoët. They would have to repeat this ceremony in all the dioceses of Brittany in due time, but this was enough for now.

During the Passing of the Peace, Budic put out his hand out to Charles. Charles went to shake it out of habit, then paused realizing it was Budic.

"It took time and patience for Bretons to become Christians. It will take time for Bretons to become Franks," Budic stated, and when Gisela nudged her brother from behind Charles not only shook Budic's hand but they finally hugged like comrades again.

Scissy

The afternoon was advancing swiftly and the tide fully out by the time Mass was complete, and all the preparations had been made. Four Aleth ships, big enough to cross the Gallicus Sea but not as large as Budic's balinger, rocked far off-shore on the waves, waiting on the last passengers. Rowboats picked up everyone off the very last block of stone on the quay-road by the Oreigle Tower, but several, including Charles and Moruuan, were delayed talking to others. When their turns came, they stood on the sand by the shore, waiting for the rowboats to return, but the swift current of the Rance seemed to drag everything out past the fortress point. Gisela could see from the ship that Charles was aggravated. A number of new sailors suddenly began launching larger boats out of the nausts into the water, and they picked up Charles, Moruuan, and the remaining few soldiers and headed out in force.

"They are the whalers of Aleth!" Budic pointed out to Gisela. "The current holds nu fear fur them! They'll get the new King and yur brother un board."

The Bishop grabbed onto Budic's arm and kept pointing. "They aren't just ferrying Moruuan out, either. Look, there are six, seven...eight whaleboats...too many for a ferry. Those whalers have joined the fleet to Tombe! Praise the Lord!"

Each whaleboat only held nine or ten whalers, but

Gisela noticed just how many people were on the four ships. Bishop Cadocanan's plea for good Christians had touched the hearts of the best, and his offer for the church to accept militia soldiers joining this fleet in place of their year's tithe won over many more of the coloni farmers. By reducing the goods they owed taxes on and letting the manor lords send willing servants and troops in their place, for the good of both God and Aleth, Cadocanan had won the town's support out from under Arastang. Now the ships around Gisela brimmed with an overabundance of sailors like fishing boats laden with full nets in a choice haul.

At least, Gisela reasoned, all these Bretons were motivated for one reason or another to be in the coming battle. The problem she saw was precisely that mix. Veteran soldiers stood by ill-trained hunters standing beside adscripti slaves with nothing left to lose.

Cassyon, Ebrulf, Comes Notker of Walloon, Captain Riquier, all of Charles faithful bodyguards were on board again. Budic's eight soldiers as well, with their distinctive high thorn cross emblems in gold. Fourteen tough soldiers, counting Charles and Budic. Maybe fifteen, if she counted Budic by size, Gisela thought to herself with a half smile. But they were only a handful amongst two hundred. Two hundred Alethians.

She looked at the Alethian men, and she wondered how many would lose faith when they came to the fight.

The Bretons of the rebellion, these Bagaudae and their kind; she had seen them up close. Too close. These Alethians were going to basically be fighting themselves, as the Breton Bagaudae and the Alethians were often from the same family. It would also be a fair fight. God alone would determine if faith or family would be stronger than coin.

The Frisian invaders of ex-king Gundebold; they were a harder lot, and bitterly war-minded. She guessed these Alethians fighting them would be about as effective as the Aquitani farmers around Mur that King Waiofar had ordered to kill Frankish soldiers with pitchforks and woods axes. At least these farmers were better armored and had steel weapons.

The Frankish traitors on their big horses; Gisela was not as concerned about them. Between her brother and the Margrave with his Pride barons, they oozed Frankish virtue. Traitors tended to melt away when confronted by strength. They would become rats once faced by real Royal troops and scurry off the field.

The Saxon lazzi; now they frightened her. They were not armored much differently than the Alethians, but they were twice as pagan as the Frisians and thrice as cruel. Something evil was at work with the Saxon mercenaries she had seen in the rebellion troops. Something that gnawed at her greatly; the kind of thing that made her glad the Bishop was with them.

And Bishop Cadocanan was on Budic's ship with her, leading prayers, stoking faith with furor. Several St Maclou white friars were with him too, priests with black robes with white hoods and waist ropes. They tended to Wido as the only wounded before them, but that would change in battle.

Amona helped the friars with Wido. She would not be left behind with the other women and children, kept from both Gisela and the Archer captain. She and Gisela were bound by a strange, warm friendship. Perhaps it was that she was a Godly nun on the prison journey by her own choice. She had sacrificed much to keep Gisela safe.

In that aspect, Amona was not alone. Copar stood near her, awaiting her slightest whim for warmth or water or a hair out of place. Lady Ogiva's ring maiden had been ordered out of the safety of Avranches to serve a Princess she had never met, yet she looked as comfortable on a rocking ship as she would be one day in the Hagia Sophia cathedral in Byzantium when Gisela was being married. Gisela looked at the ring the Lady had given her, bright billon. Copar wore its matching mate. Gisela's first lady in waiting of her own choice instead of her mother's.

Copar and Eulalie had become so attached in the past day. Good abigail companions took training and time, and if that is what Eulalie wanted, Copar was an excellent instructor. With Eulalie, it had been different. She had cried torrents in the church when Gisela told her she had to stay behind in Aleth. Her father lost, for the time being, Gisela, Amona, even her new friend Copar were leaving. Gisela finally relented, fearing her own example of running away would encourage Eulalie to do the same. The Kankaven was no place for cautious girls alone. On the other hand, Gisela thought Eulalie could use a little of that self-reliant backbone in herself, as she had benefited from some of Eulalie's caution.

Introspective Gisela was pulled aside by Budic's protective arms as sailors helped Charles up into the ship precisely where she had been daydreaming.

"Are you ready, Gisa?" Charles asked with enthusiasm as he came over the gunwale.

"Yes, Prince Karl! To the aid of the Margrave at Tombe!" she called out boldly.

"Let's hupe," Budic wiggled his eyebrows with a note of optimism.

The oars swept steadily as the fleet passed around the fortress of Aleth in the swift current, and then past the rocks of Bé and Saint Maclou. The wind was unusually cold and sharp, and Gisela with her ladies draped the bearskin over themselves and kept Wido company, everyone now huddled inside the bow-tent.

"Them Maclou friars, fix you up good like," Amona commented, pulling bearskin higher up on his chest. "You not look so pale."

Wido pulled the bearskin back down to his waist again.

"Why wouldn't Dominus Arastang let you ashore, Wido?" Gisela asked him.

"Arastang was the Comes of Vannes."

Gisela looked at him, still perplexed.

Wido shifted his weight. "We took Vannes with Royal troops a few years ago. Arastang preferred to leave Vannes rather than bow down to your Father or the Margrave, and certainly not to Dux Robert."

"That explains a lot of his resistance to helping Charles, but not you."

The bearskin crept back up his chest as he shifted again. "I was one of five Captains that took the city of Vannes. He remembered my orders to my men not to butcher the merchants of the Cohue, and he thought I had been respectful of St Patern on Méné during the surrender negotiations."

"Oh. I see."

"I let his people live, and him leave peacefully, so he let me live and leave peacefully in return."

By Varde Point the sun was sinking quickly enough blind everyone rowing, and Gisela came out from under the warmer bow-tent. The sky was brilliant blue, and the few remaining clouds were high and far south, casting a sundog to the side of the bright sun.

The Captain was coming down from his crowing up the mast to take the stern rudder. All five ships rowed steadily east, the whalers having no trouble scooting ahead and slipping around rocks closer ashore. Already bonfires burned on promontories and rocky islands ahead, and horsemen with torches paced the fleet along the shoreline.

"Look! That group there riding on top of that cliffside. The Captain says that Arastang himself is riding amongst them," Charles pointed out to her.

"He's just making sure we aren't joining the Frisian fleet," Gisela replied.

There were a lot of gray rocky cliffs, some sandy beaches, and by one passing island the old skeletal ribs of a wrecked ship sticking up out of the water. They all punctuated Charles's astute observations of Breton 'wrecking'.

Night fell with the falling sun, and by guiding bonfires they passed Meinga point and followed the coastline closer than Gisela felt comfortable, but the tides were rising high, the bonfires plain to see, and the old Captain as skilled as the pilot whales they had seen here this morning.

Finally, with a wash of cold waves and brilliant stars, the fleet arrived at a beach just below Grouin Point, and the high tide beached the ships and boats like restless children avoiding sleep.

Scouts, Charles, Budic, and King Moruuan all went the half-mile over onto Gourin, and when they returned they reported what they had seen.

There were lights on Tombe.

Sleep came to few that night, for the sea remained mischievous and the cold sharp. By the first gray light of dawn everyone awoke, for the scouts came back reporting an ill omen, a haar had formed overnight in the Dol Bay.

They had to wait for the tide to return and float their ships off the sand. When the sun finally rose, Charles and Moruuan ordered the ships to get underway despite the news. They passed out around the rocky islands of Gourin, the sea fog became easier to see.

The Captain up on the mast was yelling and cursing to those below.

"They call this the Scissy," Daev explained. "A magical forest."

"The Scissy forest is a myth!" Budic retorted.

"A myth right out of a Taliesin tale," Charles remarked, but all of them were looking at a very real forest of fog.

Gisela looked at the sea fog that crept out from the shore, surrounded Tombe and engulfed the whole of Dol Bay.

"Gwydion's trees..," she whispered.

"The sailors are afraid that demons help the rebellion and hide Tombe," the Captain's son explained to them.

"That is a lie," the Bishop insisted. "Enough of all this talk of witchcraft! Saint Aubert reported the miracle of Scissy the day the monastery on Tombe was completed. This is angel's doing, not demons! God's hand guides us to victory!"

"My father asks, will God open a pathway for us to

see to sail there?" the Captain's son asked.

"Like Moses, perhaps," Budic stated, a cross studded with hawks eye gems in his hand.

"God does favor us," Charles exclaimed.

"Does the fug part?"

"No. Look at it," Charles insisted. "It is a forest the height of trees, a sea fog no higher than our masts. Tombe can still be clearly seen above it. The Captain can guide us to Tombe from his mast, with the ships hidden beneath the fog layer!"

"Tombe will never know we're coming!" the Bishop realized. "God be praised!"

"Have the other ships send up a sailor tu guide them from the mast tup like ur guud Captain. Have the whalers form up behind us and follow us thrugh!" Budic ordered both the old Captain and his son.

Everything was translated and understood. The old Captain cracked his whip above as the rowers commenced again. Budic shouted over to a hesitant Moruuan, and he quickly grasped the plan. Whether he believed it would work or not, Gisela could not tell from his distant face.

The air grew warm as they entered the forest of fog, and the men grew quiet. Prayers could be heard all around as the rowers pulled and stroked, and the Bishop led the Friars in a deep repeating chant.

"Withdraw Satan, never advise me what is conceited. The beverage you serve is evil, drink your own poison."

Budic looked up at the fog. He could not even clearly see the old Captain on the mast anymore.

Next to the Captain's son on the steering rudder, Charles held onto a stern backstay and looked behind. He had difficulty making out the two whaleboats following in their wake.

Gisela, Amona, Eulalie, and Copar huddled together just inside the bow-tent. Voices out in the fog pleaded with God for mercy. They were all lost in the fog.

"This fog is our siren's test of courage. Bishop? Keep the Captain in your prayers."

The old Captain called down, and his son adjusted course slightly.

"Well, he must see somethin' from up there," Daev offered.

"I'm going up there myself," Charles finally stated. Budic's arm quickly found his back and held him off the mast.

"Nu room fur two men. A bad wave wuld toss yu overboard," Budic warned.

"That mast is obviously strong enough to hold a sail," Charles argued.

Budic shook his head. "A sail yes, but you are nu sailor."

The long hour passed. The fog seemed to be lighter above and darker around. They even got occasional glimpses of the ball of the sun through the fog.

The old Captain called down, and his son replied.

"Tombe grows large," Budic explained.

A flurry of orders came down from the old Captain, and the sailors listened and rowed accordingly. Soon the sound of breakers could be heard, disturbingly close in the gray haze.

Budic began talking up the mast to the invisible Captain.

"The Captain advises we go ashore on the whaleboats," Budic finally stated. "We're just off the west side of Tombe."

The Captain's son signaled for the anchor stones to be dropped and for the whaleboats came closer. The surf waves were high.

"This is like talking to God in the heavens. Where are the other ships?" Charles insisted, aggravated.

Budic called up to the Captain again.

"He can see the other ships around us. They have also stopped," Budic answered.

"If we go ashore on whalers we'll be picked off like lice," Charles complained to his clenched fist.

Budic laughed. "Hard tu see, lice."

The Captain called back down again.

Budic's faced jerked back on his neck in surprise. "He says he can see all the way up Tombe. The eel-boat huses that were there two days ago are gone. There is no one moving."

"We go ashore together on the whalers. We take the beach and that odd tree first, then wait for the rest to come ashore before heading up."

Budic nodded in agreement. "Moruuan may have a different idea."

"Then your new King should get to the shore before I do," Charles challenged Budic, almost playfully.

Gisela watched them disappear on the whaleboats into the fog. It was an eerie quiet.

"Somebody give me a bow and arrows," Wido begged from his elbows, trying to pull off the bearskin and look around.

"Stay still, Wido. If we're attacked at sea I'll hand you a quiver myself," the Bishop cautioned. Even his faith was being tested by the unknowing fog.

After an interminable wait, a whaleboat came back into view, calling out to the ship. Gisela recognized her own name being called out in Breton.

"They say Tombe is empty. They want us to come ashore, with more torches," the Bishop interpreted.

Gisela got into a whaler's boat, along with Copar and the Bishop with a friar. She thought the whaleboat smelled awful, but every piece of wood in the boat was worn smooth, and the men were kind.

They came ashore, and every once in a while the fog thinned enough overhead to reveal Tombe like a massive giant towering over them, only to shroud it again from view. Out of the fog along the shore, Charles appeared with a torch.

"They've left."

"What?" The Bishop asked.

"The Frisian's. The eel-boats, even the supplies we saw the day before yesterday, they are all gone," Charles insisted, walking like a racehorse, leading them up the pathway to the monastery. His scouts lit the way by torchlight and the odd blue lanterns.

"What is that?" Gisela asked as they started up. Something was still in the trees where the boats had been, but it was unclear in the fog.

"Dead captives. Men, women...children. They've all been hung," Charles explained, not stopping.

Gisela clutched onto Charles, and he had to stop. "Are they...mine?"

I don't know, Gisa."

The Bishop, Budic, and Daev went closer, and a scout took his blue lantern with them. Gisela took a step to join them, but Charles pulled her back to him.

"They've been slain," Bishop Cadocanan offered back to them from under the tree.

"They've been sacrificed. Luuk at the beheadings, the huuf markings in suut un the bodies," Budic pointed out. He turned a hanging body and then turned away. Bishop Cadocanan remained, saying prayers over the dead souls.

"How many?" Gisela asked as Budic and Daev returned. Budic was having trouble breathing and was in a cold sweat.

"Maybe eighteen total, all along the trees down here," the scout replied.

"One for every eel-boat?" Daev conjectured. Budic nodded in a broken manner in solemn agreement.

Gisela went to hug the big man's leg. He rubbed her head as she looked up at him.

"Was it like...like your..."

Budic nodded and coughed, and rubbed her veil as his eyes welled up.

"If the Frisians sacrificed a captive on each boat's hull, then they used the blood to paint the keel and bow," Daev offered. "It's a Saxon ritual too, for bringing good luck on the voyage."

"It looks like the luck was all the Frisians," Charles spat as the Bishop returned.

Gisela fell to her knees and prayed. The Bishop did as well, and Charles waited patiently. Budic and Daev and his guards went on up, disappearing through the fog. The scout with the blue lantern waited off to the side as well.

Part way up Tombe they popped out into bright sunshine. Tombe was angelic, the thin sea fog spreading out like a blanket onto the shore and around the bay. Gisela remembered seeing clouds in the Alps like this when she was younger.

"We can see smoke rising from Avranches," Charles advised them. Gisela peeked through the passing trees to see the smoke columns of the city to the east.

It only took minutes to climb up to the monastery gate.

"It's like walking on Olympus," Daev said as she passed. He was sitting out on the gate wall, looking out over the Scissy forest of fog towards Avranches, and he thumb pointed back towards the chapel and Budic.

They marched past the ashy remains of their signal fire into the brightly lit monastery to meet Budic and his guards coming out.

"They've cleaned the place ut," Budic insisted, tossing a still smoking candle down in disgust.

"They were here just last night, Præfectus. I saw the lights with my own eyes," a scout apologized to Charles.

"We all did," Charles replied.

"They must have seen us coming," Moruuan surmised. "Fled back to the coast in the fog."

"In this fog? Insanity," Budic shook his head. "They've nu masts tu crow from."

"Maybe they misjudged our numbers, thought us enough to overrun them," Moruuan offered.

"And maybe they are hiding just offshore to pounce upon us as we are divided," the Bishop offered instead.

"They can't have rowed intu Avranches at low tide, even un those eel-boats."

"But they could have taken the boats to Avranches yesterday, and the remaining soldiers, who lit the fires here we saw last night, walked there over the sands in the dark.

"Brenin..," Daev called out from the open monastery gate door.

Budic, Moruuan, and Charles all turned their heads

in response.

"Lord help me. I'm surrounded by royalty," the Bishop pleaded to the sky.

They all followed Daev back outside, where Gisela and Copar were on the wall of the gate where he had been, looking out to sea.

"Call out your whalers, King Moruuan," Gisela pointed out into the fog layer far below them.

More than a dozen dark forms rippled the fog, like sharks just under the water.

"The rising sun glinting off the fog swirls made them sparkle," Gisela pointed out.

Charles lined up the boats travel. "They are headed straight for Avranches. Somehow they can see through this fog."

Gisela looked at Budic. "Sorcery?" Budic shrugged.

Charles put his hand to his hip and the other on his sword hilt. "The Margrave is not here, and does not appear to have been here. We must follow the Frisians to Avranches. Let us hope we can trap them between fort and sea."

Moruuan handed Budic the great ivory horn back.

"You are King nuw," Budic responded, holding the horn back out.

"We both are for this battle, Brenin, and the horn was meant to go to King Pepin in Attigny anyways. Let it go with the Prince to Avranches for this fight," Moruuan offered. Budic took it, and they clasped arms.

They both hugged Charles, who sighed, looked at them both in the eye, and then briskly walked off back down the hill. Like a slow avalanche, one by one, the others and the guards and the last of the scouts first walked and then began to run past the gates of the monastery after him.

Bishop Cadocanan finally appeared from inside, walking slowly out into the morning sunlight. He put a hand to the wall by the gate door and prayed, then left only St Michael behind to guard Tombe.

"Skamelar fog!!!" Charles shouted out into the dull gray.

The slight wind coming off the shore only seemed to feed the sea fog more. Arms creaked with oars. Spear bottoms drummed on iroko decking. Shrouds played a strung tune, plucked by the sea.

"Curse that old codger and his tight lips! I want to know what's going on!" Charles yelled as he paced the deck.

"Raise me up," Gisela offered, then stood and looked at Budic. "Put me on a rope and hoist me up there. I am too small to be in his way, the rope will keep me tied up there, and I can call down what I see."

Charles stopped and stared at her. "Do it."

Budic shook his head as sailors tied a pulley to a halyard, ran a life rope through it and then ran the pulley up to the gooseneck of the fog-shrouded mast and upper spar. They tied the other end of the life rope under Gisela's arms. Budic took a second rope and tied it around her waist.

"They'll pull me up on this rope," Gisela stated, hugging the line around her chest. "What's this for?" she asked Budic.

"Keep angels frum flying away frum me," he replied, then tied the other end of her waist rope around his own waist.

"Mind the shrouds," a sailor begged and lifted her

up as several men took the other end of her halyard life rope. Charles grabbed her elbows, and she let go with one hand to hold his for a brief second, then suddenly she was called up to heaven away from him by the men pulling on deck. She floated up into the lighter fog and then suddenly she was above the fog at the top of the mast.

The mast top had two rings like a pulpit. The old Captain was standing on the smaller one and inside the larger one about waist high. Gisela reached for him, and his weathered old hand wrapped around her and tucked her up against him inside the ring. She clutched onto it with both hands and then gasped.

They looked like they were on a sunken boat, only the mast top and spar were in the clear, cutting through the fog. Ghostly wisps of fog danced and played around them, the sea fog higher here and there, the wind fresh. To their right and left she saw the other ships captain's also crowing. They might disappear in the thicker fogs for a minute or two, but they seemed to always reappear where they had been. One even waved to her, and as she watched, he lifted himself up on his arms on his ring and began pumping his legs, running in place.

He was running across the top of the fog.

The masts of the five ships struck up through the sea fog; lookouts over the gray sheet, crows flying over the Scissy forest.

She began calling down what she saw every minute or two to her brother. It felt like talking to fish or moles.

"How are the Frisians sailing through this?" Gisela finally asked. The old Captain did not understand, so she pointed ahead towards the Frisian fleet and cupped her hand over her brow as if looking and then shrugged. She called her question down to Budic who translated it back up to the Captain.

The old Captain laughed when he finally understood and appeared to twist yarn in front of one of his eyes, saying "Bricht," twice. Gisela had no idea what he meant.

"We're in the Sélune River," Gisela called down. "There's a lot of smoke from the hilltop of Avranches!"

"What about Pont Aubaud? Can you see upriver?" Charles asked the unseen angel above.

Gisela tried, but she could see nothing of the Pont Aubaud bridge.

"I can't see it."

The Captain issued more instructions in Breton down to his son.

"Alright, then look up the Sée River!" Charles begged.

The Captain's son ordered the rowers to alter the pace and turned the boat.

Gisela gasped again as they cleared the sheep lined woods. Avranches was at war.

"The hilltop by the fortress and town are burning furiously!"

Faces, drawn and stern, looked up at blank gray and listened.

"The attacking Bretons have formed a line, entrenched around the Avranches fort, maybe a hundred yards from the motte walls. Dear Lord, the arrows flying. So many," her voice trailed off a moment.

"I see the Frisian ships! The Frisian fleet is landing short of the Port Gilbert bridge along the Seé, where the raiders threw the torches! Many eel-boats, Karl!"

"We'll nut be a match un the grund fur that siege," Budic insisted.

"We will be on water though. We can keep them from leaving," Charles decided, and he looked at Daev.

"Blow the horn," he ordered.

"We'll give away our arrival," the Bishop suggested.

"And let Avranches know of ours," Charles beamed.

Daev looked at Budic, who nodded.

The great ivory horn of Finistère, as white as the fog, was raised up and Daev put it up to his lips.

A great blast bellowed from below, scaring her and even startling the old Captain. He began to cackle and crack his whip in the sky as below they let out a second horn blast.

The Aleth fleet appeared out of the sea fog, coming to Avranches right behind the beached Frisian fleet.

Gisela came floating down on rope wings into Charles and Budic's arms. The old Captain came down behind her.

The hillside of Avranches was before them, the Sée river curving away left. The fortress was a few hundred yards away, and there was a deep trench line of Breton's dug in along the hillside below it, sieging them inside the fort. Breton onagers snapped and jumped as they hurled stones over at the fortress, and carroscorpions launched deadly javelins at any who appeared along the top of the wall of the fortress.

Before them, the Frisian fleet was spread out along the shoreline of the Sée river, right behind the Breton siege trenches. Port Gilbert's bridge-dock that had confused Gisela on her dark ride was farther off to their left around the big wooded curve.

The cheering Frisians were advancing across the ground towards the Breton siege line. The half-naked soldiers seemed to be leading the Frisian charge and in their enthusiasm would sweep past the Bretons and carry them all right up to the walls of the Avranches fort like a human wave. Few Frisians were left by the boats, and only a handful turned to head back to their eel-boats from the charge.

"Moruuan! Have your whalers burn those eel-boats!" Charles ordered across the water between them.

The whaleboats had been prepared to take on the new eels, and they lit harpoons with tar-fire as they passed behind the eel-boats, Budic's warriors and the sailors trading arrows with the few Frisians who remained.

Daev let loose another blast of the horn, lest any in Avranches had failed to hear the last two or failed to see them fighting the Frisians.

The Breton line cheered at the horn blast, apparently confused about just who had shown up.

"They think we are more Breton's coming to help!" Charles complained.

The gates of Avranches opened, and Royal Frankish soldiers began to pour out.

"The fools!" Charles shouted in anger. "Get us ashore!"

The Breton line of soldiers suddenly turned, the Breton flags coming down, the Breton clothing being tossed off. Royal archers popped up from hiding in the Breton siege trench, facing the advancing Frisian wave, and arrows poured down from the Breton line into the oncoming line of exposed Frisians.

A stout Bishop appeared on the Breton trench walls with a great cross rising up behind him, commanding his spearmen to stand ready. Orange Frankish banners unfurled all along the trench, and the carroscorpions began turning away from the fortress and towards the advancing Frisians.

"They've tricked the rebellion!" Budic exclaimed.

"Those aren't Bretons? They're the Franks?" Bishop Cadocanan realized.

"That's Bishop Joshua Jumael and the Second, God bless his soul! They've used the Breton's own tricks against the Frisians!" Charles laughed.

"Eulalie, look! Those are our prison fathers! Helping turn the siege engines!" Gisela grabbed Eulalie's hand and pointed at the siege line as it turned.

"Stay down!" Copar begged. There were still Frisian's with bows along the shore, though the whalers seemed to be the targets. Wido, sitting up on the trunk just inside the bow-tent now, sent a few half-hearted arrows in their direction.

"Captain, sail along with the whalers! Give them

cover fire!" Charles ordered, and the ship turned, the sailors and a pair of Budic's guards all filling the Frisian shore guards with either arrows or abject fear. The other Aleth ship's archers followed suit. Militia or not, the Breton's of Aleth were very good with their bows.

The advancing Frisian wave collapsed into chaos. Only the half-naked soldiers still kept up the charge uphill. The scorpions sang and between them and the archers they did terrible damage to the rebellious Frisians. Gisela had never seen such wanton death, like mowed wheat in a field.

One Frisian group broke left, away from the trenches and around the hillside towards the Port Gilbert bridge. Another Frisian group broke right, away from the trenches and down the slope, headed for the Sélune river.

"Saxons!" Gisela cried out. The group breaking away right from the siege began dropping the big shields they had. It was indeed Saxons amongst the Frisians, carrying their cow-hide coracles as shields, and when the scorpions shot javelins through them like linen, they abandoned them in their haste.

"Land, King Moruuan! Take the battle to Port Gilbert!" Charles yelled.

"Where do you go?" Moruuan yelled back across the water.

"To the bridge at Pont Aubaud, to join the Third and cut off the Saxon's retreat!" Charles yelled, and Moruuan saluted him with his sword.

"Get us ashore, Prince," the Bishop begged.

"Why?"

"You're here to slay. We're here to save," his friars coming up behind him.

"These Frisians will not follow Christ," Charles scoffed.

"Our dying men need the rights, and the Frisians need help finding faith or assistance to go discuss their doubts with Saint Peter. Bishop Jumael will be a bit hasty in deciding for them."

The four Aleth ships all ran up onto the sand together with a great grinding noise as Budic's ship turned at the end of the eel-boat line to make another pass back by them. Several of the whalers came alongside, and the Bishop and his friars got on board the whaleboats to go ashore. A few whalers from each boat climbed aboard and bowed to Budic before joining his guards. Charles ordered one of the boats to go with them to the bridge.

"Daev, gu with them. Take Moruuan his hurn back," Budic asked his bard.

"As ya wish, Brenin."

"Time fur Brenin Moruuan tu forge his own kingly legends, and I've a feeling Gundebold went that way instead," Budic warned. "Yu can tell me the story uf his death when we meet again."

"Don't you want revenge for your brother David?" Charles asked.

"The Lord may have that vengeance."

"Prince. Beware the Saxons," Bishop Cadocanan urged back up at Charles from the whaler's boat. "They'll surrender, repent and then laugh at you, all with the same breath."

"God be with us," Budic boomed out, echoed by many of the sailors and whalers.

"God's speed," the Bishop offered, and all but one of the whaler's boats pulled away towards shore, the Bishop and Friars chasing after Moruuan's troops.

Some of the soldiers pouring out of Avranches joined Bishop Jumael, and they drove into the half-naked Frisians in a flurry of swords and shields. The rest rode out on horseback through the village, among the few burning houses sacrificed to fool the Frisian fleet, and the cavalry disappeared down the road towards the port.

"That's the Margrave and his Pride barons riding to cut off the Frisians at Port Gilbert. They'll be caught between the Margrave and Moruuan. Gundebold is about to be introduced to the Lord's vengeance," Charles patted Budic on the back.

The eel-boats were all ablaze, and Moruuan's soldiers and sailors heavily outnumbered any retreating Frisians foolish enough to try to return to the burning boats.

"Get us to the Sélune quickly!" Charles begged the old Captain, and after Budic translated he nodded and obliged. The rowers stroked fast and deep, but it was back down the Sée before they could go up the Sélune. The whaleboat, swifter, pulled out ahead of them like a pilot fish to a shark. On the ship they watched the Saxon lazzi band making its way around the Avranches hillside towards the Sélune river, receding from their view until they were lost amongst the woods, farms, and barns.

Bishop Jumael, no longer visible himself but the troops of the Avranches Second were, met up with Moruuan's sailors and soldiers. The Frisian army had been massacred and those left now fled in two separate directions. The great horn of Finistère could be heard bellowing on the far side of the fort and village. It also appeared Jumael and his troops began pursuing the Saxon group around Avranches, and

Gisela and Eulalie helped Copar and the Captain's son hang three of the blue lanterns on the backstay to give them a reference.

They finally turned up the Sélune, and it was an agonizing time against the retreating tide, with the current against them.

"More speed! We MUST beat them to Pont Aubaud and the Third!" Charles practically begged, wishing he had jumped on the whaler boat pulling ahead of them. The Captain ordered the sail unfurled and soon the canvas spread out in the breeze, the rowers still stroking, the bow wake rising along with Charles' smile, and the Pont Aubaud bridge grew closer.

It did not take long for them to realize where Bishop Jumael had gotten all his Breton siege machinery and garb. The Breton rebel army had indeed tried to attack Avranches, and they were obviously caught at the Pont Aubaud bridge trying to cross the Sélune in a tremendous battle between the Avranches and the Breton armies. Stripped bodies still littered the road and smoke still repulsed the nostrils. Eulalie began to weep, and Gisela held her. As the whaleboat came to shore ahead of them, crows took flight from the carnage and circled over the ship.

The scout up in the mast was the first to see the Saxon mercenaries group again, far to their back left. The ship would easily make the bridge before they did.

The ship rocked them backward with every synchronous oar stroke, and gently slid them forward with the sailing wind as the oars stirred air on the return. The oars looked like wings to Gisela, a great heron trying to take off over the water, the wingtip feathers just dipping in.

"I'd have preferred Tombe for this fight. It reminded me of home," one of Charles bodyguards remarked, shedding his sheath and picking at the deck with the bare sword point as the ship closed on the bridge. It was Comes Notker; Gisela remembered him from a fun hunt down in Munsterwald, it must have been two years ago now. Notker had bet her brother his Dachs dogs would find a badger before Charles' dogs did, and in trying to see whom had won, they both crawled into an entire cete of badgers.

"I'd give good coin for one of your Walloon apples if you had them. The apples here are too tart," another warrior remarked to Notker, taking out a flask and taking a long drink. It was baron Ebrulf, with his silver swans on his epaulets and etched on the sides of his ax. Gisela wished they were about to dance again instead of about to fight.

"You'll be home to Eckart Castle soon enough," Charles chuckled at Ebrulf.

"Well, I hope I'm upright to enjoy them, then," Ebrulf lamented, toasting them.

"Don't worry yourself none," baron Cassyon joked, spinning his spear in his fingers. "If you're not, we'll stick a Walloon apple in your mouth for the funeral Mass." He took the offered flask from Ebrulf.

"Oh, I can just see his mother over his body now..," Charles joked. "...Ebrulf, how many times have I told you not to eat during Communion!"

The hard men laughed a moment. Budic stepped up.

"What's ur plan, Prince?"

Cassyon handed Budic the flask.

The sail flapped once above them, and Charles

looked up at it before looking back at the Saxon band
across the fields drawing near and then back again at
the bridge drawing even nearer.

Budic took a long swig.

"The Bretons fought hard here, but they didn't burn
the bridge. They needed it. The Saxons need it. We
don't," Charles declared, declining the flask when
Budic offered it to him.

"You want to torch the bridge?" a bodyguard with
an iron laurel wreath around the top of his helm
asked, taking the offered flask from Budic's hand.
Gisela recalled hearing her father in court coaxing
stories out of Riquier evening after evening. If
anybody could be counted on to help hold a bridge in
defense, it would be a former Captain of the Porte de
Mars.

"They've spent a year building it," Cassyon added,
looking at the tremendous wooden bridge on pilings.

"They can spend a year rebuilding it too," Charles
added.

"'Which side will we be upon, I wonder," Budic
shook his head.

The men laughed again.

"You don't need to wonder about that," Notker
advised with a chuckle, taking the flask from Riquier.

"That beast will take forever to burn," Cassyon
observed out loud.

Charles looked at the advancing Saxons. "Have the
Captain tie off on the south bank of the bridge by the
whaler boat. Leave a few archers here on the ship with
Wido, and a few more on the south bank, just in case
any Saxon's try to make it across the water. The rest of
us will cross and fight on the Avranches side, with our
backs to the burning bridge. Have the remaining

archers form a line along our right, using the bank as cover."

"Those Saxons will want to cross the bridge and flee."

"When they see us and the flames, they'll swim for it here off the banks. The archers have the right. Have the sailors and whalers go across and down along the bank to our left there to surprise them and cut them down as they come down to the water.

"It'll be muddy as all hell on that bank," Riquier warned.

"They only have to hold, not charge," Charles argued. "Let the Saxons plow the muck."

"Do yu wish my men tu stand with yu?" Budic asked.

Charles thought. "I'd be honored, Brenin. When the Saxons can't cross the bridge, and the river here is denied them, they might double back on Jumael."

"Jumael advances behind them," Ebrulf noted, finally taking his flask back.

"The lazzi might prefer the flames of the bridge to Bishop Jumael's Holy wrath," Notker offered wistfully.

"Then they will be in a pinch. They'll have no place to flee without passing through one of our groups," Charles stated. Budic nodded in understanding and agreement.

"Well that's it then," Riquier stated, running his fingers over his laureled helm.

"We've no Bishop left for the invocation," Cassyon realized.

"Sister Amona, can you give us an invocation?" Charles asked.

"I can, but you need that child there, Prince. She

will talk to Christ for you better than me."

Charles and the men looked to Gisela. She pulled herself away slowly from Eulalie and Copar and stood amongst them, like an Odysseus amidst the Cyclopes. Copar was so emotionally struck by the scene she had to catch herself on Eulalie.

Gisela breathed, summoned all her courage, then kneeled in the ship amidst them as they kneeled and bowed their heads as well. The rowing stopped, and the boat rose up slightly on the sand and reeds of the south bank.

"Remember, O most gracious Virgin Mary, that never was it known that anyone who fled to your protection, implored your help, or sought your intercession, was left unaided. Inspired by this confidence, I fly unto you, O Virgin of virgins, my Mother. To you do I come, before you I stand, sinful and sorrowful. O Mother of the Word Incarnate, despise not my petitions, but in your mercy, hear and answer me. Amen."

"Amen," everyone said around her.

Charles stood, almost weeping, and softly put his hand on Gisela's head as he passed up to the bow and over the gunwale to the shore.

"L'Ange," Budic praised her with a smile, touched her head and left as well. Then one by one, the bodyguards began to grazingly touch her veil and hair as they left the ship.

Big mailed hands passed like soft brushing pillows across her bowed head, the leather fingers of the archers like feathered wings, the calloused hands of the sailors like Atenea's big furry paws, sweetly asking to please pet more. They all in passing paid homage to the Virgin of Heaven with a touch of the virgin amidst them.

Gisela's head remained bowed because her tears were running. How did priests do this? Some of these men were going to die. All of them might perish. She felt like the totem of death.

An anchor rope was tied to part of the bridge pilings at the bow, and half a dozen archers and sailors stood guard on the ship's bank for any Saxon who might make it across the bridge or Sélune.

The riverside of Port Aubaud was a jumble of half burned fish houses, salt pan shelters, and fishnet drying masts. The smoke still trailed off from smoldering timbers in a hundred thin lines towards the distant fog as if being summoned. Dead oxen, still yoked but no longer with any load, lay in deep dark pools. Men in the Breton green wool lay strewn everywhere, their shields with wheeled crosses and their short spears forming a rough pavement of road.

Cassyon pointed up into a passing fishnet, hung from the flagpole masts to dry. Caught up in the net were half a dozen dead Bretons, filled with Royal arrows.

"Jumael must have set these nets as traps," Riquier observed.

"Then someone drove them into them from off the bridge road," Charles surmised.

"There are hufprints everywhere," Budic pointed out with his great sword.

"The Margrave seems to have made it back with his Pride barons to this fight, then," Charles observed.

"Look at that. The far side of the road is covered in sailcloth," Ebrulf noticed as he crossed the road.

"They used the sails to hide an ambush from the fish houses," Charles guessed, his attention on the bridge ahead. Budic's finger silently motioned two of his guards to pass through the fish houses.

"Tu make certain there is nu second ambush," the big king shrugged.

Charles led the scores of soldiers, sailors, and whalers across the Aubuad bridge. Several sailors carried oars and drug fishnets behind them. Budic and his guards followed last, pouring the whaler's oil on the bridge and the parts of the netting the sailors dropped as they went, finally dropping the empty kegs themselves about half-way across.

As the whalers and archers divided up along the north banks, they spread the fishnet out on the bridge landing to help tangle feet. They began stacking the oars across the end of the bridge to form a wall to fight behind.

The current lifted the ship off the sand slightly, but the anchor rope to the bridge piling kept it tight against the shore. An archer on the shore put a foot on the rope just to make sure.

"Why do men before a battle speak of what they will do when it is over, as if it were plowing a field or eating a meal?" Gisela asked.

Wido tried to turn to look at her but remained silent.

"Men speak optimistically before a battle because they must believe they will win. The hope is contagious, and it bolsters their courage together," Copar explained. "Men who are pessimistic before a battle will always try to figure a way out of it instead."

"And *that* fear...is just as contagious," Wido admitted.

The first Saxons appeared coming around a boathouse.

"Luk there!" Budic called out. A wall of Royal

orange shields and tall spears appeared several hundred yards away to the right, slowly marching across the fields from Chien towards the Saxons and the bridge.

"The Avranches Third lives still!" Charles exuberantly growled through his clenched teeth. Yet another tooth in the Port Aubuad trap. "They advance down from Grand Chien. There is no way for the Saxons to slip upstream now!"

Gisela could see Bishop Jumael's soldiers of the Second and their big cross coming across the field to the far left, but they were still a thousand yards away. The Saxons were being driven towards the bridge, and the moment they realized it, they became running deer. Gisela thought their speed and swiftness seemed almost unnatural.

On the bow of the ship Wido was sitting up on a sailors trunk, and he and a pair of archers lit arrows and drew them back, sending the flaming comets out onto the bridge.

The way across the Aubaud erupted into hell.

The first few running Saxons were effortlessly dropped by the archers before they even reached the netting. The rest held back their advance until the full number could charge.

As Charles expected, the Saxons choose the Sélune bank to their left over the other options. "Better to drown than burn," Wido stated and readied arrows for any that might make it past the whalers and sailors. The old Captain, in the stern with his son and an archer guard, crossed his arms and said something.

Gisela looked to his son, an older man himself.

"Papa says our ship beckons to the Saxons like a treasure. Your Prince obviously placed it here to draw the Saxons hope of escape on it."

The brown clothed Saxons came to the bank in frightening numbers, their liripiped hoods trailing out behind them like flags. Many amongst them wore mail and thick leathers. Harpoons and spears greeted them equally, however, and a dozen Saxons careened up into the air, vaulting, skewered, kicking and screaming over into the Sélune mud like kabobed meat into a sauce. The spears and harpoons hiding down the bank had sufficiently surprised them.

The Saxon hoard turned back from the flying harpoons towards the bridge, and their own wall of thrown spears drove Charles, Budic and their guards down behind their oar wall.

"Look there!" Wido pointed. There were three heavily armed Frankish barons amidst the tattooed Saxons. "Who are they?"

"The devil himself," Gisela whispered and made the sign of the cross.

"The Dux?" Wido asked, unable to tell. Gisela remained silent.

The archers to their right fired arrow after arrow, but shields and sheer numbers overwhelmed the oar wall, and they began climbing over their own dead on the netting to jump over the oars.

Charles, Budic and their guards were waiting. The Saxon bodies began falling off the sides of the bridge, and the body parts that flew made Gisela nauseous.

Great men, kind men, loving men, now vile, cruel, deadly. Dancing, laughing, hunting; courtly men, turned butchers. Rain gutters on the bridge began to run out red, and a luckless Saxon, who had luckily made it past the steel teeth of her brother and Budic, jumped, flaming, off the bridge for his choice of fortune. The archers on the ship beside her extinguished the jumpers life in exchange for his river's extinguished flames.

The harpooners and sailors with spears climbed up the bank as the Saxons recoiled from them and pushed towards the bridge instead. Saxons would sacrifice themselves upon a thrust spear so that their comrades could kill the occupied soldier. Aleth Bretons died alongside Saxons in wrestling jumbles and bloody knots before the shield wall of the Avranches Third pressed in from the right and Bishop Jumael and the Avranches Second arrived from behind. The Saxons were completely surrounded.

The three armored soldiers quickened their advance to arrive at the oar wall in the middle of the Saxons.

"Black Lions. They're Swabians!" Wido exclaimed, pointing at the three armored Frisian soldiers among the Saxons. Two of the heavily armed barons used dying Saxons as additional shields to get over the half-tumbled oar wall, and the third followed them over, the rampant black lion on his shield blocking away Charles's sword. King Budic advanced into them. Gisela could see his great sword rising above the fight, first glinting in the sunlight, then red with death. Besides Charles, Ebrulf popped up into her view, his head back, screaming out in pain, and he and a mailed Saxon came over the side of the bridge together, plunging down into the water and mud. The flames on the bridge grew.

There would be no more dances for her and Ebrulf.

Gisela turned away from the horror, only to discover confusion.

Copar had cut her dress shorter for some reason, her cloth wrapped legs now showing, and she pulled her veil off as she turned back towards Gisela. Her hair was as red as the flames of the bridge.

"Malguen?" Gisela asked Copar, confused.

Copar's eyes flashed at Gisela in response as she drew her golden dagger and crossed the Captain's son's face and then cut the totally unaware stern archer's bowstring as she brought it back across.

Eulalie screamed as the old Captain uncrossed his arms and crumpled down onto the deck with an arrow in his back. A strange, older soldier was behind him, outside the ship as if walking on water, his hunnish bow still twanging from shooting the Captain at point blank range. Another new Breton soldier beside him sent an arrow past her head so close she felt it's wind, striking one of the surprised archers next to the unaware and still seated Wido in the bow.

On the south bank, muddy Breton men who had hidden in the cold marsh now fought with the sailors along the shore. The ship was trapped on both sides by fighting, and a burning bridge before it.

Copar helped four strange wet soldiers up over the side by the stern. Gisela wondered why they were so muddy if they could walk on water. One of the four new soldiers was struck by an arrow from Wido's remaining archer companion, and another fell to the stern sailor's blade before Copar's dagger found the sailor's back.

"Tortulfe," Gisela recognized the older soldier with the hunnish bow from the Fougères camp.

The warlord's second shot sailed past her on the opposite side of her head and struck the other archer beside Wido. Wido turned enough to get a horizontal bowshot off and hit one of Tortulfe's companions, leaving only Tortulfe and Copar facing Wido, with

Gisela, Eulalie, Amona in the middle.

Eulalie ran screaming, jumping off the ship towards the shore. The ship's archers by the bridge defeated the few cold, muddy soldiers attacking them along the shore, then from the screams realized Bagaudae assassins had used the whaler's boat to climb up over the stern of the ship. The women were intermingled with them now, though, and none wished to slay the Princess by mistake.

Wido's arrow at Tortulfe was short-shot by his pain and flew off into the Sélune. Copar grabbed Gisela by the arm, breaking her out of her confused daze.

"Who is that?" Tortulfe asked as he shouldered into his bow.

"Pepin's Princess!" Copar grinned.

"Bring her," Tortulfe ordered as he drew his seaxes and charged past her towards Wido.

Wido managed to get off another arrow despite the pain. Tortulfe blocked it deftly with one of his blades. Gisela had never seen anyone do that before.

Copar drug Gisela forward with her to cut the line keeping the ship moored to the piling, keeping Gisela between her and the shore archers. The ship lurched in the current and began to slowly spin away from the bank, the bridge's flames rising higher behind it. One sailor dove for the ship from the ramparts of the bridge shore wall, catching himself on the gunwale by his arms.

Wido tried to stand on unsteady legs, using his bow as a shield to block Tortulfe's charge. Tortulfe cut Wido's arms, but as Wido stumbled back, he grasped Tortulfe's backslung bowstring and dragged Tortulfe over the side with him as he fell off.

Copar kicked at the hands of the sailor on the bow,

sending him off into the water.

Eulalie was screaming in the river, and Amona stood up to confront Copar, who only showed her dagger and forearm and grinned.

"Don't do it, Sister."

"Save Wido! He'll drown!" Gisela begged Amona, and the heavy woman ran and jumped over the side after the injured man, and square onto Tortulfe's swimming back. Eulalie made it to the bank and the waiting friendly sailors.

The Horn of Finistère blew in the distance. Moruuan was advancing from Avranches. Gisela saw more muddy Breton soldier's heads pop up behind the ship. They were standing in the whaler boat, not walking on water.

"Malguen, what are you doing?" Gisela begged as Copar drug her back towards the stern, keeping them both down from any shore archer shot as the ship slowly spun on the tide. Gisela guessed Tortulfe and his companions had been hiding in the river marsh reeds since the Breton battle yesterday and climbed onto the whaler boat when the fight across the burning bridge got everyone else's attention. Their shivering cold made them poor fighters.

"You're coming with us, snow angel," Copar insisted, chancing a glance over the side to ensure the whaler boat was still tied up at the stern. She smiled at several ragtag Bagaudae soldiers, most of whom were either shooting at the archers on shore or trying to help the cursing Tortulfe back onto their boat.

"No, I don't think I will," Gisela replied plainly. Copar turned to see Gisela tying herself to the rudder with the old Captain's whip, and was now slowly adding more winds around her arm as she stared at

Copar. "Catch them in your hands, the Proverb said."

"Bejabbers, you little vixen!" Copar grabbed her free arm to stop her from winding more.

"Are you a margot, Malguen from across the water? Daughter of a margot, perhaps? Was Copar a changeling to fool Lady Ogiva?" Gisela asked, turning her attention to the winding and her trapped arm.

"I'm from across the water, Gisa," Copar remarked, appearing touched as well as deadly. "I was never Ogiva's childhood maiden, I lied to you about that. No better place to learn the Margrave's plans than from inside his own fort."

"A spider in the King's Palace, and no better place to learn our plans than with us on our ship. I wondered where you disappeared to during the crowd riot at Aleth."

"I had to alert my comrades," Copar confessed warmly. "So you think I'm the Faerie Queen of your adventure, eh?"

"Yes, though your mate Tortulfe makes an odd King Gradlon."

Copar grinned. "Your mate Charles will make an odd King as well."

"He's not my mate, he's my brother. You should know that."

"And he's not my mate, he's my father. You should know that, I think," Copar answered back, then got a devilish look on her face. "Gisela, come run away with us," Copar begged.

"WHAT?!" Gisela's mouth fell open, startled.

"Join my father and I with the Bagaudae. Live free with us, on both sides of the Mor Breizh. I know you don't want to go to Constantinople and be married. You can run away with us."

Gisela laughed.

"You can believe in faeries all you like," Copar tempted her. "I know your heart, dear one."

"No."

"Copar! Come on!" came a deep voice from over the side. Her father Tortulfe was back in the whaleboat.

"Don't make me kill you, Princess," Copar warned, her dagger now pressing up against Gisela's neck.

With her free hand, Gisela pulled Budic's tiny fork out of her pocket. "You will have too, and I know you don't want to. Go ahead. I'll join God, and Jesus, and my little brother Pepin, and Sacha. And I'll say a good word for you when you arrive before Christ to answer for it."

"You are a tricky one, dear love. I shan't forget you," Copar whispered, moving the blade away and instead caressing Gisela's cheek with the back of her hand before vanishing over the side in the same swift motion. Gisela began to untie her arm.

Arrows struck the sides of the ship in a loud report, and Gisela saw the sailors on the bank splashing out to help Amona pull Wido up to shore.

When she unwrapped her arm, she dropped to the side of the dying old Captain and his face-cut son, covered in blood and quivering disturbingly. She looked over the edge of the ship again.

Several of the Breton Bagaudae were rowing the whaler boat away down the Sélune, boat archers trading shots with shore archers following along the shoreline, Tortulfe looking back towards the bridge battle and Copar looking back at Gisela. They moved off swiftly with the current downriver towards the Scissy fog, Royal archers on the muddy bank side trying to follow them and shoot arrows, other whalers on the Avranches side running back to their friends by Port Gilbert to get the whalers to give chase.

Gisela looked back at the bridge, bright and aflame in an incredible blaze.

Budic was standing on the edge, looking back at her and the ship. Charles was still on the end of the bridge, standing before one of the Swabian Black Lions. The armored baron was on his knees, surrounded by soldiers and whalers, his helmet off and his sword surrendered to Charles. He was an older man, much more so than the rest had been.

Several whalers dove from the Avranches bank into the icy waters and swam over to the drifting ship. Gisela tried to help them up and tossed the cut anchor rope over the side for them. The dripping sea hands made certain she was alright, then some went to the old Captain and his son as others took the rudder to steer the drifting ship closer to the bank. Harpoons with ropes quickly passed between the ship and shore, and an army of sailors, soldiers and whalers pulled the ship back up towards the Avranches end of the bridge as Bishop Jumael, King Moruuan, the Margrave and Bishop Cadocanan joined Charles and his captured Dux. Gisela wondered if it was Tassilo or Robert who had surrendered.

Several sailors and Budic helped Gisela off the ship and up to the bridge ramp. The smoke and flames of the burning bridge rose high behind Charles.

As he helped her off the ship, Budic handed Gisela a piece of what looked like broken glass.

"What is this? Quartz?"

"Gundebold's sunstone," Budic answered.

Gisela looked puzzled. "From Fougères?"

"Moruuan took it frum him. He used it tu see

through the smoke uf the siege uf Fougères, and through the Scissy fug," Budic replied.

Gisela turned it over in her fingers. "Can he use it to see through the smokes of Hell?"

"Nut any mure. He's already departed un that journey withut it," Budic stated and stepped across the gunwale to see about the old Captain for himself.

The Margrave stood over several dead warriors. The Aleth whalers looked like an execution squad with their harpoons ready. Bishop Cadocanan and Bishop Jumael came over to put their escorting arms around Gisela to keep her from any wounded Saxon or the Dux's treachery.

"Sister," Charles introduced his prisoner. "May I present our granduncle Robert, Dux of Neustria, and the leader behind this rebellion."

"Where is Tassilo?"

"In Bavaria, unaware of all this, it would seem."

"Grandmother Rotrude will not have nice things to say about her brother's actions of late," Gisela observed.

The older armored duke barely nodded.

"Why does he still have his head?" Gisela asked her even angrier brother.

"Because he is royalty and has surrendered to the judgment of the True King instead of fighting to the death."

"So *this* is the Saxon's Fairy Princess?" Dux Robert asked from his knees.

"So you are the Black King?" Gisela hurled back.

Dux Robert almost laughed. "Gundebold did have you in his grasp, after all, that night at Fougères, and he let you go."

"You'll join him as soon as you reach our Father.

You can go serve Satan together," Gisela stated, then looked puzzled at him. "Why? Why rebel against us? Why cause so much death?"

"We were possessed by demons, and not working under our own will. You must forgive us! " Robert offered in his defense.

"As Dominus Arastang would say, convenient."

"Bishop Jumael can help you with that, I'm certain," Riquier spat, the only one of Charles' guards to survive the bridge battle.

"Arrest him," Charles ordered. "Robert, son of Lambert, Comes of Hesbaye and Dux of Neustria; in the True King's absence I now place judgment upon you for Treason Against the Crown, with the sentence of death to be carried out when we reach my Father."

The older dux went from kneeling sorrowfulness to defiant incredulity. "Ask yourselves a question," Robert stated as friars roughly lifted him up and bound his hands behind him. "Eve started the original sin by taking the apple," he pointedly looked at Gisela. "But who let Satan into Paradise in the first place? Adam or Eve?"

"Evil giant of Enoch! *Nephilim*," Gisela stated back in a voice so unusual it made the hair stand up on the arms of those who heard it. Cadocanan and Jumael beside her looked stunned.

"*Nephilim!*" Gisela growled again at the Dux, even louder and sterner, in a voice that no one recognized. The Dux cried out in terrible pain and fell down, though the friars tried to keep him standing.

"*NEPHILIM!*" Gisela finally shouted, and the great ivory horn in Daev's hands suddenly blasted out a note all by itself as she did. Daev dropped it in disbelief. Dux Robert screamed hideously as if being racked, then broke down into tears, sobbing on the ground like an infant.

The priests and friars and half the surrounding army around her made the sign of the cross.

"You are to fear the LORD your God and serve him," spouted Bishop Jumael, falling to his knees. "Cling to him and swear by his name. He is the one you are to praise, because he is, your God who carried out those great and awesome things for you that you witnessed."

Gisela calmed down and looked at Dux Robert with disdain. "It will start again with his lies, this very day. He'll cause nothing but disharmony and trouble in the months ahead as he awaits Father, and he'll be treated more royally in the wait than the good-hearted vineyard prisoners I walked with on my journey. There will be...discussions. Favors will be offered. Clemency will be suggested. Exile instead of execution, only to return us to a battlefield in our future to this very day, this very man, this very treason, again."

Charles looked at Cadocanan, who was still bloody from the fight and amazed at what he had just witnessed from Gisela. He motioned with his sword at Robert.

"God forgive him," was all Cadocanan could say, and he nodded.

Bishop Jumael nodded as well, weeping, sobbing in gleeful praise.

The stunned Margrave stepped over to Charles side.

"What do you say, my Margrave?"

"I say, I have never witnessed such a thing in my entire life. As a Comes Palatine you have the authority. You're the Prince of Neustria, Præfectus; you'll be king of Neustria one day soon. No man here would dare say a word against your judgment after what just happened here."

Budic's ship sailed back up the Sée, past the burned eel-boats, past cheering soldiers, back into Port Gilbert and Avranches, with Dux Robert hung dead from the top of the spar by the old Captain's whip. Bishop Jumael was bellowing out prayers to the ship and passing crowds.

"For this cause I bow my knees to the Father of our Lord Jesus Christ, Of whom all paternity in heaven and earth is named, That he would grant you, according to the riches of his glory, to be strengthened by his Spirit with might unto the inward man, That Christ may dwell by faith in your hearts; that being rooted and founded in charity, You may be able to comprehend, with all the saints, what is the breadth, and length, and height, and depth: To know also the charity of Christ, which surpasseth all knowledge, that you may be filled unto all the fullness of God. Now to him who is able to do all things more abundantly than we desire or understand, according to the power that worketh in us..."

Hypostasis

"To him be glory in the church, and in Christ Jesus unto all generations, world without end. Amen."

With that final prayer, the abbess left the nave of the chapel after Vespers and entered the sanctuary. She watched thoughtfully as the nuns replaced the chalice and paten and the censer and cross back upon the tables and then removed her stole and chasuble. She could not shake the unusual feelings that were settling over her this evening,

She held hands and shared praise with the other nuns as they left the sanctuary, encouraging them to go ahead to the refectory and begin work on the choir tapestry, but then herself turned through the reliquary, alone and in silence. Statues and portraits of former abbesses Balthild, Bertille, and Swanachild patiently watched over bejeweled treasures and old bones, and the Abbess's fingers flowed over marble, gold, and canvas as if blindly finding her way through a dark history. Without meaning too, she found herself back at the narthex, and she put on her thick green cope, pulled the sides around her and stepped out into the cloister.

Hanging lamps with feeble light flickered from their ceiling's perch along the hall of the cloister. The carefully tended open garden inside the cloister was under a thick blanket of snow; color, shade, and design now well hidden under flowing white form.

The snow barely drifted onto the floor between the arches on this side, and her footprints quickly became the only tracks to go this way. Her heart was craving something hard to define, and she lingered at each window under its arch, pausing and looking at the names carved on them as if they were stoic dance partners. Audion. Leodegardius. Sigisla.

She looked up into the night's heavy snowfall, the signum tower disappearing from her dim lamp lit view. Childishness struck her with a mischievous smirk, and she slowly walked her way around to the tower and entered it's lower room.

The ladder was cold to her hands, but firm and dry. She began climbing. It had been years since she had climbed up to the signum.

Up beside the great bell, the cold and flakes greeted her face. The abbey was laid out below her in a tight cluster, the few lamps inside the cloister halls giving it the appearance of a lonely island on a vast dark sea. Looking away, the gray and white of the thick clouds and snows made a dense, impenetrable fog. Chelles village spread out around the abbey towards the south, but few were the lights between it and the Marne. She looked north towards the mountain of Chalats, but the snow washed it away in the blurry darkness. The Abbess lingered there for a long while, her copa tucked tightly around her, the flakes drifting past her face, looking out at the fog from such a great height.

The journey of life alongside Christ was one of God's greatest challenges. The former Abbesses in quiet remembrance down in the reliquary did not leave life the same women that had come to Chelles Abbey. The journey had changed them, just as her journey had changed her. People who were once thought enemies became allies. Allies became enemies. Saul became Paul on God's path. When a person vainly chooses their own obstacles in life, the gates to them often remain tightly sealed and resist every siege, yet the daunting challenges and mistakes God puts in our way always seem to lead to the postern gates we didn't know about, and they open before us. The path's journey shapes us for the destination. At some point in life, everyone is a prisoner of themselves, everyone is a victim of themselves, from criminal to pope.

The Abbess climbed back down the ladder slowly. She did not wish to slip and fall. The steep ladder was an obstacle, yet it was an aide. Without it, you could not reach the bell. You could not see into the distance. But you had to climb it. One has to see God's obstacles differently. Overcoming the obstacles God has placed before us, walking away from those we have chosen for ourselves, recognizing that the ones God puts before us are to help us gain strength for horizons yet unknown, for mistakes yet unmade. Every rung of the ladder is essential. Even ogres can be helpful to you at times. At some point in life, everyone is a great hero, and a guard of their fellows. From mastiff to margrave.

The snows on the floor of the other side of the cloister drifted almost to the inside wall. In the dim lamplight from the ceiling, she saw another set of fresh footprints. They had been barefoot and hopping; that could only be Sister Nadette, who had undoubtedly come to check on her after Vespers and kindly left her alone in the tower with her thoughts when it was clear she was alright.

The journey of life alongside such women was a blessing. The ability of the convent to overcome its problems was made easier by sharing the difficulties. Men, so futilely dedicated to the solos of God's music. Men faced monsters alone as a badge of courage. Women joined together to sing the chorus, their ability to lock arms together against the challenge made them different. Strong women together never cry for want, never cry tears alone under suffering. They forgive the mistakes in each other. Men bind the wounds of war. Women bind the emotional wounds of life. God's truest spiritual army lies not with warring men but in forgiving women. To not see that was a mistake all men made at some point, from bandits to kings.

Stepping through the crunching snow, she came back to the hall that separated the convent from the monastery. She unlocked the door with her key and entered the long room. A dim candle flickered outside the door of the Abbot's foyer to the scriptorium, indicating he was still awake as well. She opened the locked door with her key.

Gisela put more ink on the quill tip.

This thus ends the story I began many pages ago. I can only trust to God and hope that your reader has done this tale justice without my voice to perfect or witness it.

We returned to Avranches as victors, but amidst such carnage. The rebellion never grew, and indeed was seemingly snuffed out with Dux Robert. As Dux Tassilo's aide-de-camp, he had convinced Tassilo that his own family was at great risk by rivals, to induce him to leave your war camp so suddenly. Tassilo appears to have been unaware of Dux Robert's plans to take over Neustria and the Marche with Frisian and Bagaudae help. Tortulfe and his daughter

Copar escaped along the foggy shore back into the Couesnon valley; the Margrave himself tracks them incessantly.

You Captains will give you a far more accurate report, but suffice it to say the Margrave had marched his armies to Harcouët, but cleverly had many of his Pride barons and squads drop off the moving train and secretly make their way to Ducey, a village on the Sélune, upriver from Avranches. There in the night they used fish nets to snare and destroy an elite squad of rebel soldiers using the coracles to come and secure the bridge at Port Aubaud for the Bretons. The Margrave believes Tortulfe may have been amongst them, and escaped. The Breton siege army was not met by a few defenders and an open bridge, but by Bishop Jumael, the full Second and Third armies, and then the Margrave with his Pride barons to end the battle, the very night we camped on Point Gouin and saw lights on Tombe.

The bodies of the Saxon mercenaries were burned upon the Aubaud bridge. The bodies of the Frisians were buried across the Sée, and Bishop Jumael led Masses for an entire week in hopes of bringing their souls, and our own, closer to God. Jumael plans to revive the monastery on Tombe, possibly from the monastery in Dol.

Captain Wido is recovering his legs and arms in Avranches, and the Margrave has made him his lieutenant of the Marche, at Charles' request. Wido remains there till fully healed, which is a good thing, for Mother sings his praises and send him blessings and funds, but has forbidden him to return to her Court for disobeying her direct orders. The great horn of Finistère remains with the Margrave in Avranches as a sign of the Franks and Bretons working there together.

Bishop Cadocanan returned to Aleth a hero. He brought back most of the prison women and children to Avranches the following week, just shortly before Mother's army showed up with Comes Ceufroy and soldiers of Andecavus and Laval. Many of the Aquitani vigneron prison families were reunited, including Maylis' father and step-mother, though we never found Eulalie's father. Nor were we ever to find the boy or body of Sacha along the coast, a matter that still breaks my heart.

Comes Hoel returned from Wales to find his son had won the family honor and seems greatly pleased. He threw a feast for us all to honor his son the new king. King Moruuan himself has begun touring the diocese of Brittany in hopes to earn the full title of Brenin of Brittany. Time will tell if he is successful, for he has many lords and lesser kings to convince, and many bishops to pray with to match Budic. He seems committed to finding peace with us. On his way, he returned the dying old Captain C'hreac'h to Brest. Gundebold's treacherous sunstone went to be buried with him, at Bishop Cadocanan's request.

Bishop Cadocanan, Bishop Jumael, Comes Budic and I took Sister Amona on a pilgrimage to Dol, where she earned an indulgence, and she was pardoned for lying before God to the corrupt Bishop of Le Mans, a harm to her that had saved my life, now healed.

With the coming of December, Charles, Comes Budic and I began an expedition to return the Aquitani prison families home to their Mur vineyards and search for survivors along the forts. We even managed to find a big Le Mans dray stallion that Budic could actually ride.

We were able to find the bodies, buried by the locals, of Julien and the Ogre at the Billé stream, but we never found the body of Atenea. All of the guards and prisoners bodies were taken to be buried properly in Ize, and mother's recompense to reeve Wibert was to elevate him to a Comes of d'Ize. At the celebration, Wibert and Charles undertook a louveterie, a grand wolf hunt according to Breton history, and over fifty-seven wolves were killed and bountied. Charles plans to make it a tradition. The bodies of Julien and the Ogre were returned to Andecavus and buried at St Aubin's with a huge Mass that even Mother and Archbishop Gravien attended.

Comes Budic has returned all the way to Mur with Charles and me, and has remained here. He has offered to pay the Romefeoh tithe of every bishop along the Loire and Maine under Tour's see. He would pay for every bishop in Aquitania as well if he could, I think. Charles thinks it is a ploy to get Bishop Gauciolenus of Le Mans to stand before the Pope. Honestly, my King, of all the saints I have heard exaggerated tales of, and all the posturing, self-aggrandizing Bishops I have run across, Budic is a saint unrecognized, and he does not seek it. He truly believes this life pales in comparison to the next. I hope you are able to meet him soon.

Next, we come to my duty. I am fully ready to marry Leo if that is still your desire. Charles and Mother both agree that Emperor Constantine V of the Eastern Empire and you began arranging my marriage only six years ago, yet nothing has been said between you about my actual age. Charles has suggested, and Mother has agreed, that the Emperor does not need know my exact age, and that we should tell him I am still too young to travel to Constantinople just yet. This would allow me time to recover from my journey and spend time with Charles and you upon your return. This would be a great boon.

Bishop Cadocanan has also made another suggestion, that according to Church Law, people unable to travel can be married by proxy in the Church's eyes, legally and spiritually. Archbishop Gravien confirms that proxy weddings can be granted in unusual cases. Perhaps, dear Father, you may find it in your heart to inquire of the Holy

Pope if my and Leo's marriage might not qualify as an unusual case, and allow me a proxy wedding so I can remain in Aachen and yet still fulfill your wishes with the Emperor?

Now we come to my forgiveness. I deeply regret running away over Pepin's death, and I am ashamed of my dabbling in folklore and witchcraft instead of grieving. My journey has taught me so much, but I do not ask for mercy in your punishment. I do, however, make every claim I may for the lives and grapevines of the Mur vignerons who I have brought back with us. These are not rebellious soldiers or traitorous lords. They are base farmers that Waiofar propped up and threatened with death if they did not guard his retreat. The captains of Mur tell me they did not even fight our forces upon our arrival, but surrendered. Surely we can have compassion for such good folk, folk who fought bravely against the Saxons and Breton rebels, folk who deserve a king of promise rather than wrath.

If you have forgiveness in your heart for me, I ask that you show me your displeasure, and instead allow these coloni, their vines and wine to remain at Mur, and serve us well. Let them be free, as Saint Gildas did growing prayer crops with Saint Illtud, when the birds began to eat their miraculous corn.

Gisela set her quill down in the ink well a moment and reflected. She looked at her ring from Lady Ogiva. The bright billon was a merrow form holding a crowned heart, as if in an offering. She looked over at her Mother's punishment for her. A florilegium of commentaries, allegories, and expositions of Hilary of Poitiers, to be copied for another psalter for the new church. On top was Psalm 1.

Blessed is the man who hath not walked in the counsel of

the ungodly, nor stood in the way of sinners, nor sat in the chair of pestilence. But his will is in the law of the Lord, and on his law he shall meditate day and night. And he shall be like a tree which is planted near the running waters, which shall bring forth its fruit, in due season. And his leaf shall not fall off: and all whosoever he shall do shall prosper.

"Not so the wicked, not so: but like the dust, which the wind driveth from the face of the earth. Therefore the wicked shall not rise again in judgment: nor sinners in the council of the just. For the Lord knoweth the way of the just: and the way of the wicked shall perish."

The Abbess recited the first Psalm as she watched the candle's flame in the glass alcove. It would be perfectly still, then pop and flutter like the wind from one tiny bird's feather, only to return to its solemn vigil.

"Ants. Rabbits. Locusts. Spiders," the Abbess whispered to herself, her eyes brightening before tearing up slightly. "It was an early winter then, too."

The jubé opened beside her, the wooden lattice of a shryving now forming a barrier between convent and monastery.

"Abbess, you are up late this eve. Does the storm trouble you?" the young abbot asked.

"No," the Abbess corrected the young man, perhaps half her age. "But we do not have enough hay in our barn to feed our cows in snow this deep. I was hoping you could ask Brother Rupert to go to Calae for more."

"It will be done in the morning, Abbess. Do you believe this snow will delay Emperor Charlemagne's arrival past Twelfth Night?"

"Perhaps, if this snow falls all the way to Rheims."

There was a long pause.

"Is there anything else Abbess?"

"No. Well, perhaps," she corrected herself, rubbing her eyes and thinking. "Have you ever been to war, Abbot?"

"War? Thank the Good Lord, no, Sister!"

The Abbess tipped her head to the side and squeezed her eyes shut with her fingers on the bridge of her nose. "You've never seen warfare in your life?"

"Bishop Belto kept Tonnerre peaceful. There were street fights outside Auxerre, if that's kind of fighting you are speaking of."

"No. No, thank you, Abbot."

"Abbess? I've not seen the war, but I've seen the warriors. I've ministered to many lost monks misplaced by the Northmen, tended many hurts and stitched many wounds they have caused."

The Abbess smiled purely to herself. "Then Chelles is fortunate to have you here. Thank you for tending to the hay. Good night." She slid the jubé between them closed, and then doused the candle with the cup.

The Abbess made her way up and out the quiet hall, back into the convent.

While the cloister was dim and the dormitory dark, the refectory was brightly lit and glowed warmly. A giant ornate choir tapestry, almost complete, stretched all around the walls. Over a score of nuns, seemingly at ease and comfort with each other's company, worked busily on the remaining parts of the tapestry. The Abbess paused as she watched them. Laughing, crying, sharing. Women in Christ, taking pleasure in doing Christ's work.

"This is so much more relaxing than the

scriptorium," young nun Sophis whispered to the nun beside her. The Abbess behind them bit her lip in silent agreement.

"We can unsew our mistakes," Rene agreed.

"Can't do that with the ink!"

"Mother Superior! Please come join us! We've almost finished!"

"Yes, Mother, oh please come!"

The Abbess smiled and stepped down into the busy women.

"The Choir Tapestry is beautiful, Mother, but Sandrine says there is a problem."

"Oh?"

"Yes, Mother. It is too big for our Choiry rood. It will wrap all the way around behind the ambulatory!"

The Abbess smiled again. "That is because it is not for Chelles. The Emperor Charlemagne is christening his new Palatine Cathedral in Aachen in the coming months. His Holiness himself is coming as well. This is destined for that rood."

"Oh, how grand!"

"This choiry tapestry will be hung there? In the Emperor's Cathedral?"

"One of many hanging there, I would suppose."

"But the *only* one from his sister!"

"Come, Mother, sew your name and date here on the last panel then!"

The Abbess slowly walked over to the empty stool and looked at the panel.

A wise man shall hear and shall be wiser: and he that understandeth, shall possess governments.

He shall understand a parable, and the interpretation, the words of the wise, and their mysterious sayings.

The fear of the Lord is the beginning of wisdom. Fools despise wisdom and instruction.

Gisela signed her letter to her father King Pepin *Your loving daughter, Gisela, Feast of St Stephen, December 26th, In the year of our Lord 763.*

The Abbess sewed her name into the tapestry for her brother, Emperor Charlemagne, *Abbess Gisela of Chelles, St Stephen's Day, December 26th, AD 804.*

End Credits & Acknowledgments

There are many people and entities to thank for the inspiration to write this series of books. On my author's website I go into great detail about the more important and subtle influences, so here let me just thank those that helped this particular book achieve its full measure.

End Credits music

I write in my head in the vineyard, and I spend a LOT of time in the vineyard with music in my ears. This is not a playlist. I have over 890 songs on my regular playlist rotation, and you are invited to go to my website and connect with me to learn more about how and why music has influenced my writing, and, if you feel like it, share how it is influencing yours.

This musical acknowledgment is in deep appreciation for the incredible artistry of the individuals and musicians below. Simply put, I could never have imagined the story of *Tynged* without these six inspirations. To not thank them here would be terribly selfish. They earned and deserve the credit.

Odin's Hill: Irminsul; nuns & fairies
Achillea The Nine Worlds

I Mett Her in the Medowe: the Breton Marche, old Roman roads
Ancient Future

Selling the Aroma Gisela's ride (BIG thank you!)
Mehmet Ergin

Lock and Load: King Budic
Dàimh

Carpe Diem: the Abbess remembers
Kori Linae Carothers

The Silken Whip: Tynged Suite (in my own little dream world)
Afro Celt Sound System

* the above artists do not support or endorse my book in any

way.

Really folks, these wonderful artists and their record labels don't even know I exist, much less that their music deeply inspired me. I can only hope they are flattered if they one day stumble over this praise.

Two musical influences to Tynged require a particular bit of explanation:

Kori Linae Carothers's piano became Gisela over the months of writing. If you want to hear Gisela's voice, listen to Kori play. Gisela would not be who she is on the page without Kori's three albums.

The Gaelic band Dàimh became a massive influence for Bretons, Eulalie & the chained vineyard workers. Playing off Gisela's theme music was Dàimh's theme music for the prisoners on the march. Early on in the research and outline process of *Tynged*, my wife and I were able to see Dàimh play live in a very intimate setting. We were perhaps 15' away from the musicians, and their performance absolutely enchanted me. It was one of the greatest live band performances I've ever heard, and I've seen a lot of great bands in concert over the ages. (I'd also listened to Afro Celt+, Hearts of Space, etc. for 20 years, and heard bagpipes in the forest mists at SCA war events, so it wasn't just a new thing.) I was already a fan of some Celtic music, but Dàimh just battering-rammed that door down to open up a whole new influence of Breton and Celtic music in this writing. Budic's bard is named Daev as a tribute to Dàimh's incredible influence on the storyline.

So, if you wish to hear how the prison train felt to me as I wrote, read and edited *Tynged*, then mix up Kori's piano tunes (particularly recommend Liberty, Midnight, & Winterstorm) with Dàimh's Gaelic tunes (recommend O Fair A-Nall Am Botal, Mo Mhaili Bheag Og & Muineira De Ramelle) and put them on the old Roman road with I Mett Her in the Medowe.

Acknowledgments

My soul-mate wife, Wendy; for being a constant sounding-board for ideas. My dear brother, Robert; for being an Atlas of support. My niece Molly, for being a big part of the inspiration for Gisela, as some of this started out as a present; I sent the first chapters to Molly for her birthday on a November 11th. To our friends, Bob & Jill; for pointers and still more memorable conversations over wine, water & stars. And my dear friend, Linneus; for artistry and unwavering support. They are, in no small part, the reasons you are reading this novel.

To Reese Antcil and Mary Luper; for inspiring courage equal to any squad of Marines, and who often benefit from long walks.

Final thoughts

Earning a living growing grapes and making wine forces you to accept criticism and praise for what they really are, and teaches you that only the year after year, long-term consistency is what really makes or breaks your body of work as an artist. Even the happiest devoted taster will still inevitably tell you about their *favorite* wine, or some extraordinary wine they just shared at a dinner party. This is the way wine is meant to be enjoyed; with a popped cork and a generous pour amongst friends.

And so it is with writing as well.

Author Bio & Wine's Anvil series

The vigneron Donald Furrow-Scott has decades of experience as a full time grape grower, cellar master, winemaker, and tasting room storyteller at his families estate vineyard, Hickory Hill Vineyards, on Smith Mountain Lake, Virginia. 200,000 hand-corked bottles of wine and over a quarter million personal tastings gives an interesting perspective into the business, the history and the tastes of the modern wine drinker.

The author Donald Furrow-Scott bottles the history of grape growing and winemaking into historical fiction novels spanning the centuries; stories with compelling notes of ancient legends and lingering hints of the supernatural. In the Wine's Anvil series, the history of several wine varietals comes to life through a series of memorable characters and their inspiring adventures.

Donald invites you to a deeper, personal barrel-tasting of his writing at www.winesanvil.com, Facebook (Wine's Anvil Novels), and Twitter (#winesanvil).

Here are the tasting notes for the current Wine's Anvil series:

In the early Iron Age novel *Wine's Anvil*, grapevines and a gifted wine-maker cross the Mediterranean on a doomed Phoenician expedition to legendary Tartessus. Centuries later, wine-making comes of age in 1st century Gaul when a retired Roman official has more than passing boats and passing travelers arrive at his Loire River waystation.

Tynged is the 8th-century story of a young Christian girl named Gisela, whose imagination runs away with her when an unexpected early blizzard buries the Loire Valley. As she is swept along with a group of rebellious vineyard workers she crosses the lines of privilege amidst a Frankish and Breton war that crosses the lines of culture, and where the Catholic Church crosses the battle lines to fill in the bureaucratic vacuum of ancient Rome.

Children of Breton introduces the trilogy of Tiran de

Laval, a 17th-century noble son whose love of wine and growing grapes casts him away from his royal roots in France. A troubling apparition and an old mentor lure him back into the Loire Valley, where he becomes an undercover investigator for an influential group of judges working for the French King.

Hard Cane continues Tiran's story as an undercover investigator posing as a wine-maker in Poitou and the Loire, with local politics growing into international intrigue as he begins secret missions for Cardinal Richelieu. His love of the Vidure wine grapes, the various mysterious women in his life and his troubling religious visions all create a maelstrom of decisions that funnel his impending future towards damnation.

King of the Son capstones the Tiran de Laval trilogy. As he wrestles with his wife's recent death and the revealing details of her diary, seemingly meant to haunt him, an old friend comes to seek his help with a vineyard mystery. When the friend is subsequently kidnapped, Tiran sets out to rescue him, beginning a journey across Western France where he is forced to defend his life from wine thieves, and his family name from the church and the royal court.

The Changeling is an early 18th-century novel introducing Barbin Fortier, an aging son returning home from a life of youthful piracy to seek peace and take his place in a failing, once noble, family vineyard. His past keeps undermining his future as he navigates a journey of change in France, change in tastes in wine and a change in his own beliefs.

The Blackbird is a mid-18th-century mystery-romance. Old wine grower Joël-Gervais de Laval finds budding love with another witness amidst the intrigue of a local murder trial. As the trial slowly begins to take on a more national flavor the lovers are carried along, away from their vines, their wines, and their insular past lives.